Isle of Broken Years

Jane Fletcher

Praise for Jane Fletcher

The Walls of Westernfort

"Award-winning author Jane Fletcher explores serious themes in the Celaeno series and creates a world that loosely parallels the one we inhabit. In *The Walls of Westernfort*, Fletcher weaves a plausible action-packed plot, set on a credible world, and with appealing multi-dimensional characters. The result is a fantasy by one of the best speculative fiction writers in the business."—*Just About Write*

"...captivating, well-written stories in the fantasy genre that are built around women's struggles against themselves, one another, society, and nature."—*WomanSpace Magazine*

"*The Walls of Westernfort* is not only a highly engaging and fast-paced adventure novel, it provides the reader with an interesting framework for examining the same questions of loyalty, faith, family and love."—*Midwest Book Review*

"*The Walls of Westernfort* is...a true delight. Bold, well-developed characters hold your interest from the beginning and keep you turning the pages. The main plot twists and turns until the very end. The subplot involves likeable women who seem destined not to be together."—*MegaScene*

"In *The Walls of Westernfort*, Jane Fletcher spins a captivating story about youthful idealism, honor, and courage. The action is fast paced and the characters are compelling in this gripping sci-fi adventure."—*Sapphic Reader*

"Jane Fletcher has a great talent for spinning yarns, especially stories of lesbians with swords. *The Walls of Westernfort* is a well written and suspenseful tale...Fletcher effectively intertwines the intrigues of the assassination plot with a young woman's inward exploration...and yes, there is romance...This book is a page-turner; you will have a hard time finding a stopping place."—*Lesbian Connection Magazine*

Rangers at Roadsend

"In *Rangers at Roadsend* Fletcher not only gives us powerful characters, but she surprises us with an unexpected ending to the murder conspiracy plot, pushing the story in one direction only to have that direction reversed more than once. This is one thrill ride the reader will not want to get off."—*Independent Gay Writer*

"*Rangers at Roadsend*, a murder mystery reminiscent of Agatha Christie, has crossed many genres including speculative fiction, fantasy, romance, and adventure. The story is an incredible whodunit that has something for everyone. Jane Fletcher, winner of the Golden Crown Literary Award in 2005 for *Walls at Westernfort*, has created an intelligent and compelling story where the reader easily gets drawn into the fascinating world of Celaeno, becomes totally absorbed in the well-designed plot, and finds herself completely enamoured with the multi-faceted characters."—*Just About Write*

The Temple at Landfall

"*The Temple at Landfall* is absorbing and engrossing tale-telling of the highest order, and the really exciting thing is that although this novel is complete and 'finished,' the door is left open to explore more of this world, which the author has done in subsequent books. I can't wait to read the next Celaeno Series volumes, and this book is a keeper that I will re-read again and again. I highly recommend it."—*Just About Write*

"Jane Fletcher is the consummate storyteller and plot wizard. Getting caught up in the action happens as if by magic and the fantasy elements are long forgotten. The world Fletcher creates, the characters she brings to life, and the rich detail described in eloquent prose, all serve to keep the reader enchanted, satisfied, yet wanting more. A Lammy finalist, *The Temple at Landfall* is surely a winner in this reader's book. Don't miss it."—*Midwest Book Review*

Dynasty of Rogues

"Jane Fletcher has another triumph with *Dynasty of Rogues*, the continuing story in the Celaeno series. This reviewer found the book clever and compelling and difficult to put down once I started reading and easily could be devoured in one sitting. Some of the characters in *Dynasty of Rogues* have visited us in other Celaeno novels, but this is a non-linear series, so it can be understood without having read the other stories...*Dynasty of Rogues* has it all. Mystery, intrigue, crime, and romance, with lots of angst thrown in too, make this fascinating novel thoroughly enjoyable and fun."
—*Just About Write*

"When you pick up a novel by Jane Fletcher, you will always get a riveting plot, strong, interesting characters, and a beautifully written story complete with three-dimensional villains, believable conflicts, and the twin spices of adventure and romance. Ethical and moral dilemmas abound. Fletcher writes real characters, the type that William Faulkner once said 'stand up and cast a shadow.' The reader can't help but root for these characters, many of whom are classic underdogs. I give the highest recommendation for *Dynasty of Rogues* and to the entire Celaeno Series."—*Midwest Book Review*

The Exile and the Sorcerer

"Jane Fletcher once again has written an exciting fantasy story for everyone. Though she sets her stories in foreign worlds where the traditional role of women are reversed, her characters (are) all too familiar in their inner lives and thoughts. Unlike the Celaeno series (which I highly recommend) where there are no men, this series incorporates male characters that help round out the story nicely... Fletcher has a way of balancing the fantasy with the human drama in a precise way. She never gets caught up in the minor details of the environment and forgets to tell the story, which happens too often in fantasy fiction...With Fletcher writing such strong work, readers of fantasy will continue to grow."—*Lambda Book Report*

"*The Exile and the Sorcerer* is a mesmerizing read, a tour-de-force packed with adventure, ordeals, complex twists and turns, and the internal introspection of appealing characters. The author writes effortlessly, handling the size and scope of the book with ease. Not since the fantasy works of Elizabeth Moon and Lynn Flewelling have I been so thoroughly engrossed in a tale. This is knockout fiction, tantalizingly told, and beautifully packaged."—*Midwest Book Review*

Wolfsbane Winter

"Jane Fletcher is known for her fantasy stories that take place in a world that could almost be real, but not quite. Her books seem like an alternative version of history and contain rich atmospheres of magic, legends, sorcerers and other worldly characters mixed in with ordinary people. The way she writes is so realistic that it is easy to believe that these places and people really exist. *Wolfsbane Winter* fits that mold perfectly. It draws the reader in and leads her through the story. Very enjoyable."—*Just About Write*

The Shewstone

"I was hooked on the plot and the characters are absolutely delightful."—*The Romantic Reader Blog*

By the Author

The Celaeno Series

The Temple at Landfall

The Walls of Westernfort

Rangers at Roadsend

Dynasty of Rogues

Shadow of the Knife

The Lyremouth Chronicles

The Exile and the Sorcerer

The Chalice and the Traitor

The Empress and the Acolyte

The High Priest and the Idol

Wolfsbane Winter

The Shewstone

Isle of Broken Years

Visit us at www.boldstrokesbooks.com

ISLE OF
BROKEN YEARS

by
Jane Fletcher

2018

ISLE OF BROKEN YEARS

ISBN 13: 978-1-63555-175-4

THIS TRADE PAPERBACK ORIGINAL IS PUBLISHED BY
BOLD STROKES BOOKS, INC.
P.O. BOX 249
VALLEY FALLS, NY 12185

FIRST EDITION: OCTOBER 2018

CREDITS
EDITOR: CINDY CRESAP
PRODUCTION DESIGN: STACIA SEAMAN
COVER DESIGN BY SHERI (HINDSIGHTGRAPHICS@GMAIL.COM)

ISLE OF BROKEN YEARS

Chapter One

"Ship ahoy!" The shout drifted down from the crow's nest.

Catalina de Valasco secured her needle and looked up, shielding her eyes.

The mast was a silhouette against the bright Caribbean sky. The sailor on lookout was obscured by the billowing sails, but Catalina caught sight of his outstretched arm, pointing north. Was it worth going to see? Regardless, her fingers were stiff, and a break from embroidery was due. Catalina folded the material, placed it on the bench, then went to stand at the railing. The other ship was no more than a speck on the horizon.

As ever, Lucia dogged her heels. "Who do you think it is, my lady?" Her voice was an octave higher than normal. Lucia had been living in dread of pirates ever since the *Santa Eulalia de Merida* left Spain, and Catalina's willingness to humor her maid had long since run out.

"How would I know?"

"I'm sorry, my lady, I was just—"

"It will be a merchantman, going about its lawful business. Pirates don't attack ships going to New Spain. They want the gold and silver on the way back." How many times did Lucia need to be told?

"If you say so, my lady. But supposing—"

"Then your repairs to my wedding gown will be wasted. Which would be a shame, after all your work." Fortunately, the rats' taste for silk had been discovered before too much damage occurred.

"Oh yes, my lady. It's nearly finished. Nobody will ever notice. I've taken lace from your second best nightgown and…"

Preparations for the forthcoming marriage could be relied on to divert Lucia's scatterbrain thoughts. Catalina was less obsessed with the subject. There was nothing worthwhile to add, and nor would there be, until the galleon reached port at Veracruz.

Instead, Catalina did her best to block out Lucia's chatter while her gaze drifted idly over the scene. It was idyllic, making any talk of danger seem ridiculous. The deck rolled gently beneath her feet. Wisps of high cloud broke the pure blue dome of the heavens. Afternoon sunlight glittered on the waves between dazzling white crests of surf. Catalina leaned over the side, hoping to spot more flying fish. Strands of seaweed swept through the dark glass troughs in the bow wave and were gone in an instant.

When she looked up again, the other ship was close enough for Catalina to pick out its three masts. It was gaining on them apace. To her annoyance, Catalina felt a clenching in the pit of her stomach. She was getting as bad as Lucia. The standard flying above the crow's nest was still too indistinct to make out. The royal astrologer had recently demonstrated a clever spyglass at court, a tube with a lens at either end that made distant objects appear close. Catalina would have appreciated one now, to dismiss her foolish worries—a shame ships did not carry them.

On the quarterdeck, Captain Giraldo was also studying the unknown ship. Perhaps she should mention the spyglasses to him as an idea for the future. He frowned and rapped his knuckles on the rail, then shouted, "Bear hard to port."

The sails rippled as the helmsman pulled on the wheel. Briefly, the distance between the two ships widened, but then, unmistakably, the other ship changed tack to follow the *Santa Eulalia*.

And still it was gaining on them.

Despite the warm sunshine, a prickling of ice washed over Catalina. She could not tear her eyes from the pursuing ship and felt rather than saw all action still around her. Sailors hung motionless in the rigging.

Ironically, after weeks of anxiety, Lucia was last to react. The maid was drawing patterns in sea spray on the handrail while prattling away. "...but if it does, I'll carry a spare pair, in case you—" until finally the silence caught her attention. She looked up and squealed, "Oh no! Oh no, no, no!"

The sound of her voice snapped the spell. "Man the guns." Captain Giraldo's command was echoed by the first mate and others.

A maelstrom of activity surged across the deck. Sailors dropped from the rigging, hand over hand. Others burst from every hatch and doorway. They threw open lockers, passing around swords and muskets. Cannons were hauled into place, gunpowder kegs rolled from storage, breastplates adjusted and tightened.

"Goddamned, whoreson pirates," a sailor spat a curse that normally would have earned a rebuke, but Catalina ignored the coarse language along with the bleats from Lucia whimpering beside her.

Her hands were clamped around the rail so tightly her knuckles ached. It took an act of willpower to loosen her grip, yet still she stayed where she was, unable to stop watching the ship get ever nearer. It sliced gracefully, majestically, through the waves, and it meant them harm.

The ship was so close Catalina could spot figures standing on the deck. A flag with red, white, and blue bands fluttered atop the highest mast. Everything was moving so slowly, yet with each beat of her heart, the gap between the ships narrowed.

Somebody was talking at Catalina's shoulder, and had been for a while, although it took a light touch to fully claim her attention. "Please, madam, you and your maid should take shelter. I beg you, go to your cabin, now. Here is not safe for you." The officer's words were polite, but his tone and his eyes added, *and you will get in our way.*

At some point, Lucia had collapsed in a trembling heap. Catalina urged her to her feet and took her hand. Their path was a chaotic dance, sidestepping and bobbing around the scrambling sailors. Before entering the passage under the quarterdeck, Catalina paused for one last sight of the looming ship with its taunting rebel flag. It was now close enough for her to hear the enemy shouts over the hubbub around her. Catalina flinched as the first musket shot rang out. Lucia took the lead and jerked her through the narrow doorway and into the tranquil gloom below deck.

Their cabin was familiar, exactly as they had left it a couple of hours earlier, with her book open on the table, and her nightgown folded on the bunk, but now it felt like a prison rather than a refuge. The walls and ceiling pressed in on her. Sounds from outside were muffled through the stout timbers, shouts, screams and musket fire—

all suddenly drowned out by the thunder of cannon. Even if she were deaf, Catalina would have felt the galleon lurch with the recoil. She staggered and put her hand on the table.

Lucia screamed and flung her arms around Catalina's knees. Once again, Lucia was on the floor.

Catalina tried to free herself. "Please. It doesn't help."

"Oh, my lady, they're pirates."

"Privateers. They're flying the flag of the Dutch Republic."

Admittedly, any difference was quite abstract as far as anyone aboard the *Santa Eulalia* was concerned. If the other captain had a letter of marque from the Dutch renegades, it was merely an excuse to steal and murder.

The cannons continued to roar, sending shocks through the ship as if it were running before a storm. Lucia loosened her grip, allowing Catalina to keep her balance more easily, but then a new quake sent her stumbling against the wall. The jolt was accompanied by a boom and the complaint of strained timber. Shouts from above reached a new crescendo. The attacking ship had made contact with the *Santa Eulalia*, ready for boarding. One way or another, the battle would soon be over.

Lucia knelt beside her bunk, praying like a child before sleeping. Her eyes were scrunched shut as she recited the words, clicking through the beads on her rosary. Catalina knew she should join her. What else could she do but pray? And yet it was impossible to think of anything other than the battle outside.

Catalina stared at the ceiling, tracking the sounds. The uproar on deck surged back and forth. Who was winning? She tried to pick out words amid the chaos. Were the commands still being shouted in Spanish? How long would the fighting last? Yet, surely the tumult above was beginning to slacken. Instead of a continuous uproar, the clamor came in bursts, with the gaps between growing longer and quieter— quiet enough to hear Lucia embark on her next Hail Mary.

Hail Mary, full of grace.

Our Lord is with thee.

Blessed art thou among women.

One last gunshot, and then there was silence.

Lucia opened her eyes. "Have we won?"

Another foolish question. Catalina bit back any answer, not that

Lucia waited for one. She kissed her rosary. "Our Lord would not let the fiends and heretics win. We are fighting for the true faith."

Lucia had not been paying attention to the state of the war if she placed any trust in divine intervention. In Catalina's opinion, the toss of a coin was as likely to be right. However, if Captain Giraldo and his men had won, someone would soon come to share the good news. And by the same token, the longer the wait went on, the worse the outlook was. Either way, hiding in the cabin was futile.

Catalina put her hand on the door latch, but then heard voices—laughter and talking, too faint for her to make out the words. She strained her ears, hoping for Captain Giraldo's bellow, a familiar voice, a phrase spoken in Spanish. Instead there were footsteps, coming closer. Another burst of harsh male laughter, but still no clue as to the victors. The footsteps paused in the passage outside.

Catalina backed away. "Who's there?"

The door was flung back. Framed in the entrance were two men. Each had a pistol in his waistband and a sword at his side. Their shirts and breeches were disheveled and blood-splattered. One had a neckerchief knotted at his throat. The taller man had a scar running down the side of his face. Neither was a member of the crew.

For a moment, nobody moved and then Lucia screamed.

The scarred pirate stuck his hands on his hips, while a broad smile creased his face. He spoke in English. "Well. What have we here?"

❖

The scene on deck was surprisingly similar to before. Everywhere, a riot of sailors made busy, some still flourishing swords, while others dug through storage lockers. Yet the atmosphere and the voices had changed. The mood was now one of celebration, and instead of Spanish, the sailors were speaking a mixture of English, German, and other languages Catalina did not know. Presumably, Dutch was one, but her parents had not included it in her otherwise comprehensive education.

Other differences were also apparent. Streaks and puddles of blood stained the decking red. A knot of prisoners, two dozen or more, sat hunched in one corner, heads down. None met her eyes, although the faces were ones she knew—as were others, on bodies lying motionless, with frozen expressions and blank eyes.

Catalina watched two pirates swing one corpse by hands and feet, then toss him overboard. The splash that followed was almost lost in the hubbub. Catalina tasted bile rising in her throat. Matias, that had been his name, she remembered. He had poured her wine the previous evening. Catalina summoned her courage. She would face her fate. Giving in to panic was not only unworthy, it was also pointless.

Her captor raised his voice. "Hey, lads. Look what I've found!"

At first, only a few heads turned in their direction. But there was no mistaking the reaction. Within seconds, silence swept across the deck; all motion stilled. And then, starting at the back, a wild chorus of cheering erupted, ending in laughter and shouts.

"There was me thinking I'd have to wait till the next whorehouse."

More laughter.

"Who gets first dibs?"

"I'll arm wrestle you."

"Careful. You don't want to strain your wrist in case you don't win."

"Nah. I think Mrs. Palm and her daughters will be having a rest tonight." The laughter reached new heights, while the mob drew closer, forming a densely packed ring.

Of course. What else would pirates do with women they captured? Catalina heard a wail. It was questionable how much Lucia understood—her English was weak—but the tones and expressions were unmistakable. Catalina tightened her jaw and drew her shoulders back. The blood of kings ran in her veins. She was a true daughter of Spain, who could trace her ancestors to El Cid, and beyond. Whatever else, she would not let this rabble see fear on her face. They deserved nothing but contempt, and that she would grant them, in abundance.

A man on her left pawed at her, clamping a hand over her breast and squeezing. As calmly as she could, Catalina turned her head to bestow her iciest stare and was rewarded when he blushed and fell back, giving rise to the loudest burst of laughter yet.

The braying faded to a rumble. Pirates shuffled aside, allowing a new man through—the captain, judging by the way others yielded their place in the front row. He was far from being the tallest man present, and his clothing would have shamed a shopkeeper, but he projected an air of command.

Like his subordinates, the captain had a smile on his lips, but it did not reach his eyes. Catalina's immediate impression was that this was a man who would always think, plan, and calculate. He was more dangerous for it, yet she found his arrival strangely comforting. He could be reasoned with, although when he spoke it was in parody.

He swept off his hat and gave an exaggerated, low bow. "Madam, allow me to present your humble servant. Captain Edward Williams, at your service. But you can call me Ned."

"I am Doña Catalina de Valasco, daughter of Vizconde Pedro de Valasco. You can call me, your ladyship."

"You're Spanish." A statement, not a question.

"And you're English, although you sail under a Dutch flag."

"Yes. I admit I'd rather serve my country. Alas, my country's not quite so keen on me. The Dutch West India Company is more generous with its letters of marque."

"The Dutch renegades are traitors, with no authority to issue those letters."

"I'll pass on your opinion next time I'm in port, but I think they might disagree."

The matter was not worth arguing. The outcome would be decided by armies, not lone women prisoners. "What do you intend to do with me?"

His smile did not falter, but something else flickered in his eyes. Was it regret or depravity? "I'm sorry, but the life of a sailor is hard, lacking in amusement. We must make the most of whatever we find. I'm sure you understand."

"I understand that you do not deserve to be counted as men, and trust the demons of hell will make you pay for your crimes, once you improve this world, by leaving it. I can only pray this happens soon."

"Indeed. Praying is the only option available to you." Captain Williams nodded to the man holding Catalina's arm. "Take her and the other one below deck and keep them safe. And I mean that. No sneaking in a quick poke. We divvy up all loot fairly while I'm—"

The end of his words was lost in a roar of catcalls and whistles. More hands grasped Catalina, hauling her back through the doorway. It seemed as if half the pirates on ship were trying to squeeze into the narrow passageway.

Over the turmoil, Lucia screeched in Spanish. "You'll regret this, you will. She's on her way to be married. When Don Perez finds out, he'll make you sorry. He'll hunt you down and hang you…hang every last one…" Her cry ended in an incoherent wail.

Catalina looked up to catch a last sight of God's clean sky. Would she see it again? Would she want to? The unwashed bodies of pirates pressed hard around her.

The blast of a gunshot made everyone freeze. Captain Williams was holding up his pistol. A halo of smoke drifted away behind him.

"Wait a minute, lads. Let's not be too hasty."

Catalina tugged herself free.

"This bridegroom of yours, would that be Don Miguel Perez of Veracruz?" Captain Williams evidently understood Spanish, although he continued in his native tongue.

"Yes, I'm betrothed to him."

"Ah." He scratched his chin thoughtfully. "Well, I guess that changes everything."

"You're not scared of him, are you, Cap'n?" someone called out.

"Oh no, not scared…never scared. It's just the only thing that gets my juices going more than a pretty woman is a big pile of money." Calculations were running behind his eyes. "You're marrying a very, very rich man, you know."

Catalina did know. Half the silver leaving New Spain ran through Don Miguel's hands. It was the main reason her parents had agreed to the match, overlooking his less than impressive pedigree.

"How much do you think your husband would be willing to pay to get you back—completely intact, shall we say?"

"That would be your area of expertise. I've never held anyone for ransom."

Captain Williams threw back his head and laughed. "God's blood, you're a cool one. I'll say that for you."

"Cap'n, you saying we can't drill her?" A confused, plaintive voice in the crowd.

"Yes. That's just what I'm saying."

"How 'bout the other one?"

Catalina resisted the urge to look around. Was Lucia still on deck? The absence of a squeal might only mean she was not keeping up with the conversation.

"No. Best leave her alone too."

"Why?"

"Because we're going to send her with the ransom demand. If she's been humped to hell and back, Don Silverarse Perez will never believe his darling bride is untouched." Captain Williams's eyes never left Catalina.

"Still…"

"Think of how many whores you can buy with your share of the ransom. So just keep it in your breeches for a while."

"Or go complain to Ellis." The call from the back was greeted by more laughter.

"Karl, take Nick and Sam with you, and find somewhere safe for her ladyship and the maid. The rest of you, I don't want to see you anywhere near the ladies. Understand me?"

A grumble of agreement answered him.

Three pirates left the crowd and ushered Catalina and Lucia back down the passageway. Once again, the muted underdeck swallowed them. Annoyingly, Catalina's legs chose now to start shaking, and nausea swirled in her stomach. She braced her hand against a wall while fighting to regain her self-control.

The youngest of the pirates was a scrawny, towheaded boy, who looked to be fourteen at most. His face had no trace of a beard. The oldest could have been a great-grandfather, and limped as he walked. Yet both were as blood-splattered as everyone else. They had clearly played an active part in the fight. The last was the scarred man who had first dragged her out.

"Where are we going to put them?" the boy asked.

Scarface pointed. "That's where I found them."

"Then might as well stick them back again." The oldest pirate pushed the cabin door open. "There you go."

Lucia rushed in, dived onto her bunk, and pulled the blanket over her head. The chances of this being a successful hiding strategy were further reduced by her loud sobs.

Catalina tried to follow more sedately, but her legs had lost all strength. Why? It made no sense for her body to betray her now, when it seemed events would turn out favorably. Surely Don Miguel would pay her ransom. She just needed to hold herself together a while longer.

When she did not move quickly enough, Scarface grabbed her shoulder and shoved her through the doorway. Without the bolstering from a flare of anger, Catalina would have fallen. The boy started to say something but stopped. She turned and glared at the pirates. Scarface smirked back at her. Only the boy had the grace to look ill at ease.

"We'll be standing guard out here," the elderly pirate said.

"I assure you, I've no plans to go anywhere." Did he think she would try to escape in the rowing boat?

"We'll get you some food once everything's sorted."

"Thank you." Although why should she thank the old man for returning goods he had just helped steal?

Catalina watched the door close. Standing in the corridor outside, the blond boy was staring at her with wide-open eyes, as if he had never seen a woman before.

CHAPTER TWO

It's all right, lad. Nick and me'll stand guard. The cap'n didn't say you had to stick with us. Go claim your share of the pickings," Karl said once the door closed.

"I don't mind staying here."

"Nobody's gonna diddle me or Nick, but you need to be there and make sure nobody forgets about you."

He had a point. Karl might be old, but the master gunner got respect, and Nick had been known to flatten men who looked at him sideways, whereas a cabin boy came right at the bottom of the heap. Yet, the Spanish noblewoman had a mixture of beauty, courage, and vulnerability that hit home. It was stupid, but Sam wanted to stay close by, even if it meant no more than staring at the door.

Nobody had challenged Captain Williams's orders, especially with the lure of Don Miguel's money, but might some oafs, using their balls for brains, try their luck? Would then leaping in as her protector win Doña Catalina's thanks? Automatically, Sam's hand fastened on the pistol, stuck in the knotted rope that functioned as a belt.

All of which was one big stupid fantasy. Nobody was going to try anything with Nick on guard. The sensible thing was to follow Karl's advice. Acting sensibly was something Sam had plenty of experience at.

"Right you are, Karl." Sam trotted back to the main deck.

Captain Williams was on the forecastle, giving his post-battle speech. "Men, you've done yourselves proud. You don't need me to tell you that. And Lady Luck's been with us. We weren't expecting much from the loot, but once Don Silverarse coughs up, we're all gonna be walking lopsided from the weight of our coin purses, just as long as nobody does anything to ruin her ladyship's value. I would say, treat her like she's your mother, but most of your mothers were whores."

"Hey! I didn't know you'd met my ma," someone shouted.

"Sure I did. Best five minutes of my life." He waited for the laughter to fade. "I don't want anyone acting the idiot, now that we've got two women on board."

Actually, there were three, but Sam was not about to correct him. She had no wish to learn how her shipmates would react.

"We've got ourselves a second ship again. It's gonna make life easier. Though we'll be a bit shorthanded until we recruit a few more lads." The captain leaned on the railing, looking down at the prisoners directly beneath him. "Which is where you fellows come in. I'm going to give you a choice. Either you can ask nicely to join me and my hearty crew, or you can get put ashore, the first place we make land."

The prisoners exchanged looks among themselves. Captain Williams had spoken in English, but even those who had not understood every word would have caught his drift. The Caribbean was a mishmash of nations. In her years at sea, Sam had picked up a working knowledge of Spanish, French, German, and Dutch, and she knew how to swear in eight other languages, including a few exotic phrases from freed slaves. A fair number of the privateers were African.

"If we let you join us, the rules are simple. You do what me, the quartermaster, and the first mate say. You work when we say work, you fight when we say fight, and you get one share of the loot for every three years you're with us. If you disagree with something you can ask for it to go to a vote. But if you get into the habit of disagreeing and make a nuisance of yourself, we tip you overboard. So what do you say?"

The offer was the same one Sam had received, ten months earlier. If her father had still been alive, they might have taken the chance that the next landfall would not be an uninhabited atoll. Without him, the best Sam could hope for was to end up totally alone in some hellhole of a town, filled with freebooters, outcasts, and slavers. Regardless, she would have needed to find work, and the sea was the only life she knew. She had told herself sailing with Captain Williams on the *Golden Goose* would allow time to look for a better alternative, although so far, this better alternative was yet to show up.

These prisoners were on firmer ground, if they had the wits to work it out. Rejecting the offer carried no risk of being marooned. Captain Williams wanted the ransom demand to get to Don Perez quickly, which meant he would leave them as close to a Spanish controlled outpost as he dared go.

However, the defeated captain would have none of it. He spoke in heavily accented English. "I can answer for my men. Not one of them will have anything to do with a villain like you, other than put a rope around your neck."

"That's very good of you, to save your sailors' breath and all, but we like to give a man the chance to speak for himself. So what say you fellows? How do you fancy a chance to put some of that gold in your own pockets, rather than ferrying it back to Spain for some rich bastard who's already got more than he knows what to do with?"

Sam could see a couple glancing sideways at their crewmates, as if trying to work out which way the wind was blowing.

The Spanish captain was not among them. "By your own words, you are nothing more than a common thief, a pirate. I'll see you hang for your crimes."

"I'd have to say you're not in a good position to be hanging anyone right now. Anyway, I'm not a pirate. I'm fighting on behalf of the Dutch Republic. I've got a very nice letter of marque from them to prove it."

"The so-called Dutch Republic are rebels against both God and their rightful king."

Captain Williams made a show of yawning. "This is boring. I've heard it before."

"Treason and heresy will not succeed. The true faith will triumph."

"So now we all know what your voice sounds like. It's time to give it a rest."

"I will not be quiet in the presence of God's enemies."

"Did you hear what I said before, about what happens if you make a nuisance of yourself?"

"I do not fear your threats."

"That's very brave of you." Captain Williams gestured to the side. "Throw him overboard."

This shut the captain up, and to give him his due, he offered nothing but stoic defiance as three crewmembers heaved him over the gunwale. A few seconds of silence followed the splash.

Captain Williams turned back to the prisoners and clapped his hands. "Right then. Who wants to be a privateer?"

❖

In the end, nine prisoners took up the offer, and the others were chained in the hold of the captured ship. The recruits joined their new crewmates in a vote. Sam guessed this was their first taste of shipboard democracy. For her, it was easily the best thing about being a privateer.

A forest of hands waved in the air. There was no need for Captain Williams to count.

"Right. It's decided. Henceforth, this ship is the *Maiden's Prayer*." The crew cheered. "We'll give both ships a quick check and patch them up if needed. Luckily, it doesn't look like anything got too banged up. I want to be heading west by sunset. We'll have to split crews, which will need juggling. Senior hands come to my cabin back on the *Golden Goose*. And, lad…" He turned to Sam. "See if you can find a bottle of Spanish brandy, in case our throats get dry from talking."

The main hold of the newly renamed *Maiden's Prayer* was two-thirds full. Most of the cargo was weapons and luxuries, intended for Spanish colonies in the Americas, all now gratefully received by the privateers. In theory, a share of the profits was due to the Dutch who issued the letter of marque. In practice, things might turn out slightly differently.

The main battle prize was the galleon herself. A month earlier, they had lost their frigate, the *Grey Lady*. Eastward bound treasure ships were too well defended for lone privateers to tackle at will, especially if the Spanish traveled in convoy. With two ships working together, the chances were greatly improved.

Sitting in the gloom below deck, the prisoners formed a row, chained together with leg irons. The links clicked with the roll of the waves. No slaves had been on the captured ship, although human freight was common enough, as the chains showed. The men scowled at Sam as she riffled though the crates. Did any now regret not joining the privateers?

"King Phillip will cleanse the seas of this filth once God grants us victory. The heretics and traitors will all burn." The Spanish was spoken loudly enough to overhear. Clearly, the man did not care whether Sam understood, but he then switched to English and raised his voice. "You, pirate. Do you not fear for your immortal soul?"

Sam did not bother answering. The war in Europe had been going on for over ten years, and could easily last ten more. It had started as a religious dispute in the German states, but had gotten quite out of hand. The Dutch had pitched in, wanting freedom from Spain, and now Sweden and England were caught up in the struggle. Who could say how things would turn out?

Sam snagged a bottle of brandy and left the Spanish loyalists to their dreams of God finally pitching in on their side. The two ships were still bound together, facing the sinking sun. Sam vaulted over the gunwale onto the *Golden Goose* and entered the captain's cabin. She caught part of a report by Donal, the first mate.

"...able deckhands. Six are Portuguese conscripts."

"So no love lost there," the captain said, smiling.

"True enough. They'd probably have volunteered to pitch their old captain overboard, given the chance."

Captain Williams pointed to a row of glasses. "Set 'em up, lad." He turned back to Donal. "What about the Spaniards?"

"One's getting on in years. Says he was a cook. The other two are disillusioned youngsters. They ran away to sea to make their fortune, but it's been too slow coming."

"Might they be trouble?"

"I don't think so."

The captain nodded. "Right. Before we cast off the grappling irons we'll transfer the prisoners to the *Golden Goose*, so I can keep my eye on them, her ladyship and the maid included. The new recruits can all crew on the *Maiden's Prayer*, to cut out any risk of them getting a change of heart and deciding to free their old shipmates. They're also familiar with the ship. Though, on second thought, the old cook can come onto the *Golden Goose*. We ought to be able to handle him if he tries making mischief and we can see what his salmagundi is like." He rapped his knuckles on the table. "Sam, lad."

Sam stopped midway though pouring a glass. "Cap'n?"

"What are you hearing? How's the crew taking today's action?"

"They're happy. We only lost four men, and we've got a second ship. They're a bit...excited about the women."

"I bet they are."

"But it's just talk. Most have already spent their share of the ransom three times over in their head."

Captain Williams laughed.

"How much can we screw out of Don Perez for her?" Donal asked.

"If you had his money, how much would you pay? You don't find a woman with looks like hers every day."

"She's pretty enough, I'll grant you that. So what's the plan? I take it you've got one?"

Plans were the captain's specialty. It was one reason why the crew voted for him. "We'll drop the prisoners with the ransom demand a couple of hours north of St. Augustine. The lady's maid can go with them, to prove we've got the discipline not to drill every woman we lay our hands on. Then we'll find somewhere quiet to hole up. We'll give him two months, then send the *Maiden's Prayer* to pick up the ransom. If he comes through with the money, we'll tell him where to find his bride and be on our way with a hold full of gold."

"Supposing he double-crosses us?"

"I've got a few other ideas." Captain Williams picked up a glass and swilled the contents, thoughtfully. "Thanks, lad. Leave the bottle. Go back to the *Maiden's Prayer* and call on her ladyship. Tell her she'll be coming aboard the *Golden Goose* with her maid. Anything they want to bring over has to be in a bag and ready within the hour."

"Aye, Cap'n." Sam left the cabin.

No doubt Captain Williams's other ideas would be inventive, but Sam would have to wait with the rest of the crew to learn more.

A lone sailor was outside Doña Catalina's cabin, supposedly standing guard. However, Hugh was curled on the floor, snoring loudly, with an empty bottle in his hand. The captain was not the only one to enjoy brandy.

Sam resisted the urge to kick Hugh. Maybe there was little risk of Doña Catalina escaping—if she had any sense, she would not set foot outside her cabin—but he was supposed to be protecting her. There were men on ship who did their thinking with their dicks whenever they saw a woman, and Hugh would not be the only one who had helped himself to a bottle. Supposing some swillbelly dog tried to force himself on Catalina?

Sam shook the drunken sailor's shoulder, but got only a cough and a grumble before the snores resumed. He was as much use as a wet paper sail in a hurricane. After passing on the captain's message, she would stay and keep watch. With a sigh, Sam stepped over Hugh's legs and pushed open the cabin door.

A single candle supplemented the weak daylight. Doña Catalina was sitting with her maid at the table. A book, probably the Bible, was open before her. At the sound of the latch, the maid flinched visibly and gave a whimper of fear. However, Catalina slowly and coolly turned her head and treated Sam to a look of utter contempt, as if she were a bad smell that had wafted in.

Sam was held spellbound by the pair of startling blue eyes trained on her. Catalina had a heart-shaped face, framed by sculptured jet-black ringlets, which were thrown into yet sharper contrast by the fine white ruff around her throat. Even compressed in a straight line, there was no disguising the fullness of her lips. The bodice on her crimson dress was thick with gold embroidery. Her sleeves were tied with ribbon and cut to reveal the cream cloth beneath. She was a picture of wealth and elegance, and easily the most beautiful woman Sam had seen in ages— although to be fair, a sailor's life did not throw up much by way of competition.

She put Catalina's age at maybe a little over her own tally of twenty years. She had previously seen that Catalina was of average height for a woman, although several inches shorter than Sam. She spoke English fluently, with a low voice, and a bewitching, musical accent.

And she was still glaring at Sam. "Well? Are you here for a reason? Or do you just want to look at me?"

There were worse ways to pass the time.

Sam struggled to find her voice. "Your ladysh…miss. The captain sent me. You'll be moving to the other ship, the *Golden Goose*, with your maid, in about an hour. You should pack a bag of things you want to take with you."

"How large a bag?"

"I don't know. He didn't say. I guess as long as you can carry it. Or I'll carry it for you." Sam forced herself to shut up. She was babbling.

"How old are you?"

"Pardon?"

"You're a child."

"No, I'm not." Although true, it hardly sounded convincing.

The contempt on Catalina's face was changing to stern disapproval.

"How sad to see one as young as you, already lost to the devil. Your mother must shed bitter tears when she thinks of you."

"My ma is dead. So is my pa."

"Yet you strive only to turn more children into orphans."

"It's not like that."

"Isn't it? Then tell me how it is."

Sam stared at the floor. This conversation was not going anywhere good. She should let actions speak for her. "Is there nothing I can do for you?"

"No."

"I could help you pack."

"You're hoping to delve through my spare undergarments?"

"No!" Though now that Sam thought about it, her face burned. She must have been blushing like a nun in a brothel.

"So young. And racing on the path to hell."

"I'm not a child."

"No. You're a monster in training."

A dozen comebacks in an equal number of languages shot through Sam's head. She bit them back. It was unreasonable to expect sympathy from a prisoner being held for ransom.

Catalina returned to her book. She appeared totally composed. Yet the warm candlelight could not mask the paleness of her cheeks, nor did the ruff hide the rapid pulse in her throat. Catalina was not as immune to fear as she acted.

Sam's anger dissolved. "You needn't worry. Don Perez will pay your ransom. Then Captain Williams will set you free. You'll be all right."

"I put no faith in your pirate captain to honor his word. And I doubt Don Perez will either."

"Captain Williams is a man of—"

"Actually, there is something I'd like you to do for me." Catalina cut Sam off.

"What?"

"Go. And please, shut the door after you."

Sam opened her mouth and closed it again. She must look like a dying fish, and hanging around was not going to make things better. Sam ducked her head in an awkward bow and left.

Alone in the corridor, with only Hugh's snores as a distraction,

Sam rested her forehead against the wooden wall and took several deep breaths. Her pulse raced and her knees were weak. So what if Doña Catalina despised her? The Spanish noblewoman was enough to send anyone's brains on the journey south.

In the days ahead, Sam knew she would need to act very sensibly indeed.

❖

Two days later, the *Golden Goose* and the *Maiden's Prayer* dropped anchor in the estuary of a river. Sunrise was approaching and the light was just strong enough to see the banks on either side. These were low and covered in a knotted mat of shrub-like trees and palms. The shoreline showed up clearly, a ribbon of white sand, luminous in the waning moonlight.

Sam rested her elbows on the gunwale of the *Golden Goose* and watched the longboat return from ferrying its load of prisoners ashore. The sound of the oars carried on the dawn breeze. The privateers would not hang around for long. A few miles farther south, a wider river led to the Spanish outpost of St. Augustine. Apart from any danger posed by the settlement defenses, there was always the risk of visiting warships.

The prisoners would not have to travel far before reaching safety, although it would require care. The land was low-lying swamp, cut by a lacework of alligator-infested rivers and streams. As long as they watched where they were going, most should survive the journey, although possibly not all.

"Sam," Captain Williams called.

"Cap'n?"

"Fetch the lady's maid. She'll go in the next boatload."

"Aye-aye." Sam headed below deck.

She found Lucia sobbing and clinging to Catalina. The maid was wearing what must have passed as outdoor clothing for a Spanish gentlewoman but was hardly suited to wading through swamps. Fortunately, there was no shortage of sturdy men among the prisoners. Someone would need to carry Lucia across the wetland. The floor-length petticoats would weigh a ton once they soaked up water. On the other hand, an alligator would have to chew through layers of starched cloth before getting anywhere close to her legs.

"It's time for you to go, miss."

The sobs got louder. Catalina pulled free from the encircling arms and captured Lucia's hands between her own.

"You must be brave," Catalina said softly in Spanish.

"I'd rather stay here."

"And I'd much rather go with you. The pirates will set you ashore, close to a friendly fort. The commander there will take care of you."

A niggle of guilt poked Sam when she remembered the alligators. Lucia stifled her sobs with a loud gulp, but showed no sign of moving.

Sam put a hand under Lucia's elbow to draw her away. "You have to come now."

Lucia took her first, teetering step toward the door.

Abruptly, Catalina said, "Please, can we have just five minutes more?"

Her eyes met Sam's, pleading. For the first time, there was no scorn, no defiance. More than anything, Sam wanted to agree, so Catalina would continue looking at her in that way, but she was not in a position to grant the request.

"I'm sorry. Captain Williams is waiting."

Even so, Sam was willing to stick her neck out and delay for as long as she dared, but she did not get the chance to say more. Immediately, Catalina's guard snapped back into place.

"Oh no. We can't keep your captain waiting."

"I'm just obeying orders."

"Is that the sop you give your conscience? Do you think it will spare you the noose when you are brought to trial?"

"No. I'll stand no chance at all, if it's a Spanish court."

"So why do you follow this life?"

"Because I have no other options."

"We always have options."

"You need money to buy options." A hard truth Sam had learned long ago. She tugged Lucia's elbow. "Come with me, miss."

Sam steered the weeping maid from the room. As the door closed, she glanced back. Doña Catalina had not moved. Her eyes were closed and the mask of icy aloofness was gone. She was a woman alone and friendless, surrounded by danger, trying to control her fear. What would Catalina say if Sam went back, put an arm around her, and told her she was not quite as alone as she might think? Was it sensible even to ask the question?

The door shut.

❖

The waning crescent of the moon hung low on the horizon. Its light was not strong enough to challenge the glittering stars, splashed across the night sky. Sam lay on her back and picked out the constellations. They had been her guide across the oceans and were as familiar to her as the lines across her hands.

Many sailors believed both stars and lines could also be a guide to the future. The port towns held more than their share of astrologers and palmists. Sam was doubtful, not least because those who relied most on fortune-tellers had the worst luck. A shame. It would be so much easier if she could only read the answers in the stars.

Where could she go for guidance? Sam felt in desperate need of it. The nature of her life at sea meant emotions and desires were something to be ignored, not prodded around. The only available women Sam ran into were the dockside whores, who never interested her. Was that not proof she had no real interest in women? Other sailors would race to the brothels as soon as the ship made harbor.

Occasionally, Sam had toyed with the idea of talking to the women—just talking—to see what advice they could give. What chance she would learn anything to justify the risk? If the truth got back to her shipmates, the outcome was predictable.

Sam had pushed the whole subject to the back of her mind and stuck a very tight lid on it. She did not need to make her life any more difficult than it already was. Then Catalina arrived, and suddenly Sam was feeling out of control. The thought of saying something not at all sensible was a worryingly strong temptation.

"What do you think I should do, Pa?" she whispered to the stars.

Where was her father's spirit? It would be nice to think he was up there, listening and watching over her. Sam smiled. If the afterlife contained a tavern, that was where to look for him, not drifting around over the ocean. Her father's idea of heaven had always come in a bottle.

Richard Helyer had not been the most cautious of men, even

when sober, but he was someone she trusted, someone she could talk to. And while his ideas might not be well thought through, they were usually fun. Such as when he returned to Devon to find his sister on her deathbed, leaving no one to look after his eight-year-old daughter. So he told Sarah her name was now Sam, dressed her as a boy, and took her with him on his next voyage.

With hindsight, his shipmates probably guessed the truth, but Pa was well liked and a good seaman. After all, a taste for rum went with the job. Everyone had turned a blind eye, until Sam had mastered playing the part of a boy. The steps she needed to take were now second-nature, and she had long ceased thinking of herself as Sarah.

Everything had been fine until their last nightmare voyage together. Bad weather and worse luck had dogged the *Portland Bessie*. An outbreak of ship fever killed half of the crew. Sam had recovered. Her father had not. Then the mainmast snapped in a storm, leaving the *Portland Bessie* limping across the Atlantic, shorthanded. A galley fire destroyed most of the supplies. Her odds of seeing land again had been dropping by the day. The situation was so poor it had come as a blessing when they were waylaid by privateers, looking for recruits. Nobody had even pointed out that boarding a British ship was not covered by the letter of marque.

Sam reckoned she had a year before she would need to part company with the *Golden Goose*. Much longer, and questions would start about why the cabin boy was showing no sign of becoming a man. With luck, she could find a place on another ship. Beyond that, she had a while longer before her face was too lined to pass as a teenage boy.

What then? Sam gave a rueful smile. Given the dangers of a sailor's life in the Caribbean, it was not worth worrying about. What chance she would live that long? And no matter which way she viewed it, her future held no place for a woman like Catalina.

Sam yawned—time to sleep. Her hammock was waiting for her below deck, but the night was warm, with no risk of rain. The air was clean and fresh, and she would not have Heinrich's snoring to deal with. In fact, it would be surprising if she was the only one spending the night under the stars.

Sam rolled onto her side, using a coil of rope as a pillow. Images of Catalina slid through her thoughts. Sam had been told her own eyes were hazel, and could seem either brown or green, depending on the light. Catalina's were ice blue—rare for a Spaniard, although far from unique. A wintry blast from them could freeze the heart beating in Sam's chest. Yet they were the feature most often filling Sam's nights. At least dreaming was safe.

Sam's eyelids closed, but before she could drift off, a murmur of voices roused her. The words were just slurred enough to suggest the speakers had been drinking.

"Are you mad? The captain will throw a fit."

"So what if he does?"

"You want to be marooned?"

"He can't do it, not over this. I know the articles. All he can do is challenge me to a duel."

Sam turned her head, straining to catch the whispers. Even without recognizing his voice, she could have guessed the last speaker was Jacob. Everyone knew he thought he had a shot at becoming captain.

The case was not clear-cut mutiny. Privateers could vote to pick a new captain, if discontent became too strong. To date, Jacob's attempts had floundered on the rocks. Mainly because nobody thought he could do a better job than Captain Williams. Jacob was a reckless fighter who believed the best answer to every problem was a sword, as now, in talking of a duel. The captain's strength was brains, not muscle. He might well lose if it came to a swordfight, but Sam's money would go on him outmaneuvering Jacob before a weapon was drawn.

"Are you sure?" a third person asked.

"Yes. It's not disobeying orders in a battle. It's not stealing from a crewmate. It doesn't risk the ship. There's nothing in the articles to say we can't drill any woman we capture."

Sam barely restrained a gasp. Of course. She should have guessed. His dick was the only thing Jacob liked more than his sword, and with both, he always wanted to be sticking it into someone.

Jacob continued. "We drill her now, and all Ned can do is challenge me, man to man."

"Some of the lads are keen on the ransom money."

"So am I, but once Don Silverarse has coughed up, there's nothing he can do about it. He'll get her back alive. He should be grateful for that. Ned plays it too safe. The lads will be happy to vote for me if I let them have some fun first."

Sam was sure he was wrong. The crew would still not vote for

Jacob, but whether or not his plans were doomed was irrelevant. By the time they fell apart, it would be too late for Catalina.

"What about the guard outside her door?"

"Not a problem. Dan's on watch tonight. And he's with us." Jacob exhaled in a humorless laugh. "So come on. What are you waiting for?"

The voices were from the main deck, directly below Sam. She lifted her head and looked around. The only other person in sight was the night helmsman on the poop deck, a silhouette against the stars. He was farther away and might not have overheard. Or he might be in with Jacob as well.

Making enemies on board was never a good idea, and Jacob was the sort to hold a grudge. The sensible thing was to lie down, go to sleep, and pretend she had heard nothing. Sam caught her lower lip in her teeth. There was no way she could stick with being sensible, but this did not mean she had to be stupid.

Sam crept down the ladder. Her bare feet made no sound on the rungs. Jacob and his friends were gone, and faint candlelight glowed from the passage under the quarterdeck. She inched forward, keeping to the deepest patches of shadow, and peered around the corner. Four men stood outside the door to Catalina's cabin, whispering, their heads close together, Jacob put his hand on the latch.

Sam had to act, and quickly. Shouting, *What are you doing?* would work. Captain Williams's cabin was at the end of the same passage, and he was a notoriously light sleeper. It would also earn Sam bruises in the days ahead, if not a knife in the back. Was she willing to put her own life on the line? Of course, if Catalina woke up and started screaming, there was no need to do anything.

Jacob slipped into the room, followed by his friends. Sam closed her eyes, praying for Catalina to call out. Slow seconds rolled by. The only sounds were the waves against the hull, the wind in the sails, and then a rustle of feathers followed by the soft boowk-bok-bok of a dozing chicken.

Food supplies on ship were holding out well. Currently, the hens were only supplying eggs to the galley. Although, by the time the *Golden Goose* returned to port, the hencoop would be empty, and everyone would have dined on roast chicken. Maybe the hens knew this, because they were the most bad-tempered birds Sam ever had the misfortune of meeting. Unfortunately, feeding them was one of the cabin boy's duties.

Sam knelt by the coop and fumbled for the catch. The faint clink when the flap opened and the squeak of the hinge roused the hens. Sam heard them stirring as she reached inside. The first chicken bobbed away from her touch, but the second was not so quick. She placed the hen on the deck and pushed it away when it tried to get back in, which went to prove that chickens were plain contrary. Normally, they were only too eager to escape.

By the time Sam released four hens, the remaining birds were excited enough to make their own bids for freedom, and the ones already out were becoming noisier as they scrabbled around, investigating anything that looked edible. She had done enough. Maybe half a minute had passed since the would-be rapists entered Catalina's cabin. Sam was not willing to allow them any longer.

She scuttled back to the quarterdeck. The silhouette of the helmsman had not moved. Had he seen her, or was he too focused on his job? Of course, he might even be asleep. If so, he would not be the only crewman to doze off at the wheel.

It was time to interrupt Jacob's plans. Sam made a show of leaping to her feet, and then shouted at the top of her voice. "HEY! THE HENS HAVE ESCAPED!"

The helmsman lurched to one side and almost fell. So he had been asleep.

Sam leapt down to the main deck. "THE HENS ARE LOOSE!"

For the first time ever, two chickens chose to help Sam. They started a fight and the angry squawks set off the rest of the birds. Then sailors who had been sleeping in the forecastle awoke. Someone threw a hatch open with a bang. The noise level was rising by the second.

Sam turned to the passage, ready to run down it, banging on the cabins. Before she could enter, the door at the end opened and Captain Williams appeared, holding a lantern. The light sent a hen squawking down the passage. It escaped between Sam's legs and fluttered into the rigging.

"The hens—"

"I heard you before, lad."

"I have to…" Sam paused. Would Jacob and his friends try to stay hidden in Catalina's cabin? What excuse could she use to ensure he was disturbed?

But there was no need. Captain Williams was sharp enough to spot the missing guard. He strode the few steps and threw the door open. Sam sidled along the passage and peered around him. Had she been quick enough?

The five people in the room were frozen in place, looking at Captain Williams. To Sam's relief, the men were fully dressed and buttoned up, and Catalina still had on a long white sleeping gown. The rest of the news was not so good. Dan stood behind Catalina, holding her. One hand was clamped over her mouth and the other held a knife to her throat. The remaining three men backed away.

Captain Williams rubbed his chin thoughtfully. "If I was to ask what's going on, do you think you could come up with some entertaining stories for me?"

Jacob did not miss a beat. "Yes, Cap'n. We were on the main deck chatting when we saw Dan take out his knife and sneak into the lady's cabin. We thought he was hoping to play in and out with her, so we came to stop him. But he got the lady and, well...you see how things stand."

Dan's expression shifted through surprise to outrage. "No. It weren't like that."

"Then how about you let go of the lady and tell me how it was?" Captain Williams's tone gave no clue whether he had bought Jacob's story.

"It weren't my idea. It was his." Dan pointed at Jacob, using the knife. "He said we could all—"

As soon as the blade moved from her throat, Catalina rammed her elbow back into Dan's gut. She dived forward, breaking free from his grasp.

Jacob was only a fraction slower. He charged into Dan, slamming him against the wall behind. The knife slipped through Dan's fingers, but before it could drop, Jacob tore it free and plunged it into Dan's chest.

Blood welled as a dark stain on Dan's shirt. "It weren't like..." He fell to his knees, gasping. "No. It—"

Jacob grabbed a fistful of Dan's hair, pulled his head back, and sliced his throat open. The spray of blood coated Catalina, who shrieked, either in disgust or horror. In the following hush, Dan's body hit the floor with a thud. A dark pool beneath him spread.

"Shame that. I was looking forward to hearing the rest of his story." Captain Williams blew out his cheeks. "I guess we need to talk this over tomorrow. Jacob, I'd like to hear again how you went to help this lady preserve her virtue. And, Sam, you can tell me about how you forgot to lock the hencoop."

"Aye, Cap'n." Of course, blame would come back to Sam. She was the last to tend to the chickens, when she fed them.

"For now, you can all go and help with the round-up. And the lady can stay in my cabin until this mess is cleaned."

"Aye-aye."

Out on deck, the hullabaloo had reached storm force. Sam returned to a scene of chaos. Were it not for the absence of gunshot and cannon, she could honesty claim to have witnessed quieter battles. Catching chickens by moonlight was not straightforward, especially when the sailors turned it into a game, laughing and whooping as they dived over barrels, skidded on wet floorboards, and crashed into each other. The capture of each hen was greeted with a deafening cheer, and a victory dance from the catcher.

In the end, most hens were returned to the coop, although three made a final bid for freedom, jumping over the gunwale to their deaths, proving that chickens were not just contrary, they were also brainless.

❖

"The thing is, you see, Jacob, her ladyship doesn't remember events quite the same way you do."

Jacob shrugged. "She was asleep. What with being woken up like that, Dan jumping on her, in the dark. It's not surprising she got confused."

Sam said nothing. The memory of Dan's death smothered any temptation to tell her own version.

Jacob had been so quick to act. Maybe blaming Dan was his fallback plan all along, if things went astray. In which case, he had jumped too quickly. He had not gotten as far as raping Catalina, but still could have stuck to his original goal of pushing Captain Williams into a duel. Except he must have heard the uproar on deck and not had any idea of what was going on. Jacob's motto—when in doubt, kill someone.

"Yep. You're right. That must be it. She's confused." Captain Williams nodded slowly, but the look in his eye said he did not believe a word of Jacob's story. "Still, it turned out all right. We've still got a full deck of cards for our game with Don Silverarse. But I'll have to give more thought to keeping our Queen of Coins safe. Just in case someone else gets ideas. So well done, Jacob. You can go."

"Aye, Cap'n."

As Jacob turned away, Sam caught a glimpse of his face. Anger and frustration were easy to read. Jacob had boxed himself in. He could not change his story now without admitting to murdering Dan.

Once they were alone, Captain Williams wandered to the porthole. For a long time he stared out, saying nothing. Sam tried not to fidget.

"That was a real peculiar turnabout last night, don't you think, lad?"

The suddenness of the question made Sam jump. "I guess so."

"Dan thinking he could get away with a sneaky game of in and out. Then him being caught by Jacob, of all people." Captain Williams shook his head. "Have you ever imagined Jacob playing the knight in shining armor, rescuing a damsel in distress?"

"No."

"Nope. Me neither. But if that isn't strange enough, just when Jacob and his mates are about to tackle Dan, the chickens get out, waking everyone up." He turned away from the porthole. "Have you ever heard anything like it, lad?"

"No."

"It's not like you've ever forgotten to fasten the hencoop before. But I guess there's a first time for everything."

"I'm sorry about that. I don't know how it—"

Captain Williams held up a hand. "You weren't paying attention. You had your mind on other things. I know. And I'm sure it won't happen again. We lost three hens, but all things considered, it could have turned out far worse. In fact, I think Lady Luck was on our side last night. So we'll say no more about it. You did all right."

Sam nodded. There was no need to speak. Captain Williams understood everything.

"So, lad. Since you slipped up with the chickens, I'm going to see if you can do any better with her ladyship. I'm putting you on guard duty. I'll pick some trusty men to run shifts with you. But I want two guards outside her door, day and night, until we have the ransom in our hold. Your first watch starts now."

"Aye, Cap'n."

Sam left the captain's cabin and walked the few steps to Catalina's door.

Birum, one of the African ex-slaves, was on guard duty. He looked hopeful as Sam arrived. "You taking over from me? Can I go?"

"No. I'm joining you. The captain wants two on watch."

"Dammit." Birum slid down the wall. "Still, now I've got someone to chat with."

Sam joined him, sitting on the floor. Birum spoke with a heavy, rolling accent, but after years with the privateers, his English was better than many of the Dutch and German crew.

"I hear Dan tried to drill her last night," Birum said eventually.

"Yup. And Jacob stuck him for it."

"The cap'n made it clear. Dan should have kept it in his breeches. But that woman, she could send any man's brain southward. I get a stiff-stander just thinking about her."

Sam did not look to check how Birum was faring at the moment. He jogged her with his elbow. "So how about you?"

"She's, she's…yup."

"Would you like to do the pillow dance with her?"

What could she say? "Well, I wouldn't mind, if…you know."

Birum gave a roar of laughter. "Dammit. I swear, you're turning red." He would not let up. "No surprise, a face like hers, turning a backdoor man into a muff hunter."

"I'm not a—"

Birum elbowed her again. "Ah. It's nothing to me. Wish there were more of you on board. Makes a shorter queue at the whorehouse when we land."

Sam knew about the rumors. Her presumed age was not so young her lack of interest in brothels could go unnoticed. Not that it was an issue for the sailors. After a month at sea, half of them would be humping each other, only to leap on the first available women when they returned to port. In fact, Sam had more trouble avoiding unwanted attention. It was such a routine hazard in a cabin boy's life, there were even songs about it.

Still Birum would not let the subject drop. "You should give women a try. It's not too late to change your mind about things like that."

A sound made Sam look up. At the end of the passage, the new recruit, the Spanish cook, was staring at her with an intense but hard to read expression. So far, Alonzo had kept himself very quiet. However, his cooking skills were drawing comments, mainly due to their absence. Even when you allowed for different national tastes, Spanish ships obviously did not expect much in the way of food.

Despite his age, Alonzo was strong and well-built, yet had shown remarkably little knowledge of life at sea. His cooking skills were matched by his rope craft. He could not tie a clove hitch or a sheepshank to save his life. Even his neatly trimmed beard marked him out from the other sailors. The current betting was that he would be put ashore at the next port and not be let back on.

Catching her eye, Alonzo gave a weak smile then stepped back, turned, and walked away.

Birum, however, remained. "When we land, you come with me. I'll find a good woman who can show you what you're missing."

Sam sighed. Which was worse, Alonzo's cooking or Birum's idea of a friendly chat? And how much longer before she got relief from either?

❖

Sam ladled out a dollop of bully stew. It landed with a watery splat and the patter of hard lumps hitting the mess tray. She wrinkled her nose. The smell reminded her of dog's breath. How difficult could cooking stew be? You soaked hard tack, dried beans, and salt beef until they were soft enough to eat, and added whatever herbs you had to hand. Yet even something this easy was beyond the talents of the so-called cook, standing on the other side of the galley.

Sam would have liked something better for Catalina's evening meal, but the noblewoman would have to suffer, along with the sailors. At least the wine was acceptable. Sam was pouring a flagon when the light dimmed. Someone was blocking the doorway. She glanced over her shoulder to see Jacob, with Gilly and Luke at his shoulder.

Alonzo had also noticed the visitors. Was he worried they had come to complain about dinner? He should be, especially when Jacob fixed on him first.

"Why don't you go and count beans for a bit?"

"Sí. Yes." Alonzo took himself into the storeroom.

Sam put down the mess tray and faced the door. Her heart hammered in her chest. All she could think about was blood spraying from Dan's throat. "You want to talk to me?"

"Just a few words."

"What about?"

"We could start with the chickens."

Sam did her best to look innocently regretful. "I don't know what happened. Maybe someone wanted to help themselves to an extra egg or two after dark."

"You sure about that?"

"No. Well, I'm sure I fastened the coop after I fed them. And the hens didn't do it themselves, though the little sods would if they could." Sam let her expression brighten. "Maybe it was Dan. Maybe he thought he could make a distraction while he did the trick with Doña Catalina."

Sam would not have dared try a line like that with Captain Williams, but Jacob did not have the captain's sharp ear. He merely scowled. "Maybe. Anyhow, the captain has put you on guard duty."

"Yes. Sixteen hours a day. I'm sick of it, I tell you."

Jacob entered the galley. Sam felt her guts turn to ice. He stood so close Sam could feel his breath on her cheek. Did he have a knife, or was he going to use his fists? But then he threw an arm around her shoulder, as if they were best mates. "Well. That's good you're keeping a watch on her."

"It is?"

"Someone has to, and you know why the captain picked you, don't you?"

"Because he's annoyed with me about the chickens?"

"No. Because he thinks you're not man enough to drill her when his back is turned."

"Um…" Jacob had no idea how right he was.

He gave her a pat on the back. "Have you ever done the pillow dance with a woman?"

"Um…"

Jacob threw back his head and roared with laughter. "I remember when I was your age. Women were strange, scary even. But once you've split a muff or two there's nothing to be scared of. All you need is to get your ramrod and bullets out and take a shot. You see, I'm not like Cap'n Ned. He thinks you're just a backroom boy. But I bet, given a chance, you could drill a woman with the best of them. And I tell you what, lad, follow my lead and I'll see you get the chance to drill her ladyship. Would you like that?"

What was it with the other sailors? Sam clenched her jaw to stop herself from saying anything rash. Suddenly everyone wanted to sort out her love life. It would have been irritating, even if they had the first idea about the truth.

Jacob patted her shoulder again and moved away. "If you want to stick with rump riding…well, each to his own, I say. But however you want to play the game, listen to me and I'll see you right."

Jacob strolled away into the sunshine with Gilly and Luke trotting like lapdogs at his heels. Sam shook her head. What was Jacob wanting, a vote if he made a bid for captain, or to set her up in Dan's role for his next rape attempt?

The storeroom door opened an inch. "He's gone?"

"Yes."

Alonzo slipped back into the galley and stood arms folded. "I was listening at the door."

"Hmm." No surprise there.

"He is not a good man." Alonzo needed to expand his knowledge of English swearwords.

"You could put it that way."

"What he said about you…a backroom boy. What is that?"

"In Spanish?" Sam shrugged. "I can think of phrases. But take a few seconds. I'm sure you can work it out for yourself."

"The captain has you watch over Doña Catalina because you do not wish to take a woman to bed? He thinks she is safe with you?"

"You'd have to ask him about that." *Actually, the captain has a good idea that I let the hens out to upset Jacob's plans.* Sam did not say it. Loose talk had a way of traveling.

"The other sailors do not like you, because of this? They make jokes about you?"

"I'm the cabin boy. Do you think they're running short of things to joke about?"

Alonzo sidled closer and dropped his voice. "I tell you, it is the same everywhere. I understand. It is hard to be a man who likes men. Hard to find a place to be safe, to find others who share your wants."

Sam shot a sideways look at him. Just how long had Alonzo been at sea? "If that's what you're after, give them a bottle of rum and half the men on board can be yours."

Alonzo frowned, as if unsure how to take her words. His expression shifted to a smile. "But all are not so good-looking as you."

Sam leapt away. Damn. She should have seen that coming. "No."

"Do not be frightened. I will be good to you."

"You ain't going to be anything to me."

"I promise. I will not tell anyone about us."

"There isn't going to be anything to tell."

"I know about boys like you."

"I bet you don't."

Alonzo continued to advance, trying to corner her. Sam would not win in a fight. He was a good five inches taller than she was, and his shoulders were as broad as any man on ship. "Please. It will be good. I have been with men before—many men. I know how to make you happy."

"No, you don't. What will make me happy is if you get back to cooking." Which was not strictly true.

"You think I am too old? I can still get as hard as any man on the ship."

Sam had run out of space to retreat. Luckily, a cook's knife was to hand. Sam snatched it up. "Not if I cut your dick off first."

"You are being foolish. You are just a child." But his eyes held a flicker of uncertainty.

"You're the fool. Since I joined the *Golden Goose* I've killed eight men. Do you want to make it nine?"

The count was open to dispute, most had been group efforts, but it had the effect Sam wanted. Alonzo took a step back and held up his hands. "You're making the mistake."

"Not as much as you." Sam waved the knife, forcing another

retreat. "You want a man to hump? There's plenty on board who'll be happy to give you what you want. But I'm not one of them."

"The other sailor said—"

"Forget what he said."

Alonzo scowled and slumped back against the wall. "You will not tell anyone about this?"

"No. You can hawk your own wares." Sam put down the knife and picked up the flagon and mess tray. "Just don't try it with me again."

"You will not say a word to Doña Catalina? Promise? Not a word?"

"What makes you think she'd care, one way or the other?" Although, as the only person on the *Golden Goose* in the habit of reading the Bible, she might know the appropriate level of hell awaiting him. Was Alonzo still a Catholic? The state of the war in Europe made things not as clear-cut as before.

"Please. Promise."

Sam merely shrugged and left the galley.

True to form, Catalina was sitting at the table with the Bible open before her.

"I've brought you dinner, miss."

Catalina gave the mess tray a look of disgust that was everything it deserved. "You call that food?"

"No. Your old cook does."

"Who?"

Sam's doubts solidified. Whatever reason Alonzo had for being on the Spanish ship, it was nothing to do with food.

Catalina's next words confirmed it. "I know supplies on a ship are limited. But nobody would have dared give me such swill on the *Santa Eulalia*."

Why was Alonzo lying? Had he gotten into a tight spot, humping one of his former shipmates, and seized the chance to part company? He was not a cook, but his lack of seacraft meant he could hardly pass himself off as a common sailor. So why had he been on the ship to start with? Not that it mattered, as long as he did not poison everyone before he was booted off ship.

"I'm sorry. I know the stew is bad, but it's all we've got."

"I would not dream of touching it. Take it away."

"You need to eat something."

"I'd rather starve."

"Please."

Catalina turned one of her ice-cold stares on Sam. "Please? You think I'm a spoiled child who needs to be encouraged to eat her dinner? You think I might mistake you for a nursemaid?"

"I just want you to be all right." Her pathetic wish for Catalina to like her was all the more wretched for having not the slightest hope of success.

"Really? You want me to believe you care for anyone other than yourself? You'd kill me in an instant if you could make a profit."

"No."

"Yes. You pirates are all the same. Murderers, thieves, and rapists."

"No. We're not."

"Prove it."

"How?"

"Next chance you get, leave this ship of depraved brutes. Find yourself an honest job."

The advice was better than Catalina knew. "I might."

"Might? Or maybe you will continue as you are now, stealing other men's property and their lives, not caring about the pain you cause."

"That's not true." She met Catalina's eyes. Long seconds drew out while Sam's heartbeat pounded in her ears.

To her surprise, Catalina was the one to break contact. Her gaze dropped to the opened pages. "Go. And take that foul slop with you."

Sam stared at the top of Catalina's head. The temptation was so strong to sit down opposite Catalina, take her hand, and tell her the truth, devil take the consequences. Would it be worth it, if for one moment, Catalina would look on her as a friend? Sam picked up the mess tray and left quickly, not giving herself time to decide if the answer might be yes, because there was no doubt what the consequences would be. Sam did not have a Don Silverarse to pay the ransom for her.

Back on main deck, Sam scraped the mess tray over the side, to poison the fishes. She leaned on the gunwale and looked down at the waves, trying to clear her thoughts. With all the tempest Catalina stirred inside her, Sam was dreading the day the ransom arrived. Catalina would be put ashore, and Sam would never see her again.

"Land ahoy."

A shout from the crow's nest interrupted her brooding. Sam

looked up. The sun was setting behind her, and purple haze cloaked the distance. Yet clear on the horizon was a smudge, piercing the skyline.

The *Golden Goose*, attended by the *Maiden's Prayer*, had been heading south-southeast, on course for the Bahamas. The Spanish had stripped the islands of natives to work in their mines. Now mostly uninhabited, they were a perfect place to hole up. However, the nearest was still two days' sailing away.

"Reef the sails. We'll take her on easy." Captain Williams gave the order. Did he know which island this was? Had it been his destination all along?

Sam stared at the distant speck until it was swallowed by the night. Somewhere, deep in her soul, something was wrong. It was an itching in her palms, goose bumps down her spine, prickling over her scalp. Shaking her head, Sam returned the mess tray to the galley and sought out her hammock. The feeling was quite stupid. And yet she was sure. Something about the island was very wrong.

❖

By dawn the next morning, the island was less than a mile off the bows. The perfect curve of golden sand was unbroken by rivers or headlands. Behind it stood a dense wall of palm trees and ferns. The terrain seemed unnaturally flat, except for the center of the island, where a table mountain punched into the sky. A shimmering haze clouded the details, but the straight sides and flat top could have been drawn by a ruler.

The previous night's uneasiness had faded but not completely gone. Sam rested her elbows on the gunwale and studied the shoreline. What was unsettling her? Nobody else had said anything. Was she the only one?

"Sam. Come here," Captain Williams called from the forecastle.

First mate Donal was with him. Both were poring over a map that was spread out on top of a locker, held down by the ship's log and sextant in opposite corners.

"What is it, Cap'n?"

"Come with me." Captain Williams walked the few steps to the bowsprit. He stared at the island. "Me and Donal have been looking at the maps. This island isn't on any of them. It strikes me somewhere nobody knows about is the perfect place to stay while we wait for Don Silverarse to cough up the coin for her ladyship."

Don't do it. The urge to speak was so strong. Sam bit her tongue.

"We'll go ashore to get supplies, but there's another matter I want you for."

"Cap'n?"

"The lady. The more time passes, the more some of the lads are going to get crazy, having to keep their hands off her. It wouldn't hurt to put temptation out of reach for a while. I want you and another couple of reliable men to take her to the island and keep an eye on her—men I can rely on not to damage her value." Captain Williams turned his head to look at Sam. "And I can rely on you, can't I, lad?" Was there the faintest stress on the word "lad"?

Sam just nodded.

"When it comes to reckoning the worth of a man, some think its balls and some think it's brains. What do you think...lad?" This time there was no doubt.

"I don't know."

"Oh, go on. Make a guess."

"Brains?"

"Dead right. The trouble is, measuring brains isn't as easy as looking in a man's breeches." His eyes fixed on Sam. "Jacob is all balls. But you've got brains, and I've got use for them."

"Thank you."

"I'm not simply sweet talking. Once we drop anchor we'll be fair set to ferry you and her ladyship ashore. I want you to keep her safe. The best man for a job isn't always a man. You follow my drift, lad?"

"Aye, Cap'n."

"Once we've finished this game with the Queen of Coins, maybe we should think about the Jack of..." He frowned. "But what's the suit? It's so hard when you don't know what suit a card belongs in."

Sam shrugged. "You can make it up as you go along. It works for me."

"That's not the safest game to play. I like to have an idea about my next few tricks."

"You don't advise laying the cards on the table?"

The smile on Captain Williams's face broadened. "Oh no. Probably best if you don't do that."

CHAPTER THREE

The Bible made it very clear. Good people who obeyed God's laws would have a nice time, and evil people would not. Catalina sighed and tried not to slump in her chair. The trouble was, the passages had limited agreement over whether the reward and retribution came in this world or the next. Some confidently promised speedy, inescapable divine justice. Others took a long-term view.

Catalina turned to the next page, seeking grounds for optimism. She felt in need of it. Her education had focused on accomplishments a future husband would find both pleasing and useful. However, enough history, politics, and current events had crept in to cause her doubts. It was impossible to avoid the suspicion that God was giving sinners a free hand in this life.

More than one hundred years had passed since Luther's rebellion against the Pope, God's representative on earth. If ever God was going to intervene, and vent His wrath on the wicked, surely this would be the cause. Yet the Protestant countries of northern Europe were prospering at the expense of the faithful. If God was not going to intervene on behalf of the Pope, what hope He would do it for her? Especially since, in her heart of hearts, Catalina knew her faith was not as strong as it should be.

She remembered Father Ortiz, the family priest, confidently announcing, "God will reveal His hand and grant victory to His chosen."

Her reply would have been better kept to herself. "In that case, God has chosen the Swedes under King Gustavus Adolphus."

Cynicism had gotten Catalina into trouble more than once. Yet clearly, victory in battle depended purely on the number of soldiers and the quality of the commanders. All the prayers spoken beforehand counted for nothing, regardless of what form they took. Catalina sunk her face in her hands. It would be so very comforting to think prayers were answered sometimes.

After a moment to gather herself, Catalina flipped farther on. Reading the Bible had limited appeal, but her only other entertainment was staring out the window, and she had seen quite enough ocean. She needed a distraction from her empty stomach, although she had no regrets about refusing the revolting swill offered her the previous night.

Foolishly, she had left her other books on the *Santa Eulalia*. She could ask the cabin boy if there was any way to fetch them, but if he managed it, she would become indebted to him, and before she knew it, she would stop seeing him as an enemy. She dared not let her resolve weaken until she was free and away.

Yet, now that she thought of it, something had changed. The motion was different as the ship rode the waves. The sun had risen and light streamed through the window, then a burst of sudden shadows flitted across the cabin wall.

Catalina went to look as another flock of seabirds swooped by. Did this mean they were close to land? She pressed her face against the thick green glass, but could see nothing apart from the sea meeting the horizon. Then she noticed what was missing—there was no wake. The ship had dropped anchor.

Footsteps sounded in the corridor. Catalina quickly returned to her chair and the Bible. The door opened, and then there was silence. Without looking up, she knew it was the cabin boy. He always took one step into the room and then stopped, staring at her as if he were a three-year-old at Christmas who has just seen the goose come out of the oven. He had not been among the would-be rapists, but Catalina had no doubt it was due to his youth. Before long he would be the same as all the rest.

Catalina kept her eyes on the page. Disregarding the pirates was the only defiance open to her. She would not ask their names, or treat any as though they were worthy of her attention. Maybe the boy had age as an excuse, but it did not take a crystal ball to see where he was headed. It was obvious by the swagger in his step and the hunger in his eyes.

"Excuse me, miss."

Catalina looked up.

How old was he? Fourteen? Fifteen? She assumed he was somewhere thereabouts. He was going to be tall, if he kept growing, although currently he had only a few inches on herself. He was lanky, all knees and elbows. His face was hollow to the point of gauntness, emphasizing the lines of cheek and jaw. Combined with the thatch of ash-blond hair and hazel-green eyes, he was almost too pretty for a male.

"Yes?"

"You need to pack some things. You'll be off ship for a while."

Catalina felt her heart jump. But no—the ransom could not have arrived so quickly. She could not stop herself from asking, "Why?"

"We've dropped anchor at an island. You, me, and a couple of others will be setting up camp ashore. You'll be safer there."

Safer was a relative term. Catalina said nothing.

"The food will be better too. I promise. We can get fresh fruit. Hunt game. I'll cook for you."

Was he expecting gratitude? None of the pirates would get any from her. Catalina had seen the trap and knew how close she had been to falling in. She fought back the memory of the men hauling her from her bed—the smell of their bodies, their breath, the touch of their hands, the way candlelight glinted in their eyes. Then Captain Williams appeared, and she had been so thankful. But he had not been there for her; he cared only for the ransom money. She owed him nothing and would ask for nothing.

She would not even request information beyond the minimum. "When do we leave?"

"Whenever you're ready. We'll be ashore for a few weeks, but the ships will stay at anchor. If you forget anything, we can send for it."

"I'll get Lu—" But Lucia was no longer with her. Either she packed her belongings herself or she asked the cabin boy. "—my things together. Give me a half hour."

"Right you are, miss." He ducked out of the cabin.

Catalina looked around. Packing would be straightforward. She could leave her church gown and wedding dress behind, also her stays. They were impossible to put on without aid. But did she want to take the Bible? Would she get bored, sitting on the beach? Was it too much to think the tropical island would be more interesting than being stuck in a cabin?

Leave it. She made the decision. She could always send for the Bible later, when things became dull.

❖

After days in the cabin, the sunlight was dazzling, blinding her. Catalina's eyes started to water as soon as she emerged on deck. She could only hope nobody would think she was crying from fear. Her concentration went into keeping her back straight and her head up.

"The longboat is on the starboard bow, just over here, miss." The cabin boy was at her side. "I'll help you down."

"I ca—"

Catalina looked over the railing. She had been about to refuse, but it would be impossible to clamber down the rope ladder unaided. In fact, even with help, it was not going to be easy. How would she maintain any decorum? And she was going to have an audience. Now that her eyes had adjusted to the sunlight, she could see every pirate on board had come to watch.

"There's a box here you can step on."

The cabin boy took her hand. His fingers were rough, gritty with dirt, and surprisingly warm. Catalina resisted the urge to snatch her arm away. She was going to need help, and rather him than any of the leering men.

From the box, Catalina was able to sit on the railing. She gathered her skirts with one hand while grasping the rigging with the other. Now all she needed was to get her feet on the ladder as gracefully as possible. However, as she swung her legs over the side, her petticoat snagged on rough wood. Her grip on the rope slipped, and she felt herself toppling. Twenty feet below, the pirates in the longboat were watching her. Catalina was suspended over their upturned faces. If she landed on the boat it would hurt, but if she dropped into the sea, would they be able to fish her out before the weight of her skirts dragged her down?

The cabin boy caught Catalina around the waist, steadying her. "Careful there, miss."

His quickness raised a cheer. "That's it, my lad."

"Give her a kiss."

"Don't stop there."

For the first time, they were close enough for Catalina to see the soft down on the boy's cheek, smell the sweat and tar on his body, feel the hard, young muscles of his arms and chest. He continued to hold Catalina while she hunted around for the first foothold.

"Are you all right now?" He loosened his hold.

"Yes. I...I don't know your name."

"Sam."

"Thank you, Sam." Anything less would be ungracious.

Catalina looked over his head, straight at Alonzo, standing amid the rabble on the quarterdeck. For the second time, Catalina nearly fell. Why was he there, with the pirates? Alonzo's eyes met hers, embarrassed, pleading, then he shook his head and took a step back, disappearing into the crowd.

"Hang on, miss. I'll help you."

Sam hopped onto the railing, grabbed a dangling rope, and abseiled down the side, moving with monkey-like agility. Presumably, he thought she was frozen with fear or uncertainty. Catalina felt him pull one foot off the rope ladder and reposition it on the loop below.

"There you go."

"Thank you." The response was automatic.

With Sam's help, they finished the ladder and settled in the boat. The half dozen pirates already there took their seats. Somebody on deck tossed down the bundle of her possessions, and four oarsmen began to row. Throughout this, Catalina was lost in a state of bewilderment.

Alonzo had been part of her life for as long as she could remember. As a youth, he had been her grandfather's squire, and as a man, her father's trusted advisor. He had played with her when she was a child and listened to her when no one else could be bothered. He had volunteered to come with her to meet her new husband, and there was nobody she would rather have along. She trusted him with her life. Despite doubts about the effectiveness of prayers, especially retrospective ones, she had offered numerous pleas that he had survived the battle. He was more than a servant; he was a friend. Of all the men who might have joined the murderous thieves, Alonzo was the very last.

Had she imagined him? Were her eyes playing tricks? The sun had been very bright. But Catalina knew what she had seen. Her surprise faded. One thing she was sure of—whatever reason Alonzo had for being on the pirate ship, it was honorable.

Catalina looked back over the previous days, when she had felt alone and surrounded by enemies, there had been a true friend close at hand, and now it was too late to talk. The *Golden Goose* was some forty yards away, with the *Santa Eulalia* behind. Both ships lay at anchor, their sails furled. The figures of pirates still dangled in the rigging, whooping and catcalling. Catalina ignored them and faced the other direction.

A perfect bow of golden sand bent away on either side. Behind was a vibrant wall of green. Far inland rose a single, flat-topped mountain, half lost in haze. The breeze carried the scent of wet soil and leaves. It ruffled the ringlets around her face, tickling her forehead and cheeks. Catalina took a deep breath, filling her lungs. The stale cabin air was flushed away.

After a few minutes, the hull of the longboat rasped on sand. Sam and the rowers jumped out and dragged the boat farther up the beach. Even so, water lay between Catalina and dry land.

"Would you like me to carry you ashore, miss?"

"No, thank you."

Catalina lowered herself over the side. The sea was warmer than she expected, but also deeper, as high as her knees. Maybe she should have given more thought before rejecting Sam's offer. Her petticoats became soaked and as heavy as lead. Each step was a struggle to stay upright. Yet somehow she managed it, fighting inch by inch. Luckily, the day was warm. Her clothes would dry quickly.

Catalina finally waddled from the sea, taking a fair amount of it with her. The inner layers of her petticoat clung to her legs like wet clay, despite attempts to kick her ankles free. With each step, her shoes squelched. The sand worked its way through the pattern of her lace stockings. She could feel the skin being stripped from her shins and heels.

Another painful step and she stopped. This was ridiculous. After checking that none of the pirates were watching, Catalina quickly removed her shoes and stockings. The sand was hot and dry between her toes. Tiny seashells crunched when she moved her foot.

Catalina stood on the beach while her dripping skirt made a wet ring around her. She was just beyond the point where smooth, wave-washed seashore met the higher, windblown banks. A dark line of dead kelp marked the boundary. On the seaward side, a tracery of bird footprints crisscrossed the sand. They were not the only creatures to have been there. Something else had left trails, like those of giant spiders, eighteen inches or more across. Were they crabs?

Meanwhile, the pirates were busy carrying supplies from the boat to a spot on the tree line. Would Sam know what made the marks? But it was unimportant. Maybe she would ask him later. Catalina continued up the beach until she reached the pile of sacks by the base of a tall palm tree.

The boat was now empty. Sam joined Catalina while other pirates shoved the longboat back to deep water and jumped in.

"It's just going to be four of us on the island," Sam said. "You, me, Ellis, and Simon. You'll be safe with us."

The only way she could imagine feeling safe was if Alonzo joined them. What chance he would be able to? "Will it just be you, or will others take turns?"

"No. Just us. The captain picked Ellis and Simon because...well, they like each other a lot, and there's no risk of them bothering you."

"How about you? Are you going to bother me?"

"No, miss. I'm...No. I won't." A faint blush rose on Sam's cheeks.

Catalina lowered herself to the sand and adopted as ladylike a position as was possible. Teasing Sam was petty, but strangely entertaining.

The camp on the beach was soon set. The pirates erected a canvas awning to shade the supplies, and Catalina was given her own screened-off section, which allowed her privacy when wanted. However, the two older pirates made it clear they intended to sleep some way off, behind a dense clump of ferns. Sam showed no interest in joining them.

Catalina was still barefoot. She sat, leaning against the palm tree and wiggling her toes in the sun-warmed sand. It felt good, although she should move into the shade. If she did not take care, she would become as tanned as a farmhand. On the voyage across the Atlantic, Lucia had continually nagged her not to endanger her complexion. Catalina did not want to meet her future husband looking as if she had just come from milking the cows.

Staying pale was not an issue for common-born pirates like Sam.

The cabin boy's face appeared even darker by comparison with his mop of ash-blond hair. Currently, he stood a short way off, staring out to sea. The scene was pretty enough. Sunlight glittered on waves, rolling gently over golden sand. The sky was deepest blue, with just a few puffy clouds drifting by. Even the pirate ships looked worthy of a painting, bobbing on the ocean.

Sam had also discarded his boots and stockings, displaying the sharply defined muscles of his calves. His knee britches were worn, loose and shapeless, but hinted at narrow hips. His shoulders were no broader than a child's, yet to fill out, though it would surely come. In a couple more years, he would be a well-built and very attractive man.

Catalina looked away. Not for the first time, she wondered what Don Miguel Perez was like. All she knew of him was his name, that he was a good Catholic widower, aged forty-five, and extremely rich. How would he fare as a husband? That was, if this marriage actually happened. Would it be third time lucky?

Her first betrothed was the only one she had met. Although, since he was three at the time and she had just turned six, her memories of him were blurred, and she had no idea what sort of man he might have become, had he lived that long.

Poor petit Chevalier Gaston. He had been heir presumptive to the Comte du... Catalina frowned. What had been his uncle's title? It had been somewhere in France starting with an A. However, the marriage was not to be. Their parents were waiting until Gaston was old enough to make his vows. That day had been drawing close, but then a riding accident claimed him, aged thirteen.

For her next prospective husband, her parents picked Freiherr Leopold of Bohemia. Yet it had turned out no better. Freiherr Leopold had been an active military man, in an age when military men did not get much chance to sit around idle. He had not even been able to attend their betrothal and had sent a junior officer to stand in his place.

There had been numerous plans for Leopold to visit Spain and solemnize their marriage, but always something would crop up—a battle to fight, a treaty to negotiate, an audience with Pope Urban VIII. After four years of delay, finally he had been on his way after concluding business in Rome. But his route went via Genoa, which was in the middle of a plague outbreak, and Freiherr Leopold got no farther.

All of which was becoming delicate for Catalina—twenty-one

years old and still unwed. Her parents agreed to the first offer they received and put her on the next ship bound for Veracruz and New Spain. No more waiting for babies to grow up or soldiers to clear their commitments.

Sam's voice pulled Catalina back to the present. "We didn't bring food, since there'll be better here. I'll see what I can find. There's always fruit and eggs. Birds too. Some of these islands even have wild pigs and goats running round. Then we'll get a fire going."

Catalina's mouth watered. However, she just nodded. No need to let him think she was grateful. She watched Sam prime and ready his pistol. His hands moved with practiced skill. He had done this before, many times.

And fired his gun.

And taken the lives of honest folk.

Sam was a killer, and if justice was served, would end up hanging from a rope around his neck. The letter of marque was a poor excuse, granted by rebels without lawful authority to issue it. Catalina tried to swallow away the tightness in her throat. She refused to feel anything other than disgust for the pirates. On the day she heard of their capture and death she would rejoice—Sam included, despite his youth. She watched him stick the pistol in his waistband and take a step toward the trees.

A breeze sprung up, growing ever stronger and raising spiraling sand devils across the beach. Overhead, the sky darkened, changing in seconds from blue to lifeless, gunmetal gray. The ground lurched. A pirate cried out in alarm, and Sam dropped to his knees. On the open sea, the water started to froth and bubble, like the contents of some monstrous cauldron.

Catalina got unsteadily to her feet as another quake shook the ground. The horizon was covered by churning rolls of mist. The sun had vanished. In the gloomy half-light, the sea was growing wilder. Raging vortexes pitted its surface. As Catalina watched, the first ship ripped free of its anchor and started to turn in drunken circles, like a leaf sucked down a drainpipe. The *Golden Goose* rolled on its side. The bows dipped beneath the water, and then the masts. Tiny figures of doomed pirates dropped from its deck into the unforgiving waves. Roaring wind drowned out their screams, but closer at hand, she heard Sam give a wordless cry.

Now the other ship, the proud *Santa Eulalia de Merida*, was caught in a whirlpool. The Spanish galleon was a larger ship, but equally helpless in the maelstrom. On the beach, the waves retreated, drawing back quicker than a man could run. The newly exposed seabed was littered with the wreckage of countless ships. This had happened before, many times.

Sam grabbed Catalina's arm. "Come back. The water will return." He tugged her toward the trees. "We need to—"

As abruptly as it had risen, the wind dropped. The sky turned blue. The waves rippled gently back over the sand, hiding their grim secret. In the space of a dozen heartbeats, the scene returned to how it had been before, except, instead of two ships, there was just debris floating on the ocean.

Sam released her arm. "What the…"

"Was that an earthquake?" Catalina had read of such things.

"I don't think so. Not like any I've heard of."

Sam stumbled toward the sea. Catalina began to follow, then stopped and stared around. She expected a landscape of carnage, a world ripped open, devastated by the tempest. But apart from part of the awning being blown away, nothing had changed. Except she was now marooned, and regardless of whether Don Miguel paid the ransom, it was one more marriage that was not going to happen.

The two older men were farther along the beach, standing motionless. Abruptly, one shouted and pointed out to sea. Something was moving in the water, a swimmer. At least one pirate had escaped the sinking ships. Sam and the others rushed to his aid. Catalina stayed where she was. Her heavy skirts would make her more hindrance than help.

A niggling worry poked at her thoughts, an awareness she could not put her finger on. Absurd after what she had witnessed, but something had changed, something important, something that should be obvious. She tried to pin it down, taking in the ocean, the sky, the beach.

Some way off, a second pirate was crawling from the sea, on hands and knees. Catalina watched Sam help him to his feet. A third body was rolling in the surf, but this one was inert, either unconscious or dead.

Catalina turned around. The line of trees was the same as before. Maybe a branch or two was snapped, and a fine coating of sand dusted the leaves. Was it her imagination or was the weather warmer? The sky might be hazier, clouds more in evidence, but shadows still lay sharply defined on the sand.

That was it. Catalina looked up for confirmation, as if it were needed. She had been right. It was obvious.

The tempest had lasted only a few minutes, five at most. Before it struck, she was sitting in the sunshine, with her back against a tree. Yet, if she returned to the spot now, she would be in shade. The sun was past its zenith. Afternoon had arrived. Hours had gone by in an instant. But how? Catalina knew she was not mistaken.

What had happened?

❖

Catalina sat beneath what was left of the awning, watching the search for survivors, although she could tell all hope had gone. The weather had turned unusually warm for March, making it easily the hottest day since leaving Spain. Her ringlets stuck to sweat on her face and neck. She found a water flask and took a long drink. What were her options? Did she have any? She rested her head on her knees.

Nine souls had survived the shipwrecks, dragging themselves to safety. To Catalina's joy, Alonzo was among them. She must talk to him and find out what was going on. Set against this, the leader of the would-be rapists also lived. Catalina had felt sick, seeing him stumble clear of the waves. She was keeping her distance, not that it would do any good.

Her memories of the attack were confused. In truth, she had gone from being asleep, to being terrified, to being stunned and sickened in the space of a minute. Yet in that time, she had formed the impression this man was the ringleader. He had certainly been the quickest to react, murdering his companion and inventing a story.

Meanwhile, between sifting through the wreckage, the pirates were arguing over what had happened. It was a waste of breath. The more Catalina listened, the clearer it became that none had any idea. Despite being just as clueless as the others, the rapist ringleader's voice was loudest and most confident. Of all the pirates, Catalina would have most wished him on the bottom of the ocean.

Another cause for regret, Captain Williams had gone down with his ship. Not that Catalina saw him as an ally, but he would have imposed order. She could have counted on him to think and plan. He might even have found a way off this island. Who knew what the pirates would do without him? Catalina buried her face in her hands. Actually, she could make a guess.

"My lady? Are you well?" Spoken softly words in Spanish.

"Alonzo. What's going on? Why are you here with them?"

He knelt by her side. "Did you think I'd abandon you?"

"No. Never."

"When the captain said we could either join or get put ashore, I knew it was the only way I'd be able to stay and protect you. Not that I've made a good job of it." His voice filled with sorrow. "I'm sorry, my lady. Surely it was the hand of the Blessed Virgin that released the hens that night. I was asleep. I helped recapture the birds, but knew nothing of what else had occurred until I heard the news the next day. Forgive me. I should have kept a better watch on you."

Catalina grasped his hand. "It wasn't your fault. I'm pleased you're here with me now. Your devotion is the only hope I have."

"Hope? My lady. It's bad…it's…"

"What?"

"I fear for you. The pirates. For now, they're preoccupied, they're shaken, but soon, they'll recover. I fear what they'll do to you." Unshed tears filled his eyes. "My lady, I'm sorry. It would be better if you died, to preserve your honor, unsullied. I…" He thumped his fist onto the sand, fighting for self-control. "I am always your servant. If you ask, I will…" He did not need to say more.

"No. I'm not asking, not yet. Not until there is no alternative." Would it count as suicide? What would Father Ortiz say?

"What can we do?"

"We can't stay here."

Catalina looked over her shoulder. Tangled plants formed an unbroken wall. Could they hide in the jungle? Would it do anything beyond delaying the inevitable? Yet it would give them time, and with time maybe she could think of something. The only other options were to sit and wait for the pirates to remember she was there, or to ask Alonzo to perform one final service.

Her shoes and stockings were dry. While putting them on Catalina asked, "Do you have a weapon? A knife? A pistol?"

"No. The captain didn't entrust me with one."

Catalina looked to the seashore. The pirates were still busy, paying her no attention. She had a little time yet. A quick search produced a second water bottle and a compass. There was gunpowder and lead shot, but the only weapon was a knife. The blade was eight inches long, just like the one the ringleader had used to slit his companion's throat. She handed the knife to Alonzo. If would make his task easier, if they were reduced to their final option. As a former squire, he would know how to use it effectively.

Shouting on the beach grew louder and more raucous. Catalina froze, thinking she had been spotted. But no, the pirates were arguing among themselves. No surprise the ringleader was in the midst of it, and his voice was the most blaring. By the look of it, a fight could break out, and possibly more bloodshed. Was it too much to hope the pirates would all kill one another? Could they be so senselessly violent?

"Come. They're distracted. This is our chance," Alonzo said.

Ferns formed a dense hedge, but the leaves were soft and easily pushed aside. Catalina squirmed through. After a few steps, the light was reduced to a green gloom, and the undergrowth thinned out. Even so, she would not be able to move swiftly in her current gown. Catalina took a deep breath, forcing herself to think rationally. This was no time for foolish modesty.

After Lucia went, Catalina had been forced to dress unaided, which required simplifying her attire. The laced corset and wicker farthingale had been sacrificed. Of all her clothes, the pale blue gown and petticoat she currently wore were easiest to put on. They also came off quickly. It was the work of seconds to strip to her knee-length smock.

Alonzo looked away but said nothing.

The compass pointed away from the beach, toward the center of the island. Catalina frowned. She would have said due north was to her right, but the needle was steady. They did not want to be running in circles.

"Let's go." Catalina led the way.

The air was thick and humid and smelled of decay. Tree trunks rose like the pillars of a cathedral. Ferns formed a carpet, cut by ribbons of bare earth. The chatter of birds floated down, along with the rustle of leaves in the breeze. Something small scurried off through the undergrowth as she passed.

Catalina paused and glanced back. A sliver of sea was visible between the trees, etched in dazzling sunlight. The pirates' voices had faded into the rush and sigh of the ocean. Still, there was no sign her flight had been noticed. They should make the most of their chance. Together, she and Alonzo pushed on, into the heart of the island.

CHAPTER FOUR

D o you want to back that up with something?" Jacob snarled.
Ellis stood his ground. "I say it goes to a vote."
"Is that so? Well, I'm voting with this." Jacob brandished his knife.
"You can't fight your way to being captain."
"For one, we ain't got a frigging boat for anyone to be captain of. For two, let's see how good you are at telling me what I can't do when you're holding your guts in your hands."

Despite all she knew of Jacob, Sam was still surprised events had come to this so quickly. She looked around the ring of spectators. Who would support Ellis? Who would cave in to Jacob? It was so damned stupid. Had everyone lost his brain?

Something was deeply wrong with this island. Sam had known it before setting foot ashore. The storm was like nothing she had ever seen. A dozen whirlpools did not suddenly appear and vanish. The sun did not jump across the sky. The word "magic" was running around in her head. She did not want to believe it, but what other explanation was there?

Sailors were superstitious by nature. Sam had long ceased being surprised at their gullibility and the credit they gave to blatant nonsense. Yet now, the one time when tales of krakens, mermaids, and sea sprites might carry weight, and they were acting as if everything was normal, as if what had happened was no more than a freak storm.

Nobody had mentioned the sun. Instead, they were quarrelling over who got to pick which pile of flotsam they looked under next, in a pointless search for survivors. No one else had made it to the beach.

The twelve of them, plus Catalina, were all who were left, and with unknown dangers ahead, they could not afford to lose anyone else.

Ellis had not yet pulled his own knife. He had to know he would stand no chance against the younger, bigger man. Jacob knew this too, which was why he was not about to give way. The only thing he need fear was if everyone ganged up against him. How likely was that? Sam checked each face again and realized one was missing. Where was Alonzo? She knew he had crawled from the sea.

Sam looked to where Catalina had been sitting in the shade of the awning. She was gone—completely gone. The only people on the beach were the squabbling band of sailors. Neither Catalina nor Alonzo were anywhere in sight. Without thinking, Sam started toward the camp.

She went only a few steps before the others noticed. "What's up?"

"I—" Sam stopped, cursing herself. She should have thought before moving.

Of course, Catalina had fled. Jacob would not think twice about raping her, and he would not be the only one. There was not even the promise of a ransom as a reason to hold back. Catalina was wise to have run when she had the chance.

Sam turned back, trying to act casual. She wanted to give Catalina the best head start, but it was too late.

Simon also noticed Catalina was missing. "Hey! Where's her frigging ladyship?"

"Dammed bitch." Jacob spat, then gave a bark of laughter. "Right, lads. She wants to make a game of it. We get to play hide-and-seek. Who's up for the hunt?"

After a moment to grasp his meaning, everyone cheered. Even Ellis joined in eagerly, to Sam's surprise. His lack of interest in women was well known.

The sailors charged over to the camp. Spotting the bent ferns where Catalina had pushed her way through was easy. Whooping and laughing, the sailors followed after, vanishing into the greenery. Jacob's voice was loudest. Within seconds, Sam was alone on the beach.

What could she do to help Catalina? Sam searched for anything to give a clue to her plans—if there were any. Several bags were upended on the ground. A knife had been in the supplies brought ashore, but Catalina would need more than that for defense.

Nobody had mentioned that Alonzo was also missing. His preference for male lovers made it unlikely he had abducted Catalina, and he lied about being a cook. So what was his role, both then and now? Might he be her guardian? It would explain why he was on the galleon, and why he volunteered for the *Golden Goose*. In which case, he was there to offer Catalina his help and protection. Sam felt an absurd stab of jealousy. It did not matter. Catalina would never look to her as a savior.

An outburst of shouting erupted in the jungle. Surely they could not have found Catalina so quickly? She must have got farther away than that. Sam dived through the wall of ferns. Leaves slapped her face, but after a few steps, the undergrowth became sparse, deprived of sunlight by the dense treetop canopy. A few yards away, the sailors were clustered around a bundle of material.

"Look, lads, she's ready for us. She's stripped already." Jacob held up the pale blue satin. "Spread out and search. Everyone, prime your pistol. When you find her, let off a shot. And no having a sneaky in and out without giving your mates a chance."

"So who does go first?"

Jacob grinned—and why not? He had what he wanted. The others were letting him take the lead. "We'll talk about that when we've found her. So what are you waiting for?"

The sailors cheered like children playing football, and raced off, all in different directions.

"Wait. Shouldn't we stick together?" Sam shouted.

Jacob was the only one to stop. He grabbed a high branch and swung around, half hanging, ape-like. "What, boy? You scared? Think you're not man enough?" He laughed. "Follow me if you want. I'll show you how to drill a woman." Then he too charged away.

Shouts echoed through the trees, getting fainter. Already, the sailors were out of sight, and once again, Sam was left alone. Her insides knotted. She pressed the sides of her head between her hands. Think. That was the first step. Think. She needed to, because no one else was.

Around her, clumps of knee-high ferns were broken into islands by rivers of brown leaf litter. Larger, thick-stemmed plants held up multi-fingered leaves, as if worshiping the light. Ropes of vines hung in coils from the treetops. During her years at sea, Sam had visited dozens of Caribbean islands. This one was not different to the eye, but she could feel her hair stand on end. Something was so very wrong.

Jacob would never make a good leader. He was a joke compared to Captain Williams. This island was unsafe. Two ships had been lost, along with most of the crew. Who knew what other dangers might lurk here? They could not afford mistakes. Yet Jacob was thinking with his dick. He had them running off on their own just because he wanted to hump a woman. The fact the woman was Catalina was irrelevant.

Or maybe not totally irrelevant.

Sam sucked in a deep breath. Whatever danger lay in wait, Catalina was also at risk. Alonzo might want to protect her, but he could not guarantee her safety alone. Sam had to find them before anyone else did. But which way?

The crack of a pistol shot broke the peace beneath the trees. Seabirds took to the air, complaining. She was too late. Someone had found Catalina first.

Sam raced through the jungle in the direction of the gunshot. She hurdled fallen trees and burst through clumps of matted shrubs. To her right, another sailor's path was converging with hers.

"Who's there?" he called out.

"Me. Sam."

She came to where a fallen tree had torn a ragged hole in the canopy. Sam stopped in the patch of sunlight, gasping to catch her breath.

Simon joined her. "Do you know who fired the shot?"

"No."

"I don't either."

Sam had guessed as much. She raised her voice. "Hey. Is anyone here? Who signaled?"

No answer.

"It sounded like it came from around here," Simon said.

Two more sailors arrived, crashing through the undergrowth. "Who fired their pistol?"

"We don't know."

Sam was about to shout again. She drew a breath and stopped. A dozen feet away, on the other side of the fallen trunk, a pair of boots stuck out from beneath a clump of ferns. Sam hopped over the tree and parted the leaves.

Jacob was lying facedown, his shirt soaked in blood. One of the other sailors knelt and turned him over. Jacob stared, wide-eyed but unseeing, at the sky. No need to check for breath. He was dead. Shot in the back.

Nobody said anything. Sam turned away to avoid meeting anyone's eyes. She could prove nothing, but no wonder Ellis had been happy to go along with Jacob's insane hunt.

❖

"What should we do with him?"

"We could carry him to the shore."

"Why?"

Sam sat on the fallen tree, playing no part. She wondered if the other sailors shared her suspicions about Jacob's killer. If so, none voiced them aloud. Simon had even gone so far as to mumble about "an accident," and nobody contradicted him—which might be how things stayed. Was anyone unhappy enough at Jacob's death to want to push the point?

The only thing giving Sam cause for doubt was that Ellis had not appeared. She expected him to turn up, gasping as if from running a distance, and feign innocence. In fact, four sailors had not yet joined them. Where were they? They must have heard the pistol. What chance one of them was the killer? After all, Ellis was not Jacob's only enemy. It might even have been Simon, acting on his bedfellow's behalf.

The sailors rambled on. "We can't just leave him here."

"Don't see why—"

A shot rang out, sounding about a quarter mile away. *Damn.* In her shock at Jacob's murder, Sam had forgotten about Catalina. That must be where the rest were.

The other sailors brightened. "Hey! They've found her."

"Let's go." Simon waved them on. "We can come back for—"

A second shot sounded, followed by a scream. The smiles vanished. Sam jumped to her feet. The voice had not belonged to a woman. Had she wronged Ellis? Was there an unknown killer on the island, hunting then down? Where was Catalina?

Simon was the first to speak. "Look lively, lads. There's trouble."

"Wait." Sam was again ignored.

They had no idea who or what they faced. Charging in recklessly was stupid. Yet within seconds, Sam was once more left alone. In the distance, a renewed clamor of shots and shouts ended in an agonized cry, cut short. Sam pulled her pistol from her belt. Was there any point following Simon and the rest?

Sam looked at Jacob's lifeless face. He had been a bastard without a conscience, a fool without any understanding of how much ability he lacked. His death was no great loss to her, or anyone else. Was there, somewhere, a mother who would mourn him? Sam doubted it.

She was about to turn away when she noticed, a few feet from his head, the unmistakable imprint of a small foot—a dainty woman's foot. Jacob might have been a fool, but he had not been running blindly through the forest. He had been tracking Catalina. Sam set off, following the footprints.

She had been traveling a few minutes when a fresh uproar erupted. Sam stopped to listen. Repeated gunfire was mixed with shouts and screams. Simon and the others had joined the battle, and judging by the sounds, they were not finding it easy. The sailors were all veterans of countless fights, both on and off the sea. It would take more than one lone foe to better them.

The island was not uninhabited. Sam had heard the tales of cannibals and headhunters. She had lumped them in with myths of mermaids and sea monsters. But why should she be surprised? This was clearly a place where magic ruled and nightmares came true.

As suddenly as it started, the sounds of battle stopped. The silence that followed was the most worrying part. Sam was very familiar with her crewmates' celebrations. The sailors were not cheering, which meant they had lost, and were either dead or prisoner. Would the unknown enemy now be content with the victory, or would they come looking for her?

Sam started to run. Ferns snatched at her legs, vines slapped her face, and then a tree leaped into her path. The jolt as she crashed into it knocked her back to her senses. This was more than stupid. She had no idea where she was headed, and was as likely to blunder into a trap. On top of this, she was leaving a trail a blind man could follow and making enough noise to alert anyone with a pair of ears. Sam rested her hand against the trunk, waiting for her heartbeat to slow.

The jungle was silent. No hint that she was being followed. Sam moved on carefully, watching her footsteps, trying to make no noise. Then she caught a distant sound, a clicking, like someone sucking their tongue off the roof of their mouth. "Tck-tck-tck, tck-tck-tck." It was not birdsong, she was sure. An insect or a secret code? More than one mouth was making the sound, and all were coming in her direction. She had to find somewhere to hide, and quickly, a dense patch of greenery, a hole in the ground, anywhere.

Sam moved on, searching. A glint in the leaf litter caught her eye. She grimaced as she picked up a brass compass. At least she would know which direction she was going when she was overtaken. All the time the clicking was getting closer. "Tck-tck. Tck. Tck-tck." Was it some strange language? How long did she have?

High above, the canopy of leaves was dense enough to hide in, but would she be able to climb, even with her experience of shimmying up masts and swinging though rigging? The clicking was getting closer by the second. "Tck-tck. Tck."

Sam could feel panic rising. She went from trunk to trunk. Which would be best? The last thing she expected was for a knotted rope to drop, no more than ten feet away.

"Up here. Skjot."

Sam skidded to a halt.

A second voice, Catalina's. "That's one of the pirates."

Sam started to climb. Above her, she saw the rope disappearing into the canopy.

A third person spoke. "We don't leave anyone for the hunters."

Sam felt the rope being hauled up with her on it. Still, she continued to climb with all the speed she could muster. A few seconds more and she arrived at a fan of branches. Palm fronds were interwoven between the limbs, forming a circular platform in the air. It felt secure, if not completely firm.

Five people were already there, including Catalina wearing just a loose smock and stockings. Sam tried not to stare. The smock was embroidered and obviously expensive. It covered Catalina from chest to knees, but still left more skin exposed than anything Sam had seen her wear before. There was even a hint of cleavage between her breasts. Someone kicked Sam's foot, reminding her she was not alone. The someone was Alonzo, who scowled at Sam though he said nothing.

She turned to the others. The three strangers were dressed in loose-fitting breeches that did not reach their knees. They had woven reed sandals on their feet. Two wore simple sack-like shirts, while the other was bare-chested. Aside from their clothing, their appearance was as different as it was possible for three men to get.

The bare-chested one had the look of the native islanders. His skin was the color of tanned leather. He had solemn dark eyes and a thoughtful expression. Thick black hair was wound in a knot on top of his head. His body was tattooed with bands of intricate patterns, snaking across his chest and around his arms.

The biggest was a giant of a man. He had a thick mane of long yellow hair. His bushy mustache and beard could not hide his broad smile. The absence of lines around his eyes put him in his mid-twenties, several years younger than his native companion. He was the one who had been pulling up the rope with her on it, an action not requiring any great effort on his part.

The last of the three was easily the oldest, aged fifty or more. His hair was receding and gray at the temples. He had clearly made some attempt to shave that day, with mixed success. Small nicks marked his round face. He blinked at her through a pair of spectacles, which made his eyes appear smaller than they truly were. Sam had seen such lens devices before, although not with side arms to hold them secure on the wearer's face. It struck her as a sensible addition.

Sam opened her mouth, but the oldest man held a finger to his lip and whispered, "Shush. Wait until the hunters have moved on."

She peered down through the leaves.

"Tck-tck. Tck. Tck-tck-tck."

The source of the clicks was now directly below, although Sam could see nothing. A blur of movement caught the corner of her eye, gone before she had a chance for a proper look, but Sam saw that she had been watching for the wrong thing. These hunters were not human. They were too small, too quick, and with too many legs. Another bush rustled and twitched, and then another. How many were in the pack? Yet already the clicks were moving away. Whatever sort of creature these hunters might be, they were not in the habit of looking up for their prey.

The party in the treetops waited until the sounds had faded.

The blond giant was the first to speak. "Close. Ja." He let out his breath with a sigh.

The other two men also relaxed.

"Who are you? Do you know what this place is?" Sam asked.

The native gave a smile and said, in softly accented English, "My name is Yaraha. Welcome to the Isle of Broken Years."

The name was not one Sam had seen on any map. What had she been expecting? She was in the land of fairies. No doubt, unicorns and dragons would show up next.

The oldest man spoke. "Catalina and Alonzo had just introduced themselves before we spotted you." His English was fluent, but although he appeared European, his accent was as unfamiliar as Yaraha's. "You are?"

Before Sam could speak, Catalina answered for her. "He's a pirate."

"He?" The man looked at her, clearly confused, then shrugged. "Okay."

Oakie? Had he called her that? "My name's Sam. I'm cabin boy on the *Golden Goose*. Well, I was before it sank."

"Yes. That has a habit of happening to ships around here. But you were the cabin boy?"

His tone made it a question and there was stress on the word *boy*. He knew she was a woman. How had he seen through her so quickly? Even Captain Williams had taken a year. However, he did not seem about to challenge her. He continued, without waiting for an answer. "I'm Charles Wooten, navigator on the *Okeechobee Dawn*."

"Did your ship sink too?"

"The *Okeechobee Dawn* isn't a ship. Not as you'd think of it. She's a seaplane. Fortunately, Babs was able to bring her down safely, even after the engines cut out. But she won't be able to take off unless the electromagnetic interference lets up." About a third of what Charles said made sense. Was it due to his peculiar accent? He pointed to the blond man. "This is Torvold Olavson, he's a Viking. He's one of the few people to have the misfortune of being shipwrecked even before getting to the island. He paddled his way here on a raft he'd lashed together."

"How. Do. You. Do?" Torvold said each word separately, like a child who has been practicing.

Charles grinned. "He's been here less than a year and is still learning English. But don't let him wind you up. He's actually getting quite good at it." He gestured to the native. "Yaraha was blown here from the mainland by a storm. He was one of eight in a fishing canoe. And that was..."

"Eleven years ago," Yaraha said. "Now there's just me and Piracola left."

Charles asked. "So, you three, what year was it for you?"

"What year when?" Sam's confusion was not easing.

"What year when you got here?"

"Last night."

"Do you know the date?"

"March the 20th, 1631." The start of an idea crept into Sam's head. "Broken years?"

"Yup. That's it. The island keeps hopping back and forth through time. Won't stay still. That's what causes the whirlpools and the like. The whole island gets sucked out of one year and splashes down in another. Time is getting sliced and diced. The Isle of Broken Years was the name one of Yaraha's friends gave it. There are others. You can pick which you prefer when you know more."

Catalina looked as stunned as Sam felt. "That doesn't...It's...You mean you've all come from different times?"

Charles nodded. "I know. It takes some getting used to."

"How?"

"If we could answer that, maybe we could escape. Liz knows more than anyone. Save your questions for her."

"There are others here?"

"Yes. Liz has been here longest. She was a scientist with a team who wanted to investigate the Bermuda Triangle." Charles gave a wry smile. "She's the world expert on it now, even if she's just turned up more questions than answers."

"How many are here?"

"It'll be fifteen, including you three."

"There were other sailors from my ship. They're the ones you'd have heard..." Sam's voice died at the sight of Charles's expression.

"I'm sorry. They wouldn't have gotten the better of the hunters. Were they friends of yours?"

Catalina scowled. "They're pirates and murderers."

Charles glanced between Catalina and Sam. "That may be, but we don't judge here. We can't afford to. We have to work together and let go of old scores."

"They deserve to hang."

"Possibly. But we'll all die soon enough." Despite his grim words, Charles sounded cheerfully resigned. "The hunters don't differentiate between honest folk and crooks. This island's a dangerous place. We've all lost friends. So, like I said, Sam, I'm truly sorry."

Sam caught her lower lip in her teeth and nodded. How did she feel? There were a few sailors on the *Golden Goose* she might have called friends, but none had survived the sinking. Of those on the island, were there any whose death touched her deeply?

"What are these hunters?" Catalina asked.

"Madison calls them bio-robots."

"A bio-robot? What's that?"

"You can ask Madison when you meet her. But I can't guarantee you'll be any wiser afterward."

Torvold gave a snort of laughter. "Madison. They say she talks English. I am not so sure. Lady Gagger, the book of faces, neck flicks. I think she makes up things to trick me."

"In that case, she's doing the same to me," Yaraha said with feeling.

Charles grinned. "If it makes you feel any better, she's just as baffling for me and Babs, and we were only eighty years before her."

"So where...when are we now?" Sam asked.

"No way of telling, unless someone new arrives and they avoid the hunters."

Torvold peered over the edge of the platform. "Talk of the hunters, they are gone now. When do we go down? When do you think it is safe?"

"It's never safe. Still, I'd vote for waiting in the roost till morning. The hunters are always more active after a time jump," Charles added for Sam, Catalina, and Alonzo. "They come looking for new castaways. But they're unpredictable. Old Town is the worst spot. We think it's where their nest is—that's if they have a nest. The closer you are to Old Town, the less warning you get after a jump."

"How far away is this Old Town?" Sam asked.

"The opposite side of the island. We're as far away here as we can get. Not that it means much. Some jumps and they'll be out here in minutes. Other times they don't show up for hours."

Yaraha said, "I agree with Charles. We should wait until tomorrow before returning to the Squat."

"The Squat?" Sam could not tell whether he meant it as a place name or an activity.

"That's what someone called it a long time ago. It's where we live, on the middle island."

"There's another island?"

"Yes. In fact, there are three in total. We have to cross the inner sea to get to the Squat."

"The hunters don't go there?"

"No. Otherwise we would not be here to talk to you," Yaraha said with a smile.

"So why don't you stay there? Why come here, if it's so dangerous?" Catalina voiced Sam's next questions for her.

"Food. We were on our way back from the farm when the island jumped."

"Farm? Would you have any food you could spare?" Catalina's eagerness was obvious.

Sacks were hanging from a nearby branch. Yaraha lifted the nearest one down and took out papaya and avocados. "Here's fruit. Mainly we harvested maize and potatoes, and I caught a pair of ducks. We also have eggs if you don't mind them raw."

"Fruit will do. Thank you so much. I couldn't eat anything last night." Catalina directed a glare at Sam.

Don't blame me. It was your friend Alonzo's fault. The not-cook had been silent throughout the conversation, sitting beside Catalina. His only contribution was to frown anytime anyone dared look in Catalina's direction. Had Charles and the others noticed? Alonzo gave the clear sense he saw himself as a guardian. If it had not been his official role on the Spanish ship, he had now taken it on himself.

Torvold shook the branches, making the platform sway. "You think the hunters are less to fear than we fall off when we sleep?"

"Won't be the first time I've slept in a roost," Charles said. "We can take turns on watch. Make sure nobody rolls over in their sleep. It wouldn't be a bad idea to wake anyone who's snoring too loudly. The hunters can hear. They've never shown any interest in climbing trees, but I don't want to learn the hard way that they can."

Sam took a bite of papaya and looked up through the lattice of leaves. The moon was a silver disc, set in the darkening sky. She could not restrain a gasp, nearly choking on the fruit. Any doubts about Charles's story vanished.

"What is it?" Yaraha asked.

"The moon. It's full, but should be past the last quarter." Sam shook her head. "I don't know why it's so shocking, after talk of jumping years, but…" She shrugged. "I suppose, as a sailor, the stars and moon are your guide. If you can't trust them, then you're totally lost."

Sam kept staring at the moon while she ate the fruit. Had she ever imagined it was possible to be this lost?

Sam and Charles took the first watch. Darkness claimed the sky, but the moon cast enough light to pick out the curled shapes of sleeping figures. After years spent clambering though ship's rigging, Sam had a good head for heights, but some of the group were clearly uneasy and had taken a long time to settle. Alonzo had placed himself between Catalina and the rest, as if fearing they might assault her in the night.

Sam's ears were trained for the "Tck-tck-tck." Yet time passed, and she heard nothing except for four sets of breathing and the sounds of the night forest—a rustle of palm fronds in the breeze, the thrum of soft insect wings beating the humid air, and the distant rush of the ocean on the beach.

Charles was so still, Sam was beginning to wonder if he had drifted off, but then he said, "You are a woman, aren't you? I'm not wrong?"

"How did you know?"

His teeth showed white in the darkness as he smiled. "It's to do with fashion. The markers you look for, when you first meet someone, and make a split-second judgment. When fashions change, you can't simply pick up on clothes and hairstyle. You have to look at the person.

I saw you and immediately thought you were a woman. It threw me when Catalina called you he."

"What was it about me?"

"Not sure. The way you move, or something in your eyes, your jawline. Maybe all it takes to mislead people in your time is to hack off your hair, ditch the skirt, and shimmy up a rope. I'm used to women with short hair, wearing pants, and acting like tomboys. I'm also used to women who want to go and explore the world. You'll understand when you meet Babs."

"Are you going to tell the others?"

"Do you want me to?"

Sam's gut reaction was to say no. But did it matter? "What would people here say about it?"

"In what way?"

"Would they think I was unnatural?"

"Oh God, no."

"Would they want me to..." Sam tried to think what she would least like about being treated as a woman.

"Sit indoors, do the cooking, and knit booties for babies?"

Apart from being unsure what booties were, it seemed about right. "I'd hate it."

He chuckled. "You're going to get on well with Babs."

"I won't be expected to act like a housewife?"

"It'd be more problematic if you did. The island is deadly. I'd say no one lasts long here, except Liz is doing okay. We all take our share of the risks. We can't carry fainting maidens. Catalina will probably have more problems than you." He glanced at where she lay sleeping. "What made you decide to pass as a boy?"

"My pa. When my aunt died there was no one to look after me, so he took me to sea with him. He disguised me as a boy. I've been living as one ever since."

"How old were you?"

"Seven or eight."

"Sam is short for Samantha?"

"No. I was Sarah." How long since she last thought of herself by that name?

"And you were a real pirate? Yo-ho-ho and a bottle of rum, and all that?"

"Yo-ho-ho?"

"Robert Louis Stevenson. I guess he was a bit after your time. But you were a pirate?"

"We were privateers, in theory. The captain had a letter of marque from the Dutch Republic."

"You didn't regret your father taking you to sea?"

"No."

"Was it fun?"

"In parts, I guess."

Sam leaned back and stared at the stars. It felt good to be able to talk, without the need to lie and guard every word she said. Sam had loved her father. Her heart ached at his death, but beyond that, she had not realized how much she missed simply having somebody she could relax with. For the last year she had been always on guard, watching herself. It was over. She need never play at being cabin boy again.

"You can tell them I'm a woman." Sam made the decision.

"Why don't you tell them yourself?"

Sam smiled. Indeed, why not? It would be fun to see Alonzo's expression—Catalina's too, come to that. "I might."

"Then I'll leave it to you. Sleep on it."

"Thanks. I will."

CHAPTER FIVE

The rope swayed as Catalina negotiated each knot. This was despite Alonzo standing at the bottom, holding it steady for her. Halfway down, and it felt as if her arms were about to pop from their sockets. Her hands were skinned raw. Reaching the treetop platform yesterday would have been impossible if Torvold had not hauled her up. She should have asked him to lower her now, but it was too late. He was already on the ground. Catalina made the mistake of looking down. Her head swam. She refocused on the rope and felt with her foot for the next knot.

Were it possible, Catalina would have sworn the rope had grown longer overnight. Each step was torture, a never-ending nightmare. The ground came as a surprise when she finally reached it. Catalina staggered and needed Alonzo to steady her. Her arms and legs were shaking, her hands throbbed, but it was over. She took a step back and gave Alonzo a grateful smile.

The final person was Sam. He dropped down the rope, hand over hand, barely using his feet at all, making light work of what had been such an ordeal for her. Not that it was appropriate to compare herself to a cabin boy.

Charles secured the end of rope around the tree trunk. "For the next time we need a roost."

Sam watched him do it. "It's certain there will be a next time?"

"Count on it."

Yaraha swung a sack over his shoulder and pointed. "The boat is this way."

Torvold grabbed two others, ready to follow.

"Wait. We must take more care," Alonzo said. "Doña Catalina should be in the middle."

"Why? Can she not walk where she wants?" Yaraha asked.

"We must be ready to protect her."

Torvold laughed. "We cannot protect. If the hunters come, we all run. Very fast."

"Doña Catalina is daughter of Vizconde Pedro de Valasco. She—"

"If she cannot run, then she should learn."

Charles joined in. "There are no viscounts here. Catalina is just another person. That's all. She takes her chance with the rest of us." As if to emphasize the point, he handed them both a sack.

Alonzo was temporarily speechless, although he soon recovered. "How da—"

Catalina had also been surprised, but she put her free hand on Alonzo's arm. "It's all right. Without them, we'd be dead." Charles was not being deliberately unfriendly or provocative, merely stating facts. After her time with the pirates, it was easy to spot the difference.

Alonzo still glared at Charles, but then took Catalina's bag from her and stalked off, carrying both. "I know how to treat a lady."

Everyone ignored his muttering, although Charles and Sam exchanged an amused look, as if sharing a joke over it. What did it say about the castaways if a pirate was more favored company than a noblewoman? Catalina already knew Sam was no gentleman, and neither were the others, it would seem.

However, a seed of discomfort sprouted. The memory resurfaced, of her and her friends, mocking their grandparents' outdated views. Not decades, but hundreds of years stood between her and the castaways. It was naïve to expect them to obey the social rules she was used to. *When in Rome...* If she did not want to become a figure of ridicule, she had to be willing to change. Alonzo meant well, but he would also need to adapt. Although, she had to admit, she was grateful not to be burdened for the walk. Her legs were still unsteady.

Fortunately, Yaraha did not set a fast pace. He moved with a stealthy grace, watching and listening. His feet made no noise. Catalina wished she could draw more confidence from his obvious familiarity with the jungle, or Torvold's strength, or Alonzo's loyalty. She tried to keep up with them, while Charles and Sam brought up the rear, each carrying a sack.

Catalina knew the island had not changed from the day before, but now it felt far more ominous. Had the air always been so thick? Every shadow held a threat. Splayed leaves were monstrous hands, reaching for her. She jumped at a dry click, but it was just a stone striking another. Catalina felt her heart trying to climb up her throat. The pirates had frightened her, but they were a known, comprehendible danger. These hunters belonged only in nightmares. Then, amazingly, she heard Sam laugh. Of all sounds, it was the last she expected. Catalina glanced back.

Sam and Charles were strolling along, as if on a leisurely jaunt in the countryside, clearly at ease. In fact, Catalina had never seen Sam look so relaxed and cheerful. Even the way he walked was more animated than before. There was a spring to his step, a fluidity to the set of his shoulders.

Sam held something in his hand. Catalina thought it might be the compass she had dropped the day before when she was surprised by voices calling from the treetops. She slowed a little to catch what Sam was saying.

"This is wrong. North has to be over there."

"Probably is," Charles agreed.

"But the compass is pointing this way."

"It will be pointing to the center of the island. It's the electromagnetic interference. That's what killed all the instruments on the *Okeechobee Dawn*."

"That was your ship?"

"Our seaplane."

"What's that?"

"You'll see."

"It had instruments that could die?"

"If they ran out of juice."

"Juice?"

"Or got zapped."

Sam was silent of a while. "Do things here ever start making sense?"

"No."

The jungle ahead was becoming lighter. Before long, the group emerged beside a wide river. Or was it? Surely the waterway was too big for the island. The opposite bank was a quarter mile distant. Yaraha had spoken of an inner sea, so was this an inlet? The water stretched in both directions, curving gently inward. A vague memory nagged in Catalina's head. She should recognize this. But how?

"Here is our wonderful boat, the *Inflatable*," Torvold said.

The craft was unlike any Catalina had seen before. It was bright orange. The sides looked as though they were made from tubular cushions. It had three benches to sit on, but no rowlocks. At first, she thought there were no oars either, but then saw two small paddles on the floor. It would take a long time to cross if that was all they had.

"How does it float so high in the water?" Sam clearly was also unfamiliar with the type of boat.

"There's air inside. Like a balloon," Charles answered. "That's why it's called the *Inflatable*. Really it's a description, not a name, but we've got to call it something."

The boat was tied to a stump. Yaraha slipped the mooring rope loose and towed it to where a rock formed a natural jetty. From the way the *Inflatable* responded, it was surprisingly lightweight.

Yaraha held the boat steady for them to board. "Watch out for fish in the water. They're nasty."

"How nasty?" Sam asked.

"Like piranhas with extra teeth and a sore head," Charles said, laughing. "They're another of Madison's bio-robots. They're not really fish. You couldn't eat one, but the same doesn't work in reverse. Your chances aren't good if you fall in, and I'd recommend keeping your hands inside."

Alonzo dropped the sacks he had been carrying in the *Inflatable*, then turned to make a show of helping Catalina. The boat rocked as she took a seat, and she was grateful for the helping hand, but Alonzo's manner was excessive. He clearly intended his actions as an example of good manners for the others. It was not going to work. Catalina could tell from their expressions. Maybe she should say something to him when they had the chance for a private chat.

Meanwhile, Sam prodded the side experimentally. "Oilskin?"

"Rubber."

"What does it rub?"

"Rubber is the stuff it's made of."

"Oh." Sam picked up one of the small paddles. "This is it?"

Torvold's grin split his beard in two. "You are a sailor, ja? Watch. You will like this. Oh yes, you will like this."

He knelt by a box at the rear and pulled hard on a cord coming from it. The sudden eruption of noise made Catalina jump, and she barely restrained a squeal. The sound would have resembled that of an angry bee, if bees could produce the same volume as a church bell. The *Inflatable* surged forward. Catalina clung to the side as spray whipped her face. Amazingly, they were moving as fast as a galleon in full sail.

Torvold threw back his head and roared with delight. "So far I have rowed. Heave-ho, heave-ho. So many seas. Of all the wonders I have seen, I tell you, this is the best. The very best. My grandfather was a wise man, but even he had no tales of anything so good. If I could take it back to my home, I could ask for gold beyond counting."

"Until the gas ran out," Charles said.

"Always, you spoil my dreams."

"Then dream on, my friend."

Catalina tried not to watch the water for signs of the deadly piranhas. She did not need to frighten herself more. Instead she divided her attention between the two shorelines. Now that she was out on the water, the uniformity of the twin curves was unmistakable. If the inner sea maintained the same arc in both directions, it would meet itself, forming a complete ring, with the flat-topped mountain in the center. That could not be natural—concentric rings of land and sea set around a mountain?

Catalina gasped in surprise. Of course she recognized it. Why had it taken her so long?

"Charles, you said about other names for this island."

He smiled at her. "Have you thought of one?"

"Yes. I've read Plato. This is Atlantis."

❖

Even from a distance, the differences between the two island rings were obvious. The outer one had been a jungle. The one they were approaching was a garden. The land was laid out with clipped formal hedges and flower beds. The trees stood in ruler straight rows. However, the plants were unlike any Catalina had seen before.

The grass, if that was what it was, shimmered purple-red. The trees were thirty-foot-high blades of yellow and white. The flowers might have passed for orchids, except they formed clusters, with each flower the size of a plate.

Set among the beds were numerous flat-topped structures, all built from the same yellow stone that lined the waterfront. The top of the embankment was only two feet above sea level. Tides must not be an issue here.

Catalina saw a knot of people gathering on the quay, clearly attracted by the sound of the rowing box. Torvold did something to cut the noise to a low drone. The boat's speed slowed accordingly, and they coasted toward the waiting group.

"We were starting to worry about you."

"Us? We're fine. How could you doubt it?" Torvold shouted back.

"We picked up some newbies," Charles added. Catalina assumed the term related to her, Alonzo, and Sam.

The side of the boat bumped the wall of the embankment. Yaraha threw the mooring rope to one of the watchers and sprang ashore. Another native with an identical topknot exchanged a few words with him in a lilting language Catalina did not recognize. Everyone else seemed to be speaking a variant of English, although she had to listen carefully to be sure in some cases.

Catalina again accepted a hand from Alonzo to step onto the quay. She was all too aware that, just like an embarrassing dream, she was meeting a collection of strangers while dressed in her underwear. Admittedly, her state of undress was more in keeping with the castaways' loose, knee-length breeches and shapeless smock tops than her gowns, but it did not make her feel any less awkward.

A new person joined the gathering, an elderly woman with curly white hair and a face crisscrossed by lines. The skin on her hands sank between her knuckles and was dotted with liver spots. Yet her eyes were sharp and she carried herself with resolve. She was the leader of the castaways. Of that, Catalina had no doubt.

"Welcome to the Squat. My name's Elizabeth Anderson, but I answer to Liz."

Out of habit, Catalina started to curtsy before remembering her clothes did not lend themselves to such formalities. "I am Catalina de

Valasco, daughter of Vizconde Pedro de Valasco, and this is my family retainer, Alonzo Ortiz."

Liz patted Catalina's shoulder. "No need to stand on ceremony, dear." She had a strange accent, similar to Charles, although with more of a nasal twang. She turned to Sam. "And you are?"

"Sam. Sam Helyer. I was cabin boy on the *Golden Goose*. The ship has sunk, and I'm the last survivor." Sam hesitated, as if making a decision. "So I've missed my chance to tell my crewmates I'm not a boy. Probably just as well. I don't think they'd have been happy about a cabin girl."

While people around her laughed, Catalina needed long seconds to be sure she understood what Sam had just said. But there could be no doubt. She was dimly aware of Alonzo at her side giving a low growl. Mostly, Catalina just felt her jaw drop open.

❖

Catalina had assumed the yellow buildings were houses. They had clearly been made for a purpose, yet they were devoid of windows and doors. The walls were built from large blocks, cut and assembled without mortar, creating wavelike patterns in the stone.

"This is the Squat." Liz's wave took in a group of buildings, set around a purple lawn. "I guess you're wondering why we call it that."

Catalina nodded out of habit. In truth, the only thing she was wondering about was Sam. Was he…she really a woman? It was hard not to stare, looking for signs.

"I don't know who first gave it the name, probably someone from the twentieth century. Squatting is a slang term, meaning to take over an empty building. The owners have gone, so now we live here."

"These are houses?" Sam asked.

"Right enough."

"Where's the door? How do you get inside?"

Catalina glanced across. Of course, the pitch of Sam's voice did not belong to a child, or a man. How had she not noticed it before?

"Like this." Liz marched along a broad flagstone path, leading straight to the nearest wall, where curves in the stone formed the outline of an arch.

Five feet off the ground, a small black circle broke the uniformity of yellow. The disc was inset, and possibly made of glass, judging by the way light shimmered over it. Liz waved her hand in front, without touching. Immediately, a vertical crack split the arch and the two halves slid apart, vanishing quickly into the wall on either side.

Catalina jumped back. The day had contained too many surprises. She did not know how much more she could take.

Liz put an arm around Catalina's shoulder and gently urged her forward. "Don't worry, dear. You'll get used to it."

They entered a large room. A warm light filled the space from no obvious source, casting no shadows. It was as if the entire ceiling was a lamp. In the center, a fountain splashed into a basin, surrounded by a high circular bench.

"This is the common room. We gather here for meals and the like," Liz said.

The aroma of cooking was enough to make Catalina forget all else. There was only so far that fruit could go to assuage the hunger gnawing her stomach. "Does that mean we might get breakfast?"

The others were following, carrying sacks from the *Inflatable*. Yaraha spoke. "It does. I'll cook. Torvold can put the supplies into storage."

Charles laughed as he handed over the sack he was carrying. "Believe me, that's the safest way around. Torvold has many talents, but cooking isn't one of them."

"You do not like my food?"

"Has anyone, ever?"

"Humph." The exchange was in good spirits.

"Do you want breakfast, Charles?" Yaraha asked from the doorway leading to an adjoining room.

"No. It's okay. I'll find Babs. Catch you later." He smiled, patted Sam on the back, and left. Torvold followed Yaraha from the room.

Catalina snuck a longer look at Sam. Questions seethed in her head. The pat had been a gesture of support. Had Charles known Sam was not a boy before she made her announcement on the quay? But what was Sam? A girl? A woman? How had Sam kept her secret from the other pirates? Or had she? It was easy to imagine the sort of woman who would choose the company of vulgar sailors. But no—Catalina remembered the way the pirates treated her. They had not known.

"Okie-dokie. First things first." Liz clapped her hands for attention. "We need to put you in the book. Take a pew."

Catalina's parents had ensured she was schooled in every language a prospective husband might speak. She had thought her command of English was good, but now she was at a loss.

Sam was just as confused. "Take what pew where?"

"I mean, sit down. Make yourselves at home."

The circular bench had a cushioned top and was clearly intended as a seat. However, it was too high. Catalina did not see how to get on while maintaining decorum, nor would she be able to rest her feet on the floor, once up there.

Neither of these issues were a problem for Sam, who jumped up with a backward hop, and then sat, cross-legged. Was she really a woman?

A band of daylight fell across the floor as the door opened and a man and a woman entered the common room. Catalina thought they had been among the castaways on the quay. The man was tanned, middle-aged, and bald. The woman was younger, and had the dark skin and curly black hair of an African.

Meanwhile, Liz opened one of a grid of hatches on the side wall. She called out, "A bit of advice, never leave anything lying around. The caretakers will assume it's trash and you'll never see it again. Always put stuff you want to keep in a locker, like this."

"Can't you tell them not to?" Sam asked.

"They aren't human and don't take orders." The man who had entered held out his hand. "I'm Floyd."

Without getting up, Sam leaned forward to grasp it. "Sam. From the *Golden Goose.*"

"US Coast Guard."

Sam frowned. "Did you say useless coastguard?"

Floyd laughed. "No. U. S. United States."

"Which means?"

Liz rejoined them, holding a large book. "It means you're from before 1776." She held up a finger. "No, don't tell me. Let's see how close I can get. You can introduce yourselves while I find the page."

Floyd looked as if he was made from a series of balls, strung tightly together, with a round face, and round bulging muscles. He had to be in his fifties but was obviously still fit and active. What time period had he come from? But some things did not change. His straight back, along with the set of his shoulders, marked him as a soldier.

"You were in the army?" Catalina asked.

"Yes, ma'am. Started in the 29th Infantry Division, finished in the Coast Guard." He touched a forefinger to his brow. "Sergeant Floyd Lombardi."

"You'll have been in his boat already. The *Inflatable* came with him and his comrades," the woman said.

"While poor old *USS Donahue* sank." Floyd assisted the African woman onto the bench. In her case the help was doubly needed, since she was clearly in the middle stages of pregnancy.

Once seated, she leaned back with her legs outstretched. Her shift top rode up over her gently bulging stomach. She smiled at them. "My name is Kali." Her voice was deep and rich.

Catalina guessed Kali was a similar age to herself. She had seen Africans before—many at court owned slaves from across the known world, as far away as Japan—but this woman acted with none of their deference, and not just in her relaxed pose. Kali's eyes met hers in honest, open appraisal. No viscounts, no special people, and it would seem, no slaves. Catalina's grandmother would have been shocked. Fortunately, Catalina was not her grandmother.

"I'm Catalina, and this is my fam—friend, Alonzo." Most likely, there were no family retainers.

"Right, found it." Liz had a forefinger on the open book. "So let's see, last jump, Atlantis had been stable for eighty-two days, which means…" She traced across the page. "You're from 1625, give or take."

"March 1631," Sam said.

"That's not bad. Maybe I can shave Nate's numbers a little." Liz sounded thoughtful.

"Nate? Is he one of the people here?"

"He was, but he's long gone. He was first to spot the link between the date and the gap between jumps. The further back in time we go, the longer Atlantis stays put. Nate started plotting a graph. The trouble is, the points were concentrated at one end, which left a lot of extrapolation to do. There've been castaways like Madison, who managed to get herself shipwrecked during a ten-minute window in 2016. At the other extreme, the longest Atlantis has ever gone between jumps is 4,172 days, but nobody arrived then, and they wouldn't have had a clue about the date, even if they had. Like Yaraha and Piracola. They're pre-Columbus, so they've never heard of Pope Gregory, or his calendar."

"I couldn't give a date either," Kali said.

"She escaped from a slave ship on its way over from Africa," Floyd added.

"Yes, dear. But we know you were roundabout 1780." Liz looked up from her book "From the point of view of fine-tuning the graph, we hit lucky with Torvold. He was a bit hazy about dates, but his father was foster brother to Leif Erikson. He could give enough clues to put his arrival at 1010 AD. It dropped a point on the graph centuries earlier than anything we'd had before, and confirmed what everyone suspected. The graph was an exponential curve that shoots to infinity at about 1200 BC—the Late Bronze Age collapse."

Liz sounded triumphant, but was she still speaking English? Then she laughed. "Oh, listen to me. You probably haven't got a clue what I'm talking about, right?"

"Ah. No."

"Never mind, dear. Just do what everyone else does and nod. Humor me."

"We do listen," Kali said, her tone gently teasing. "We take you very seriously. If we ever get off this island, it will be due to you and your graphs."

"Not much hope of that, I'm afraid."

"Never give up hope."

Liz shook her head sadly and turned to another page in the book. She dipped a quill in an ink bottle. "Anyway, we need to enter you three in here. So, your names again, in full."

"Sam Helyer."

"Catalina de Valasco."

"Alonzo Ortiz."

Liz put down the quill and put the book aside for the ink to dry. "I'm the thirty-ninth person to be record keeper since a castaway named Ivan started this journal. Some of my predecessors were a touch lackadaisical and there are a few gaps along the way. On top of that, no one has any idea how long Atlantis was jumping around before Ivan got here. Still, each sunrise I put one more mark on the tally sheet, and for what it's worth, the day count of your arrival is 88,413."

"That many? It must add up to centuries."

"Oh, it does, dear. We're at 242 years and counting. Hundreds of castaways have come and gone before us. And I don't expect we'll be the last."

Yaraha and Torvold reappeared, carrying trays. "Time to stop the chatter. I've made Spanish omelet."

The food smelled good and tasted better, but Catalina could not work out why Yaraha called it Spanish. She had never eaten it before in her life.

❖

For Madison, something being cool had nothing to do with temperature, and the word "like" was a form of punctuation. All sentences ended on a high note. She had volunteered to show Catalina, Alonzo, and Sam around the buildings that made up the Squat and help them choose accommodations.

Although Madison was in her mid-twenties, she possessed the sort of happy enthusiasm rarely seen in anyone past the age of five. She was the only castaway to have her own style of dress, although it amounted to little more than exposing as much skin as possible, while preserving a minimal level of decency. Alonzo was clearly having trouble knowing where to look—or where not to look.

Madison had a knot tied in the hem of her smock top, so her midriff was on display. The castaways' knee-length breeches were called shorts. In Madison's case, the name was particularly apt. Her light brown hair was held back from her face by a cloth band tied around her forehead.

Madison's left hand flapped up and down. "This is, like, a condo."

Catalina looked around, trying to work out what this meant. She had given up asking for translations. A few feet away, Sam stood with her back to Catalina, possibly doing the same.

A woman. Catalina was swamped by shock every time she thought about it. And yet now that she studied Sam, were the signs there? Did Sam's hips sway more when she walked? Was her jawline too delicate? Her face was boyish but fine-boned, and intriguing. Catalina remembered Sam's arm around her waist, saving her from falling into the sea—arms that were hard and strong, but also smooth. Catalina forced herself to look away. Sam had become far more interesting in ways hard to understand.

Alonzo stayed at the entrance to the building, glaring at Sam with unmistakable disgust. Admittedly, the Bible forbade women from dressing as men, but it was a minor clause and hardly explained the strength of Alonzo's reaction. Was it important, and should she talk to him about it later?

Meanwhile, the tour continued. "Three of the boys live here. They're cool, and there's plenty of space if one of you wanted to join them. Or if any of you are a couple..." Madison left the sentence hanging and looked at them brightly, waiting for a response.

After a few seconds of silence, Sam asked the question. "How can one person be two?"

Madison laughed and clapped her hands. "Oh, you know. An item. Involved with each other. In a relationship. Lovers."

"Married?"

"Doesn't have to be official, honey. You know—try before you buy."

"Do you suggest Doña Catalina—" Alonzo's eyes bulged. His voice choked off in outrage.

Nobody had spoken of Madison as a woman of easy virtue, and there had clearly been no insult intended. Was it really just different morals from different times? Catalina sidled toward Alonzo. She did not want him to say or do anything until she had a better grasp of etiquette among the castaways.

Madison was unperturbed. "One thing I've learned here is that people don't change. When it comes to the itch, no matter when you're from, girls will be girls." She gave Sam a bright smile and added, "Or boys."

A sound like the mewling of a newborn kitten interrupted them, "Meea, meea, meea." Catalina almost fell as a creature scuttled into the building, looking like nothing so much as a giant spider. It was the size of a large dog but had six legs and another pair of appendages, folded in front. The body was bulbous, the head just a bulge on top. If it had eyes, they were not obvious. Its skin was mottled white.

"What is it?" Catalina could hear her voice cracking.

"Oh, don't worry, honey. It's just a caretaker. They're, like, harmless."

"Caretaker?" She had imagined something far more human.

The creature ignored them. It lowered its body to the ground and ran back and forth, mewling all the time. Where it passed, the ground was left clean—a footprint, a blown leaf, a scrap of paper, all vanished. Then it scuttled to one side of the room, opened a panel, and probed with one of its front appendages. Catalina had no idea what it was doing, but then noticed one corner of the room had been slightly darker than the rest. Within seconds, the ceiling returned to a uniform glow. The caretaker replaced the panel and left. A last "Meea, meea" faded away.

Catalina was shaking but tried to smile. "That saves work, I guess."

"Yes and no. We don't have to clean up our own shit. But they won't let us change anything. Years back, someone had the bright idea of growing normal plants over here, so they, like, brought seeds over from the outer island. As soon as they sprouted, the caretakers dug them up. They won't even let seabirds build nests here. That's why we have to go over for food supplies and play dodge the hunters."

"We can't eat the plants here?"

"Uh-uh. No way. If you're lucky they just make you puke your guts out."

Catalina thought she got the idea.

"Liz reckons it's all, like, alien. You know, from another planet."

Sam looked surprised. "The wandering stars? You think they're responsible for the poisonous plants here? How?"

"You're all from a long time ago, aren't you?" Madison caught her lower lip in her teeth, clearly thinking. She then clasped her hands together. "Right. Well, you know the stars? They're really other suns, but a long, long, long way away. And planets like ours go around them. You know this world is a planet, right? Anyway, we think other people live on those planets. Except they aren't people like us. They're aliens."

Madison was clearly making an effort to communicate. It was unfortunate this made her sound as if she were talking to three-year-olds. Catalina studied her face, trying to tell whether she was teasing them, but Madison's smile held nothing but sincerity. *I'm in Atlantis, having jumped though time, with monstrous spiders that clean the floor.* Put in perspective, what was so hard to believe about people living on worlds in the stars? Even Catalina's father had thought the church a little too quick to dismiss Galileo and Copernicus.

Madison returned to adult mode. "Anyway. Like I said, Yaraha,

Piracola, and Jorge live here, but there's plenty of space if you want to move in. Or we can check out the other condos. Tell you what, I'll show you what the digs are like."

She bounced across the room and into the sunshine with Catalina and the others trailing, bemused, in her wake.

❖

Madison's tour ended in the kitchen. "We all take turns to cook. Charles is in charge of the roster. He'll let you know when it's your turn."

"All of us?" Sam sounded apprehensive. She was looking at Alonzo.

"Yup. Everyone. Don't fret. When it's your turn, somebody will, like, show you how the hotplates and ovens work. It's a cinch."

"It's not my cooking I'm worried about."

Sam spoke under her breath, but clearly enough to be heard. Alonzo's scowl deepened. Something had gone on between them on the pirate ship, that much was obvious, but Catalina could not imagine what part cooking played.

"Okay, that's it. Catch y'guys later." Which presumably translated as good-bye from Madison.

Catalina wandered back to the room she had chosen. The walls were a uniform light gray, and there was nothing she could do to personalize it. Any changes would be undone by the caretakers. The bed was a large raised platform with a cushioned top. A bureau to one side had built-in lockers to store bedding and any other belongings she wanted to keep. A small side room had waste and washing facilities. Catalina stood in the doorway. Madison had strongly hinted they should make use of it at least once a day. So why not now? *When in Rome...*

Catalina pulled off her clothes. Standing completely naked felt indecent, even with the door closed. She dropped her smock in the laundry bin and pressed the wall button. Water fell like rain from a pattern of holes in the ceiling. It was warm and scented, exactly as Madison had claimed it would be. What was unexpected, though, was how pleasant it was, flowing over her skin.

Catalina had intended only the briefest of washes, but ended up taking ten minutes. At last she pressed the button again, and a hot wind blew from all sides, so she was dry within seconds. When she retrieved her smock from the bin it too was spotless and faintly perfumed.

The control panel on the bedroom wall was another source of wonder. It looked like glass covering a pattern, but bars changed color as Catalina ran her finger back and forth, and the lighting changed accordingly. Another bar caused air to blow from vents, not just hot, as in the washroom, but also cold.

Catalina did not understand how it was possible, and yet Madison had clearly seen nothing remarkable in any of this. Was it due to living in the Squat for years, or did the Earth she left also have such daily marvels?

Catalina sat on the side of the bed and looked around in amazement. The room might appear Spartan, and would be improved by rugs, ornaments, and paintings, but it had a level of cleanliness and convenience she had never dreamed of.

She was still playing with the lighting when a bell rang out, the signal for dinner. Catalina headed back to the common room. Maybe she would have another shower before bedtime.

❖

Sitting on the circular bench between Alonzo and Kali made Catalina feel like a small child. Her feet dangled a foot clear of the floor. However, the only other options were to sit on the ground or eat standing up. Fortunately, the meal more than compensated. The stew with corn dumplings was better than anything Catalina had eaten for a long time. She finished and sat, wondering if there was any left for a second helping.

"You liked that?" Kali asked.

"Yes, I did. Very much."

"My Ricardo, he's a good cook, don't you think?" She indicated the man sitting on the other side of her.

Ricardo smiled and lifted Kali's hand to his lips. He was, at most, a couple of years older than Catalina. His skin was not as dark as Kali, or even Yaraha, but it was evident his ancestors were not all from Europe. His features hinted more at the Americas than Africa, but could easily be either, or both. His hair was black and straight. He was tall, thin, and very quiet. Catalina was yet to hear him say a word, yet the warmth in his eyes when he looked at Kali was unmistakable.

There was no need to ask whether Ricardo was the father of her baby, though the absence of both church and priest in Atlantis made it unlikely they were married in any formal sense. Father Ortiz would have been horrified, but Plato would not, and Catalina knew who was the more astute thinker of the two. She remembered Madison's offhand attitude. *When in Rome...* Catalina suspected she would need to remind herself of the proverb frequently over the following days.

"You did well with the cooking." Catalina raised her mug of water in a toast to the chef. The absence of wine was her only complaint.

Ricardo ducked his head and mumbled a response. It took a moment for Catalina to realize he was speaking Spanish. His accent was every bit as odd as the others were when speaking English.

"Could you repeat that, please?"

Judging by his frown, he found her Spanish equally strange. He cleared his throat and switched to English. "I said, I'm pleased you liked it. My brother, Jorge, is a better cook than me. It will be his turn the day after tomorrow, so you'll see for yourself."

Kali barged him gently. "Always you say your brother is the best at everything. You should not put yourself down. You are my first choice."

"He's cleverer than me."

"No, he's not. He is older than you, that is all. Anyway, you're much more handsome than him." There was laughter in Kali's voice.

Catalina looked around. "Is he here?"

"No. Jorge is off fishing with Torvold and Piracola," Ricardo said.

"I thought we couldn't eat the fish."

"Not the ones in the inner sea, but there's a canal through to the ocean. They have taken the *Inflatable* out and won't be back until nightfall. Jorge is prepared to take the risk for fresh fish."

"What risk? Can the hunters swim?"

"No. Thank God. But if they are on the open sea when a time jump happens..." He shrugged. "If any boat can survive, it is the *Inflatable*, so Jorge tells me. But then, he told me it would be safe to land on this island, when it showed up where none was supposed to be."

"You came from New Spain?"

"Honduras. But yes, I think it was once part of the area called that. My brother and I, we were…" His expression became shamefaced. "Floyd does not approve, of course. It was his job to stop people like us. We were smugglers, you see. Mostly cocaine."

"Is that a sort of drink, like brandy?"

"No, it's…" Ricardo sighed. "It no longer matters. That world is gone. Now we are here and must all work together."

At her shoulder, she heard Alonzo mutter, "Even with abominations."

Automatically, Catalina found herself seeking out Sam. What had she done to fire up so much hostility? Catalina spotted her sitting on the floor with her back to a wall, talking to Charles and another woman, presumably Babs.

Babs, if that was her, was appreciably younger than Charles, maybe in her early thirties. She had angular features and a mop of curly auburn hair. Sam must have said something amusing, because both of them burst into laughter—a low bass woof from Charles and peals of giggles from Babs.

"Are you tired, cariño?" Ricardo was speaking to Kali.

"A little."

He cupped the side of her face. "Come. You need to lie down."

"I am not that far gone yet."

Ricardo leaned forward and whispered something in her ear. Kali's smiled broadened. She looked at Catalina. "You must excuse us. Rico wishes to…show me something."

He offered a hand to help Kali from the bench, then gave a nod to Catalina and Alonzo. "Good evening, señor, señorita. It was a pleasure to meet with you."

"And you. Good night."

Catalina watched them go, then stared at her empty plate. It probably was too late to get another helping.

"Allow me to clear away for you, Doña Catalina." Alonzo had misinterpreted her sigh.

While waiting for his return, Catalina looked around the room. Sam and Babs were talking, sitting cross-legged on the floor facing each other, like a couple of children. Except, even as a child, Catalina would not have acted in such an undignified manner. It was not hard to imagine what her parents would have said. Yet nobody was looking at the two women with disapproval, or even surprise. Most unexpected of all, watching them, Catalina felt a strange, conflicted set of emotions that she struggled to put a name to.

Somewhere deep inside was an urge to talk to Sam, even if it meant sitting on the floor. Giving in to this was a bad idea—she knew it. Just thinking about it made her nervous, but not the same sort of nervousness the pirates or the hunters invoked. Had she ever felt this way about anything or anyone? It made no sense.

Their time on the pirate ship had allowed plenty of chances for her and Sam to speak. She had not been interested then, and Sam was exactly the same person as before. What would they talk about anyway, with Alonzo standing at her heels like a guard dog? Better if he was not present. Yet the thought of being alone with Sam made the nervousness swell.

Catalina pressed her hands flat on the bench to still them. She must concentrate on something else. So—if not Sam, who should she talk to? On the other side of the fountain, Liz was sitting with a man Catalina had not yet met, which was as good a reason to join her as any.

Liz looked up as Catalina approached. "Hello, dear. Take a pew. Let me introduce you to Horatio."

He struggled off the bench and inclined his head in a crisp bow. "First Lieutenant Horatio Barnwell of Her Majesty's Royal Navy, at you service, madam."

Here at least was a gentleman. Unfortunately, his appearance was not as trim as his manners. Horatio clearly was someone who enjoyed his food. His smock top was twice the size of that worn by anyone else, and was still tight over his stomach. He was clean-shaved, aged about forty, and of a little below average height for a man. His mousy brown hair was tied back in a pigtail. His tanned face still held a trace of pink. Catalina thought she could identify an English accent.

"Her Majesty? Queen Elizabeth?"

"Queen Victoria."

"You came from a later time than I." This seemed like a safe guess.

"I arrived here 1838."

"It was 1631 for me." They had lived two centuries apart. It still made Catalina's head reel.

"I was on the HMS *Pendragon*, Vengeur class, ship of the line. Spiffing old lady. We had seventy-four guns. Forty were thirty-two-pounders set over three decks. And for eighteen-pounders we had—"

Liz put a hand on his shoulder, cutting off the catalogue of navel armaments. "Do you want to hear something I've just learned about Horatio, that makes me absolutely pig-sick jealous? Though I guess it'll mean nothing to you."

"Umm...do you want me to tell her anyway?" Horatio asked.

"Yes. Go on."

"Righto." He blinked a few times. "Well, we were anchored off Hobart, Australia, when a British survey ship dropped anchor. Of course, we invited the captain over for dinner. A decent fellow. He brought a friend, the ship's naturalist. Sort of thing we did dozens of times, that's why I didn't say anything sooner. Didn't think you'd be the slightest bit interested."

Liz sighed and shook her head. "Horatio has lived here fourteen years and didn't think to mention before now that he'd had dinner with Charles Darwin."

"How was I to know he'd become so jolly famous?"

"Charles Darwin is famous?" Catalina asked.

"Just about the greatest scientist ever." Liz paused, thinking. "Except maybe Einstein."

Alonzo returned from the kitchen. Without being asked, he offered an arm to help Catalina up beside Liz. The top was comfy enough to sit on, but again Catalina's feet were dangling in midair. She was finding it irritating.

"Why is the bench so high?"

Liz gave a laugh. "Most likely because it wasn't made for humans. Has anyone said to you about the aliens?"

"Yes, Madison did."

"Did she make sense?"

"In part."

"Well, there's a first! Anyway, the aliens were a tad bigger than us. Must have been about nine feet tall."

Now that Catalina thought about it, everything in the Squat was oversized.

Liz continued. "My guess is the aliens lived on this inner island.

The plants—they aren't native to Earth. They made themselves a little home away from home here."

"A copy of their world in the stars."

"That's my bet."

"What were the aliens doing here?"

"Absolutely no bloody idea. Gerard had all sorts of theories, but never any proof."

"Gerard?"

"My husband." Liz's face twisted in a sad smile "He's been gone now, thirty-eight years."

"I'm sorry."

"His own stupid fault. He went digging around in Old Town one time too many and never came back."

"Old Town? Charles mentioned it. He said it's where the hunters have their nest."

"Nest is a guess, but it's where you're going to find more of them, quicker than anywhere else."

"Why did your husband go there, if it's so dangerous?"

"Gerard wanted to learn the secret of Atlantis." Liz pursed her lips. "We all did once, but I grew out of it."

Horatio shook his head. "I'm not so sure. If you saw half a chance, you'd be jolly well onto it, quick as a flash."

"You reckon?" Liz raised her eyebrows. "Maybe. But I'm not holding my breath." She returned to Catalina. "There were seven of us on the *Thalassa*. Scientists. Explorers. We were an international team. You won't pick up on my accent, but I'm a Kiwi, from New Zealand. Gerard was French. Karim, Sofia, Ben, Mitch, and Ziggy were the others. We were investigating the Bermuda Triangle."

"Which is?"

"A region of the sea where boats and planes keep going missing. We found it right enough. Gerard just wouldn't stop searching for more."

"What is so important about Old Town that's worth the risk?"

"Stuff written down, books, and the like. The outer island was where the humans lived. It used to be mostly farmland, but it's overgrown now."

"Humans?"

"Yes. Who knows why the aliens had them here, though to my mind, the hunters point to them being slave workers. The hunters were to take care of runaways. Now that the aliens have gone, they go after everyone."

"But what did Gerard think there'd be on the outer island? What would slaves know?"

"No doubt quite a lot less than what the aliens did. However, since nobody knows the first thing about the alien language, we'll never understand anything we find from them."

"What language did the slaves speak? Where did they come from?"

"How good's your history?" Liz waved her hand. "Never mind, dear. Quick version. Back in the twelfth century BC, the first Mediterranean civilizations were doing nicely, then something happened. Empires collapsed, everything went backward—trade, literacy, art. Cities vanished. It's called the Late Bronze Age collapse. Nobody knows what happened, or why, but when the dust settled, the Greeks had a new alphabet and started telling stories about Atlantis."

"The ancient Greeks were here, with the aliens?"

"That's what Gerard was chasing. There are Greek inscriptions all over Old Town. He brought back pages and pages of writing."

"What does it say?"

"We don't know. That's what made it all so bloody pointless. The daft bugger." Pain and anger crackled in Liz's voice. "Sofia was the only one who knew Greek, and she didn't last out the first day here. I knew the names of the letters. That's all. They get used in science. Pi for circles. Lambda for wavelength. I could sound out one word, and one word only—alpha, tau, lambda, alpha, nu, tau, iota, sigma. Which told us absolutely bloody nothing we didn't already know. We were in Atlantis. But Gerard kept going back, searching for more, bringing it here. We've got it all stacked in the Barn. He was hoping one day someone would turn up who can read Greek."

Catalina cleared her throat. "My parents knew when I married I'd be mixing in foreign courts, so they taught me French, Italian, English, and German. When they discovered I had an ear for languages, they added Latin, for Mass, and Greek. I'm not sure why Greek, except I could read Plato and Homer in the original. Maybe I could have a look at what you have, tomorrow."

Liz stared at Catalina with surprise, but then nodded slowly. "Indeed. Why not?"

❖

Jorge was a shorter, stockier, and much louder version of his younger brother. He had a ready smile, and a sparkle to his eye. Currently, his eye was definitely on Catalina. Jorge snapped off a pink and white flower as he passed, then turned and presented it to her with a dramatic flourish.

"For you, señorita, though your beauty eclipses it ten thousand fold."

"If she wanted a flower, she could have picked one herself," Piracola said.

"You have no poetry in your soul."

"I also have no plant mess on my hands."

He had a point. Thick yellow sap dripped from the broken stem. Jorge sighed and tossed the flower head at Piracola's feet. Piracola kicked it away.

"Ugh. Now I have mess on my foot."

"Then wipe it off."

"Like this, do you mean?"

Piracola balanced on one leg, while trying to wipe his foot on Jorge's shorts. A spirited hopping battle followed. It was childish and amusing, but mostly childish. Who would think the two men were nearer thirty than thirteen?

Piracola looked similar enough to Yaraha they also could have passed for brothers. Both had bodies decorated with bands of tattoos which they obviously liked to display, although Piracola's were fewer in number and of noticeably poorer quality. Did this signify something? Catalina thought it probably did.

Currently, Piracola was playing clown to Jorge's jester. They made an entertaining duo, although Catalina was pleased Charles was with them. Normally, she could count on Alonzo as chaperone, but Horatio and Torvold wanted to see what salvage had washed ashore from the wreck of the pirate ships. Sam had agreed to go in the *Inflatable* to help them find the spot. That Alonzo also volunteered surprised Catalina, given his hostility to Sam.

Catalina could have waited for Alonzo to return before investigating the Greek texts, but curiosity got the better of her. The material Gerard retrieved from Old Town was, apparently, stored in a barn a quarter mile from the Squat. When they overheard Charles offering to show her the way, Jorge and Piracola enthusiastically tagged along as well.

Catalina was about to walk on, when a sound stopped her. "Meea, meea." A caretaker had come to tend to the damaged plant.

"We call them caretakers," Charles said.

"I know. We saw one yesterday. I was just wondering what sort of creature has a floor-sweeper on its stomach."

"They aren't really alive. Madison says they're bio-robots. Before she came, they were known as flesh golems. We've adopted Madison's name." Charles grinned. "It sounds less gruesome."

"What are they?"

"An artificial life form. But saying that doesn't leave us any wiser."

Jorge abandoned his tussle with Piracola. "Hey. I will show you."

He bent, grabbed two legs, and then, with a sharp pull, flipped the caretaker onto its back. The six legs waved wildly in the air, making it look even more like a huge spider. The pitch of the mewling raised a note or two. Despite an unsettled feeling, Catalina leaned forward for a better look.

The underside of the caretaker was nothing like she had expected. Instead of bulging, off-white skin, there was a concave surface of shiny black glass. Dots of blue light traveled back and forth in the depths. Now that she was closer, Catalina could also hear a low monotonous humming.

"Look here." Jorge caught one of the front appendages and held it out to show the disc of black glass on the tip. "This is another magic bit. Don't ask me how, but it can fix anything."

"And kill seagulls," Piracola added.

"It's dangerous?"

Jorge laughed. "Not to us. And you have me and my bold friend here, ready to lay down our lives for you."

"We are?" Piracola sounded surprised.

Jorge nudged him and said in a false whisper, "It's what you say to ladies. Normally, you don't mean it, but for a beauty such as Catalina…" He winked at her.

"Could the caretakers hurt us if they wanted to?"

"Possibly," Charles answered. "But they never have. And they only go after seagulls when they try to build nests on the inner island."

"But you should see them when they do. Whooph." Piracola mimed an explosion.

The sound of another caretaker made Catalina jump. She stepped back anxiously, but the new arrival merely set its fellow back on its feet and scurried away.

"See," Jorge said. "They never hurt us. We play a game to see who can get the most caretakers upside down at the same time. If I had flipped the one who came just now, in a minute, two more would arrive to right them both. Flip those two and you will get four arriving. And so on."

"I always win the game," Piracola said.

"He does not."

"Nearly always."

Jorge laughed. "One time, Piracola and I worked together, flipping them. I wanted to know how many caretakers there were. We got to nearly two hundred, but by then they were arriving so quickly we couldn't keep up."

"Anything to keep the children entertained." Charles smiled and continued through the gardens.

A short way on, Catalina spotted a row of buildings. Unlike the houses in the Squat, the roofs were domed rather than flat.

"What's in there?"

Charles shook his head. "We don't know."

"Has nobody looked?"

"We can't get in. The doors have a keypad."

"A what?"

"It'll be easier if I show you."

Charles turned aside. The path ended at a blank arch, much like those at the Squat. However, rather than a black disc, a rectangle was laid out in a grid of one-inch squares, six rows deep by four across. Each square was marked with a symbol.

Catalina took a closer look. "That's the Greek alphabet."

"Press a key."

Catalina felt the alpha button click and heard a soft chime. "What does it do?"

"Best guess is you need the right code sequence to open the door."

Jorge started tapping buttons. "You would not believe how many hours I've spent doing this. Maybe some day I'll strike lucky." He grinned over his shoulder at Catalina. "You could help me. Do you think I might get lucky with you?"

Judging by his tone, the words had an alternate meaning, and one Catalina did not need a translation for. The look in his eyes was enough—just as well Alonzo was not present.

"Or me?" Piracola was not to be left out.

Catalina worked to hide a smile. "I'm sure it will be better if I leave it in your hands."

Jorge gave a good-natured laugh. "That's something else I've spent hours doing."

Catalina returned to the building. "You've no idea what's in here?"

"None at all," Charles said. "We can't even be certain the Squat was originally housing. It seems to be bedrooms and a kitchen. But did the aliens sleep? Did they cook their food? We just don't know."

After a few minutes more, they reached another building, far and away the largest Catalina had yet seen.

"Allow me to present the Barn." Charles waved his hand over the opening disc and stepped back.

Catalina felt her jaw drop. Inside was one enormous room, the size of a cathedral. At a first glance, the space was empty, but it was just an effect of the scale. Numerous objects were assembled—parts of statues, parts of machines, tables, carts, things Catalina could not put a name to, all dwarfed by the building.

Catalina shook her head. No...not the size of a cathedral. The height might be similar, but the floor space could have held the largest cathedral in Europe a dozen times over. How did the roof support the span? The name "Barn" could not do justice to the imposing space.

Only once inside did she notice footprints in a thick layer of dust on the floor. "Don't the caretakers clean in here?"

"No. There seems to be some sort of 'Do not touch' order in place for them."

"Why?"

Charles just gave an expressive shrug in answer. "Whatever the reason, people have used the Barn to store things they don't want to lose. Not just Gerard, others before him, maybe even going back to when the aliens were around." He walked to a long table. "Here's the stuff Gerard brought back, but you can look at the rest as well. Somebody must have put it here for a reason."

"I know why this wasn't thrown away." Jorge held up a small statue. "Look at it. Gold." He moved to another object. "And this. What do you think it's worth?"

"Here?" Charles laughed. "Slightly less than freshly caught fish, which we have a use for. You can't even put the statue in your room to make it look pretty. I don't think the caretakers understand the concept of 'priceless art object.'"

Jorge sighed. "Of course, you're right. But I know why somebody collected all these things. They had not given up hope of leaving Atlantis, and they wanted to go home a rich man. Some days I come here, just to share the dream." He put his hand on Piracola's shoulder. "But whoever made the collection, he was not like my friend here. I'm still not sure he understands about money."

"And no doubt he's all the happier for it," Charles said.

Catalina joined him at the table. Most of the surface was covered with engraved tables, scrolls, pamphlets, sheets of paper, and even stacks of books. Texts Gerard had collected, risking his life, in the hope of meeting someone who could read it—someone like her.

"What was Gerard like?"

"I don't know. Babs and I arrived six years ago, long after he went missing. Floyd has been here second longest, but even he never met Gerard."

Laughter and the clash of metal rang out. Jorge and Piracola had found shields, swords, and helmets and were playing like boys. Catalina watched their antics. They were two attractive, friendly young men. They would not be her parents' choice of a husband for her, but her parents' choices had all suffered from singular misfortune and were no longer relevant.

Madison had been so casual in talk of taking a lover. However, neither man interested Catalina in the slightest. They were wasting their time with her. She caught her lip in her teeth. Might they stand a better chance with Sam? And why was that thought so unpleasant? Hurriedly, Catalina picked the nearest sheet of paper. The large handwritten words were underlined twice.

"What does it say?" Charles was clearly trying to sound calm, but could not disguise his eagerness.

Catalina studied the words. It was not the classical Greek she had been taught, but simple enough to understand. "Something along the lines of, *Whoever has borrowed my mixing bowl, can they return it immediately.*"

CHAPTER SIX

The canal might have passed for a natural river, if its sides were not so straight. Trees and shrubs overhung both banks, and trailing vines hid the stonework behind coils of green. In places, roots had broken through the walls, allowing earth and rocks to cascade into the water.

The series of bridges spanning the canal were also in poor repair. Sam looked up as the *Inflatable* passed beneath one. Daylight peeked through a large crack. "I take it caretakers don't visit the outer island."

"I've not seen any, just those wretched hunters," Horatio said. "And I'd be jolly happy if I never saw them again, I can tell you."

He and Sam were on the foremost seat, watching the banks slide by. The bow of the *Inflatable* was noticeably deeper in the water than on her previous trip. At the stern, Alonzo was as far from her as possible. He sat next to Torvold, who was in charge of the outboard motor, as it was called. Torvold was in good spirits and launched into what was, presumably, yet another Viking rowing song.

Horatio smiled at him. "The poor chap is going to be heartbroken when the gas runs out."

"Which gas?"

"The fuel the motor burns. To be honest, I've no idea why they call it gas. It's really a type of oil."

"Where does it come from?"

"What we're using now came from Babs and Charles. Floyd and his comrades had brought the *Inflatable*, but their supply ran out ages before I arrived. People were rowing between the islands, and the *Inflatable* was in dry dock, so to speak. Well, it was in the Barn.

Have you been there yet? You should visit. Amazing place. Anyway, six years back, Babs turned up in her seaplane. It had enough gas to take her and Charles…" He frowned. "A jolly long way. Not sure how far, but getting to Atlantis hadn't made a dent in the tank. It was Liz who thought of trying the seaplane gas in the *Inflatable*. Floyd says it runs a bit hot, but that might be due to it needing a service." The frown deepened. "I'm not quite sure what he means by that."

"Not a religious service."

"No. Probably not."

"Babs and Charles didn't mind giving up their fuel?"

"We share whatever we have, and they've got no use for it. Besides, otherwise they'd have to take their turn rowing. It was no fun, I can tell you, what with the wretched fish nibbling the paddles. We still have plenty of gas left. The pinch will come when there's just enough to get the *Okeechobee Dawn* back to the mainland. It's still our best hope of escape."

"Babs has promised to show me it when we get back. It's hard to imagine a machine that can fly."

"I know, and I saw it land. Amazing. Quite amazing. A good show that Babs brought it down on the inner sea. It doesn't get whirlpools when we jump."

"How long have you been here?"

"Fourteen years. Only Floyd and Liz surpass me. We're all the last of our crews. The *Pendragon* was on her way home, back to Portsmouth when we spotted the island. The captain sent me ashore for provisions. Rotten luck all round." Horatio gave an awkward one-shouldered shrug. "I don't suppose I'll ever see Portsmouth again."

"It's the risk we sailors take when we go to sea." Where would Sam call home?

"My father didn't give me much say in the matter, what with him naming me Horatio and all." At Sam's questioning look he continued. "I suppose he was a bit after your time. Lord Horatio Nelson was British Admiral at the Battle of Trafalgar. He died heroically at the point of victory, defeating the combined fleets of France and Spain."

"Some things never change." If the English were not fighting the Spanish, they were fighting the French. Although, taking both on at the same time sounded ambitious.

"The fighting had calmed down in my time. Mostly, we were up against pirates and slavers." He blinked at Sam. "I was talking to Catalina last night. According to her, you were one. A pirate that is, not a slaver."

"I was a privateer. I'll agree there's not much difference when you're on the other side."

"Well, it's all in the past now. We're on the same side here."

"Have you told that to Alonzo?" Sam had noticed the savage looks he was sending her way. She was surprised he had agreed to come on the salvage trip with her.

A sudden movement caught her eye. "Is that—" But Sam had her answer even before she could finish, not one of the deadly hunters, but a goat, munching on leaves.

"There are pigs and goats around. The farm stock gone feral. I've been told there were cows too, but the jungle didn't suit them, and they died out."

"The hunters don't bother them?"

"Oh no. Luckily, the sheepdogs have reverted to acting like pack wolves. Otherwise the goats would have jolly well overrun the place and eaten it bare."

"Are the dogs dangerous?"

"Best avoided, I'd say. Their ancestral memory might hold a few friendly instincts toward us, but I don't advise putting it to the test."

More goats were now visible. Sam watched until they were out of sight. "A shame we didn't have a musket with us. Roast goat would be nice."

Horatio tapped a storage box under the bench. "We have AK-47s, and let me tell you, they are to muskets what the outboard motor is to rowing. If the goats are still around on the way back, maybe we can bag a couple."

The end of the canal was fast approaching. Soon the sides fell away on either side and they were on the open ocean. Torvold steered them close along the shoreline. "First sign of the jump, and I zip onto the beach. Quick as green mustard." This was possibly the direct translation of a Viking saying. If any craft could outrun the whirlpools, the *Inflatable* probably had the best odds. Would it be quick enough?

Sam looked out to sea. The familiar horizon taunted her, water touching sky. "We could leave, couldn't we? As long as we were far enough away when Atlantis jumped. The rest of the world is still out there."

"Indeed. Some brave souls have taken their chances and headed off."

"Did it turn out all right?"

"No way of knowing. It's not just when we are. We aren't even quite sure where we are. Atlantis isn't a real island, you know. You can tell from the lay of the land it's man-made...or alien-made, maybe I should say."

"It moves?"

"It floats."

"Floats?"

"When a hurricane hits, an invisible dome protects us, but you can feel the ground rocking."

"You'd still have the sun and stars to navigate by."

"But no idea how far to reach land. Plus, if you make it there safely, what will you find? Liz told you about her graph? The longer you have to get away, the less chance it'll be anything like the world you left. Even Yaraha and Piracola decided to stay, rather than take their chance with measles and enemy tribes."

Sam was about to trail her fingers in the water, then remembered Yaraha's warning.

"Do the bio-robot piranhas ever come out here?"

"No. And normal fish don't swim into the inner sea. Don't ask me why."

"The campsite. There she is," Alonzo called out.

Sam had been too caught up watching the horizon. She turned to the beach. Sure enough, there were the remains of the awning she had helped put up, just two days before. Torvold steered the *Inflatable* to shore.

More wreckage had washed on the beach while she had been gone. Dotted among the flotsam were the pallid bodies of her former crewmates. Sam slid her feet over the soft wall of the *Inflatable* onto the warm sand. She tried to ignore the stench of rotting flesh and the flies hovering above each corpse.

Horatio and Torvold started on nearby crates. The bodies would be checked as well, but for now Sam decided to start with the unloaded supplies. She knew they were useful, and it would give her a chance to build herself up for the task. Sam had searched corpses before, but never of people she could put a name to.

The scrunch of feet on sand followed her. Alonzo was close behind. When he saw her turn her head, he deliberately averted his eyes. Sam clenched her teeth. His hostility was becoming tiresome, and she was no longer willing to ignore it. She reached the awning, then swung to face him.

"What's wrong? Have I done something to insult you?"

"Why do you ask?"

"Because I'm getting sick of you scowling at me."

"And I sicken with the sight of you."

"Then look somewhere else."

Alonzo took a step closer and dropped his voice. "You tempted me. Was it a joke, to make a game of a man's weakness? I have prayed to the Lord to take away this sickness from inside me. Every day, on my knees. With God's help, I thought I had defeated it. For three years, I had not given in to the temptation. Then you play your tricks. You pull me back into the hell of the devil's own lust. You set the trap for me."

"It's not my fault if you can't live up to your own standards. I didn't do anything to trap you."

"Yes, you did. The Bible says, 'A woman shall not wear that which belongs to a man, nor shall a man put on a woman's clothes, for all who do so are an abomination to the Lord your God.' People like you, who defy nature, you hope only to pull others into your sin."

"I wasn't trying to pull you in anything. I don't care what you do, as long as you're not doing it with me."

"You made a fool of me."

"You made a fool of yourself. I was minding my own business."

"You break the divine law, and I pay the price."

"Your guilty conscience isn't my problem. Go back to praying for forgiveness. Wipe me from your mind. It should be easy enough. I assume I'm no longer a temptation for you."

"I would wipe you from the world, if I could."

"So why have you followed me?"

"I am not following you. Doña Catalina had to leave her gown here, to flee the foulness of your fellows. It is not right for a noble lady to walk around dressed as she is now." Alonzo barged past Sam and through the wall of greenery, striking out with his fists as if the ferns were an enemy.

So that was it. Alonzo wanted someone to blame for everything he could not accept about himself. She should have guessed. Shaking her head, Sam knelt on the sand and yanked the nearest sack toward her. The bottom snagged on a root, wrenching it from her grasp, and spilling its contents.

Sam heard the angry hiss, an instant before the band of black, red, and yellow slithered from the neck of the open sack. No warning. No chance to back away. Sam froze. The head was scant inches from her hand, weaving back and forth. The forked tongue flicked out, tasting the air. Any movement might bring a strike, but maybe, if she stayed very, very still, the creature would slide away.

Snakes were rare on the islands, poisonous ones even more so, although they were common on the mainland. How had this one arrived? Was it an unwilling stowaway, carried on a floating log, or had the aliens released it for some unfathomable reason? Regardless, the type was one Sam had heard of, and for all the wrong reasons. She struggled to remember the sailor's doggerel, about the way the red and yellow touched. The nose was black, which was a bad sign.

The wall of ferns rustled. Sam raised her eyes, the only part of her body she dared move. Alonzo stood there, staring at her with surprise that shifted into understanding. Sam felt her guts tighten in a knot. His chance to be rid of her—walk away and leave it to his vengeful God.

Without a word, Alonzo put down the bundle of clothes, picked up a fallen palm frond, and pulled a knife from his belt. Once the spiky leaves were gone, all that remained was the central stalk, three feet long. Slowly, Alonzo moved closer, holding it out like a sword. Of course, he could jolt her arm, giving God's vengeance a helping hand. Instead, he deftly thrust the stalk under the looped body and flicked the snake away into the undergrowth.

Now it was safe to start shaking. Sam sat back on her heels and closed her eyes. "Thank you. I'm in your debt."

"You are surprised."

"I didn't know what you'd do. You just said you wanted to wipe me from the world."

"I am from a noble family. Poison, in all its forms, is a weapon only for cowards. When I kill, I do so honorably, with my sword, man to man. I would not expect someone like you to understand."

"Because I'm a pirate, because I'm a commoner, or because I'm a woman?"

"Even a woman can know the meaning of honor."

"And I'm a lost cause."

His lip curled. "Your words. But you spoke of debt. If there is any honor to you, much though I doubt it, I ask this. Say nothing to Doña Catalina of the trick you played or my weakness in falling for it."

"I'll think about it."

The chances of Catalina swapping gossip with her were slight enough. Alonzo's taste in lovers was hardly likely to crop up. No matter. He had just saved her life and she owed him that much—not that she was about to make promises to the arrogant fool. Sam watched Alonzo walk back down the beach. Anyway, even if she were to swear an oath, it was not as if he would place any trust in her word.

❖

"Do the wings flap?"

Sam had taken it for granted that they would, but now that she saw the *Okeechobee Dawn*, she was not so sure.

Babs gave one of her high-pitched giggles. "Don't be silly. Of course not."

"Then how does it fly?"

"Do you see the two propellers on the wings?"

"The things that look like windmills?"

"Yes, them. They spin around and pull the plane along. The air rushing over the wings gives the lift."

Sam was unconvinced. The seaplane, with its two sets of wings, looked far too heavy to fly. She was surprised it could even float. It had to be top-heavy. Sam crossed her arms and studied it.

The *Okeechobee Dawn* was moored with its nose overhanging the inward facing embankment close to the Squat. Just like the outer jungle island, the alien garden formed a ring. Another circle of sea separated it from the central mountain. Except, now that Sam had a clear view, she was questioning whether the flat-topped shape was really a mountain.

From where she stood, it looked like nothing so much as a tower—if you could accept a tower hundreds of feet high, and a half mile across. The sides rose like the layered buttresses of a castle.

Babs had come looking for Sam soon after the *Inflatable* returned. She was thirty years or so in age, with a round face, a thick mop of curly auburn hair, and a mass of freckles. She fired out words in rapid bursts, broken by giggles. Her manner shifted from steely confidence to bubbly humor and back so quickly, Sam was getting dizzy keeping up.

"Come on. I'll show you the cockpit." Babs tugged Sam's arm.

"Do you have one of those in there?" Sam was confused. Why on earth would they be staging cockerel fights?

"Of course. How else could I fly it?"

"Do you need to examine their entrails?" Surely the *Okeechobee Dawn* did not use superstition for navigation.

"Whose entrails?"

"The bird that lost, I guess."

"What?" Now Babs looked confused.

"Tell you what, show me the cockpit, and see if we can sort it out."

Babs stepped onto the wing using a strut as a handhold and opened a small door on the hull. Sam followed. The seaplane rocked under her feet, but was clearly far more buoyant than she had expected.

The cockpit turned out to be a tiny room at the front of the seaplane, with two leather strap chairs and more dials, levers, knobs, and buttons than Sam had ever seen collected in one place.

"Why do you call it a cockpit?"

"Because that's what it's called."

What other reason was there for any name? "You and Charles would have sat here together, all the way around the world?"

"That was the plan."

"It's small for two people."

"I know. It's a good thing we get on so well. Though I don't doubt we'd have fallen out once or twice before we got halfway to China."

"Fallen out of the seaplane?"

"No silly. Fallen out with each other." Babs giggled and flipped a small lever. A hiss like an angry cat filled the room. "Static. I keep hoping."

"For what?"

"It's a radio. It allows me to talk to people far away. Or would, if the interference cleared." She ran her hand over a bank of dials, as if stroking a pet, or a lover. "It's so sad to see her earthbound. This baby was born to fly. Come on. Let's go back outside."

They returned to the quay. Babs plonked herself down, with her legs dangling over the edge.

Sam joined her. "What's that in the middle? It's not a real mountain, is it?"

"Is anything here real?"

"It looks like a tower, but how can any building be that big?"

"You should see the skyscrapers in New York."

"The what?"

"Big buildings. Maybe not wide as this one, but just as high."

"Do you know what's inside?"

"No. Folks have paddled over, but it rises sheer from the water. No doors. No windows. No way in."

They sat in silence for three seconds, which, Sam had learned, was as long as silence could last with Babs around.

"Do you know what I'd really like right now?"

Sam could not begin to guess. "What?"

"A cigarette. God, how I miss them."

"Cigarette?"

"Tobacco."

"I don't know how it matches a cigarette, but there's tobacco and a couple of clay pipes in the salvage we brought back this afternoon."

Babs squealed in delight and threw an arm around Sam's waist. "You're a gem among women. Do you know that?"

Sam freed herself. "Thanks, I guess."

"I don't suppose you had champagne as well?"

"Champagne?"

"Fizzy wine."

"No. But we found some bottles of rum."

"And a dead man's chest?"

"That's not a serious question, is it?"

"No." Babs sighed, then picked up a pebble and tossed it into the water. "It's a shame. I had it all planned. A triumphant return. My name in the record books. All the papers there, taking photos."

"Papers?"

"You know, newspapers."

Sam did not know. Was it worth asking what photos were? She let it go.

"I named her the *Okeechobee Dawn* because we took off from Lake Okeechobee and flew into the dawn sky. We were going to keep flying east until we saw dawn rise over Okeechobee again." For once, Babs voice was serious. "Mostly east, anyway. First stage was to New York before the Atlantic crossing. We barely got out of sight of land when everything went haywire."

"What made you decide to do it?"

"Do what?"

"Fly around the world."

"It's all Amelia Earhart's fault."

"What did she do?"

"Inspired me. I heard her give a talk and wanted to give it a go. Charles was assigned to the Air Service during the Great War. He was just a tad too old to be a pilot, but he was taught how to fly. I nagged him into giving me lessons and Pops into buying me a secondhand seaplane." She tilted her head to Sam. "At this point you're supposed to say 'Rich Pops.' Which he was."

"Who's Pops?"

"My father. What did you call yours?"

"Pa."

"Don't suppose either of us will see them again."

"I won't for sure. My pa's dead."

"I'm sorry."

"It's been a year. An outbreak of ship fever. I'm lucky I survived." Did death have to be the final word? Sam toyed with the fantasy of leaving the island and timing it to find Pa again, as a young man. Not that there was any way to arrange it.

"Do you have other family?" Babs asked.

"No. Ma died when I was a baby. I don't remember her at all. Aunt Wilmot looked after me, until she died too."

"Wilmot. Now there's a girl's name you don't hear anymore. Is Sam short for Samantha?"

"No. I was Sarah as a baby. Samantha wasn't a name in Devon when I was born. Pa called me Sam when he took me to sea with him. It could have been short for Samuel. I don't know if he thought about it." Pa had not been the thinking kind. "Is Babs short for something?"

"Barbara. Barbara Helen Vera Maria Weinberg."

"That's quite a lot to shorten."

"You can say that again."

Was this a genuine request? Before Sam could ask, she was interrupted by a shout.

"Hey." Madison trotted toward them. "Can I hide with you?" She sat without waiting for an answer.

"Who are you hiding from?" Sam asked.

"Guess."

Babs gave a snort of laughter. "Jorge or Piracola."

"Jorge has reset his sights on Catalina, so Piracola is stepping up the moves. He's been hitting on me for the last hour straight."

Babs elbowed Sam. "Would you like a translation on that?"

"A hint would be nice." Sam had an idea what Madison meant, but wanted to be sure.

"Women have always been outnumbered on Atlantis. Not so much from recent times, but the earlier centuries give a big imbalance. Before you arrived, there was just us two, plus Liz and Kali. Anyone nominally female, who's got at least one of her own teeth left in her head, ends up with a string of admirers. And if she's young and pretty, it could turn into a free-for-all."

Young and pretty described Catalina well enough. Just as well Alonzo was taking his guard duties seriously and had retrieved her clothes.

Babs continued. "Don't say we didn't warn you if you turn around and find you've got a line standing behind you. Although maybe you can play the pirate thing and scare them off."

"You know, you being a pirate. That is just so cool," Madison cut in. "I used to have a mega-crush on Johnny Depp."

"A crush?" Sam asked.

"I thought he was ultra sexy."

"He was your lover?"

"Don't be silly. He was a film star."

If she asked Madison what a film star was, would she end up any wiser? They must play a part in astrology, and that was never a straightforward topic. She turned to something easier. "You don't find either Jorge or Piracola attractive?"

"Jorge is fun, but I don't one hundred percent trust him. He comes on friendly, but he's only out for number one. Piracola is, like, thirty going on three. I want a grown-up. With him, I'd feel I had to be wiping his nose and making sure he's been to the bathroom." Madison pursed her lips. "Yaraha is more my style. He's always thinking. Except you never know what he's thinking about. Which is kinda cool on one level, but scary on another. Torvold is just plain batshit crazy. Ricardo's been taken, and I don't move in on other girls' boyfriends. Can't say much about Alonzo yet, except he's too old. Horatio has the sexy British accent going for him, but not much else. I mean, like, don't get me wrong, he's a nice guy, but not my idea of hot. Floyd would be really cute if he was twenty years younger—"

"And wasn't gay," Babs said.

"What's wrong with being gay? Isn't that good? Or is it another slang term?" Sam was confused.

"It's slang. A term I've picked up from Madison," Babs said. "It means he's only into other guys."

Sam thought for a moment. "You mean a backroom man?"

Babs and Madison dissolved in fits of laughter. Madison patted Sam's shoulder. "That's it, sister, you got it."

"It doesn't shock you?" Babs asked.

"I've spent my life at sea. After a few months with no women around…well, none they know of, most men aren't so particular, especially after sharing a bottle of rum."

Again, Babs and Madison shrieked with laughter.

"It doesn't bother you either?" Sam asked.

Madison shook her head. "All that crap is so done with. The only people who get their panties in a wad are, like, the Fundamentalists." She rolled her eyes dramatically. "And who gives a flying fuck about them?"

"I was one of the bright young things." Babs shrugged. "You know, anything goes."

Sam thought of saying something about Alonzo, but regardless of how they might respond, she would keep his secret.

Madison said. "My friends Dave and Bobby were gay. I was, like, visiting them during summer break. Bobby's friends had a boat and said they'd take us to the Bahamas. We were in the middle of the ocean when the island popped out of nowhere. We almost sank right then. If we'd had any sense we'd have turned around pronto. But we'd been smoking weed and everything was a giggle." She drew a deep breath. "Anyway. It was a shame, because Dave and Bobby had just got engaged. So you see, when I come from, gays can even marry. It's all cool."

About half of it made sense. Sam turned to Babs. "You and Charles aren't married, are you?" She noticed his name had been left off Madison's list.

"Oh, no. He's a sweetheart, but he's just a family friend. My mom and his wife go way back." The laughter left Babs's face. "I bullied him into the flight. I knew he didn't want to leave Clara and his family. It was just me being…" She shrugged. "It was what I wanted to do. So I went for it."

"Your parents didn't object?"

"I'm an adult. My parents didn't get a say. Well, Pops could have refused the money, but he knew I wouldn't talk to him for months if he tried it."

"They didn't insist on a chaperone?"

Babs's smile returned. "It was the twentieth century. Women were free to do what they wanted."

"But not as free as they were by my time. The pill saw to that," Madison said.

"Which pill?"

"The pill. Like, take one each morning and you'll never get pregnant, no matter what you do." Madison pouted. "It puts a damper on things here. Makes me think twice. Giving birth without a doc on hand. I just hope it goes okay for Kali." She perked up. "So come on. I've given my view of the talent on offer. Who do you get the hots for?"

Babs thought for a moment. "Torvold. I like crazy."

"And you?" She turned to Sam.

"I'm—" Sam stopped with her mouth open and no idea what she was going to say.

"Are you gay? It's not like I'm making assumptions, what with you passing as a boy. Well, maybe I am a bit. So are you?"

"Can women be gay?"

"Of course they can."

So was she? It was not as if the idea had never crossed her mind before. However, her only experience was the whores outside brothels, trying to attract business. The sight of the women, kissing and fondling each other's breasts, had stirred up the other sailors, but to Sam it had seemed crudely false. She had been repulsed not attracted and had wanted nothing to do with it. Then she had met Catalina and the doubts had come back, full force. Maybe kissing another woman would not seem so sleazy and empty without the chorus of jeering sailors.

"I don't know."

"How can you not know?"

Babs wrapped an arm around Madison and shook her in mock wrestling. "Maddy, you're trampling across the centuries. Give Sam a chance. She only just got here. You should allow her at least three days to catch up with five centuries of social change."

"Careful. You don't want to fall in." Sam peered at the water under their feet. There was no sign of piranhas, but they did not sound like something you wanted to take chances with.

"You're right." Babs released Madison and scooted back from the edge. "I'm going to clean up before dinner. It was fun talking to you ladies. Catch you later."

"You too." Madison also got to her feet, then bent down to bring her head level with Sam's. "When you do work it out, let me know." She held up her hands. "Not that I'm interested in that way. Girls are just for friends with me. But I'm nosy."

Left alone, Sam sat staring over the water. For the first time in her life, she had sat as a woman, chatting with other women. It had been fun, if more than a little confusing. Questions whirled in her head. Softly, for her own benefit, Sam whispered, "Madison, if you work it out first, can you tell me?"

❖

When Sam left the *Okeechobee Dawn*, the sun was sinking, covering the scene with golden light. The only sounds were the cries of seabirds and the slap of waves against the quay. With evening approaching, a light breeze took the edge off the heat.

Sam was getting used to purple grass. It no longer looked quite so garish, and the scent of the flowers was sweet and clean. She should give up thinking and just enjoy life. With all its dangers, Atlantis was an improvement on the *Golden Goose*. The people were friendly, she was free to be herself, and the food was better.

Sam was passing the building where Catalina and Alonzo had taken lodgings, when the door whooshed open. Catalina stood there, dressed in the pale blue gown she had worn when she came ashore.

She looked startled. Her hand moved, as if to close the door again, but froze before she completed the action. She was clearly caught between conflicting impulses. Then, in an instant, Catalina's composure returned. Her shoulders went back; her chin went up. Her face adopted its normal mask of calm detachment.

Catalina left the building, advancing sedately up the path. Her bearing was so perfect, Sam was left to wonder if she had imagined the moment of uncertainty.

"Good evening, Sam."

"Good evening, Catalina." Sam was surprised at how steady her own voice sounded. "You look..." Nice? Was that really what she wanted to say? "More like yourself."

"It was good of Alonzo to think of me."

Having said all that politeness required, Sam expected Catalina to now ignore her and walk away. Catalina had made it clear she felt nothing but scorn for the entire crew of the *Golden Goose*. Yet, amazingly, she stayed, while a hint of her unease returned. Something must have been on her mind. Awkward seconds passed.

"Are you—"

"Did the—"

They both started talking at the same time.

"Please, go on. You were about to ask something," Sam said.

"Just whether you're finding life here agreeable?"

Just that? Where was this going? "Um...yes. Apart from things trying to kill me. But that's not so much of a change."

Catalina's face softened in a smile. The effect on Sam was immediate. Her heart leapt. Her hands broke into a sweat. Suddenly, she remembered just how much she wanted Catalina to like her. This was followed by a vision of the whores' cheap show. She had to be very careful, at least until she had sorted out where she stood. The sensible thing was to make her excuses and leave. Catalina was clearly putting effort into improving things between them. Sam knew if she stayed she was likely to say or do something stupid and ruin any hope of that happening. Yet, for once, Sam had no intention of being sensible.

"It's all new for me, or it was until I encountered your former shipmates. My life was very safe before then."

"I..." Sam swallowed. Apologizing would sound feeble or insincere and possibly both. She could hardly claim it had all happened by accident.

"You were going to ask something of me," Catalina said.

"Only whether you had learned anything from the Greek writings."

"Oh, that. It was—" The sound of footsteps interrupted her.

Alonzo strode toward them. "Doña Catalina, please allow me to escort you to dinner." He spoke in Spanish, while glaring at Sam. "I trust no one has been bothering you? A noble lady should not have to endure the foul manners of ruffians."

This was much easier to deal with. Sam smiled. "Better foul manners and a pure heart than the other way around, wouldn't you say?"

She was amused by his surprised expression. Did he think she only spoke English? Alonzo quickly controlled his features, but this was obviously just a thin mask over fury and fear. "What would you know of purity?"

"Enough to see through it, when something nasty is hiding underneath." Sam walked away.

So much for just enjoying life.

CHAPTER SEVEN

Had she just made a fool of herself? Catalina watched Sam disappear behind a row of tall, bladed shrubs. What was it about her? Catalina closed her eyes, exasperated with herself. From the moment she had learned the supposed cabin boy was actually a woman, she had not been able to get Sam out of her mind. Why? Sam was still a pirate and a thief. What difference did her sex make?

"Doña Catalina?" Alonzo was trying to catch her attention.

"Yes?"

"My lady, I trust that..." Alonzo paused, clearly hunting for the right word, "that ruffian said nothing to disturb you."

"No. We were just talking." Catalina put a hand on his arm. "Thank you for your concern. But our situation means we must put the past behind us, as far as is wise."

"Then be wise. You cannot trust her."

"I don't." Annoyingly, that was part of the attraction.

"She's a liar."

"I don't doubt it."

"My lady..." Alonzo was pleading with her.

"What is it?"

"Of all the foul villains, she's the last I would have wanted here with us."

"Why?"

Alonzo ran a hand through his thinning hair. His agitation was unmistakable. "When I was on their ship, trying to pass as one of them, I got to see how they are, how they act. My lady, I've witnessed crimes I wouldn't assault your ears by describing. That Jezebel was among the worst, although I didn't know she was a woman then. She pulled a knife on me, threatened me with mutilation."

"Why did she do that?"

"You wouldn't waste time seeking a reason, if you'd seen what I have. They don't need a reason to take a life. Bad enough for men, but for a woman to forsake the natural modesty and gentleness of her sex— it's beyond understanding. Her heart is soaked in villainy. She will lie to you and distort all that's good and true. You mustn't listen to her, my lady. You mustn't listen to her."

"Alonzo?" Catalina had never seen him so fervent.

"She'll lie about everything. She'll lie about me."

"And I will not believe her."

He pressed his hands over his face.

"Alonzo? You need to calm down."

He drew a shaky breath and let his hands drop. "I'm sorry, my lady."

"Are you all right?"

"Yes, my lady. Of course." He would not meet her eyes, but his expression cleared. He held out his arm. "Please. It's time for our evening meal. Let me escort you to dinner."

Alonzo's loyalty was beyond question. It would be more than foolish to ignore his warning. She was a descendant of El Cid. It was beneath her to play the part of a moth, circling a flame. Yet, sometimes, it was so tempting to play with fire, and Sam was burning in her thoughts.

Catalina tried to clear her mind. She placed her hand on Alonzo's forearm, and they strolled through the alien garden.

❖

Giddy sheep we were to dance in wine when he poured honey in our ears.

Catalina frowned at the line of text. Maybe a literal translation was not the best. Most likely it meant something along the lines of, *He flattered us into making fools of ourselves by drinking to excess.* Or the sentence might need the even looser translation of, *We were too quick to celebrate when he gave us the good news.* But what was the news, or the flattery? The writer gave no clue. Catalina picked up the next sheet of paper.

The sound of footsteps made her look up. Catalina hoped Jorge was not coming to offer more flattery of his own. Not that she had anything to fear, with Alonzo dozing at the end of the table. However, Jorge was an unwanted distraction. In the right conditions, he could be amusing company, but currently she was far more interested in the Greek texts.

The new arrival turned out to be Liz. "Hi there, dear. I've come to see how you're getting on."

"Slow progress."

"Have you been able to make head or tail of anything?"

"Bits."

Liz pulled a stool over and sat down. The normal-sized furniture confirmed other humans had made the Barn their workshop. But was it before or after the aliens left?

"Anything you feel ready to share?"

What could she offer Liz to show her husband's life had not been thrown away on a fool's quest? "Mostly it's trivial notes. Requests for supplies, lists of people, even some gossip."

"Have you looked at the books yet?"

"I started, but they're difficult to follow. I thought I'd begin with the notes until I've developed more feel for the language."

"But this is all in Greek, the books included?"

"Oh yes. It's not the classical style of Plato or Homer, but it's all written in an archaic version of the language."

"I guess it's something. We couldn't even be sure of that much, before. Anything else?"

Catalina cast her eyes over the papers. "To my mind, it points to the Greeks not being slaves or prisoners here. Not all of them, anyway. They were educated and free to exchange letters with each other, which means they were privileged and trusted. I've known slaves who can read and write, of course. The Moors even have their own Arabic alphabet, the same as the Greeks do here. However, nobody makes books just for slaves to read."

"Really. Well, you've got the advantage on me there, dear. I've never met a slave." The tone was the harshest Catalina had heard from her. Had she just said something to upset Liz?

"Never?"

"Slavery is completely illegal, speaking from the standpoint of

1980. It was banned centuries ago in the British Empire, which New Zealand was part of at the time. The rest of the world followed suit, except for a few countries who took a while longer to come on board."

"But how can the world function without slaves?"

"Very easily. The same way it can function without kings and emperors."

"You said New Zealand was part of the British Empire."

"The word is was." Liz emphasized the last word. "The British Empire has gone, along with all the other European empires. Some kings and queens might have managed to keep their arses on a throne, but they lost all real power. Most countries were republics, in practice, if not in name."

"Like the Dutch?"

"The Americans were a better model. You've got some catching up to do. History from my point of view. I guess you could call it futury." Liz leaned back and sighed. "Sorry, dear. I shouldn't have snapped at you. Different times. Different ideas of right and wrong, good and evil."

"Surely good and evil don't change?"

"Ideas about them do. For me, and anyone from my time, slavery is as evil as you can get. It's right up there with eating babies for breakfast. We believe everyone is created equal."

"But some races of men are—"

"Whoa. Stop right there." Liz held out her hand. "Everyone is equal. No ifs, no buts. I know it's the world you come from, but you need to drop any ideas about some people being innately better than others, or you're going to end up in a shitload of trouble with folk here. Everyone is equal and has the same rights. Male or female, black or white, rich or poor, and as Madison would add, gay or straight."

"Commoner or noble?"

"You can put that on the list too."

Catalina mulled over Liz's words. It sounded like the sort of ideal Jesus might have championed, yet in her estimation, priests would be among the people most resistant to accepting it. Could the human race really be weaned from hypocrisy?

"It would be nice if people could be taught to act that way. But you say in your time it was true. Everyone was treated with the same respect?"

Liz's mouth twisted in a rueful smile. "Well, I admit we haven't been able to knock the idea into some people's thick heads. But we're working on it. A lot of appalling things were done by sick bastards with ideas about who does or doesn't deserve to live, because of the color of their skin, or the shape of their nose. We don't want to make the same mistakes again. And when it comes to Atlantis, there aren't enough folk here to start counting some as less than fully human."

"So Kali and Yaraha…"

"Are exactly the same as you and me. Doesn't matter if your dad was Lord Whatsisface."

"Some people are more able than others."

"True. And some are braver than others, or kinder, or more honest. But each of us has only one life to live. Everyone deserves a fair crack to make something of it."

How did she feel about that? Her heritage was a source of pride to Catalina, something she could draw on for strength. Yet, whatever the name de Valasco might mean to her, in truth, her position in Spain relied purely on money and her father's influence at court. Neither of these existed in Atlantis. So what was she now? Catalina smiled as the answer came to her—someone who could read Greek.

Catalina glanced up the table. Alonzo was still asleep at the far end. "I think he might be unhappy. He's been in service to my family since he was a child, and his father and grandfather before him. Honor and duty are everything to him, and he can be a little rigid."

"Then he's going to have to learn to bend. But we'll give him time to find his feet first."

"Thank you. I wouldn't want him to have trouble on account of his loyalty to me."

"No probs."

Catalina thought she knew what the expression meant, more from Liz's tone than the words themselves. It was a shame she could not have similar audible clues when translating the texts.

Liz added. "Religion is something else you might have trouble with."

"I know. The Protestants have been rejecting the Pope's authority for over a century. I don't expect everyone here to be true Catholics."

"That is just the start of it, dear. Some of us aren't even true Christians."

"The Pope decreed those who follow Luther aren't—" Catalina

broke off at the sight of Liz's expression. "That isn't what you mean, is it? Yaraha and Piracola are still heathens. Before Columbus there were no missionaries so—" This time it was Liz's laughter that stopped her.

"To be honest, I don't have the faintest idea which gods those two follow, if any. They haven't shared that side of their culture. Torvold might still worship Thor and Odin for all I know. Babs's family were Jewish, but she's happy to admit she's lapsed. And I stopped putting any faith in the whole thing before I left kindergarten."

"You're not a Christian?" Catalina could not keep the shock from her voice. At the end of the table, Alonzo stirred.

"I don't count myself as one, no. But religion's the issue that's caused more ructions here than anything else. So the rules are, you're free to believe whatever you want and pray to whoever you want, however you want, if it makes you feel better. But you give the same courtesy to everyone else, and you don't try to convert them to your faith."

"You care not for the state of your immortal soul?" Alonzo said.

"I'm happy to take my chances."

"The Pope has decreed—"

Liz held up her hand. "Uh-uh. What did I say? Keep it to yourself."

Alonzo was still willing to argue. Catalina could tell from his face. She cut him off with a change of topic. "Just before, you quoted Madison about different groups of people. What did you say, gay or something?"

"Oh, you can ask her. I'm done lecturing for today." Liz pointed to the table. "Back to the writing. You think the Greeks were partners with the aliens in whatever they were doing here?"

Catalina took a moment to regather her thoughts. "Yes. That's how I see it."

"But you've had no luck with the books?"

"No. Some look like instruction manuals, but it's impossible to make sense of them. I think my translation skills need polishing."

"Well, dear, it can't help if you're going from archaic Greek into medieval Spanish and from there to twentieth century English."

"It's more than that. Take this for example." Catalina flipped open the nearest book and read the first line. "*Instructions for reviving the distribution of reserve potency in extreme situations.*" She looked up. "What can that mean?"

Liz stared into the air, a frown knotting her face. After a lengthy pause she said, "That bit about reserve potency. Could it be read as *emergency backup power supply?*"

"It could, I suppose. Does it make a difference?"

Liz laughed. "I think we should have someone with recent technical knowledge work with you tomorrow. They might not be up to speed on alien tech, but they could help with the guesswork."

❖

An hour later, Catalina was going cross-eyed. The Greeks might have been literate, but some had clearly not grasped the importance of letter formation. The strange numerical clock on the wall said there was plenty of time before dinner, but Catalina could not face any more. She pushed back from the table and stretched her arms.

"Are you all right, my lady?" As ever, Alonzo was not far away.

"Yes. I'm fine, but I've done enough for today."

"Please, allow me to escort you to your room." He offered his arm.

Catalina hesitated before accepting. Part of her welcomed the display of gentlemanly good manners, reassuring in this strange new world. His arm was both literally and figuratively something to hang on to. Liz's comments gave her cause to think again, but then she placed her hand on Alonzo's arm. They could start weaning themselves off the familiar etiquette another day, when she was not feeling so tired.

The ground outside was damp and puddles dotted the flower beds. It must have rained recently, but for now the sun was shining between puffy white clouds. The air smelled fresh and clean.

As they approached the Squat, Catalina heard shouts, laughter, and an occasional high-pitched whistle. They turned a corner and saw the entire population of Atlantis gathered on the large purple lawn. Everyone was engaged in some sort of game, except for Liz and Kali, who were spectators, seated on a couple of crates at the side.

Liz smiled at Catalina and shifted over to make room for her. "Take a pew. It's good you've shown up. I was thinking we ought to send someone to let you know what's happening."

"And what is happening?"

"Five a side football. Soccer. They're playing twentieth century against the rest. Charles is referee because he was born in 1888 and has a foot in each camp. Your side's losing, by the way, two goals to nil. They can do with someone to cheer them on."

"Who organized this?"

"Nobody. Jorge found a ball in a locker, and the rest just happened. I'm sorry you missed the start."

The excited shouts reached a new peak. Torvold was running full pelt while kicking a round ball before him. When Floyd moved to cut him off, Torvold chipped the ball across to Sam. Was it any surprise the ex-cabin boy was playing like a man? However, Madison and Babs were also in the game.

Catalina settled beside Liz. "Is it fair? The twentieth century side has two women, whereas the other only has one. Won't the team with more women be at a disadvantage?"

"Depends on the women. Anyway, the twentieth century has Jorge and Ricardo. They're the only two who've played much soccer before. As I said, we're winning."

To underscore the point, Jorge kicked the ball to his brother. Ricardo swerved left then right before thumping the ball past Horatio, who appeared to be tasked with guarding a twenty-foot gap between two trees.

Charles blew a shrill note on a whistle. "Goal. Three–nil to the twentieth."

"Are there rules to this game?" Catalina asked.

"Yes. But most of them are being ignored."

Several men had removed their shirts, not just Yaraha and Piracola. Catalina had never seen so much flesh on display before. Yet it seemed innocent, like children at play. The men's bodies glistened with sweat as they ran barefoot. Everyone was clearly enjoying themselves, and both Liz and Kali were laughing at the antics.

Catalina glanced up at Alonzo. "Do you want to sit down? I don't know if there's another crate around."

"No, my lady. No." His eyes were fixed on the players. Then he shook his head and turned away. "I…I must go to my room. Please excuse me." He appeared flustered.

"Are you all right?"

"Yes, my lady. I trust it's acceptable if I leave you with Doña Elizabeth."

"Yes, of course."

"I will see you at dinner." Alonzo hurried away.

Catalina was wondering whether she should follow and assure herself all was well, when another burst of shouting reclaimed her attention. Sam had the ball, using her speed to get by first Floyd, then Madison. She booted the ball high across the lawn, over the head of Babs, who was filling the role of gap guarder for the twentieth century.

Charles blew the whistle again. "Goal. Three–one."

The game continued. The rules appeared to be straightforward, although questions arose. "Why are Horatio and Babs the only ones who pick the ball up?"

"They're the goalies. The only ones allowed to touch the ball with their hands," Liz answered.

After more of the game Catalina asked, "Why does Jorge keep shouting 'offside' to Charles?"

"It's one of the rules everyone bar him is ignoring. Don't worry about it."

And later still. "Is Torvold allowed to pick Ricardo up like that?"

But this time Liz was laughing too hard to answer.

Catalina found her eyes continually drawn to Sam. She could not help watching the way Sam moved, the sunlight on her face, her speed and fluid grace. Sam might have been a dancer. Catalina drew a deep breath, as if she could by an act of willpower command her heartbeat to slow. What had come over her?

Sam wore the same breeches as before but had loosened the ties around her knees and rolled the hem up so they were more in keeping with the shorts worn by other castaways. Her shirt was no longer tucked into her waistband, and the buttons at her neck were undone. Her stockings and boots were gone.

Catalina twisted slightly, feeling the satin stick to the sweat on her back and chafe her neck. She knew she should be grateful to Alonzo for retrieving her gown, but half of her wished she could dress like the others. They looked so at ease.

Catalina remembered the excitement of getting a new gown, reveling in the cut and the color, the soft warmth of velvet and fur, the sheen of satin and silk. But how much had been due to imagining how other women would see her? Catalina assumed women of the twentieth century did not dress in shorts and loose shirts all the time. What could she wear to impress Babs, or Liz, or Madison? What could she wear to impress Sam? And why should she want to? When had she started caring about the opinion of a cabin boy on a pirate ship? That question at least was easy to answer—as soon as she had gotten over her surprise that Sam was female.

The game ended with the score five–three to the twentieth century, but no one on the losing team was downhearted, judging by the talk of a rematch. Ricardo trotted across to claim a winner's kiss from Kali. Torvold, Floyd, and Jorge pulled on their shirts and wandered away, jostling each other and laughing loudly while they argued some point about the game.

"Well, dear. It's my turn to cook tonight, so I'll love you and leave you. Just don't expect anything fancy for dinner." Liz levered herself to her feet.

Ricardo picked up the crate Kali had been sitting on and carried it away. Catalina looked at the other one. How heavy was it? Should she try to pick it up? She became aware of Sam at her shoulder.

"I'll take care of the crate. It's empty, but we might need it again. We don't want the caretakers clearing it away."

"Thank you."

Sam followed after Ricardo. After a moment of wavering, Catalina hurried to catch up. "You did well, scoring two goals."

"Mostly luck, I think."

"It looked like fun."

"It was."

Catalina studied Sam's face in profile. White-blond hair clung to the sweat on her forehead. Her skin was flushed from the exercise. Her eyes were downcast as she concentrated on her footing, but this only drew attention to the length of her eyelashes. The firm line of Sam's jaw had made her a convincing boy but did nothing to lessen her attractiveness as a woman.

Catalina played a bizarre, disorientating game with herself, superimposing the way Sam looked before onto how she appeared now. Both images were identical. How could they not be? And yet so very different. As with the Greek texts, interpretation involved more than simply seeing what was in front of your eyes.

"Did you enjoy watching?" Sam asked abruptly.

"It was entertaining. Had you played before?"

"Not much. Football isn't suited to onboard ship. Balls get lost overboard."

"Yes, I imagine so." They walked on in silence. Catalina tried to think of something else to say. "What made you go to sea?"

"My father."

"He wanted you to become a sailor?"

Sam laughed. "It wasn't quite like that. Either he took me with him on his ship, or he abandoned me to fend for myself. I was a young child at the time."

"Was he a pirate?"

"No. Pa was an honest merchant sailor, till the day he died."

"So why did you join the crew of the *Golden Goose* after his death?"

"Because otherwise I'd have died as well."

Had Sam really been faced with no other option? *She will lie about everything.* Alonzo's words echoed in Catalina's head. He was more reliable than any pirate. Catalina knew anything and everything Sam said was probably untrue. Yet this did nothing to dampen the excitement she felt, due to nothing more than walking at Sam's side. If anything, the sense of courting danger only made it worse.

Ricardo and Sam stacked the crates in a storeroom at the communal building. A boar carcass and several brace of seabirds hung from hooks on the ceiling, and a rack of fish stood to one side. The room was surprisingly cold. Catalina's breath formed clouds of white steam, but before she could ask about the temperature, Liz shooed them out of the kitchen area. Ricardo and Kali wandered off, arm in arm.

Catalina tried to think of an excuse to make Sam stay. She wanted to talk, with no idea what to talk about. This was not a good idea. She should leave but did not want to.

"Did you like being a sailor?"

"It was all I was used to."

"The pirates were terrible men—evil. How could you bear living among them?"

Sam shrugged. "Some were. Most weren't. They were much like any other crew I've known, except they were better treated by the captain, and there was always a chance the next day you'd either make your fortune or be killed."

The chances Sam also had lived with. "Was it exciting?"

"Sometimes."

"Frightening?"

"Sometimes."

"Do you miss it?"

Sam thought for a while. "No. Though it's only been a few days."

"True. It feels far longer."

There were other questions Catalina wanted to ask. How had Sam managed to conceal her true sex in the confines of the ship? Was she offended at the way Catalina had spoken to her, back then? Did she want to be friends now? Could they spend more time together? What was she planning on doing after dinner? Of course, the question she should ask was, why did you threaten Alonzo with a knife? Catalina had no doubt he had been telling the truth.

"I need to go," Sam said. "I'm sweaty after the game. I should wash before dinner. The castaways put a lot of importance on getting clean."

"I've noticed."

The stress placed on hygiene was extreme, even if the wonderful supply of hot water turned bathing into an unexpected and quite indulgent pleasure. Catalina had washed more in the previous two days than she would have in a year back in Spain.

Liz evidently overheard them and shouted from the kitchen. "You better hurry. You'll only have time for a quick shower."

"Right. Thanks." Sam trotted away.

Catalina was left alone. Talking to Sam was not wise. It was not safe, or constructive, or appropriate. But it was fun. Catalina had no idea why, but it was so much fun.

CHAPTER EIGHT

The size of the Barn caught Sam by surprise. She stopped in the doorway.

"God's blood, it's big!" Maybe not the most original thing to say, but nothing else came to mind.

Yaraha laughed. "Do you know, that's not so far from my own words the first time I came in here."

"The inside can't be bigger than the outside, can it? That would be impossible."

"I'd warn against dismissing anything as impossible. It's proved a fatal mistake for other castaways. But no. Like you, I wondered the same thing, so I measured it. The outside is exactly the same size, but it's harder to judge scale without the sky over your head."

Sam stepped forward slowly, her eyes fixed on the ceiling. Would having the sun or a few clouds for comparison make any difference? "Why did the aliens need to make a building this big?"

"Why did they need to make the Isle of Broken Years at all? They're no longer here to ask."

Sam lowered her gaze. "You don't use the name Atlantis. Why?"

"Because a name should mean something. What does Atlantis mean?"

"An island in the Atlantic ocean?"

"There are hundreds of such islands. Somewhere this unique deserves its own name. Time is broken here, and in turn it breaks us. Even if I choose to mock myself with childish dreams of escape, the broken years shatter any hope of returning to my family. I'll never again see my beloved Obenayo, or my father and mother. I'll never again hold my infant son in my arms. And even if it was possible, how could I look into their eyes, knowing what I do now? My people are doomed. Their shadows will fade from the land. Their voices will fall silent. My children, my grandchildren, might have lived out their lives. But the end is written, and my heart breaks on the story of the years unfolding."

Yaraha's words flowed with the rhythm of poetry. His eyes were closed, his face impassive. Sam would not have been surprised to see tears flow down his cheeks, though none came.

"Is the future really that bad for your people?"

"Yes. One of Madison's companions—Jeff was his name. He was so proud to be one-eighth Seminole Indian. He'd made a study of the first people in the land he called Florida. Before he fell prey to the hunters, he told me many things that I cannot unhear. My people will go down in history as a vanished tribe called the Timucua. And neither he nor I had any idea what that name might mean, if anything." Yaraha looked at her, and surprisingly, he smiled. "Come tell me. What does 'Sam' mean?"

"It doesn't mean anything. It's just my name."

"Exactly. Names should mean something."

"Does yours?"

"Yes. It means 'panther.'"

"So how did your folk know whether someone was talking about you or a real panther?"

"The same way I knew you hadn't really seen God's blood when you walked though the door." He put his arm across her shoulder and urged her onward. "Come. I'll show you some of the impossible things stored here."

If she was being honest, Yaraha's stories about the contents of the Barn were just an excuse to be there. However, since Sam could not read English, let alone Greek, asking Catalina about her work might not have been as believable.

Already, Sam had spotted her, sitting to one side of the entrance. Catalina's head was bent over one end of a long table. She must have heard Sam and Yaraha enter but was showing no reaction, unlike the other two present. Alonzo had his arms crossed and was scowling furiously—no change there. However, Floyd smiled, got to his feet, and stretched until the muscles in his back cracked.

"You okay without me for a bit?" he asked.

"For the moment." This time Catalina looked around. Her eyes met Sam's and held, for the space of a heartbeat, before returning to the papers spread before her.

Floyd sauntered over. "How's it going?" Which, Sam had learned, was his way of saying hello.

"She wanted to see the Barn."

"You know to be careful. You don't want to end up like poor Alice." Floyd tilted his head in Sam's direction. "Long time back, she was in here, digging around. Said, 'What's this button?' Next moment she was nothing more than a pile of ash."

"Really?"

"Would I lie to you?"

"Yes," Yaraha answered for her. "You should not take everything Floyd says seriously."

Sam had already experienced Floyd's sense of humor. Even so, she decided to be careful about what she touched.

Floyd was clearly not at all offended. He laughed and slapped his leg. "Careful, buddy, you'll be giving this little lady the wrong idea about me."

Floyd was actually no taller than Sam. However, his shoulders were twice as broad, and she would have strained to touch her fingers around his biceps using both hands. His neck was nearly the same width as his bald head. He owed the muscles to an exercise routine he performed without fail every morning. Floyd had said he used to play linebacker at college, but gave no more details. Sam assumed linebacker was a game something like soccer, but requiring more in the way of arm strength.

"What were you going to show her first?" Floyd asked Yaraha.

"What do you recommend?"

Floyd grinned and pointed to a set of shelves. "It's not the most exciting, but while we're here, we can check out Jorge's hoard. If ever he gets back to when he came from, he plans on being a rich man."

"He doesn't stop dreaming," Yaraha said.

"Nope."

The collection was, to Sam's mind, an uneven mix—bowls, bracelets, coins, scrolls, and tiny statues. Some items were gold, but others were base metal or carved from stone. Taken together, they would have filled two sacks.

Sam picked up a carving of a warrior brandishing a shield and spear. "Does he think these are valuable?"

"Yes. And he's probably right. Collectors would pay a fortune. He also has a pouch of diamonds stored somewhere," Floyd said.

Sam replaced the figure, and Yaraha led them deeper into the Barn. He stopped by an enormous metal claw attached to the top of a thirty-foot-high gantry.

"Watch this." Floyd picked up a black metal glove and put it on.

The claw jerked into life, swiveling in Sam's direction. The talons opened, reaching, grasping for her, to the sound of an inhuman howl. Sam leapt back and fell, tripping over her own feet. Even as she hit the ground, she realized the claw was mimicking the movement of Floyd's hand. The howl was the screech of metal on metal.

"It made me jump as well, first time." Yaraha offered a hand to help her up.

"I think it needs to be oiled." Floyd removed the glove and held it out to Sam. "Do you want to give it a try?"

"Maybe next time." When her heart was not beating nineteen to the dozen.

A short way farther on was a bench with what looked like a row of dead spiders lying on their backs. They were the size of dinner plates. At the end of each upraised leg was a tiny windmill, similar to those on Bab's seaplane.

Yaraha took down a box from the shelf above. "What did Madison call this? A drain?"

"Something like that," Floyd agreed.

The box made Sam think of the *Okeechobee Dawn* cockpit, set with levers, dials, and buttons. Yaraha flicked a switch with his thumb. Immediately, one set of windmills turned into a blur. The drain rose from the table and hovered in midair. The sound of humming made it seem even more like a giant insect.

Floyd nudged Sam. "Look at the screen."

He pointed to a rectangle of black glass standing on a nearby easel.

This had also come to life, showing a moving picture, the drain's-eye view of the world.

The drain zipped across the Barn, turning the display into a dizzying whirl. When the picture settled, there was Catalina's face, filling the screen. She tilted her head to one side and gave a confused half smile, then twisted in her seat to look over at them. Sam wondered whether she should wave or apologize for disturbing Catalina's work, although it had been all Yaraha's doing. Meanwhile, the screen now showed her left ear.

The drain shot along the table to hover in front of Alonzo, who merely scowled.

"Careful, buddy. You don't want to crack the glass, pulling a face like that," Floyd called out, laughing.

Alonzo took himself far too seriously. Would it be worth letting him know he was not the only man in Atlantis who preferred other men? Not that Sam could imagine anything happening between the two. Apart from their choice of bedfellow, they had nothing in common. Floyd was friendly and outgoing, and Alonzo was not.

Yaraha brought the drain back and passed the control box to Sam. After crashing it four times, she finally got the drain to hover.

"Why's it called a drain?" Sam asked. Did this name mean anything?

"You'll have to ask Madison."

They put it back with the others and were about to move on when Catalina called out, "Floyd, can you have a look at this for me?"

"Sure thing, honey." Floyd touched his forefinger to his eyebrow and flicked it in Sam's direction, his way of saying good-bye.

The tour continued without him. Yaraha pointed out a set of contraptions that could repair and inflate the *Inflatable* if it suffered a leak. A mechanical head, a rack of swords sharper than Sam would have believed possible, a life-sized model of a puffed up man with a bowl on his head, children's toys, half-assembled tools. The contents of the Barn stretched away into the distance. It would take months to see it all.

Several times Sam caught Catalina looking their way. Were they disrupting her work? She was about to suggest they leave the rest of the Barn for another day when Yaraha picked up an oval board, a yard in length.

"How good is your sense of balance?"

"Pretty good, I think. Why?"

"You should try this. But it would be better if we go outside. The grass will be softer if you fall off."

"Falling off shouldn't be a problem, as long as you don't expect me to balance on it edgewise." A thought struck her. "Or does it move?"

"Oh my word, yes, as Horatio would say." Yaraha started for the exit.

Sam hurried to catch up. "You speak English well."

"Thank you. Piracola and I have lived here eleven years, and we've had good teachers, even if they can't agree on what certain words mean. I've found it wisest to avoid using bum and fanny."

As they passed the table, Catalina looked up. "Are you going?" She did not sound impatient or irritated, despite Sam's earlier doubts.

"For now," Yaraha said. "Have you learned much from this writing?"

Floyd cut in, before Catalina had a chance to reply. "That those old Greeks sure had a way with words. Never use three where you can squeeze in sixteen." He nodded at the object in Yaraha's hands. "You're giving Sam a go on the hoverboard?"

"Yes. Do you want to come to watch?"

"It's up to the lady." He smiled at Catalina.

"You can come too." Sam spoke on impulse.

Alonzo did not give her a chance to answer. "Doña Catalina has important work to do. She does not wish to be taken away from it."

You could let her speak for herself. Sam bit back the words.

"Alonzo's right. I need to concentrate."

"Right. Well. Another time then."

"Another time." Catalina gave a warm smile. "Maybe you can show me later."

Sam felt the air leave her lungs. She braced one hand on the table until she felt steady enough to walk. How could one smile affect her like that?

"Come on. We'll find a good spot, well away from the water. We don't want you falling in." Yaraha walked away.

Sam followed but stopped by the doorway to look back. Catalina had returned to work and was pointing something out to Floyd. At the end of the bench, Alonzo was glaring at Sam with pure, undisguised hatred. It was just as well looks could not kill. Sam was sure he had a private name for her, complete with meaning.

❖

The caretaker appeared out of nowhere, racing along the path. Sam barely avoided tripping over it. Her foot came down awkwardly, twisting her ankle. She did not hold back from letting the bio-robot know exactly what she thought of it, using one of her more exotic phrases.

A ripple of laughter came from the other side of a large bush. "Where did you learn such language? I'm shocked."

Sam hobbled forward. Kali was sitting on a crate in the shade.

"Sorry."

"I hope you don't teach words like that to my child."

Sam felt her cheeks burn. Her embarrassment was increased to see Catalina also present. Was there any risk she would understand as well? Fortunately, Catalina was looking at her with nothing but surprise. As ever, Alonzo was close at hand, although he was currently stretched out on the grass, taking an after-lunch nap.

"I promise I'll watch my mouth in future."

However, Kali's smile broadened. "I don't mind really. It's good to hear my own tongue spoken. And anyway, it's the goat I feel sorry for."

Sam gave a shamefaced grin and carried on, but before she had gone two steps, she heard movement.

Catalina had stood and was following her. "I'm going back to the Barn. May I walk with you, if you're going in that direction?"

The request was so unexpected, Sam struggled to find her voice. "Um…yes. You don't want…" She glanced in Alonzo's direction.

"We can let him sleep."

This was fine by Sam. They started walking, side by side. "I'm sorry about cussing just now."

"I guessed that's what it was. But I didn't understand a word. I assume you were talking African?"

"One of the languages. There's dozens, maybe hundreds. If anything, Kali knowing it was surprising. And I can't say much. Just a few handy phrases."

"For when you get run over by a caretaker?"

Sam laughed. "Something like that. We had crew on the *Golden Goose* picked up from slave ships. They might not have been the most expert sailors, but they were fired up for revenge. What I said just now was what some would shout going into a fight. It's all I know how to say."

"You speak Spanish?"

"A little. Like with French, German, Dutch—enough to get along with other crew members." She looked at Catalina. "I don't speak any of them half as well as you speak English."

"I can thank my parents for that."

They turned a corner. Their destination was in sight, but a scene of frenzied activity stood between them and the Barn. This must have been where the caretaker had been rushing to. A dozen were hard at work, digging up the path. Flashes of blue light lit the sides of the hole. Smoke drifted out, although the smell was more like rotten cabbages.

Catalina wrinkled her nose. "What do you think it is?"

"I don't know. Probably best to give them a bit of space." Sam pointed at the row of bushes bordering the path. "We can cut through there."

Sam pushed back the leaves. Without thinking, she reached back to offer Catalina assistance over the uneven ground. Catalina took her hand and continued to hold it even after they were on pavement again. Sam's head was totally scrambled. They walked the short distance remaining in silence, while she struggled to pull her thoughts together.

Catalina's hand felt smooth and delicate, although her grip was surprisingly firm. It might be sensible to let go, although Sam did not think she was the one doing the holding. Did Catalina know what she was doing? Did she mean anything by it? And if so, what?

They stopped at the door. Catalina released Sam's hand and stepped back. "Thank you for your assistance."

"You're welcome."

Catalina moved away, not meeting Sam's eyes, but then she stopped and turned back. "Sam?"

"Yes?" She felt her heart pounding. What would come next?

"Alonzo said…"

Sam clenched her jaw. Nothing good was going to follow from that beginning.

"He said that, on the pirate ship, there was an incident between you two."

Had he admitted taking other men as lovers? If this was the subject on Catalina's mind, did it have any part to play in them holding hands? The idea died as quickly as it flashed into her head. Alonzo would never confess to Catalina. Sam just nodded.

"He said you threatened him with a knife."

Yes. Of course. That would be the slant he put on the tale. Sam folded her arms, waiting for more.

"I wondered what you had to say."

"What has Alonzo told you?"

Catalina looked uncomfortable. "You don't deny it?"

"Would there be any point?" Sam sighed and took a step back. "You should ask him, but I doubt you'll get much in the way of an answer."

She turned and walked away. Her fingers still tingled. Why had Catalina held her hand for so long? Although, to be honest, she had no idea of courtly manners. Maybe Spanish noblewomen walked around all the time hand in hand. It certainly was not sensible to interpret Catalina's actions any other way, since with Alonzo in the picture, things were not going to end up looking pretty.

❖

"Bad news, folks. We're getting low on corn and potatoes." Liz addressed the room at breakfast. "We need to send a food expedition to the farm tomorrow. Which three are next on the roster?"

"Me." Ricardo was the first to speak up.

Kali was sitting beside him. She pressed their joined hands to her chest. Ricardo slipped free and wrapped his arm around her shoulder, pulling her against him. His lips brushed the top of her head. "I'll be fine, cariño."

"Who else?"

"Me," Madison said.

"And me. I think. Maybe it is so." Piracola looked around anxiously, as if hoping someone would disagree with him.

"No maybe about it, son." Charles waved a notebook in the air. "Your name's on the list."

"Don't we send one of the newbies? I thought we worked them into the roster."

"We can," Liz said. "Usually they get time to settle in, but they've been here a fortnight. So, who gets replaced?" she called to Charles.

He flipped open the notebook again. "Madison."

Piracola's face fell. Clearly, he had been hoping to avoid going.

Liz faced to the side where Sam was sitting. "We'll put you three newbies' names into the hat and draw one out. Then—" She got no further.

"What! You think to send Doña Catalina into danger? You would have her dig in the fields?" Alonzo's voice shook with outrage.

"Only if she wants to eat."

"She is not a farmhand. She is a lady and—"

"She's one of us, and she takes her chances like the rest. Even Kali won't get let off the roster for another month or two."

"You are—"

This time it was Catalina who interrupted. "No. Liz is right. I'm not..." A pink flush rose on her cheeks. "I don't want any special treatment."

Still Alonzo would not shut up. Sam felt a rush of annoyance. Could the fool not see he was embarrassing Catalina?

"My lady, please do not be so...so..." Alonzo turned to Liz. "If you will not stop this barbaric nonsense, I demand we do not play with drawing names. I will go."

"Wait up there." Sam was not going to let Alonzo run away with the award for chivalry, when Catalina was involved. "I'm game for this as well. It can be between him and me."

"I spoke first."

The argument held the promise of becoming very childish, very quickly. "Then we can both go." Sam turned to Liz. "As long as that doesn't cause a problem."

"No. No problem at all, dear. You'll be able to carry more back." Liz clapped her hands together. "Okay, so there'll be four going. Piracola, Ricardo, Sam, and Alonzo." She smiled at them grimly. "Stay safe, guys."

❖

Dawn was turning the horizon yellow and orange when they assembled on the quay the next morning. With Charles's advice, Sam had packed the things she would need the previous night. Her rucksack contained a machete, empty sacks, a whistle, a medical bag, and enough food and water to last two days. She dropped it in the *Inflatable* and yawned. The other tools they needed were stored at the farm.

Alonzo was already waiting when Sam arrived. He turned his back as soon as he saw her. Ricardo was busy, making his good-byes to Kali. The pair stood a short way off, arms wrapped around each other. Kali's head was on his shoulder, her eyes closed. With nothing else to do, Sam watched the sunrise.

Piracola trotted up, yawning. "Sorry. I slept for too long."

He hopped into the rear of the *Inflatable* and started adjusting the outboard motor. Sam sat beside him, and Alonzo went to the front. Ricardo was last in. He broke away from Kali after a last kiss.

"Right. Off we go." He looked back. "I'll be back soon, cariño. Don't worry."

Kali stepped back from the edge as the outboard motor ripped into the early morning peace. "Full throttle" was the phrase Torvold had used on the salvage trip. The boat sped away across the water, leaving Kali as a lone figure on the quay, waving.

The early morning air was chill. Sam held the neck of her shirt to keep out the breeze, and peered into the water, trying to see through the bow wave. Once, she caught a glint of movement under the surface, multiple forms, moving swiftly, chasing the boat. A rush of ice prickles flowed down Sam's spine, and she turned her attention to the approaching shoreline.

The jungle looked darker and denser than Sam remembered. Piracola silenced the outboard motor, and the *Inflatable* coasted the final few yards, until it bumped against the rock jetty. Ricardo picked up his pack and jumped ashore, followed by Sam, then Alonzo. Piracola was last, holding the mooring rope.

"Right, we'll—"

Leaves along the shore flapped in a sudden gust of wind. A tremor ran through the ground, and up Sam's legs. The light dimmed. Who reacted first?

"She's jumping," Ricardo shouted.

Sam looked up at a gunmetal sky. The wind strengthened, buffeting them, and a second stronger jolt made the ground buck.

"No! She's—" Piracola's words changed to a broken stream in a language Sam did not know, but she did not need a translation.

Piracola was crouched down, stretching out to grab the rope floating away from him. A third shock kicked the ground from under Sam's feet. She landed on her knees. Piracola also fell forward. His chest hit the rock and his arm plunged, elbow deep, into the water. In an instant, Ricardo was at his side, hauling him back.

As Piracola's hand cleared the sea, a rush of water chased it upward. The rising wave separated around silver fangs set in a lipless mouth, and then splashed back. A razor fin broke the surface of the water and vanished.

Piracola knelt on the rock, holding his hand against his chest. A dark trickle of blood ran down his wrist and dripped onto the rock. "I'm okay. Just a scratch. But the boat…"

The *Inflatable* was now thirty feet from shore, driven by the swirling gusts. Yet already the world was settling. The light hardened into black and white. The wind dropped and the ground became steady. Sam looked up again. The gray had gone, replaced by the black of night, strewn with stars. A full moon hung overhead.

"We're stranded." Sam fought to keep the fear from her voice, although her stomach had turned to ice.

"It won't be for long. We'll be okay," Ricardo said. "When we don't return, the others will come looking for us."

"They won't give us up for dead?"

"Kali won't." He spoke with certainty. "I don't think the others will either. Can you imagine Torvold forgetting the *Inflatable*? We just need to stay safe until then."

Safe. "The hunters will be out soon." Sam remembered the warnings.

"Yes. So we need to get to a roost as quickly as possible."

"Where's the nearest one?"

"Not far."

Piracola got to his feet, still cradling his hand.

"Are you sure you're all right?" Ricardo asked him.

"Yes. Yes." Piracola shook out his arm and cast one last vengeful look at the departing boat. "I'll lead."

Piracola might seem immature at times, and Sam had noted his command of English was not as good as Yaraha's, but no one could fault his woodcraft skills. She had no idea how he navigated through the jungle. Even with a full moon, the darkness under the canopy of trees was total. Piracola moved like a ghost, whereas the cracks of twigs under her own feet were like thunderclaps. Sam had trouble merely following his lead. All the time her ears were trained for the sound of clicking.

Sam ran into Ricardo's back. He had stopped. "This is it. We're here."

She heard the rasp of rope being untied, and then the creak as someone began to climb. Soon they were all sitting on a platform identical to the one where she had met Charles, Yaraha, and Torvold. The moonlight was stronger in the treetops, enough for Sam to see the others.

Ricardo settled back on his elbows and sighed. "Do you know what's the second worst thing about time jumps?"

"What?" Piracola asked.

"The jet lag. How do I persuade my body it's not morning anymore, and it would be a good idea to sleep?"

"Why do you call that jet lag?"

"It's because of—" Ricardo broke off, then dropped his voice to a whisper. "Of course there is the very worst thing."

Then Sam heard it too, coming softly from the forest floor, some way off, but getting closer.

"Tck-tck. Tck. Tck-tck-tck."

"Thank the good Lord. We made it in time. Now, everyone, hush."

Sam lay awake all night. Judging by the restless shifting, the others fared no better. Then her eyelids grew heavy just as the sun was rising.

Piracola muttered and sat up. "What are we to do today?"

Ricardo sighed. "We can stay here and try to sleep, or we can go to the farm as planned."

"Is it safe?"

"Is it ever? But people won't be expecting us back for a day, so they won't come searching. And if we don't get the food now, we'll have to come back another time. I'd rather be finished with it."

Sam looked over the edge of the roost. The forest floor was emerging from the darkness. Nothing was moving. "I think the hunters have gone."

"For now. So, do we want to vote on the farm?"

Surprisingly, Alonzo was first to speak. "I am for the farm. I wish to be done as soon as I can. Doña Catalina may be in need of my aid."

With what? Sam bit her tongue and merely nodded.

"Okay. The farm it is."

Once again, Piracola took the lead. Sam and Ricardo walked behind him, side by side, and Alonzo hung back at the rear. Sam glanced over her shoulder and was rewarded with another angry glare. If she promised to keep his guilty secret, would it improve matters between them? Did she care enough to make the effort? Sam sighed.

"What is it?" Ricardo asked.

"Oh, nothing." Alonzo's opinion was not worth worrying about. "Ricardo. That's a good name. My father was also called Richard."

"You said was?"

"Yes. He died, a year ago…well, it was a year when I arrived here. You know what I mean."

"Yes. And I'm sorry for your loss."

"Was your father still alive?"

Ricardo's lips twisted in an expression of contempt. "I don't know, and I don't care. He left my mother when I was a child. Abandoned us. And even when he lived with us, he was rarely sober enough to do more than kick me out of his way."

"Then I'm sorry for what you never had." Pa might have been a prize drunkard, but Sam had never doubted his love for her.

"Jorge is six years older than me. He's been a better father. Always he has looked out for me and our sisters."

"How many sisters?"

"Three." Ricardo grimaced. "Of course, I wonder what became of them. I pray they found good husbands."

"How old were you when your father left?"

"Seven. Jorge was thirteen. Too young to become the man of the household. I know he can seem foolish, with his dreams of escaping and becoming a millionaire, but you must remember where we come from." Ricardo's voice dropped. "I remember him trying to be a man, trying not to cry when he couldn't put food on the table for us. He'd tell us stories, promises of all the money he'd bring home one day. We were going to live in a mansion on our own private island. We were going to have cars, and boats, and maids to do all the work."

"Is that what made him turn to smuggling?"

"Of course. What other way is there to become rich in Honduras?"

"He talked you into joining him?"

"No. I don't think it was what he wanted. But once the drug lords get their claws in you, your options become limited."

"Drug lords?"

"The big criminals who control the drug trade."

Sam frowned in thought. "You mean drugs like opium?"

"Yes. Though things have moved on from there."

"Did the custom's men put a high tax on it?"

Ricardo laughed. "All trade in drugs was completely banned."

"Really?" Sam shrugged. "Wasn't in my day. Why was it illegal?"

"People become addicted. People take too much and die. People are so wasted, lying in the street they cannot go and do a day's work."

"I'd heard opium can be dangerous, the same as rum and beer. Folk in my time would have said it was your own lookout for taking it in the first place."

"It isn't so simple. The angriest Jorge has ever been with me was the day he caught me sampling the merchandise. He cried. He would not cry as a child, when he could not feed us, but he cried that day and made me swear I would never do it again. He did not want me to end up a shambling fool like our father."

"Would you have made your fortune as smugglers?"

"No. We were small fish. We made enough money to flash around at home, but never enough to get away. Before long we would have been caught, and then spent many years, rotting in jail, if we weren't killed by a rival gang."

"Then maybe it's not so bad you came here."

A smile of pure joy spread over Ricardo's face. "No. Because if I had not come to Atlantis, I would not have met Kali. I love her so much."

"And she loves you."

"Yes. But I don't know why. I'm not clever, or brave, or handsome, yet she says she sees all that in me."

"We use to say that love is blind."

"Ha! We still do."

"Though I don't think Kali has to be completely blind in your case."

"I don't know. When I think of what was done to her. I'm amazed she's willing to let any man touch her." Ricardo's voice grew hard. "You know her story?"

"I heard she escaped from a slave ship, taking her to the New World."

"But not how she escaped?"

"No."

"She's beautiful, don't you think? The crew of the slave ship thought so. They freed her from her chains, cleaned off the below decks filth, and used her." The fury in his voice made it clear what those uses were. "And when they were not using her like that, they had her work for them, cleaning and cooking."

"They trusted her about the ship. Weren't there weapons she might have got her hands on?"

"She was a child. They weren't frightened of her."

"How old was she?"

"Eleven, maybe twelve. She's not sure. The ship stopped to pick up water. Kali took her chance and dived overboard. She swam ashore and hid."

"What happened to the slavers?"

"They were lucky. They sailed away before Atlantis jumped again." Ricardo's hands formed fists. "Never before had I known what it is to want to kill someone. If I could hunt them down through the centuries, I would not rest until every last one lay dead. But Kali..." He sighed. "She makes me happy. I worry for our child. Atlantis is no place to raise children. But I cannot put it in my heart to regret what we share."

The trees ended. They stood at the edge of an expanse of low growing plants, surrounded by a solid fence. It was clearly a field of vegetables. However, the plants did not lie in neat rows. Off to her right was another area, filled with ripe maize.

"Do we tend this?"

"Minimally," Ricardo said. "We make sure the fence is strong enough to keep the goats out, and we remove the worst of the weeds, but we don't bother plowing. Everything is left to self-seed. The farmland used to cover most of the outer island. The forest has taken nearly all of it. Yet there's still enough to feed everyone in the Squat twenty times over. We do all right."

On the other side of the fields, Sam could see the remains of silos and other buildings. Even as crumbling ruins they stood as high as the surrounding trees. Discarded farm machinery rusted in the open, where it had been left. Sam walked over to inspect the nearest example.

"These are plowshares." Sam had never worked on a farm, but had no trouble identifying the curved blades.

"Yes."

"But there's twelve of them bolted together. It's huge. What sort of horses could pull it?"

"They probably had a tractor."

"A what?"

Ricardo smiled. "When we get back to the Barn, I'll see what I can find to help me explain. For now, we need to work. But first there is something I must tell you newbies." He looked over his shoulder to check that Alonzo was in hearing distance. "If you look there, there, there, and there. Do you see the roosts?"

"Yes."

"The hunters know we come to the farm, so they show up sometimes unexpected. All the while you're working, keep your ears open. First click, drop everything and warn the rest. You've got a whistle?"

"Yes."

"Three quick blasts and run for the nearest roost. Likewise if you hear someone signal, or if the island jumps. Don't hang around and take chances. This is where we lose the most people." He drew a deep breath. "Okay. Let's make a start."

❖

Sam swung her machete. The sapling snapped after three blows. She stood, wiped the sweat from her eyes, and yawned. Her mouth felt like she had been chewing sand. Fortunately, water was not rationed. Piracola's pack was in the *Inflatable*, but everyone else had theirs. Furthermore, the farm had a clean pond. Sam opened her flask and took a long drink.

Ricardo was right. Her body refused to believe it was afternoon. Her head was strangely light, and the ground bobbed under her feet, as if she was aboard a ship. She would have to ask why he called it jet lag.

Sweat trickled down her back and soaked into her waistband. Her skin felt dusty and sticky. Two weeks ago, she had never heard of a hot shower. Now, it was a hardship to be without one. However, the work was nearly done. Their harvest was in the sacks ready to be carried back.

Sam put the cap on her water bottle and fought back another yawn. A few cuts with the machete turned the sapling into a stake. Sam used it to reinforce a section of fence then continued pulling up the more obvious weeds.

A high-pitched whistle shrilled across the farm. Sam froze, spade in hand. At the other side of the field she could see Piracola working. The whistle came again, but this time she recognized it—just a bird. One more false alarm. Her pulse slowed. Sam shook her head and moved on.

Another bird joined in. Then a flock of gulls took to the air, complaining in a riot of harsh, screeching. Sam raised her head, looking to where they had been perched. The treetops were swaying in a fresh wind, sending down showers of leaves. Then Sam felt the ground shake. Why would Atlantis not stay put?

The light was changing. The sun was gone. Sam stuck her spade in the ground. She had managed to get herself as far from the scattered roosts as it was possible to get. Which was closest? Sam stumbled forward, trying to make haste over the heaving ground. She fell twice in the gloom, sprawling face-first in the dirt. The ladder over the fence was like climbing rigging in a gale. She bruised her knuckles, misjudging a handhold.

By the time she reached the knotted rope, the worst was over. The wind dropped and the ground steadied. Sam paused for a second to catch her breath, listening. No clicking. No rustling in the undergrowth. She had made it.

Sam hauled herself to the top, to find that she was not alone in selecting this roost. Of all people, why did it have to be Alonzo? Judging by his expression, he was even less happy to see her. "Why are you here?"

Sam sighed. "You know that's a silly question, don't you?"

Did she have any options? Sam glanced back down, but changing to another roost would be an act of insanity. The sun had moved and was now low on the horizon. Soon it would be dark. They did not have to talk. They could sleep until it was safe to leave.

"You wanted to follow me?"

"Why would I do that?" When Alonzo did not answer, Sam shifted to the far side of the platform and lay down with her back to him. "I'm going to sleep."

Yet, despite her tiredness, Sam's mind would not settle. Her heart was pounding, her chin and knuckles stung where she had grazed them, and she could not stop listening for hunters. The minutes drew out.

"You want to throw taunts at me. This is all your plan." And now, of all times, Alonzo wanted to have a conversation.

Sam rolled over. He was in the same spot with his arms wrapped around his raised knees. The last of the sun's rays lit the side of his face.

"Yes. Of course. Mind you, it was a bugger arranging the time jump so Piracola lost his grip on the boat."

"You think to laugh at me."

"What on earth gives you that idea?" Sam gave full rein to her irritation.

"I do not have to listen to you acting as the fool."

"You started it."

"No. It starts with you, dressing as a man to defy God. The Bible tells us how it should be for men and women. You chose to fight the will of God. Only evil can come from your sins. Can you say it is not so? Can you say your heart does not burn with lust for other women?"

Sam took a sharp breath. Unbidden, the image of Catalina's face hung before her. "No. I won't deny it. I do desire women as lovers."

The words were heavy on her tongue, but in giving them voice, a weight went from inside, just as when she had admitted her true sex to Charles. Saying the words was a release. Sam laced her fingers behind her head as a cushion and stared through the leaves at the darkening sky. Why had she ever felt confused when it was so obvious?

"You smile. I see you. I repent my sins, but your kind always cover yourselves in evil. Ever you seek to spread your foulness."

"My kind? Spreading foulness? You're just the same. I'll bet I'm the only woman you've ever offered to get your dick out for."

"You are without shame. A whore."

"No, I'm not, remember? I said no to you. If I was a whore, I'd have said yes, and charged you." Despite being angry, Sam was enjoying herself. "You were the one begging for it."

"You played the trick on me."

"Trick you? Into what? Acting in a less sinful way? Except I don't see any sin in you humping other men, as long as you leave them alone if they say no. And I'm not the only one who thinks that way. Have you talked to the others here?"

Alonzo choked audibly. "You…you have told them how—"

"No. You saved my life. If you want me to keep it a secret, then I will. You have my word on it."

"What does the word of a woman such as you count for?"

"Do you know, I thought you'd say something like that. But you should talk to them. Ask Charles or Liz what they think about men and women having lovers of the same sex."

"They would be sickened." His voice crackled with misplaced certainty.

"No, they wouldn't. And do you know how I know?" Sam swiveled around and sat facing him.

"How?"

"Because I've talked about it. Floyd's the same as you. He's a lover of men. The people here know it, and they don't care. If you'd spent less time playing mother hen to Catalina and bothered talking to people you'd have heard it too. He had a lover called David. They were together for ages, until David was killed two years ago. Floyd puts on a brave face, but everyone knows he's still mourning David. They feel sorry for him, but that's it. Just like they'd feel sorry for Kali if something happened to Ricardo."

"Why do you say this?"

"Because it's true? Because you ought to hear it? Why do you think I'd say it?"

"You think to tempt me."

"Don't be stupid. Why would I tempt you? To do what?"

"You are a devil, sent to test me. Now I see it all." Alonzo's voice grew in strength and conviction. "This island is a test. It is the work of the devil. He knows my weakness and he wants to trap my soul in lies. Your words are the lies. But at last I see the truth."

Alonzo got to his knees and crawled across the roost. Sam first thought he was coming to attack her, to push her off the edge. Instead he grabbed the rope and swung his legs over the side.

Sam scrambled to stop him. "No. Don't be an idiot."

She tried to grab his arm and haul him back to safety. Alonzo wrenched himself free and swung back at her. Whether or not it was intended, his fist connected with Sam's face, stunning her. By the time she recovered, he was no longer on the roost. The rope creaked.

Sam scuttled to the edge. Alonzo was already a third of the way down.

"Where are you going?"

"What does it matter? Anywhere that you are not. I wish to pray in peace and beg forgiveness for my sins."

"You mustn't. It's dangerous."

"The only danger comes from you. This is all the trap of the devil. I need fear nothing. I should have known from the beginning this was a trick. Jump across time. Monsters. Flying machines. Atlantis. The name is a myth for children. I was a fool to listen." He was getting close to the ground.

"No, Alonzo. Come back."

He looked up. The last glow of sunset lit his face. Was it certainty or insanity she saw there? Faintly, Sam heard the distant sound. "Tck-tck. Tck-tck-tck. Tck-tck."

"Alonzo. Listen. The hunters. They're coming."

He laughed and dropped the final few feet. "Your made-up devils do not give me fear. The Lord is my guardian and my shield. I see through your lies." He strode into the jungle.

Sam swung her legs over the edge, about to follow. The clicks were closer, louder. "Tck. Tck-tck-tck. Tck-tck."

Sam stopped. What could she do, other than die with him? She closed her eyes and rolled back onto the roost. Even if she caught up with Alonzo, she could not force him to return. She could not carry him up the rope.

The clicking passed beneath the tree and moved on, heading in the direction Alonzo had taken. Sam buried her head in her hands, until a wet tickle on her upper lip caught her notice. She wiped away blood—a nosebleed, and she would most likely have a black eye as well.

The first scream ripped through the forest.

A second scream came, fading to a gurgling, choking groan, and then there was silence, except for the sigh of the breeze in the branches and the thudding of Sam's heart.

❖

To her surprise, Sam fell asleep sometime after midnight. She woke with a crick in her neck and a chill seeping into her bones. However, the sun was peeking over the treetops. Soon, warmth would return to the world. All around were the sights, sounds, and scents of dawn in a tropical forest. Sam pressed her hands over her eyes. If only she could blot out the memory of the previous night.

Something was moving around below. Sam rolled to the edge of the platform. She could see ferns shaking, but there were no clicks, no sounds of danger. Listening more carefully, she made out a noise like snuffling breath—a piglet? Then came men's voices. The piglet fled.

Ricardo strode into view. "Sam. Alonzo. Are you there?"

"I am." Sam dropped down the rope to join him and Piracola.

"Where's Alonzo? Didn't he make it up?"

What could she say? "He did, but then he...he had a fit of madness. He decided the entire island was an illusion, created by the devil to tempt him. He climbed down and walked away."

"Couldn't you stop him?"

"How? He wouldn't listen to me." Or maybe she had said too much, and he had listened to all the wrong bits.

Both men were staring at her. Sam was aware of soreness where Alonzo had struck. She raised her hand and gently examined her face. Flakes of dried blood were rough under her fingers. Her nose was painful but not broken, as far as she could tell.

"This was what I got when I tried to stop him from leaving."

"You fought?"

"Not exactly. We argued, but I don't think he meant to punch me. I was trying to pull him back onto the roost and he shoved me away."

Now Ricardo was peering at her hands. Sam held out her knuckles.

"This isn't anything to do with it. I ran into the fence when Atlantis jumped, before I'd even reached the roost."

Did he believe her? Ricardo said nothing, but his eyes held doubt. Sam turned and stared into the jungle. "We should look for him."

"There's no point. You will not find enough to be worth burying," Piracola said.

"I have to see."

Sam started in the direction Alonzo had taken. After a few seconds, she heard Ricardo and Piracola follow. They walked in silence. How far had Alonzo gone? Sam tried to remember how long before he screamed. No. That was something she wanted to forget.

Piracola tapped her arm. "Over there. See how the bush is bent back?"

Sam did not but was happy to accept his word for it. Thereafter Piracola took the lead.

When they found more traces of Alonzo, Sam did not need Piracola to point it out. Blood was splattered across the tree trunks, shoulder high and more. Ferns were crushed flat, and stained red. Then Sam saw half a finger, lying on the ground. She took another step and stopped.

Shards of bone littered the blood-soaked soil. Skin and guts draped from surrounding plants like neckerchiefs hung out to dry. Sam saw an eye, peeking from under a bush, then realized only a third of a head was left behind. Her stomach heaved.

"It is not a good way to die," Piracola said.

"What are the hunters?"

"I have seen them clearly, three times. They arc…" He shrugged. "They are not something you can fight."

Ricardo put a hand on Sam's shoulder. "Come. There's nothing we can do. We should collect the food from the farm and go. It would take a day to gather his remains, and all the time we are here, we risk joining him. There is no graveyard in Atlantis."

No graveyard, but no shortage of corpses.

❖

Sam shaded her eyes, looking across the inner sea. "Do you think they'll have missed us yet?"

"Probably not. Hopefully, they'll start to wonder in a few hours more." Ricardo stood at her side.

"Could we signal them?"

"How?"

"Smoke." Piracola sounded like someone who has just woken up. "We can make a fire."

"Do we have a tinder box with us?" Sam asked.

"Better than that." Ricardo slipped the pack off his back and pulled out a small tube. When he pushed a button on the side, a two-inch flame shot from the end.

They made a simple hearth on the sand using a ring of stone and collected dry tinder. Once a small fire was blazing, Piracola half smothered it with wet leaves. He dipped an empty sack in the sea, taking care not to get his fingers close to the water, then wrung it out. With Sam's help, he used the damp sack to cut the column of black smoke into a series of balls.

Ricardo divided his attention between them and the inner island. "Now we just have to hope someone is watching."

Piracola grinned at him. "You are joking, right? Kali will not have left the quay while you've been gone."

Sam felt a tightening in her gut. Who, or what, else might be watching? "How long do you think it'll take them to get here?"

"Won't be quick. Even if Piracola is right and Kali has seen the signal, they'll have to get a canoe from the Barn and paddle over." Ricardo pursed his lips. "If we're lucky, an hour."

And if luck was not with them? Sam turned to the forest and closed her eyes, concentrating on every faint sound. Minutes dragged out. Would the hunters see their signal? She should have thought quicker. She should have said something earlier. Now all she could do was hope. Then her ears picked up something else. At first, it was faint, like a mosquito, but the volume grew by the second. The *Inflatable* was coming, full throttle.

Ricardo and Piracola had gone to sit on a fallen log, a short distance away. Their heads were close together. Had they been whispering to each other? Sam could guess the subject. Maybe later she could think of a way to persuade them she was innocent of Alonzo's death—once she had persuaded herself. At the moment, it was not her main concern.

"The *Inflatable* is coming."

The boat was heading straight for them, traveling so fast it bounced from wave to wave, sending up plumes of spray. If the passengers were not holding on firmly they risked being tossed overboard. Somehow, Kali had wrested control of the outboard motor from Torvold, who was sitting hunkered down in the middle, next to Horatio.

The *Inflatable* showed no sign of slowing as it approached land. Was Kali planning on driving it ashore? Sam was starting to feel anxious, but at the last moment, Kali brought the *Inflatable* around and leapt out while it was still moving, straight into Ricardo's arms.

Torvold and Horatio took more care, docking at the rock jetty.

"How did you lose the *Inflatable*?"

"Where's Alonzo?"

They spoke at the same time.

"The hunters got Alonzo." Piracola glanced sideways at Sam. "As for the boat, that was me. I dropped the mooring rope when the jump came."

"Oh, I say. Dashed rotten luck…on both counts," Horatio said.

"How did you find the *Inflatable* so quickly? We thought you'd have to get us in canoes."

"That was Kali's doing. She'd borrowed my spyglass and was watching for you…well, watching for Ricardo, but you were with him, so it was the same thing. She spotted the *Inflatable* drifting yesterday afternoon, or morning, or before the last jump anyway."

While they talked, Torvold had been busy, putting the sacks in the boat. "I had to take a canoe and row for it. Me, rowing! Then we came to see if you were at the shore, but you were not. We were ready to come back this morning, and we saw the smoke, and Kali was off, quick as green mustard. I tell you, she drives crazy fast." Which was saying a lot, coming from him. "But Alonzo, that is bad news. I think Catalina will be hit to the heart."

Sam was already anxious about how Catalina would take the news, but that was not what stoked her growing unease. They were standing, chatting, when they should be gone. Sam wanted to shoo them onto the *Inflatable*. She was about to say something, when she heard a distant sound. "Tck-tck-tck. Tck-tck." It was not her imagination.

"Quick. We have to get away."

"What is—"

Then the others heard it too. Within seconds, they were in the

Inflatable. The motor roared into life with Torvold at the helm. Kali had her arms around Ricardo and was showing no sign of ever letting go. Sam looked back at the shore, but nothing appeared, and soon they were too far away. She should mention never to use smoke signals again.

"How did the wretched hunters catch poor Alonzo? Why wasn't he with you?" Horatio asked.

Sam turned to him. "After the second jump. We were at the farm. He made it to a roost, but then he...left again."

Ricardo loosened his grip on Kali and leaned forward, examining Sam's face. "You do not know why he climbed down?"

"I told you. He convinced himself Atlantis wasn't real. He thought demons were tricking him, and he could pray it all away."

"And you couldn't stop him?"

"I tried to, but I couldn't overpower him and make him stay." Sam felt a twinge of annoyance. "I've already told you this."

"You weren't friends. Anyone could see that."

"No. We weren't. That doesn't mean I'm happy he threw his life away." She met Ricardo's eyes. "What? Do you think we had a fight and I pushed him off the roost? Even if he'd survived the fall he wouldn't have been able to go wandering off on his own."

"Yes. Of course, you're right. I didn't mean to sound as if I was accusing you. But it was such a crazy thing to do."

"I know." Sam stared at her feet. "I just keep wondering what else I could have said to him."

Horatio patted her shoulder. "I'm sure you tried your best."

Nothing else was said until they docked at the inner island. A small group of castaways was waiting, Catalina among them. Sam saw her eyes go from face to face as they left the *Inflatable.*

Her eager expression turned to confusion. "Alonzo? Where is he?"

Ricardo took her hand. "I'm sorry."

"What?"

"The second jump, we were at the farm. We all got safely to the roosts before the hunters came. But Alonzo returned to the ground and they caught him. I'm so sorry."

"Why? What made him do that?"

"I don't know. I wasn't at the same roost as him. Sam was there and spoke to him, but she has no more answers than I do."

"You?" Catalina turned on Sam. "You were with him? Why didn't you save him?"

"I tried. There was nothing I could do. I couldn't make him stay."

"What made him want to leave?"

"He…" What could she say? *He thought I was a demon?* "He convinced himself Atlantis was a test set for him by the devil. He thought he could pray it away."

"You're saying he was mad."

"No." Or was she? Had guilt driven him mad?

"Your face. I see the marks. You fought with him."

"No. I mean yes. He hit me, but we weren't fighting. I was trying to stop him from climbing down."

"You're lying."

The hostility in Catalina's voice burned like salt on a raw wound. Sam opened her mouth, but no words would come out.

"You attacked him, threatened him. He told me you'd done it before."

"No."

"I don't believe you. What did you say to him?"

"I said…" The words stuck in Sam's throat. If she had not challenged him, Alonzo would not have felt threatened. If she had not tried to make him face the truth, he would not have had a reason to flee. She had taunted him, and she had enjoyed doing it.

Catalina shouted in her face. "You did this. I know it. He told me not to trust you. You're a thief and a murderer. You murdered him. You will pay for it. I promise, you will pay for it."

CHAPTER NINE

The sound of waves slapping against the quay was a rhythmical background to the darkness. Night had fallen and a blanket of cloud covered the moon. However, there was no need to carry lanterns. The pathways of the inner island were lit by streams of tiny blue lights floating overhead, and the buildings were washed by up-facing beams of warm yellow. The cornerstones of the embankment also glowed, marking the edge between land and sea, but not so brightly as to cut into the utter blackness beyond.

Catalina sat on a patch of grass, staring at nothing. She could not see the outer island, but it was there, the nightmare in the dark. She could not tear her thoughts away. Her dress was getting crumpled, but she did not care. Alonzo had brought it back for her. Maybe she should take better care of it. Yet the sense of remorse was not enough to bring her to her feet.

Why had Alonzo done it?

Catalina hugged her knees. Sam had played a part. Of that, she had no doubt. But she could not deny Alonzo had not been himself recently. The dry humor, the playfulness, the calm certainty had been absent. He had carried a deep-rooted hatred of Sam, and yet had given no reasons that did not apply equally to the other pirates.

It was not simply that Sam was the only one to survive. If she did not know better, Catalina would have said he was frightened of Sam— which was absurd. Alonzo had never been frightened of anyone. Yet something had passed between them. That much Catalina was certain of. But what? And had it played any part in his death?

The sound of soft footsteps made Catalina turn her head. Kali was strolling along the quay, her path slow and aimless. She was also looking into the darkness, but as she reached Catalina, she paused.

"Do you mind if I stop with you a while?"

"No. Of course not." Catalina had not wanted company, but Kali was not one of the people she wished to avoid.

Kali carefully lowered herself to the ground.

Catalina offered a hand. "Are you all right?"

"Oh yes. I'm only five, maybe six months gone. My mother did a full day's work on our farm the day before I was born. In another three months you can help me." Kali's smile was white in the darkness. For a while they sat in silence.

"You're mourning your friend."

"Of course."

"You had known him a long time?"

"All my life. He was my grandfather's squire, before I was born."

"You must feel his loss keenly."

"I do." Tears filled Catalina's eyes.

"We all know the pain of losing those we love. Some might say I abandoned my family, but the choice I had was no choice at all. The sailors had me cleaning the ship's galley. I was emptying a bucket of slops when the captain called to raise the anchor. The sailors were busy, none were watching me, and the beautiful island was so close. I dived over the side and swam. I reached the beach and looked back, thinking they'd send the longboat for me, but the ship sailed away. Who knows if they even knew I'd gone? I watched it slip over the horizon. In the hold was my mother, my brothers, my aunt, my nephew. I never said good-bye."

"You knew they were still alive."

"That was not living, and people died in the holds. I think the only reason they didn't leave them to rot was they didn't want the rest of their merchandise to grow sick. My sister was thrown overboard when she died, to feed the fishes."

"I..." Catalina did not know what to say.

"But it's you who have lost today. Your wounds are still fresh. Tell me about Alonzo."

"You met him."

"Tell me a memory of him from your childhood that will make you smile."

Catalina thought. "I must have been six or seven. I had a cold and couldn't go out. I felt so sorry for myself. One of the hounds had given birth. Alonzo brought three puppies to my room. Small black furry bundles. We spent the afternoon playing, throwing a ball between us so the pups ran back and forth, sliding into each other and wagging their tails and licking us."

"Did he have children of his own?"

"No. He never married. He'd been with my family so long he was more a friend than a servant. He volunteered to come with me to meet my new husband. He risked his life joining the pirates as the only way to stay close and protect me. And that's why I don't believe he'd have abandoned me, throwing his life away."

"Do you seriously think Sam killed him?"

Catalina shook her head, in confusion rather than denial. Her initial certainty had faded, leaving only a tangle of conflicting emotions. Nothing made sense. "I don't know. I don't have any evidence, but I'm sure she was involved."

Kali placed a hand on Catalina's shoulder. "For what it's worth, I spoke to Piracola. He tracked the route Alonzo took after he left the roost. Alonzo was on his own, and he wasn't running away from Sam. Piracola said his footsteps were of a man striding through the forest. Alonzo wasn't stumbling along in a daze. He thought he knew where he was going, but he wasn't in a wild rush to get there. Piracola is sure Alonzo was acting as though he did not think himself in danger. Which agrees with what Sam said."

"So he was mad, delusional?"

"Atlantis has driven people mad before. This island robs us of our families, our homes. My poor Rico is tormented now. The last two jumps were close together, less than a day apart. From Liz's graph, we know the date was about 2005. If there was just a way for him to have left, he could have been reunited with his sisters, his friends. Merely twelve years would have passed in the outside world. Yet we only can know the date when we're no longer there."

"A cruel jest."

"Yes. Yet Rico and I have each other. I'm sorry you'll never see your beloved again."

Catalina frowned. "Who?"

"Your husband. Had you forgotten him?"

"No. Not really. But I'd never met him, so…" She shrugged.

"What?"

"My parents arranged the marriage. They hadn't met him either. It was all done by emissaries."

"You didn't object?"

"It was expected. I'd always known my husband would be picked by my family, either for politics or money, preferably both. And this was the third time."

"You've been married three times?"

"No. My two previous husbands-to-be died before the ceremony could take place."

"You must have been very young."

"I was six the first time. Older than my betrothed. He was three."

Kali shook her head. "This was not the way of my people."

Catalina's thoughts returned to Alonzo. "I don't think being lost in time was what troubled him. He had no family to return to."

"But he was troubled?"

"Yes. I think so."

"Do you have any idea what it was?"

"No. Except I know Sam was involved. He said she had threatened him before, with a knife."

"Did he say why?"

"No."

"You should ask her."

"Can I believe a thing she says?"

"Has she lied to you before?"

Catalina shrugged. "Not that I know. But Alonzo warned me against trusting her, and he was an honorable man. Sam is just a pirate."

"Was. She was a pirate. Now she is a castaway, like the rest of us."

"And if she does not change her ways?"

"There have been murderers on Atlantis before, and thieves and liars."

"What happened to them?"

"Sometimes they were exiled to the outer island, sometimes they became leader and did whatever they wanted. You should ask Liz. She knows more about the history of those who have gone before us.

But one thing I would say." Kali turned her face away, staring into the darkness. "The good and the bad. Atlantis will claim us all in the end. There were six others with Liz on her boat, forty-five years ago. Floyd arrived with five comrades. Yaraha and Piracola's canoe held eight. I've been here nine years, and I've lost count of those who've come and gone. We follow in the footsteps of the dead."

"You make it sound hopeless."

"It is." Kali wrapped her arms over her stomach. "I didn't plan this child. Much as I love Rico, it wasn't what I intended. Will either of us live to see our child's first steps? Hear the first words?" She turned to Catalina, her eyes empty of emotion. "None of us are going to get off this island."

❖

The words which test the purity of gold are with Tydides. Two faces are offered to us by the other ones. We must raise a shield over their unseen target. Behind the hall of books when this sun falls into the sea, we will join together and talk about where to aim our thoughts. Friends who wear their hearts on the outside only should hear this.

The writing was scrawled on a slip of paper that had been folded multiple times, the sort of thing that might be passed from one hand to another when guards were not watching. Gerard had brought many similar notes back from Old Town. Mostly, they concerned trivial matters—so trivial Catalina had previously ignored them. But that evening she had taken a pile of fragments to her room, to distract herself when other thoughts became too painful.

The pages were spread out around her. She sat cross-legged on her bed, wearing only her loose smock. Her blue satin gown was draped over the storage cabinet. Catalina looked up from the paper and considered it briefly. It was too hot for the weather, especially with the stiff high collar. Her smock was more comfortable. The full-length embroidered gown had to make her appear ridiculously overdressed, compared to everyone else. But it was her last gift from Alonzo, and she did not want to cast it aside.

Catalina rested her chin on her cupped hand and returned to the note. Normally, Liz, Floyd, or Madison worked with her, but she did not need twentieth-century engineering input on this. She was sure the issues were political, not technical. Several interpretations were possible, but the one she kept coming back to was:

Tydides has the proof. The aliens are going to betray us. We have to block whatever they are up to. We shall meet at the rear of the library today at sunset to make plans. Only tell those you trust completely.

The note was interesting, but how important was it? It definitely held implications about the relationship between the Greeks and the aliens—assuming they were the other ones referred to. Of course, it might be about something as minor as discovering their opponents intended to use underhand tactics at the next soccer match, or whatever sport the Greeks had taken part in.

Catalina picked up another scrap of paper.

You will teach pigs to sing sooner than you will talk me into your bed.

She smiled. That one at least was easy to decode. A third note was far more cryptic.

Go in my likeness.

This was followed by a word she did not recognize. Catalina frowned. Was it even a word? A mnemonic? It seemed decidedly short on vowels, although with the poor penmanship of some Greeks it was hard to be sure. If the delta at the beginning was really a carelessly scrawled alpha, then the word would be *asblof,* which still did not mean anything, and did not sound at all Greek. Was it a word in the alien language? Catalina tried saying it aloud a few times.

She riffled through more papers until the name Tydides caught her eye. What was his role, chief rebel or soccer team captain?

The page had suffered water damage. Several words were smudged, as if by raindrops. Catalina raised the light in her room to maximum and returned to the bed.

[...] jar holds all we have for the thoughts Tydides has set on his bow. Four [...] of destruction we ask you please to [...] for him to hold when the night [...]. The detailed drawing of the [...] of all has Meriones in his rooms for life away from [...] eyes. A path to victory if we find not, my [...] says our names [...] will write in his book.

Catalina held the paper at an angle, trying to catch the best light. The first splash was the worst, leaving only a faint trace. Yet it was possible to imagine the words might be *Pandora's jar,* one of the rare allusions to Greek mythology she had come across, and obviously not suffering from Erasmus's mistranslation. In which case, *Pandora's jar holds all we have for the thoughts Tydides has set on his bow* could mean *Tydides's plan is our only hope.*

A knock disturbed her.

"What is it?"

The door slid open. Liz stood outside. "Can I come in?"

"Yes. Yes, of course." Catalina made space for her, shuffling the papers into a pile.

"I wondered how you were doing. You left the dining room rather sharpish this evening."

"I wanted to read these."

"And avoid somebody?" Liz took a seat on the end of the bed.

"Maybe."

"You still think Sam was responsible for Alonzo's death?"

"I think she's not saying everything she knows."

"None of us do that, dear."

Catalina picked at a loose thread on her smock while she tried to order her thoughts. "Kali said there've been criminals here before."

"Still are. Ricardo and Jorge are drug smugglers. Sam might be considered a pirate, depending on who picks the judge. I managed to notch up an arrest for disorderly conduct at an anti-nuclear demo when I was your age. Floyd could be looking at a death sentence."

"Floyd? I thought he was a sort of policeman."

"He was."

"Then wasn't he supposed to uphold the law?" Catalina struggled to imagine what serious crime Floyd might have committed.

"It all depends when and where he is. In the wrong court he'd be in serious trouble. Even in New Zealand, in my day, he'd have been breaking the law, although it could only be a question of time before it all got repealed. The old anti-sodomy laws were on their last gasp."

"Oh yes, that. I hadn't given it much thought."

"You knew then?"

"It came up when we were working on a translation. I told him he'd have gotten on well with the ancient Greeks."

"You're not bothered? People from a strict religious background can have issues."

Catalina shook her head. "Maybe because I've been reading Greek philosophers since I was a child. I've always preferred their questions to the priests' certainty. Even being told not everyone here is Christian, part of my surprise was at how little it bothered me when I had time to think."

"Then you're doing better than some. Jorge and Ricardo took a while to come around. But the point is, we all come from different times, different backgrounds, and with different moral codes, and we all have to get along. If it's not harming you personally, then mind your own business."

"Although secondary smoke inhalation isn't so easy."

Liz blew out her cheeks. "You're telling me. But Babs has agreed not to smoke her bloody pipe when Madison is in the same room. And Madison had promised not to comment on the smell of tobacco on Babs's clothes."

Catalina smiled. The argument had gone on for days, and had, to her mind, reached silly proportions. Her thoughts returned to more serious concerns. "But they're all side issues, aren't they? Somebody getting murdered might not harm you personally, but you can't ignore it."

"You've got no evidence Sam was responsible for Alonzo's death, and it's hard to see what she could have done. Worst case, she lied and told him the hunters wouldn't hurt him. But I don't think he was such a fool to believe her, even if she did."

"What if we found evidence?"

"Then we deal with it when we need to. Kali's right about some of the people who've lived here. For a while, the first mate from a crew of slave traders set himself up as dictator. There was a man who strangled a woman who used to be his lover. And at least six people have gone missing in odd circumstances, leaving a finger of blame pointing one way or another. Each time, folk dealt with it the best way they could. We don't have the resources to start locking people up. All we can do is exile them to the outer island. That's a death sentence, and life here is too short anyway."

"Kali said much the same thing. She's worried for her baby."

"In what way?" Liz's voice held a sudden sharp edge.

"That she and Ricardo won't live to see the child grow up."

"Oh well, yes. That would be a worry for her."

"Is there something else?"

"No. No. Of course not."

Catalina stared at Liz. "Why do I get the feeling this is another example of somebody not saying all they know?"

"I don't know what you mean."

"Yes, you do."

Liz's expression wavered. "Please. I don't want to talk about it."

"About what? You seem on the point of tears."

"Honest. It's nothing." Liz was blatantly lying.

"Say that while you're looking me in the eye."

"Promise you'll say nothing to them."

"I promise. Now, what is it?"

"Most likely nothing, just me being a goose."

"You've already said that—except for the goose bit."

Liz sighed. "It's the records. They can be patchy. But with all the people who've been here, you'd think there'd be more mention of children." She shook her head. "Occasionally, the records have said that a woman is pregnant, but then nothing. No note of a baby's birth or anything about them as children, growing up."

"What do you think happens?"

"The caretakers. They tolerate us on the inner island, but it's clear they were programmed to treat us as temporary visitors. The way they tidy up after us. I can't believe the aliens couldn't put anything down for fear of losing it. I think humans used to come over to help with work in the Barn, maybe the kitchen too, and were allowed to walk around outside. Essential jobs, but nothing more. That's why the caretakers undo every change we make."

"You think the caretakers are a threat to us?"

"Not us." Liz drew a deep breath. "If we're right, the inner island is a little home away from home for the aliens, a copy of their world. We're the only Earth species the caretakers don't treat as vermin. You've seen them go bananas when seagulls try to nest here. They'll tolerate a level of human presence, but that's as far as it goes."

"Babies are human."

"Do the caretakers know that? Anyway, babies aren't essential. When Kali came here, she was just eleven or so, and she confused the caretakers. You could see that. They'd follow her around, dithering. Then she grew another inch or two, and they left her alone. I'm frightened they think children are rubbish, literally."

"Kali and her baby could live in the Barn."

"It won't work. Someone found a litter of puppies on the outer island and brought them back. The caretakers hunted them down. It's the only time they'll go into the Barn. I'm guessing they have special vermin eradication programming."

"That's awful."

"Beyond awful. But I may be wrong. Hopefully, I'm just worrying over nothing."

"You don't think you should warn Kali and Ricardo?"

"There's no point. If I'm wrong, I'll just scare them needlessly. And if I'm right there's nothing they can do."

"They could build a tree house on the outer island."

"They might want to give it a go. But they'd be lucky to see out half a year. The hunters mostly come out right after a jump, but you can never rule them out of the picture."

"So we have three months to find a solution."

"I admire your optimism, dear. But if you manage it you'll have done better than anyone who's come before."

Catalina picked up a sheaf of papers. "I've got one advantage. I can read this."

"Have you found anything new? Come on, give me a reason to hope."

Hope—forever locked in Pandora's jar. "Maybe. There's hints of something. Like this letter here." Catalina picked up the water-stained page, holding it again to the light. "Some of it's hard to read, but I think it says, *Pandora's jar holds all we have for the thoughts Tydides has set on his bow. Four apples of destruction we ask you please to rob for him to hold when the night falls. The detailed drawing of the center of all has Meriones in his rooms for life away from unwelcome eyes. A path to victory if find we not my heart says our names Hades will write in his book.*"

"And what do you think it means?"

Catalina had become familiar with some technical phrases. The apples of destruction had featured in one recent manual she had read with Madison, and other parts she could guess at.

"I'd say it goes, *Tydides's plan is our only hope. We need you to steal four of the explosive charges and get them to him tonight. Meriones has the core schematics hidden in his lodgings. If we can't succeed in this, I fear we are all going to die.*"

❖

Catalina leaned back in her chair and yawned. "I need to take a break. Get some air."

"I'm cool with that. When would you like me back here?" Madison asked.

"After lunch will be fine."

They separated outside the Barn. Madison headed toward the Squat. However, Catalina turned in the other direction and strolled along the embankment. The weather was cooler. Presumably, it was winter. The year was not worth making a guess at. Clouds were building over the outer island, and a downpour would come before evening, but for now the weather was pleasant.

The outward facing embankment of the alien island was just over three miles in circumference. Floyd ran a complete circuit each morning, before the day warmed up. Catalina had no intention of running, and certainly not in her blue gown, but the rhythm of her steps helped the flow of thoughts.

Once she had started looking, Tydides's name cropped up often, mostly in technical notes. He had obviously played a major role in whatever had been going on. Frequently, even people from the twentieth century could not begin to guess what it meant. The aliens must have had him in their confidence, and whatever he had learned caused him to doubt their motives.

Would Tydides have known why Atlantis started jumping through time once the aliens left? Would he have known how to stop it? Those were the big questions, along with, where would he have written the answer down? Would they be able to make sense of it, if they found his notes? And finally, where should they start looking for this hypothetical notebook? This last question was the easiest. The answer was wretchedly obvious.

Catalina stopped and looked across the water. Directly across from where she stood were the ruins of Old Town. The jungle was encroaching, but not enough to hide the buildings lining the waterfront. The town was extensive and might easily have once housed thousands of people. Why had the aliens needed so many?

Admittedly, the writing made it clear not all humans were treated the same. Some, such as Tydides, were favored scientists; others were servants, farm laborers, and even the subject of experiments. From what she had learned, while the more fortunate had luxury quarters in the center of town, many humans lived in prison barracks. How hard would it be to find Tydides's home? Was it worth taking the risk to search for it?

So many questions.

Catalina turned her back on Old Town and retraced her steps. The castaways were gathering at the Squat, although lunchtime still had a while to go. Liz, Charles, and Horatio sat on crates in the sun, chatting and playing cards. Kali lay on her back, sleeping on the grass. At the other end of the lawn, Ricardo and Jorge were playing a new game. This one involved much running around, barging each other, and bouncing a ball. They had tied a wire hoop to a tree trunk.

Catalina continued walking. A short way farther on was a lookout tower with a zigzag stairway leading to an open-sided deck thirty feet above ground level. A cover shaped like an oyster shell, curved over the top, and a pair of circular sitting areas jutted from one side. These seats struck Catalina as precariously suspended in midair, and she avoided them. However, the deck itself was sturdy enough, and one of her favorite spots. Even though only the stairs and sitting areas had guardrails. Presumably, the aliens had no fear of heights or falling.

When Catalina got to the top, she found she was not the only one there. Sam was sitting on the edge of the deck, with her feet dangling over the sea below. Catalina almost turned around, but that might look like running away, and she was not the one with something to hide. She settled for turning her back on Sam and taking in the view over the Squat. They had not exchanged a word since the *Inflatable* returned from the outer island without Alonzo, and that was the way Catalina wanted things to stay.

She heard the sound of movement, but did not look around. Sam's footsteps came close. Doubts sprang into Catalina's head. Was this really a sensible place to be? Was she about to be thrown off?

"You can't keep on acting as if you don't see me."

Catalina risked a sideways glance. Sam stood with her arms crossed defiantly. "I don't see why not."

"I wasn't responsible for his death, you know."

"I know no such thing."

"So what do you think I did to make him leave the roost?"

"I don't know. But you played a part. You fought. You hated him."

"No. I disliked him, I admit it, but I didn't hate him. He hated me."

"Do you know why?" At the silence, Catalina turned to face Sam and repeated, "Do you know why?"

"Yes."

"Then tell me."

"I can't. I gave him my word."

"What?" Catalina took a step closer. "You did something to cause him offense, and then you promised you wouldn't tell me what it was? That's nonsense. You're just ashamed to admit it."

"No." Sam was also looking angry. "I didn't do anything."

"He hated you for no good reason? You expect me to believe that?"

"He had a reason, but it wasn't good, and it wasn't my fault."

"You'd slander his name."

"No. I'm saying nothing."

"You know why he wouldn't stay in the roost with you."

Sam merely shrugged in answer.

"You know why he killed himself, and you won't tell me."

"Dying wasn't in his plan. He thought Atlantis was an illusion and I was a demon, sent by the devil to tempt him."

"You're lying. When he warned me about you it wasn't because of diabolical enchantments. He said you threatened him with a knife. Can you deny it?"

"That was on the *Golden Goose*. I was defending myself."

"You're accusing him of attacking you!"

The muscles in Sam's jaw bunched, and she turned to leave. "Oh, forget it. Believe what you want. Forget I spoke."

"You can't just walk away."

"Watch me." Sam started down the steps.

She was unbearable. Catalina wanted to grab her and shake the story out of her. And then what? If she knew the truth, all of the truth, would it ease the pain? Sam was hiding something. Maybe learning the what and the why would not make her any happier, but Catalina could not go on stoking her anger in ignorance. Sam had to speak.

Catalina was about to chase after her when a motion on the lawn below caught her eye. Two caretakers were slowly, stealthily, creeping out from behind a bush. Catalina almost ignored them, but their behavior was so unlike their normal bustle. And then, with horror, she realized they were approaching Kali. Catalina felt her insides turn to water. One caretaker stopped, shuffled strangely on its six feet, and backed away. The other continued until it was within touching distance. It extended one of its front appendages so it hovered over Kali's distended stomach.

Catalina was too far away to have a chance of reaching Kali in time. She tried to shout a warning, but her voice was a strangled croak. The effort to drag air into her lungs made her rib cage feel about to shatter. Then Kali moved, shuffling her arms and shoulders in her sleep. The caretaker bobbed up and down twice and scuttled away.

Catalina was shaking. She clung to the rail to hold herself up. Her legs had lost all strength.

Sam was at her side, holding her. "What's up? Are you unwell?"

"It's..." Catalina turned her head, looking across the water. The overgrown buildings were out of sight, hidden behind the curving shoreline. "I'm going to talk to Liz. I have to explore Old Town."

❖

"You sound just like Gerard." Liz's face held the expression of a woman who knew she was going to lose, but still felt she had to make the effort.

"Is that a bad thing?"

"It got him killed. The daft bugger."

"It's not as if avoiding Old Town would have guaranteed a long and happy life."

"Just because you're sitting in a lion's den doesn't mean it's a good idea to set yourself on fire."

The two of them were alone in Liz's room. Catalina had not given herself time to change her mind. As soon as her legs were working properly, she had dragged Liz from the card game. Maybe she should have taken longer to prepare her arguments.

"Trying to find out more about Tydides isn't a pointless activity. It might be our only chance to get away from Atlantis."

"Might."

"What other hope is there?"

Liz ran a hand through her gray hair. "Is there any point asking you to hold off until after you've gone through all the papers in the Barn? You never know what might turn up."

"It will take years. Kali's baby doesn't have that long."

"Getting yourself killed won't do Kali or her baby any good."

"Are you going to forbid me to go?"

"No. That's not my place. The rest might treat me as leader, but there's never been a vote or anything. You're an adult and free to go where you want."

"It doesn't mean I don't value your advice."

"Even if you've made up your mind to ignore it?"

Had she made up her mind?

Liz sighed and shook her head. "Ah, maybe you're right, dear. I've spent too long losing friends. I've lost hope."

"It's in Pandora's jar."

"I'd always thought she had a box."

"That was a mistranslation."

"Really?" A sad smile lifted one corner of Liz's mouth. "You'll be asking for volunteers to go with you?"

"I hadn't thought about it. I'm not sure if there's any point more people risking their lives. It's not as if a large group could fight off the hunters."

"Or even an army."

Yet, now that she thought of it, company would be comforting. "A second pair of eyes might spot something I miss."

"I'd say to take two others with you, three tops."

"If I get the volunteers."

"Oh, you'll get them right enough, dear. I know these nutters. Come on. It's lunchtime. Let's tell them the news." She linked arms with Catalina. "If you come across Gerard's bones over there, give them a good kick from me."

The communal room was full. Piracola was chef of the day, which was usually interesting, if not always totally successful. Catalina waited until everyone had finished eating. "Can I have everyone's attention, please?"

Around the room, people broke off their conversations.

"I'm going to Old Town. I want to look for the home of one of the Greeks, a man called Tydides, because there's a chance, just a faint chance, he'd have known what was going on with Atlantis, and why it's time jumping. If we can discover that, maybe we can work out how to stop it. I'm willing to go alone, but if anyone wants to come, I wouldn't mind company."

Torvold had jumped to his feet, even before Catalina finished talking. He punched the air with both hands. "Yes. I shall go with you. Together we will hit the donkey."

"You mean kick ass," Babs shouted from the other side of the room. "If you're short on numbers, I'll go, but it wasn't on my to-do list."

"I'll go," Floyd called out. "You might need a techie. Anything's piece of cake for me, after Omaha Beach."

Catalina drew a breath. "That's great. Two will be fine."

"Make it three," Sam said. "Torvold has strength, and Floyd can help with the science stuff. But if you want someone who can climb into places, I'm your best bet."

Catalina stared at her. Why was she putting her name forward? Sam had volunteered to go with Alonzo as well. Before Catalina could say anything, Liz clapped her hands.

"Okay. That's enough risking their necks. You four can sort out when you want to go. Have someone drop you off in the *Inflatable*. They can wait offshore to pick you up again."

"I'll do that." Babs raised her hand.

Catalina nodded. Of course, they would need someone to man the boat, because there was every possibility that no one who stepped ashore would ever be coming home.

CHAPTER TEN

The buildings rising sheer from the waves looked quiet and peaceful—romantic even, draped in trailing vines. Unlike the inner island, this waterfront was not lined with a quay. Floyd and Torvold paddled the *Inflatable* along the wall, hunting for a place they could disembark. Babs had cut the outboard motor some way out so as not to announce their arrival.

Dawn was an hour past, but the sun was hidden. The weather was overcast and humid, sounds muted in the sluggish air. Rain seemed likely before long.

Sam's ears were trained for a "Tck-tck-tck," but it was hard to hear anything over the pounding of her heart. Why had she volunteered? Sam smiled at herself—that was one question she had no trouble answering. She wanted to win Catalina's trust, even her gratitude. Maybe this was impossible, but for her own self-respect, she had to try. She had to make amends for Alonzo. Her taunts had pushed him too far.

Sam glanced in Catalina's direction. Her appearance was still surprising. Catalina had turned up in shorts and a loose shirt. Her hair was tied back. Of course, scrambling around ruins in the long blue dress would be awkward. Casual clothes allowed far more freedom of movement. They were not so beautiful or elegant, but they made Catalina appear less delicate. Sam could not decide which look she preferred. Catalina had an empty pack slung over her shoulder, for anything she might find. On her feet were a pair of oversized boots. Strips of padding stuck out around her ankles.

Despite being dressed like everyone else, Catalina was the only one not carrying a weapon. Sam had a long machete at her side and a coil of rope. She would have liked one of the amazingly sharp swords from the Barn, but could not find a scabbard capable of keeping it safe. Floyd had an eight-inch knife in his belt and an AK-47 strapped to his back. Somewhere, Torvold had found a huge, double-bladed war-axe, which he was so busy admiring he had not found time to argue about control of the outboard motor.

"There," Babs said in a sharp whisper. "A marina."

A wide channel cut between two buildings, giving access to what had once been a square harbor. The water was dotted with the rotted remains of jetties. The wooden boardwalks were gone, leaving only jagged posts, sticking out of the waves like fingers. At the far side, a flight of steps came down to the water's edge. Floyd was the first ashore, followed by the rest. Sam came last.

"First sign of a jump, come running. I'll be here, waiting for you. I promise," Babs said. "Stay safe, guys."

"You too." Floyd made a fist with his thumb sticking up.

They climbed the stairs to street level and reached the edge of an open plaza. Before them, five roads fanned out. It was a dead city, fighting a long, losing battle with the invading forest. Plants grew in cracks between flagstones, and the buildings were wrapped in shrouds of green. The closest formed a semicircle, six or seven floors high. The towers loomed over the plaza with an oppressive weight. The only movements were flocks of birds wheeling overhead, black dots against the cloud. More seagulls perched in empty windows. Their cries and the slap of waves against the harbor wall were the only sounds.

"Which way?" Torvold asked Catalina.

"I need to find an inscription, to work out where we are."

He nodded and smiled. "So which way?"

Catalina pointed to the largest building. An impressive staircase led to its doors. "We'll start there."

Standing on the steps, Sam could not get rid of the sensation they were being watched. She felt a prickling between her shoulder blades. It was ridiculous and childish. Watching in silence was one thing the hunters never did.

Catalina struggled to push aside a mat of hanging vines. When he saw what she was doing, Torvold added his strength.

"That's enough." Catalina rubbed dust and dead roots from the exposed stonework. Sam could see letters carved on a plaque.

"What does it say?" Floyd asked.

"It's the central gymnasium. Tydides lived a few blocks clockwise from here."

Sam did not know what sort of distance a block might be, but it sounded like good news. They left the plaza and crept along, staying close to the buildings. Rationally, it made no difference whether they walked down the middle of the street, but Sam wanted a wall at her back. They passed open doorways—air coming from them smelled of mold and decay. The silence was unnerving. She found herself trying to look in all directions at once.

At the end of the road was a T junction, where Catalina turned right, back toward the sea. At first this seemed to be a dead end, but a narrow passage took them through to an avenue. The line of trees down the middle might once have been ornamental. Most had died but not before their roots had buckled the pavement and cracked the low walls around their bases.

They walked for another five minutes. Apparently, a block was longer than Sam had expected.

"How much farther?" Floyd asked.

"I'm not sure." Catalina looked troubled. "I may have gone wrong. I couldn't find a map, just a few clues I put together. We need to get to the Anemoian Bridge."

"What does it look like?"

"A bridge, I suppose. In Greek mythology, the Anemoi were the wind gods, Boreas, Zephyrus, and others."

"A wind bridge?"

"Like Bifrost?" Torvold said. "The rainbow bridge to Asgard?"

Catalina frowned. "I'm expecting something a little more substantial."

"Where does this bridge go?"

"It didn't say. All I know is Tydides complained about people on it singing loudly and waking him up one morning."

"So it must have gone by his bedroom," Sam said.

"As long as he was in his own bed," Floyd added in an undertone.

Around the next corner, the road opened onto another plaza, similar in size to the one where they landed, although the buildings here were lower. All were a uniform two floors high, with a balcony lining the front. In the center of the plaza was a lookout tower, identical to the one near the Squat.

"Perhaps if we climb that we'll be able to see this wind bridge from the top," Sam said.

Catalina chewed her lip and said nothing.

"Unless someone has a better idea, I'm with Sam." Floyd adjusted the strap of his gun and set off.

Crossing the open plaza felt so exposed. The prickling down Sam's spine returned full force. It was stupid, no one would be watching, yet the urge to run was overwhelming. The others clearly shared her unease, and their pace picked up noticeably as they scurried over the worn flagstones.

When they reached the tower, the absence of caretakers was obvious from the state of repair. The handrail was loose, although there was no sign of rust. Sam prodded the bottom step with her toe. "Do you think it's safe?"

"Easy to know." Torvold jumped onto the next step up and stamped his feet. "Right as jolly old rain." He bounded up the stairs.

"You've been talking to Horatio again." Floyd followed more slowly.

"Why not? He is my friend." Torvold had reached the top and looked down at them.

"Can you see the bridge from up there?" Catalina called.

Torvold's head vanished briefly. "No."

They joined him on the deck. As with the other tower, the two circular sitting areas gave the impression they were floating in midair. Both were six feet across and surrounded by a rail, with a small gap for an entrance. Each could easily have held ten people. The seats were positioned with the rail as a backrest, meaning the occupants would all be facing each other. Directly opposite the entry points were control panels, with keypads.

Sam went to the edge of the deck. She was just high enough to see over the surrounding buildings. On three sides, the ruins of Old Town stretched into the distance until they were swallowed by the jungle. To the east was the inner sea, dull gray in the sullen light. The huge tower in the center of Atlantis was a black block against the clouds. There was no sign of a bridge anywhere.

"Catalina. Come have a look at this." Floyd had entered the right-hand circle.

"What is it?"

"One of those keypads. There's writing as well."

Catalina gingerly sidled through the entrance gap, clearly unhappy about the lack of support.

"What does it say?"

Catalina took a while before answering. "It says this is the Anemoian Bridge. And it says, *Enter destination code.*"

"Could the keypad make a bridge appear?"

"How?"

Sam stayed outside but peered over the guardrail. "Look. There's no plants or damage inside. The caretakers must have been looking after the seats."

Floyd frowned. "Why these and nothing else in Old Town? But you're right. Towers like this are dotted over both islands. They must have a reason to be here."

A breeze stirred the sluggish air, making hair tickle Sam's forehead. "They're not guard posts. The seats face inward. But it seems a strange place to have a meeting."

Dead leaves skittered across the deck, driven by a stronger gust. Sam turned her head to follow the noise, even as the wind picked up, growing stronger. A tremor shook the ground. Sam felt her guts turn to ice. She looked up. The thick clouds made the change less noticeable than normal, not that she needed confirmation. "She's jumping."

Torvold shouted a stream of words that were, undoubtedly, curses in Norse.

"Back to the *Inflatable.*"

Sam was moving, even before Floyd spoke. The next quake hit as she reached the top of the stairs, sending her stumbling. The handrail wobbled when she grabbed it, about to give way. Sam pulled back and took a second to steady herself. Breaking her neck in a fall was not going to help. She raised her eyes. On the far side of the plaza was movement, things flowing over the ground. Was it weeds swaying in the wind? But then a small shape broke free, scuttling from one building to another.

"We won't make it."

Everyone froze, then Floyd tugged Sam's shoulder. "Come back.

Away from the edge. The hunters don't like climbing. Maybe they won't come up if they don't know we're here."

What other hope did they have? Catalina returned to the circle of seats. She grabbed the guardrail for balance with one hand while stabbing at the control panel with the other. The guardrail began to hum faintly; lights flickered into life at foot level.

"What did you do?" Floyd joined her.

"I pressed the button marked *Power*."

"Anything else obvious?"

"No."

"So what now?"

Torvold hefted the war-axe and took up position guarding the entrance to the circle. "We see how many I can take with me. Ja?"

Floyd nodded slowly and slipped the AK-47 from his shoulder. "I'm with you, buddy."

Sam drew the machete from its scabbard. Was there any point? But at least she would die fighting.

The tower continued to shake, making the loose handrail clatter and groan. The wind whistled under the roof. But at last, the world calmed, the tremors stopped, and bright morning sunshine flooded the observation deck. It was a short while after sunrise, date, as ever, uncertain. The sky was washed blue, without a trace of cloud.

The roof was a curved hood over the deck. It was lowest on the side opposite the seats, where it was supported by three stumpy posts. In the fresh dawn light, the effects of time were obvious. A beard of vines dangled from the upper edge. The interior had once been white, but now was coated in dirt and cobwebs. Patches of green and orange lichens spread out from the joints with the support posts. A band of rust stains formed a pattern at head height.

Or was it rust? The six red marks seemed too deliberate to be natural. Sam's reading skills did not go beyond being able to sound out letters and numbers. She could pull information from a ship's log, but would not claim to read English. However, to her eyes, the marks looked very similar to the Greek she had seen.

"Catalina."

"What?"

"Are they Greek letters?"

"Where?"

Sam pointed. "On the wall, behind you."

"Yes. They are. So what..." Catalina turned back and spoke aloud as she punched keys, "Kappa. Iota. Mu. Omicron. Rho. Beta."

Nothing happened. Catalina's shoulders slumped.

Floyd patted her arm. "Guess it was worth a try."

Sam walked up to the letters, and brushed the cobwebs away. The paint was old and flaked under her hand. It had to mean something. Someone had written it for a reason—but what? Was it the writer's name, so everyone would know who had been there? Sam had heard of people doing that.

The fourth letter was a tall oval, shaped like a zero. Close up, Sam could see there was a line down the middle, obscured by a water stain.

"Catalina. Did you see this?"

"What?"

"This line on the fourth letter. Does it have any effect?"

"Where?"

Sam traced it with her finger.

"Yes." Catalina's voice picked up. "It means it's phi, not omicron."

Sam kept studying the letters, searching for other hidden lines. Then, from the ground below, came a series of clicks. "Tck-tck, tck-tck-tck, tck-tck." The sound became a chorus as more hunters joined in. Sam took a step back, her eyes fixed on the top of the stairs.

"Sam!" Floyd shouted.

Sam took another step backward. The clicks were growing louder, swelling in a clamor. "Tck-tck-tck, tck, tck-tck."

"Sam. Quick. Get in."

She glanced over her shoulder. The circle was moving, slowly drifting away like a giant hover board. Already it was two feet clear, leaving behind a space where it once had been docked, like a bite taken out of the side of the deck.

Torvold stood in the entrance gap holding out his hand. "Skjot. Jump."

Sam dropped her machete and ran. The platform was picking up speed, leaving her behind. Five feet of nothing now lay between it and the deck. Another two steps. Sam's foot landed at the edge and she launched herself off. Her left hand caught the guardrail, but the other flailed at air. Then a strong hand gripped her wrist, steadying her, though her legs were still swinging free. More hands seized her shirt and hauled her over the rail and down into the space between the seats. Sam landed on her head.

She squirmed between the three pairs of legs until she could get her feet under her. A helping hand from Torvold pulled her upright. The flying platform rocked gently, like a rowing boat, but showed no sign of tipping over. Sam looked back to the deck.

A swarm of creatures were surging through the entrance to the stairs. Sam knelt on the seat, folded her arms on the rail, and studied them while she got her breath back. If the caretakers made her think of spiders, these were crabs—crabs with two sets of foot-long pincers, shaped like curved sheep shears. A tide of them flowed over the deck. But the flying platform was going ever faster, and the scene behind dwindled.

"Wind bridge. Air Bridge," Catalina said. "It makes sense. It means we were in the right place."

Floyd nodded. "Tydides's home must be under the flight path."

They crossed the inner sea and passed high above the alien island. Sam thought she could pick out the Squat, but things looked very different from the air. Babs's *Okeechobee Dawn* was easier to identify, moored by the quay. Sam smiled. This sort of view must have been one Babs was very familiar with. "Does anyone have any idea where we're going?"

"Somewhere away from the hunters. That's good enough for me," Floyd answered.

An empty platform passed them going in the opposite direction, presumably to fill the slot they had left. Sam twisted round and sat on the seat. Ahead was the huge central tower, filling the skyline. For the first time, Sam was close enough to pick out details. The tower looked as if it had been bolted together from vast uneven blocks with knots of twisted pipework running around the outside.

The platform was rising, heading for a round opening. With the rising sun in their faces, it was impossible to see far, but the tunnel clearly went deep inside the tower.

Floyd pursed his lips. "Well, I guess it answers that question."

❖

The flying platform emerged from the end of the tunnel into daylight. They had reached a huge circular pit at the heart of the tower. The space was several hundred yards across and over a hundred feet deep around the edge. The floor put her in mind of an open cast mine she had seen, descending ever deeper at the center, in uneven, offset layers. The walls on all sides were black and sheer. Bands of dark glass might have been windows, except Sam could not see in.

The flying platform began to descend gently as soon as it was clear of the tunnel, heading for another docking tower. However, this was far larger than those they had seen before. Instead of two flying platforms, it had room for two dozen.

As they got lower, the black walls hung over them. The tower had seemed impossibly large before, but now Sam understood its true scale. She had never felt so small—a dust mote, drifting through a cathedral.

The platform docked on the tower, the footlights turned off and the humming stopped. Floyd was first to stand. "So that's how you get here. Shall we investigate?"

"Of course." Catalina looked eager. "Tydides's notes made it clear he did most of his work here. I'd assumed we couldn't get inside. This is going to be better than anything I'd hoped for in Old Town. Anyway, we don't want to go back until the hunters have gone."

Old Town had been dead, but this was not. Sam could feel it in her gut. "Are you sure you don't get hunters here?"

"Not according to what I've read. The hunters were to keep common workers in check, and the aliens didn't allow them here, except for…" Catalina shrugged awkwardly, "people they were going to use in experiments."

"What sort of experiments?"

"I don't know. Tydides wasn't involved."

Sam imagined she felt as an ant might, dropped into a sand castle on the beach. The scale was impossible to make sense of. The others must have been feeling something similar. Sam saw their heads moving left and right as they went down the steps, trying to take it all in. Was someone playing games with them?

The docking tower was a stone's throw from the wall, and joined to it by a walkway like a gangplank. Sam peered over the edge. Due to the cutaway layers in the floor of the pit, there was a clear sixty-foot drop below her. Meanwhile, the sun had climbed high enough to peek over the top of the wall. Light was dazzling on the black glass. They would be roasted by midday.

The walkway led to a door. "Ah." Catalina pointed to a line of Greek over the nearby keypad. "It says, *No entry to people without a permit.* That probably means us." She tapped in a sequence of letters, then shook her head. "That was the key code that got us here. I suppose it was too much to hope for."

Floyd put his hands on his hips. "That's a shame. I guess this is as far as we go."

The walkway extended a short way on either side, forming a balcony. Sam wandered along the right-hand spur. "Hey! Look at this." A line of marks running up the wall turned out to be a series of round holes, each with a bar across the middle. "It's a ladder. We can climb to the top. If nothing else, it should be cooler up there."

Torvold was unimpressed. "You think I can make like a spider? Why?"

"There'll be a nice view, I bet." Floyd slapped his shoulder, then turned to Catalina. "Do you want to come or stay here?"

Catalina eyed the ladder. "I'll stay here."

"I stay too." Torvold thumped the handle of his axe on the ground for emphasis.

"Suit yourself, buddy."

The rungs provided secure foot and handholds. Sam reached the top and waited for Floyd. He moved away from the edge, breathing heavily, and rested his hands on his knees. Sam was surprised. Floyd always seemed so fit.

"Guess you've got a good head for heights, Sammy."

"Spent half my life in ship's rigging."

"Rather you than me." He straightened up and patted her shoulder.

Like the surrounding islands, the top of the tower formed a ring. A hundred yards or more lay between the inner and outer edges. The only features were groups of small buildings, scattered around the outside.

Floyd pointed to the nearest cluster of four. "Do you want to go see?"

"Sure."

The ground was covered in black tiles and sounded hollow under their feet. The only marks were a splattering of white bird droppings. Obviously, caretakers were not cleaning up there. Gusts of wind snapped at their clothes. Sam checked that the sky was not turning gray, but it was just the sea breeze.

The smallest of the structures in the group was a triangular block with a door and keypad on the vertical face. "The way up for folk without monkey genes." Floyd smiled at Sam.

Two huts had doors opened by simple disks rather than keypads. The first was empty. The other held a wheeled cart. Floyd slid into the driver's seat. He pointed at some writing. "I'm guessing these are the instructions. We better get Catalina to have a look-see first before touching anything. I don't want to be tossing a coin for the brake when I'm heading for the edge."

"Won't it need a horse?"

"No more than the *Inflatable* needs paddles."

The last building was forty feet long and open on the outward facing side. A bank of three benches ran the entire length. Judging by their height, the gallery was intended for aliens.

"For sitting and taking in the scenery, I guess." Floyd hopped onto the bottom row and leaned back to rest his elbows on the bench behind. "I can see why."

The view was certainly impressive. Both encircling islands were laid out below. The vibrant green of the outer ring contrasted with the yellow and purple inner one. Beyond them was the blue ocean. Sunlight glittered on the waves, turning the horizon silver.

Sam spotted objects lying on the middle bench at the far end. When she got closer she saw they were a tin cup, a pair of short tubes joined together side by side, and a pistol being used as a paperweight. At least, she assumed it had been a paperweight, there was little now left to hold down, just a few tattered fragments. A weathered bag lay on the ground nearby.

"What is it?"

"Someone was here." Sam paused. "And still is."

In the well between the benches was a human skeleton, clothed in threadbare rags. The remains lay on its side, knees bent as much as the space allowed, a hand under the skull. It looked as if the person had lain down to sleep and never risen.

Floyd joined her. "Oh. I see. Wonder who it was." He picked up the bag and pulled out a notebook. The paper was yellow with age and the ink faded. He turned it to the light. "G. Dupuis. Wasn't that the name of Liz's feller?"

"I think so." Sam sucked in a breath. "I half hope so. Liz would like to know what happened to him."

"We'll take this to her and the rest of the stuff. It should all go back to Liz."

"How about the remains?"

"We'll ask. We don't tend to go in for funerals much here. We rarely have a body to bury. She might like to see where he died."

Sam picked up the joined tubes. "What's this?"

"Binoculars. Like Horatio's telescope for two eyes. Look through them. You'll see."

Sam focused on the inner island. Tiny shapes were moving, just big enough to recognize. "Hey. I can see Horatio and Kali. That's amazing."

"A shame we can't signal that we're okay. They'll be worried, what with the jump." Floyd toyed with the pistol. "We could let off a shot, but they wouldn't know what it meant."

Sam lowered the binoculars. "We should save the bullets. We don't know we're safe." She pointed to the skeleton. "What do you think killed him?"

"It wasn't the hunters. He's still in one piece. Maybe he was sick. There might be a clue in the book." Floyd flipped open the cover. "I don't suppose you speak French."

"Don't you?"

"Just what I picked up going though France, after D-Day. Are you any better?"

"I can get by. You learn a bit of everything in the Caribbean."

He held up the book. "Can you read it?"

"Oh no. I can't even read English."

"What? Not at all?"

Sam shook her head. "I can find what I need in the ship's log, but that's it."

"You should have said. Someone would have given you lessons."

"Why? What do I need it for?"

"Believe me, Sammy. You need to read."

"Why?"

"Because everyone should be able to read."

Sam let it go. Maybe this was one of those different time, moral issues Liz talked about. "I'm sure Catalina speaks French. And she can read."

Floyd nodded and dropped the tin cup, pistol, and notebook in the bag. "Let's get back to the others and see if there's any info about what happened to him."

"Yes. Until we know what killed Gerard, we should stick together."

Sam looked across the open tower top. Nothing was moving, yet it was not safe. Something had killed Gerard, and there was no reason to think it had gone away. His bones gave no clue. Despite the rising heat, ice prickled Sam's skin. She hurried to catch up with Floyd.

They found Catalina and Torvold sheltering under the docking tower, the only shade available. The temperature was getting uncomfortable.

Catalina opened the notebook. "Yes. This is Gerard's. He was keeping notes about his exploration of Old Town." She turned a few pages. "He was putting together a map. Shame we didn't have it before."

"Does it say what happened to him? Why he didn't return to Liz?" Sam asked.

Catalina flipped to the back of the notepad. "This is it. He says… oh." Her expression froze.

"What is it? What killed him?"

When Catalina did not answer, Floyd put a hand on her arm. "Is there something dangerous around?"

Catalina shook her head. "No. That's not it. There's nothing here."

"So what's wrong?"

"Gerard was like us. He saw the code letters and used them, but he couldn't go back. The key code doesn't work for the return journey. He was able to collect rainwater to drink, but there was nothing to eat and he couldn't leave. There's literally nothing here. He starved."

❖

The flying platform did not fly. Catalina's shoulders slumped. "We had to try."

"Damn." Floyd stretched his arms along the guardrail and rolled his head back. "You're sure you put in the right code?"

"Yes. Gerard wrote it down in his book. And he tried things like typing the letters backward, and swapping them around before he gave up and..." She bit her lip. "It's so sad. Him sitting up there, able to see Liz. Watching her day after day, and all the while knowing he was going to die." Catalina left the keyboard and dropped onto the seat. "And we're going to do the same."

"Only if we can't find a way home." Sam was not ready to surrender.

"Gerard couldn't."

"He was on his own. And he didn't know Greek."

"Do you truly think that's going to help?"

"Sam's right." Floyd sat up straighter. "You're one big advantage we have over Gerard. So think about the letters that got us here. Could they mean anything? Stand for anything?"

"No. They're totally random."

Torvold leaned forward, resting his hands on the shaft of his upturned axe. "Humph. Must have taken a lot of time for study. Everywhere there are doors with keypads. My grandfather was a wise man, but even he could not remember so many codes."

Floyd shook his head. "It wouldn't have been like that. Madison and me talked about it once."

"She made sense?" Torvold looked surprised.

"Yes."

"Such wonders!"

"I can see each destination probably has its own key code. There's only about a dozen docking towers total, mostly on the inner island. Folk could have carried a map. For doors, it's more likely everyone had their personal code. That way the controller could set who was allowed through, on a door by door basis, maybe even check up on who'd been where."

Sam laughed. "Don't give ideas like that to the merchant captains. They always want to keep a fix on everyone. The best thing about being a privateer was getting a say in the running of the ship."

"In Iceland, we also—"

"Go in my likeness." Catalina sounded excited.

"Pardon?"

"Go in my likeness. I saw it written on a note. It could mean, *Pretend to be me*, or *Use my code*. And there were some random letters after it." She jumped up. Her hand hovered over the keypad. "No. It wouldn't be a docking station code. It would be for the doors." She was away and running down the stairs before anyone had a chance to move.

Sam caught up with her at the end of the walkway.

Catalina had her face buried in her hands. "What was it? Asbolf? Except it may really have been a delta. So—"

She pressed a sequence of keys. Nothing happened.

Floyd arrived. "You think you know a key code to get us in?"

"Yes. I thought the letters might be a mnemonic, so I..."

On her third attempt, the door opened.

CHAPTER ELEVEN

The long corridor stretching before them was built to alien proportions, twelve feet high and fifteen wide. A series of doors lined the pale gray walls on either side, each with a keypad beside it. The floor was seamless white. The only decorations were three horizontal bands—red, orange, and green—running the length. As in the Squat, the ceiling emitted an even light.

"According to what Tydides wrote, it should be safe in here." Catalina spoke as much to comfort herself. "And Gerard wasn't attacked by anything."

"He never came inside." Sam squared her shoulders and marched through the door.

If she was being honest with herself, Catalina was happy not to be first in. With even more honesty, she knew somewhere, deep inside, she was pleased Sam was with her. Catalina tried to squash the treacherous emotion. She had to remember Sam was untrustworthy—not that telling herself this before had ever had any effect.

Catalina tried the key code on the first five doors she passed. Two of them opened. However, the rooms inside were bare and empty. The door at the end of the corridor was the only one without a keypad. It slid back when Sam waved her hand over the control disc. They passed through and emerged on the upper balcony of a large circular room. In either direction the walkway sloped down, forming ramps to the lower level. Exits led away in several directions.

A sudden blur of movement shot out from directly under where Catalina stood. Her heart thumped against her chest. But it was just a caretaker, scuttling through the room and away. Catalina rested her arms on a handrail until her pulse returned to normal. "That made me jump."

"Me too." Floyd patted her shoulder.

Sam was sidling down the walkway. She hung over the top rail and craned her neck, as if to see where the caretaker had come from. "They don't clean up top. They left Gerard's bones alone. Do you think they'll tidy up after us inside?"

Torvold tightened his grip on his axe. "I will keep good hold of Freydis until we know."

Floyd looked at him. "You've named the axe Freydis?"

"Why not? It's a good name. My grandfather was a wise man. He said your weapons were your friends, and friends need good names."

Floyd grinned and shook his head. "If you say so, buddy." He pointed to the lower level. "If we're in luck, that's just what we need." In the middle of the floor was a rectangular plinth with a sloping top.

"We do?"

"Yes. Come and see." Floyd trotted down the ramp and beckoned Catalina over. "What do you make of this?"

Catalina stared at the black glass surface. It was too low to be a lectern, and not level enough to be a table. "What do you think it is?"

"Just that this looks like the right spot to have—" Floyd tapped the glass. Immediately, lights flowed over the glass. "—a map. Ideally, there should be a circle with 'You are here' written by it."

Catalina bent for a closer look. In the middle was a flashing red dot and the words, *This place is having you now*. She pointed to it. "I'd say that was close enough."

"What else can you make out?"

Sam joined them and put her finger on the map. "That's the entrance, and that's the corridor we walked—" As she ran her finger across the glass the scale changed, expanding at a dizzying rate. Sam stepped back and held her hands up. "Sorry. I'll leave it to you."

Catalina soon discovered the display had its own perverse logic. Nothing behaved quite as she would have liked, or expected. She turned the map off twice by accident, and once on purpose as the only way to get back to the starting point. Everything was written in cryptic Greek, except for during a few minutes of confusion after she tapped on an icon labeled, *Use clear words*, which unhelpfully hid all the text completely.

After a half hour of frustration, Catalina finally felt bits were starting to make sense. "If I read this right, we came in on level 124, and we're now on 125. The farther down I go, the harder to understand everything gets. But on the top floors, the most promising sounding rooms are here, *Daily rooms for living people*, and here, *Providing people access to food*. Which I read as, *Temporary human accommodation*, and *Kitchen for humans*."

"I want to see the kitchen." Torvold spoke first.

"A kitchen might be more of a torment than anything else, if there's no food." Floyd folded his arms. "It's a long shot, but we might find emergency supplies in a medical center, if there's one here."

"Surely any food would have rotted away long ago," Sam said.

"Not if it's the caretakers' job to maintain the stocks."

"There are clinics." Catalina scrolled across the map. "But the nearest one is four floors above us, and a quarter way around the tower, *Performing art beside the sick bed*. There's this, which is nearer, *Keeping the condition of good body*, but that sounds more like a gymnasium."

"Okay. Let's try the kitchen. If nothing else, it might have water, which is more urgent. It's the old rule of threes. A human body can survive three minutes without air, three hours without heat, three days without water, and three weeks without food." Floyd studied the map, then pointed to a corridor. "That way?"

"Yes." Catalina stared at the display, trying to memorize their route. "But it's a maze, and we don't have a ball of yarn."

❖

Fortunately, maps were fixed to the walls at major intersections. They were smaller than the one in the entrance foyer, but obeyed the same confusing logic. After going astray a few times, Catalina felt she was finally getting a grip on navigation. According to the map, the kitchen was two levels directly above them. All they needed were stairs.

Catalina tapped in the key code to open a door and was faced with a dead end. "Oh." She returned to check the nearest map, to see where she had gone wrong, but she was not mistaken. It was the right door.

"What is it?" Floyd asked.

"This symbol." Catalina pointed to the map. "According to the key, it means *Movement through the levels.* I was thinking it would be a staircase, but it's just that empty room over there."

Floyd laughed. "Is that it? Come on."

"Where are you going?"

"Up. I'm betting it's an elevator."

"A what?"

"You'll see." He herded them into the small room. "We just need to tell it which floor."

"How?"

Floyd pointed to a row of colored buttons. "Did you notice the level we entered had red, orange, and green lines painted on the walls, but down in the foyer, the bottom line was blue?"

"I did," Sam said. "I wondered if it meant something."

"Right. I'm betting it's like color banding on resistors—colored bands relate to numbers. When Cat showed us the kitchen on the map, up in the corner were three big dots in a row—red, orange, and yellow." Floyd pressed the corresponding buttons in order.

The door swished shut. Catalina felt her innards jump, as if she were on a seesaw. After a few seconds, the door opened on an identical corridor. In fact, without Floyd alerting her, she would have thought they had not moved. However, the bottom stripe on the wall had changed color. If Floyd was right, the door she wanted was straight ahead.

"Let's hope whoever this key code belonged to had access."

He did, but the room inside was nothing like the familiar kitchen in the Squat, with ovens, hot plates, and cold rooms. Instead it was laid out in a regular array of tables and chairs, sufficient to seat thirty humans. Three of the walls were plain. The other was inset with four large control panels, flush with the wall. There were no doors to other rooms, or stores. If it was not a kitchen, how did it provide food?

"Where do you cook?" Torvold was just as confused.

Floyd went to the nearest panel. "They look like vending machines to me. You press these buttons to say what you want, and the food comes out here." He pulled up a flap. The rectangular cavity behind was empty. "This screen would tell you what your choices are. And I'm thinking it doesn't look promising. What does it say, Cat?"

The display was blank except for a single line of scrolling text.

"Hard to tell. I wish it would stay still." Catalina followed the words across the screen to where they disappeared, only to reappear again on the other side. On the third time around, she read out, *"Status granary empty. Feeding restricted..."*

"Out of stock. I could have guessed." Floyd moved away.

"Wait, there's more." Catalina waited for the words to reappear. *"Feeding restricted to extreme situations."*

"Emergency rations only?"

"Could be. It says, press alpha."

A pyramid shaped package dropped in the cavity. Catalina lifted the flap and took it out. The three-inch pouch felt like paste or liquid in a soft skin. Floyd also got a pyramid and tore a hole at the top. When he squeezed the sides, a brown paste oozed out, looking like mud.

"Do you think it's safe to eat?" Sam asked.

"No more dangerous than starving, which is our other option." Floyd sniffed the paste. "Doesn't smell like it's gone bad. Here goes nothing." He squeezed the pouch into his mouth and grimaced.

"What's it like?"

"Never going to win any awards." Floyd went to where a half basin was fixed against the wall and pressed a button on the side. A jet of water shot six inches into the air. After taking a long drink, he brushed his mouth with the back of his hand. "Let's just say I understand why it only gets eaten in emergencies."

Torvold opened a pyramid and took a sniff. "What do you think it is?"

"I'd guess a blend of vitamins and nutrients."

He tasted it cautiously. "New tree ants? Hate to think what old ones are like."

❖

They spent the rest of the day exploring. The tower had a transport system for getting around the floors, which Floyd likened to a subway train. They came across huge vats of pink liquid, banks of cryptically labeled controls, knots of pipework, and strange objects none of them could even guess a use for. The key code worked for about one in six of the doors they tried. Luckily, these included what Floyd called the restrooms.

Keeping the condition of good body, turned out to have a row of large beds, each one surrounded by multiple mechanical arms, ending in soft, rounded fist shapes. The temperature was noticeably warmer and more humid than elsewhere.

Floyd broke out laughing. "I'm guessing *Alien massage parlor* as a translation."

They spent the most time in a viewing gallery where the long wall was covered by dozens of screens. These could be used to watch different corridors. Since nothing was happening, apart from an occasional caretaker scuttling by, even this had limited use. However, Catalina took reassurance in that nothing looking remotely dangerous appeared.

The most potentially useful room was a tool storage, containing saws, lathes, hammers, workbenches, and a hose that shot out a tongue of flame. The outer and innermost rooms had windows, giving views over the islands and the central pit. They arrived at one in time to catch the last of the sunset. The thick glass added a purple tint to the colors.

As the last rays faded, Sam turned from the window. "You said there were living quarters, didn't you?"

"Yes. There's some not far from here." Catalina had checked on the last map.

The accommodation consisted of a dormitory lined with lockers and enough bunk beds to sleep sixteen people, plus two adjacent washrooms. There was also a small common room with tables, chairs, water fountain, and food dispenser.

Catalina finished her third pyramid of emergency rations for the day. It was not getting any more enjoyable. The flavor was bland, with an acidic edge and a strange metallic aftertaste. "I hope this paste will keep us alive long enough to escape, otherwise we're putting ourselves through an unnecessary ordeal."

"Don't worry. We'll get out of here."

Torvold thumped the ground with the butt of his axe. "Sam is right. Never give up. And if we die, we go into Valhalla together, side by side, singing."

Floyd leaned back, balancing his chair on two legs. "Didn't you convert to Christianity, Torry? I thought the Pope sent missionaries."

"I tell you, this Pope person gave big trouble in Iceland. The king of Norway pushed in with his nose. Then the Althing said we would become Christian. No arguing. When I said I would follow the new god, Leif was so happy, he gave me a boat to be captain. But, to say the truth, after I die, I would rather feast and drink in Valhalla than sit around being good with angels."

"Leif? That would be Leif Erikson? The man who first discovered America? Well, first except for Yaraha's people who were already there."

"Ja. My father's foster brother. He called it Vinland. Liz tells me America is the same place. Leif made camp and sent me to sail south and find how big it was. But my ship ran into a storm." Torvold smiled. "Ah, Leif. He would be happy to know he is so famous. Always, he wanted to be the big hero. Much less messy to find a new land than die in battle."

"You can say that again."

Torvold frowned. "Do you want me to?"

"No. It's a figure of speech. It means I agree with you. There's nothing good about war."

"I do not go so far. A man can test his courage in battle. Better to die on your feet."

"Maybe in your day. But for my generation?" Floyd shook his head. He patted the AK-47. "Remember, we were up against weapons like this, and worse. D-Day, I was two weeks short of my twentieth birthday. We got blown apart on the beach. Each day since is a bonus for me. It's a day a lot of my buddies never got to see."

"So no more war for you?"

"It wasn't that easy. Guess it never is. After the war, I went back to college, majored in engineering, but I couldn't settle. I volunteered when the Korean War started. The nightmares made sense there. When that was over, I joined the Coast Guard. Six months later, I ended up here." Floyd smiled sadly. "And when I wake up tomorrow, it will be one more bonus day for me."

"Bonus days? That's a good way to look at it." Sam was staring at the food pyramid in her hands. "My bonus days started when I woke up and felt a little better than I had the day before. My pa didn't wake at all, along with half our shipmates. But war? All Europe was going to hell in my day."

"My day too. That's what D-Day was about."

"Pa tried to keep us out of it. The people doing most of the dying weren't the ones who were going to get the prizes if their side won. That was the best bit about being with the privateers. We all got a fair share of the loot."

Loot. A fair share of the spoils from murder. Catalina worked on controlling her face. Sam was a pirate. Why was it so easy to forget that?

Meanwhile, Sam crumpled her pyramid into a ball and tossed it at the aperture for waste disposal. She missed and the empty pouch bounced off the wall and ended up in a corner of the room. Sam scowled at it. "Tomorrow, I'll see if I can find the door onto the roof and have a go at bagging a seagull. That paste makes Alonzo's stew taste good." She glanced at Catalina. "I'm sorry. I know what he meant to you, but I'm sure he'd be the first to admit he couldn't cook."

"What do you know about the sort of man he was, or his abilities?" Catalina could hear the venom in her own voice.

"He told us…Oh, nothing. Forget I spoke. I'll try to think next time before I open my mouth." Sam got to her feet. "I'm going to shower before bed." She left the room.

"Good night." Floyd avoided meeting Catalina's eyes. "So, Torry, what do you think's a good name for a rifle?"

He clearly did not want to get involved in an argument between her and Sam. Not that Catalina intended to drag anyone in. She made her own good nights and went to the bunk she had selected, taking Gerard's notebook with her. Reading should help her settle before sleep. However, concentrating was impossible. In the end, she put the book aside. If she would be spending days trapped with Sam, she was going to demand some answers.

The sound of a hot air dryer meant Sam had nearly finished her shower. By an unspoken consensus, Torvold and Floyd used one washroom, leaving the other for the women. Catalina waited inside the door for Sam to emerge from the stall. She was pulling down her shirt as she turned around and saw Catalina. Sam's expression changed from surprise to confusion to irritation.

"If you want to accuse me again of murdering Alonzo, can you wait till I've had a decent night's sleep? It's been a long day, what with the time jump and being chased by hunters. And to be honest, I didn't sleep well last night, thinking about visiting Old Town."

"It wasn't a guilty conscience keeping you awake?"

"No."

"Of course. You don't have a conscience, do you?"

Sam ran a hand through her spiky hair. "So what is it? You think I fought with Alonzo and threw him off the roost when the hunters turned up? You think I could have overpowered him?"

"Not on the ground, but the way you climb, you're more ape than human."

"While I was hanging by my feet from a branch, I gave him a good shove? Are you serious? He wasn't even trying to get to another roost. He was heading off into the jungle. How could I have made him do that?"

"I don't know." Catalina could feel her conviction weakening. Yet Sam was not guiltless. She knew it. "You said something to him. You can't deny it."

"Yes. We talked."

"About what?"

"He had problems and blamed me, but it wasn't my fault. I wasn't responsible."

"What problems?" Catalina advanced until she was within arm's reach of Sam. "You know what was upsetting him. Why won't you say?"

"Because I gave him my word I wouldn't tell anyone."

"You want me to believe he'd share a secret with you he wouldn't tell me?" The idea was ridiculous. Sam had to be lying.

"I found out by accident, sort of."

"You were spying on him. You overheard him talking."

"No. And it wasn't what he said as much as what he tried to do."

"He said you attacked him with a knife. You forced him to do something." Although what that might be, Catalina could not begin to guess.

"I didn't attack him."

"You threatened him."

Sam merely shrugged by way of answer.

"Anything Alonzo said or did under duress wouldn't count against him."

Sam stayed silent.

"Anyway, I don't believe he'd put any faith in a promise from you. He was a man of honor. He didn't strike bargains with criminals."

"Well, you're right there. He said my word was worthless."

"If he wouldn't accept your oath, then you're not bound by it."

"Believe it or not, my word means something to me." Sam's expression softened. "And I owe him. I disturbed a snake hiding in a sack. Alonzo got rid of it, and probably saved my life. Keeping his secret is the only way I have to repay the debt."

"Would he want you to keep it from me?"

"You more than anyone else."

"Why?"

"Because he cared what you thought of him."

"You're saying he was guilty of some awful crime." Catalina could not believe it.

"Only in his own mind."

Catalina slumped against the wall and buried her face in her hands. Much as she wanted to deny it, the honesty in Sam's eyes was undeniable.

"How can I honor his memory if I don't know the truth? Was I to blame? Had he gone mad and I was too bound up in myself to notice?"

"No. You were even less at fault than me. It was all in his head."

Catalina looked up, heedless of the tears filling her eyes. "What had he done? Please, you can tell me. An unaccepted oath is not binding."

Sam hesitated, wavering.

"You had a disagreement on the *Golden Goose*?"

Sam nodded.

"Enough for you to draw a knife?"

Again a nod.

"What?"

Sam stared blankly at the wall. At first, it seemed she would still keep silent, but then she drew a deep breath. "I only pulled the knife when he wouldn't accept that I had no wish to become his bedfellow."

"Bedfellow?"

"Yes, you know. The pillow dance. Play in and out. Do the trick."

Catalina shook her head. "Alonzo didn't know you were a woman."

"That's the point." Sam shrugged. "It's a hazard of being a pretty boy on a ship full of men who're missing female company. Up till last year, I had Pa looking out for me. And on the *Golden Goose*, privateers have rules about giving respect to everyone in the crew.

Even so, Alonzo wasn't the first who'd needed to be persuaded I meant what I said."

"Are you sure you didn't misunderstand him?"

"Very sure."

"It makes no sense. I can't believe the absence of women would have affected Alonzo in that way. Back in Spain, some even nicknamed him 'the monk.' He never married, and was known not to visit houses of ill repute."

"I can believe that. He had no desire for women to start with. He made it clear his choice in lovers was for his own sex. If I'd been a man and said yes, it wouldn't have been his first time."

"You're lying." But Catalina had no faith in her own words and was speaking on a reflex. The truth was written on Sam's face.

Unsurprisingly, Sam reacted with a flash of anger. "Fine. Believe whatever you want." She reached for the door controller.

Catalina put out a hand to stop her. "No. No. I'm sorry. It's just that Alonzo was such a devout follower of the church. The strength of his faith put mine to shame."

"That was his problem. He saw his desire for men as evil, a sickness inside him. But that didn't stop him once he was alone with me on the *Golden Goose*. When he learned I was really a woman he decided it was all my fault. I had passed as a boy just to tempt him. The guilt was eating him up. Pushing the blame onto me was the only way he could cope."

"But that's just stupid...stupid." Catalina balled her hands into fists. Had she ever wanted to hit something so badly? "It wouldn't matter here anyway."

"That was my mistake. I told him about Floyd and that nobody in Atlantis would care." Sam shook her head. "That was when he decided I was a demon sent from hell. I admit it. I was taunting him. I felt grateful for him saving me from the snake, but I'd lost all patience when he tried to make everything my fault. If I'd kept my mouth shut, maybe he'd have learned to cope with it. You could have talked to him. But I was so angry, I kept pushing him. I told him I was the same. That when it came to lovers, I wanted my own sex."

The words knocked the air from Catalina's lungs. Her knees threatened to buckle. Would Sam notice she was having to brace her hands on the wall to stay standing?

However, Sam showed no sign, wrapped up in her own memories. "That was the last straw for Alonzo. Everything I said had to be part of a trap set by the devil to snare his soul. He thought if he prayed hard enough, everything would go away. He climbed down from the roost, and I couldn't stop him. I'm sorry." Sam opened the washroom door. "But if that's all, if you don't mind, I'm tired and it's time for sleep. Good night."

After Sam left, Catalina stayed where she was, leaning against the wall while her breathing returned to normal. *I told him I was the same. That when it came to lovers, I wanted my own sex.* Catalina closed her eyes as the shock rolled over her again. With hindsight, everything was so obvious.

Catalina had always known the form her marriage would take. She would wed whichever nobleman her parents picked for her and bear enough children to satisfy the requirements of inheritance. Then, if her husband had the inclination, he would take a mistress or two, and she would sit with her friends, smiling behind her fan at the handsome young men in court, until she got too old to remember why she was smiling. For romance, she would listen to ballads sung by minstrels. It was what every noblewoman in Spain did. Admittedly, Catalina had not yet felt the desire to smile at handsome men, but she was sure it would come in time.

She had never wondered whether she wanted to marry the man her parents chose, any more than she had wondered whether she wanted to breathe air. Her path through life was fixed from the day she was born.

Being shipwrecked on Atlantis had changed everything, or should have. The old path had gone, but Catalina still had not considered what might replace it. Then one sentence, and Sam had gone from being intriguing to scrambling every thought in her head. *I told him I was the same. That when it came to lovers, I wanted my own sex.*

Heedless of decorum, Catalina slid down the wall and sat on the floor. So when it came to lovers, what did she want? A silly question, given that she had just been knocked sideways by the answer. She had no experience, no guidance, on how to navigate this new path. What were the way-markers, the milestones, the hurdles?

One thing Catalina was sure of, though, a false accusation of murder did not make a good starting point.

❖

The map was making more sense. The room descriptions were as cryptic as ever, but after a morning bent over the plinth in the foyer, Catalina had achieved several breakthroughs. One of the most useful was learning how to enter a key code and see which rooms it granted access to. If nothing else, it saved the time and effort of checking doors in person.

The bad news was that the unknown Greek had been quite junior. Only a small number of rooms were not grayed out, concentrated in one section. Nothing at all was lit up below floor 134, red, yellow, green in color. Had Tydides ever committed his personal code to writing? Surely he would have had greater access, though it was possible no human was trusted to any great degree.

Catalina rubbed her lower back. A dull ache had been growing for the last hour. Maybe she should take a break. She thought about the alien massage parlor. However, it would be a dangerous experiment. What counted as a soothing rub for an alien might shatter human bones.

She shrunk the map until she could see one entire floor of the tower. At this scale, no labels were readable, but it did give a depressing view of the magnitude of her task. There were thousands of rooms, each with a cryptic description. She would need months to decode them all, in the hope one might be useful.

There must be a way to narrow down the search. Catalina folded her arms and considered the entire map. Where was the most likely place to find the docking station codes? It did not help that she had no idea what the purpose of the tower was, or what any section was supposed to do.

Catalina tapped her way up the tower to the floor with the pit level entrance. The docking station was a small rectangle, barely visible at the end of the walkway. If there was a control room for the Anemoian Bridge, it would make sense if it overlooked the docking station, regardless of whether there was any benefit to be gained by it. Humans would be happier if they could use their own eyes to see what they were supervising. Would aliens be any different?

Footsteps sounded just as Catalina found what she was hoping for. She looked up to see Sam rounding the corner and quickly looked down again—not that she was able to focus on the map. Catalina's eyes refused to obey her. Any hope of stringing a coherent thought together vanished. Her entire concentration went into managing her expression, so she did not look like a drooling idiot. Catalina finally understood why ladies at court spent as much time peering over their fans, as they did using them to cool down with.

They had not exchanged a word that morning. Sam had shown no wish to, and Catalina feared making a complete fool of herself if she tried. The lyrics to various songs taunted her. Once they had seemed ridiculous. She could not imagine feeling so obsessively immature. Now, the words perfectly captured the insanity she was feeling.

"Any luck?" Floyd asked.

"Some. How about you?" Did anyone notice her voice wobble?

"We got these." Floyd held up a brace of seagulls. "We're going to rig a barbecue with the blowtorch."

Catalina nodded, despite having no idea what either a barbecue or a blowtorch might be.

Torvold peered over her shoulder. "You say you have found something?"

"Yes. Here. *Commanding the roads of the wind.* I think it's a control room for the flying platforms. It has to be our best chance of finding the return code. But there's a problem."

"What?"

"Our key code won't let us in. Whoever it belonged to wasn't authorized."

Floyd joined them at the plinth. "It's still the best lead we've had so far. We'll check it out after lunch."

Catalina risked a glance up and saw Sam standing with her back turned. This should have been a relief—less pressure on maintaining her self-control—but all Catalina felt was disappointment. Why did things have to be so awkward? Would the others think it odd if she made herself a fan?

❖

Catalina would not have believed how good burned seagull could taste. A caretaker showed up with a fire douser when an alarm went off, but this was not until the cooking was finished. The door swished closed after it left.

Catalina nibbled the last meat from a drumstick. She spotted something lying in the corner, Sam's crumpled pyramid from the evening before. "The caretaker didn't clear away the rubbish." She pointed using the bone.

"They must be more tolerant of humans. They don't need to remove any trace of us." Floyd said. "It didn't try to dismantle my barbeque either."

"I'm not taking the chance with Freydis." Torvold had his axe propped against the wall beside him.

The caretaker had also shown no interest in the seagull remains. The pile of bones and feathers lay on the end of the table. Did this mean they would not treat babies as vermin? It would be good news, as long as they mastered the flying platforms. The disadvantage was they had to clean up their own mess from lunch.

On reaching the corridor outside the control room, Catalina tapped in the key code. As expected, it had no effect. Floyd passed the AK-47 to Sam and picked at the edges of the door experimentally with his knife. "If we could get our hands on one of those explosive charges, I bet we could take this off."

"If the key code won't get us into the control room, I doubt it will open the armory or wherever it is they're kept," Sam said.

"True." Floyd stepped back. "Let's check the rooms on either side."

They had to go four doors right before they reached one the key code opened. This room had a bench up the middle and a row of tall lockers on opposite walls. Floyd pulled out a strange blue garment. It looked as if a long sleeve shirt and a full-length pair of breeches had been joined into a single item of clothing.

"A boiler suit. Could be useful. Our supply of clothes is getting threadbare. Before long we'll all be running around buck naked." He smiled and put the suit back.

Catalina tried hard not to think about what Sam might look like in the nude. To distract herself, she went to the window. The glass was free from imperfections, but as seen before, it gave a purple tinge to the world outside. The deck of the docking station was one floor below, the perfect height for a clear view of any activity.

"Does it open?"

Catalina flinched at the sound of Sam's voice by her elbow. "I don't know. I can't see a latch."

The window covered the entire side of the room and was made from a single pane. There was no frame holding it secure, rather the glass attached seamlessly to the floor, ceiling, and walls.

Floyd joined them. "It looks fixed to me. Cat, you can't see something like, *Push here to open*, can you?"

"No. The only sign is the room description, *Exchanging clothes for team B*." Catalina left the window and started opening the lockers. Maybe someone had scratched their key code inside.

She was halfway along when Sam said, "I've got it."

"What?"

Sam indicated the AK-47 she still had on her shoulder. "I'll go to the deck on the docking station and shoot out the window. The caretaker didn't want us to set the place on fire, and I bet they won't ignore broken glass. If the rest of you wait in the corridor, you can follow it in when it comes to do the repair."

Catalina was unconvinced. "Will it let us?"

"Don't see how it can stop us." Torvold hefted his axe.

Floyd shrugged. "I say it's worth a try. Do you want me to go, Sammy?"

"I think I can hit a window this big at close range."

"Take Gerard's binoculars, to make sure you aim at the right one. They might help see through the tinted glass."

"I'll go with her." Catalina spoke before she had time to think. "An extra pair of hands."

Sam shrugged. "All right."

They walked through the corridors without saying a word, while Catalina tried to think of something to say, something trivial and safe. Nothing came to mind.

"Do you mind Floyd calling you Cat?" Sam broke the silence.

"No. He shortens everyone's name, though I guess he can't do much to yours."

"He lengthens it and calls me Sammy."

"Do you mind?"

"No. But some people get funny about their name. That's why I asked."

"We should start calling him Flo." She hesitated. "You can call me Cat, if you want."

"You can call me Sammy, if you don't mind taking the extra time over it."

Sam smiled and Catalina's stomach flipped, as if she were in an elevator. She concentrated on walking in a straight line. It had been less difficult facing down a ship full of pirates. The last door opened, and they emerged into daylight with the docking station straight ahead.

From the deck, using just her eyes, the dark glass completely blocked sight of what lay inside. However, through the binoculars, Catalina was able to make out the faintest details. She identified the lockers in the room they had just left. Four windows along, the control room had something like a desk against the window, and possibly a wall display at the side with the occasional blinking light.

"That's the one."

Sam rested her elbows on the guardrail around a flying platform. Catalina studied her face as she rested her cheek against the stock of the AK-47. Sam's lips were slightly apart, her expression calm, purposeful, serious. Catalina felt in danger of gawking but could not drag her eyes away.

Sam gently squeezed the trigger. A blast like thunder made Catalina jump. Echoes bounced around the walls of the pit.

"We'll see if that does it." Sam adjusted something on the side of the rifle and rested the barrel on the railing.

The control room window had not broken completely, but now a spider web of cracks radiated out from the middle. Catalina trained the binoculars, hoping to catch sight of the door opening. "How long before a caretaker arrives, do you think?"

"It came pretty quickly when the smoke alarm went off. I doubt we'll have to—Oh damn."

"What?" Catalina lowered the binoculars. "What is it?"

"There." A caretaker was scuttling up the wall, looking even more like a giant spider than normal. "I didn't think about them doing repairs from the outside."

The caretaker dissolved the fractured region. Without the glass, it was much easier to look inside. The wall display was clearly a map of Atlantis, but Catalina could not make out any writing, even through the binoculars. The caretaker began filling the hole with new glass, working from the outside in, for all the world like a spider spinning a web. Once its task was complete, it dropped down the wall and vanished back inside.

"I guess we should go give the others the bad news," Catalina said. "Unless you have any more ideas."

"Yes. Yes, I do." Sam held out the AK-47 "Have you fired this before?"

"No, but it doesn't look hard."

"It isn't. See. This is the safety catch. Leave it like this at all times, except right before you shoot."

"Me? Why can't you?"

"Because I'm going to be over there." Sam nodded at the window.

"What?"

"When the caretaker removes the damaged section, I'll climb in and open the door for Floyd and Torvold."

"How? What will you hold on to? Supposing you fall."

"I won't. Remember, I'm more ape than human."

"I didn't mean it."

"I've been called worse things. The ladder goes nearby, and I've got this rope from the Barn." Sam was wearing the coil diagonally across her body. Light shimmered over it, as if it was made from liquid metal.

"Rope? It's more like string. It won't take your weight."

"It'll take you, me, Torvold, and even Horatio, all together. I've no idea what it's made of, but it's unbreakable."

"You're insane."

"I've been called that before too." Sam placed the rifle in Catalina's hands. "Push the safety lever down as far as it will go. This is the front sight and this is the back. You line them up with the window and squeeze the trigger. That's all there is to it."

"I need to—"

"You'll be fine. Wait until I wave. And try not to shoot me."

"I…" She got no further. Sam was gone, leaping down the stairs three at a time.

Catalina watched her dash across the walkway and scramble partway up the ladder to the roof. Sam stopped at a point well above the window height and tied her rope to a rung. Catalina had no idea how she managed it, dangling one-handed. Just looking made Catalina's mouth go dry and her hands shake. A fall would be fatal. Catalina did not know if she would ever summon the courage to say half the things to Sam that were running through her head, but how would she cope if she never had the chance?

Sam dropped back down to control room level, then twisted around and waved.

Catalina drew a deep breath. She did her best to copy Sam's pose. Lining up the sights turned out to be not quite as easy as she had expected. She squeezed the trigger. Nothing happened—of course, the safety catch. Catalina pushed it down and tried again.

If the gun had sounded like a crack of thunder when Sam fired, this was a cannonade. A dozen explosions, each one following so quickly the blasts merged into a continuous roar. Every bang slammed the butt back painfully into her shoulder.

Catalina released the trigger and the explosions stopped, although all she could hear was the sound of ringing. She had hit not only the control room window, but also the one above, and the one above that. Sam was still in place on the ladder. Her shoulders were shaking, clearly from laughter rather than fear.

A caretaker arrived. Sam waited until the cracked glass was gone and the caretaker was working on the section farthest from her. To Catalina's horror, she saw Sam was no longer holding on to the ladder, but instead had both feet braced against the wall. With a kick, Sam launched herself sideways, swinging first away from the control room and then back. Another kick, and Sam twisted around the edge of the hole and dropped into the room. She made it look so easy.

Catalina was gripping the rifle so hard her hands ached. It took an effort of willpower to pry her fingers loose and return Sam's cheery wave. She waited just long enough to see Sam let in Floyd and Torvold, then she slowly and carefully made her way to join them. With luck, her hands would stop shaking by the time she got there.

Torvold opened the door when she knocked. "Come in, champion gun shooter. Sam is telling us of your newfound skill."

"She hit the window, and she didn't hit me."

"And mastered fully automatic fire. We heard it in the corridor. You didn't push the safety down far enough." Floyd was also laughing. "So, Cat, has it been worth it?"

As she had seen from the deck, the wall display was a map of

Atlantis. Rather than cloth or material, it looked to be painted on glass, similar to the maps, although it was positioned high on the wall. Even the aliens might have had trouble reaching the top. Clearly, it was not intended for touch control.

Catalina went to the desk, which was covered in controls. Each had two labels, one unintelligible, the other in Greek. It took a few minutes to spot a likely contender, *Revealing the epithet of terminals.* She pressed it.

Lights sprung up on the map. The location of every docking station was marked and beside each one was a six-letter code.

"Oh, yes. It was worth it."

Catalina typed the key code. If this did not work, what next? However, the keypad lights flashed blue, and the flying platform gently disengaged from the docking station. She looked up. The sky was darkening. Sunset was not far off, but they should be back at the Squat before nightfall. People would be surprised to see them and even more surprised at their news.

They would be able to tell Liz about Gerard. Catalina hoped knowing what had happened to him would give her comfort. The flying platforms would let them move freely between islands. They would not need the *Inflatable* and could save fuel. Visiting the farm would be safer. Kali and Ricardo could raise their child in the tower.

The tower—the most important news of all and the hope that one day they would escape. Was it too much to hope they would learn how to control the jumps, or even simply work out what year they were in? Could they stop whatever was preventing the *Okeechobee Dawn* from working? Then they could use the fuel they had saved and fly away with Babs. The first thing was to find more key codes, now that she knew what to look for.

The platform was approaching the side of the pit. As it entered the tunnel, Catalina heard Sam say, "We'll be back." They all would. Catalina was going to crack all its secrets.

CHAPTER TWELVE

The blaze of afternoon sunlight in her face dazzled Sam. She held a hand up to shield her eyes as she stepped up onto the roof. The air was hot and humid after the controlled conditions inside, but the salt in the air smelled good to her. It always would—the sea was in her blood.

She looked back through the doorway. Three stairs down, Liz had not moved. Her expression was tentative, and quite out of character. She was clearly trying to summon her resolve.

"You can come back another time, if you'd rather."

Liz sucked in her breath. "No. I've spent too long as it is, putting it off. Eight days is more than enough. Let's get it over with." She climbed the last few steps.

"He's over here." Sam pointed.

Nothing else was said until they stood by Gerard's remains.

"Oh, you daft bugger." Liz slumped onto the bench.

"We didn't know what you'd like us to do, and when you said you wanted to see where we found him, we thought we'd wait."

"Thanks. He's been here thirty-eight years. He wasn't going anywhere." Liz looked out to sea. "That's the Squat over there?"

"Yes."

"He had his binoculars? You can see folks with them?"

"Yes."

"So he sat here, watching us until he died. Poor bastard. I didn't even wave to him." Tears spilled down her face.

Sam hovered anxiously. What should she do? She was no good at times like this. Someone else should have volunteered to guide Liz.

She patted Liz's shoulder. "Are you all right?" A silly question, but she did not know what else to say.

"Yep. I'm fine. Just give me a mo." Liz dashed a hand across her eyes then leaned down. She slid a tarnished ring off Gerard's finger bone, then sat, holding it in the palm of her hand. "Bloody cheap wedding ring. We weren't going to do it, you know—get married. It was out of fashion with our friends. Then we were in Las Vegas, got drunk, and woke up the next morning with curtain rings on our fingers. I still stuck with calling myself Liz Anderson, rather than Madame Dupuis."

Liz leaned down again. In removing the ring, she had brushed away debris and revealed a folded note under Gerard's hand. The paper was yellow with age but had been sheltered from the weather. One short word was written on the outside in faded ink. Sam could see it started with an L, but without recognizing a letter, she would have guessed what it spelled.

Liz sat, staring at the paper in her hands. When she made no move to read it, Sam asked. "Do you want me to go?"

"If you don't mind, dear. I'll be fine up here with Gerard. I think I know my way back, though we didn't have a ball of yarn with us. If I'm not down in an hour you can send out a search party."

"Right." Sam patted her shoulder once more.

Catalina was hunched over the map in the entrance foyer. She kept her head down. "Was Liz all right?"

Sam restrained a sigh. Since their return from the tower, Catalina had been acting oddly, refusing to look in her direction whenever possible. Sam had hoped revealing Alonzo's secret would change Catalina's opinion of her—which it clearly had, just not noticeably for the better.

"Mostly. She wanted to be left alone with him."

"I can understand that."

"She said she ought to be able to find her own way back, and something about a ball of yarn."

"That's from Theseus and the Minotaur."

"Who?"

Catalina glanced up for the barest split second. "It's an old Greek legend. The Minotaur was a monster, half man, half bull, that lived in a maze called the labyrinth. Theseus was the hero who killed it. His lover gave him a ball of yarn to unwind on the way in, so he could find his way out afterward."

"Right. Well, I guess we don't need the yarn, since we have maps."

"And no Minotaurs."

"That too."

"Anyway, I'm pleased you're here. There's something I'd like you to do for me."

"Sure. What?"

"You'll need this." Without looking up, Catalina held out a scrap of paper.

It was a key code. Sam was getting used to Greek letters. "Anything special about it?"

"It belonged to someone called Meriones. He's the most senior person I've found a code for. It gives access to more rooms than anyone else's. He's the only one who can get the elevator to go to the green floors."

It had been obvious from the start that floor numbers in the tower got higher the lower you went, which must have made sense to the aliens. It also seemed likely the first number, or color, related to function. The top twenty-six red floors were domestic, from what they could tell. The thirty orange floors below were stores. To date, nobody had gotten any lower. The key code used to summon the elevator controlled which floors they could reach.

"Is that where I'm going?"

"Yes. Floor 464. Green-purple-green. It's where Tydides had his workroom. I'm fairly sure I've pinned it down." Catalina tapped the map. A room lit up. "I want you to pick up every book and piece of paper you can find. There's a bag over there you can take."

Sam looked at the map. Despite being many floors below the bottom of the pit, the middle of the tower was still empty. She pointed to the central void. "Is anything there?"

"It says, *Comparison of everything driving mechanism.*"

"Do you know what that means?"

"No."

"Does Floyd or Liz?"

"No." Clearly, Catalina wanted her to go.

Sam was not sure which was worse—Catalina accusing her of murdering Alonzo or Catalina acting as if she was not there. At times,

Catalina even seemed to deliberately plan things for them to be together, just to make a point of ignoring her. Sam was getting rather tired of it.

"All right. I'll be back soon."

Sam set off for the nearest subway station. She had spent a chunk of the previous week in the maze of corridors and had begun mastering the maps. Sam felt sure she could find the workroom.

"Oh, and um…"

"Yes?" Sam turned around.

For the first time, Catalina was looking at her. She smiled awkwardly. "See you later." And went straight back to the map.

The corridors of floor 464 were markedly different from those Sam was familiar with. The air felt heavier, thicker, and carried a faint smell of oil and cat piss. The lighting was a few notches lower, with an odd tint that made the green and purple lines on the wall seem to glow. The floor was dull green and dimpled.

Sam stepped out of the elevator into an octagonal area twenty feet across. Corridors led away to her left, right, and straight ahead. A map was fixed to a wall nearby, but Sam did not need it. The route was easy enough to remember. She settled the strap of the bag over her shoulder and headed down the hallway on the left.

Tydides's workroom was nearby, just around the corner after the first intersection. Sam stopped at the door and pulled out the note with the key code. A sound like a bubbling rumble of thunder echoed down the deserted corridors. The bass roar ended on a rising whine. Sam turned her head, trying to identify the source. Was it some sort of machine? But whatever it was, the sound had stopped.

The room was in darkness, but as soon as Sam stepped inside, the ceiling started to glow with normal, white light. The door shut behind her. Sam looked around. Tydides's workroom was smaller than she had expected, although not cramped. A wide table ran down the middle, littered with scraps of finely worked metal. A long desk took up part of one wall, and above it was a shelf, filled with books. Sam could see it would need more than one visit to collect them all. Maybe she could bring Torvold next time.

A chair with small wheels on the legs was pushed under the desk, and on either side were a set of drawers. These held a mixture of small instruments and what was surely rubbish. Why had Tydides kept a tray full of buttons, tiny bolts, and bent wire? However, the top drawer on the right contained two notebooks. Scrawled inside was a mess of text, diagrams, and tables of numbers. The writing meant nothing to her, but Sam was certain they were Tydides's working notes, jotted down. The scribbling would surely be of more interest to Catalina than the books on the shelf. She slid both notebooks into her bag and moved on.

At the end of the room, farthest from the door, stood three tall lockers. Hanging in the first were two of the boiler suits, bright red in color. Sam opened the second locker and found herself face-to-face with a grinning skull. She leapt back and almost fell. Her heart tried to burst through her rib cage. The bag hit the floor with a thump. The skeleton stayed put.

Sam leaned her elbows on the central table while her pulse returned to normal. In her time at sea, she had dealt with many dead bodies. The unexpected surprise had startled her, but in the run of things, living beings were the only dangerous sort. The dead were no longer a threat. Sam returned to the locker.

The man had been wearing one of the red boiler suits, which had helped keep his skeleton together. The material had stood up well to both the passage of years and to having someone decay inside it. Even so, Sam did not imagine many would happily wear it now. A search of the pockets produced a writing instrument, six small copper discs, two seashells, and a folded letter. Everything else had turned to dust. The letter Sam put in her bag. There was no clue to the cause of death.

The final locker was empty. Sam was about to close the door when a minor discrepancy caught her eye. Was it her imagination or was this floor slightly higher than the others? She stood back to compare. The difference was no more than an inch, but it was there. The locker had a false bottom. Sam used the skeleton's pen to poke around until she was able to lift the corner of a thin metal sheet.

Underneath lay a wad of paper, covered in writing and fine line drawings, a short metal stick with jewel-like buttons on the side, and a bizarre glove with four fingers and two thumbs. It was made from the soft bendable material the castaways called rubber. Sam had no clue what it was for, but someone had thought it worth hiding. The glove went into her bag with the rest.

After another ten minutes, Sam was ready to leave. The only thing left was to select as many of the books from the shelf as she could carry. But which ones to take first? Sam pulled down a couple and flicked through them. The problem was, she had no way to know what they were about. She grabbed five at random. The rest could wait.

The bass roar sounded again. This time much, much nearer. It might even be in the corridor outside. Instinctively, Sam backed away from the door. Now she could also hear the clump, clump, clump of footsteps, far too heavy to be human. A wheezing whine, like an old dog. A clink of metal. What was it? All the time, the footsteps got louder. Sam cursed herself. With the dangers of the outer island, why had they assumed the tower was safe?

Sam's back touched the wall at the end of the room, next to the lockers. Had the thing in the corridor killed the dead man? Regardless of whether it would help, Sam stepped into the empty locker and pulled the door shut. The pounding footsteps were now directly outside the workshop. Sam held her breath. The steps halted. Another roar. Sam listened for the sound of the door opening, but then the steps resumed in the same, steady rhythm. Slowly, the sounds faded.

Sam let herself out of the locker. Of course, there was no saying whether the creature was dangerous. It might merely be a different sort of caretaker, but she had no wish to put it to the test. Sam filled her bag with as many books as she could squeeze in—it would have to do. She was not coming back.

She stopped at the door. If only it were possible to edge it open and peek out. Sam summoned her courage and waved her hand over the control disc. The door whooshed aside. The corridor was deserted.

Sam crept out, trying to make as little noise as possible. She got to the intersection and peered around the corner. The elevator was just fifty feet away. Nothing was moving, no sounds except the whisper of ventilation fans, no sign that anything had passed by since she was last there. Sam stepped forward and heard the thud of heavy feet.

She could go back to the workshop, but where would that leave her? Sam ran. She reached the keypad as the roar rang out again. This was no caretaker. She stabbed at the keys, and in her haste hit the wrong button. Again, she tried the key code.

Another roar, and now the pounding beat of running. The elevator door opened. Sam hurled herself in and hit the colored keypad. Any floor would do, other than the one she was on. Sam struck a third button and looked up.

People might have thought it was a man with a bull's head, if they had never seen a bull and could accept a man ten feet tall, with four arms and mottled skin of silver and bronze. The flat face, with its short curved horns, was angry, bestial, but intelligence glinted in the red eyes. It was naked except for a loincloth. The bulging muscles were shockingly inhuman. Each hand held an axe like the one Torvold had found. And it was charging up the corridor toward her, roaring.

The door closed. Sam heard the Minotaur smash against the outside and the clang of repeated axe stokes. The caretakers would have repairs to make. Could the axes inflict enough damage to stop the elevator from working? Then Sam felt the lurch as it began its assent to the world above and sunlight. She was safe, as long as the Minotaur could not work a keypad.

Sam leaned over the rail. She could imagine she was in the crow's nest of a huge, invisible ship. Of course, there was no bow wave or flock of seagulls swooping over the ship's wake. There was no snap and creak of the sails, no smell of tar. The flying platform did not pitch and yaw beneath her feet. Yet the view to the horizon was the same, as was the wind raking though her hair, and the taste of salt on her tongue.

Sam looked back to the docking station she had just left. The sun was high and puffs of cloud drifted overhead. Sparkling waves rolled onto yellow sand. From the air, the green outer island looked like a tropical paradise. It was a shame about the hunters. Sam had not even taken the risk of disembarking, but had immediately tapped in the return code.

Four docking stations were spread around the outer island. Along with the one in Old Town, another was, fortunately, at the site of the farm they still harvested. The inner island had eight, despite its smaller size. The flying platforms had obviously been mainly for the aliens to use. Now the castaways had them, and Sam was not the only one to spend hours flying from station to station. They all had their own copy of the map. How long before she got bored with flying? It was easy to understand Babs's obsession.

The destination was drawing near, the docking station closest to the Squat. Sam thought about going somewhere else, but maybe it was best not to overdo things. She did not want the fun to wear thin.

The deck of the docking station was warm under her bare feet. Sam wandered to where it jutted out above the sea and sat with her legs dangling over the edge. The sun felt good on her face. Maybe she should go to the tower and continue exploring, although this was not as appealing as it had been. The Minotaur had not shown up on the upper floors, but it might have friends around.

At the sound of feet on the stairs, Sam glanced over her shoulder and saw Catalina step onto the deck. Was she going somewhere, or was it another carefully contrived opportunity to act as if Sam did not exist? Either way, there was no point in saying anything. Sam returned to looking at the sea.

"That isn't a safe place to sit."

"Pardon?"

"Where you are. If you fell into the sea…well, you wouldn't get out again."

"I'm not going to fall. I've ridden a crow's nest through a hurricane."

However, Sam could see she was making Catalina nervous. She scooted back from the edge and swiveled around to sit, cross-legged. "There. Happier?" Although she had every intention of returning to her former position once Catalina left.

"Yes. Thank you."

Catalina took a step toward the nearest flying platform, and then turned back. "Is it all right if I sit with you for a while? Or would you prefer to be left alone?"

Sam was so surprised it took a while to work out her answer. "No. I mean, yes, I don't mind you staying."

Catalina dithered, as if wondering whether to leave after all but finally sat down facing Sam so their knees were only a foot apart.

She looked so different from the first time Sam had seen her. Instead of the elegant embroidered gown, she wore the shirt and shorts of the castaways. Her hair was no longer sculptured ringlets but was tied back in a ponytail. Her skin was tanned and devoid of paint or powder. Yet there was still the stamp of a keen mind in her eyes and a defiance to the set of her shoulders and head. She was also the most beautiful woman Sam had ever seen. Being near Catalina put a huge strain on Sam's ability to think straight.

The silence dragged on while Catalina stared at the deck. Sam was starting to wonder if this was a new, extreme way to make a point of ignoring her, when Catalina said, "I'm sorry about sending you down to the Minotaur last week."

"That's all right. You didn't know it was there."

"And I'm sorry I accused you of murdering Alonzo."

"I was the nudge that pushed him over the edge."

"No. It wasn't your fault."

"Um…thanks."

"We haven't got off to a good start. I saw you as one of the pirates."

"I was."

"You're better than them."

"They weren't all bad."

"The men who wanted to rape me?"

"Well, yes. Jacob was a bad one."

"I didn't see much difference between him and the rest. If the hens hadn't escaped that night, we both know how events would have gone. Alonzo said the blessed Virgin Mary came to my aid."

Sam opened her mouth and then closed it. Was it a good idea to explain how far from the truth Alonzo had been?

Catalina continued. "I was hoping we could make a fresh start and become friends."

Sam's mouth went dry. Before she could summon her voice, there was the clatter of more feet climbing the stairs.

"This is so cool. I've got to show her." Madison's voice.

"I think you will have better luck showing her than trying to explain." Jorge's head appeared, followed by the rest of him.

Madison was a few steps behind. "Awesome. You're still here."

Catalina shifted around. "Me or Sam?"

"You. Sam can come too, if she wants. But you have just got to see this."

"What?"

"Back in the Squat." Madison offered a hand to pull Catalina to her feet. "You know, ever since I got here it's been bugging me. No computer terminals. I'm thinking, like, they had to have them. Right? I mean, they probably had tablets, or something alien that did the same thing. But you must have seen around the place, the screens on the walls. I've been thinking, like, I just know it's a terminal, but how to turn it on? Then I saw the hand Sam bought back, and I think, duh, it's got bio-security. The Greeks must have made a silicone copy of an alien handprint. So I put it on, touched a screen, and ta-da, we're online. Except I can't read a word of it."

"Pardon?" Catalina had evidently made no more sense of it than Sam had.

"I told you you'd have to show her," Jorge said.

Madison looped an arm though Catalina's and led her back to the stairs. "I know you haven't seen a computer. But it's like if you broke into my home in Austin and were looking for books. There'd be a couple of magazines you'd pick up. But you'd miss my e-book reader. You'd probably think it was, like, a really boring cheese board or something." Her voice faded away, with her still talking about texting, streaming, uploads, and various other words which sounded as if they ought to be English but were completely lost for meaning.

"That Madison, she is so enthusiastic, but makes so little sense, don't you think?" Jorge said.

"I guess she knows what she's saying."

Jorge laughed and leaned against a rail. "But it's all good. We've gotten into the tower. We're starting to wheedle out the aliens' secrets. I know everyone laughed at me and my hoard of treasures. But I can feel it. We're going to get away from this island, and I'll live out my life as a rich man. It is all good." His eyes were fixed on the sky, or maybe a vision of all the things he would buy.

Sam turned her head. Down on the ground, she could see Catalina, still being treated to a breakneck monologue as Madison towed her along. Could she and Catalina become friends? That would be good too.

❖

"Okay, everyone. I guess you've heard we have news for you."

Liz did not need to raise her voice. At the sight of her and Catalina getting to their feet, conversation around the common room died. Rumors had been spreading all day. The few people who had not yet finished their evening meals hastily gobbled the last mouthfuls. Sam shifted to the side slightly so she could have a better view.

"I'll leave it to Cat to do most of the talking. I'll just chime in now and then, making a pain of myself." Liz turned to Catalina. "It's all yours."

"Thank you." Catalina stepped forward. "The papers Sam brought back from the lower floors have been very useful. Apart from what's in them, they've helped tie together clues from elsewhere. Up until now, I've had more guesswork than anything else. The trouble is the Greeks weren't writing things down as a record of events. Mainly they're notes between people, and they don't bother explaining things both parties already knew. However, I've pieced together enough to build a coherent story. There's holes, but they're more about motives than what happened. We don't have much of an idea why the aliens acted as they did. The humans are more straightforward."

Liz added, "It's possible, even if we had an alien here, it couldn't explain. There's no reason their logic should make sense to us."

Catalina nodded. "As for what they did, as others worked out, the aliens came here from the stars, over three thousand years ago. They created Atlantis as an artificial island and rounded up humans to work for them. They were here for about a hundred years. I'm afraid the computer terminals aren't much help. I've spent a few days looking at them, but the writing isn't in any language I know. I assume it's alien. But judging by the diagrams and pictures, Atlantis was a research outpost. They were working on various things. Most we don't understand. However, some aliens were studying humans and the state of our culture at the time."

"I'll chip in here," Liz said. "Their main technique was what's referred to in the scientific world as buggering things up. A bit like an entomologist taking the queen out of an ant colony to see how it falls apart without her. The upshot is what archaeologists call the Late Bronze Age Collapse. Dozens of cities were destroyed. Most civilizations around the Mediterranean vanished. We don't know how much the aliens did directly and how much was due to them knocking everyone off balance. I guess it didn't matter to the poor bastards at the time who were too busy dying to make notes."

Catalina took over again. "The aliens also studied individual humans. For some reason, they focused on the Greeks. Most were slaves or the subject of experiments. But in the later stages of their time here, the aliens either selected the brightest or enhanced them to make humans more intelligent. There was a group of forty or so, including Tydides and Meriones, who were educated in alien technology. Maybe the aliens needed their help, or maybe they wanted to find out how good humans were at learning. Or maybe it was some reason that won't make sense to us."

Sam suspected the motive was something nasty. The hunters were programmed to kill humans, and that did not point to love, friendship, and respect between the two species.

"The trouble really started when the aliens were getting ready to leave Earth. Tydides learned about it, and he also learned that when the aliens left, Atlantis would sink, and everyone on it would drown. Some common slaves were returned to Greece, taking the legend of Atlantis with them—who knows why—but the scientists were all earmarked to go down with the island. Maybe the aliens were worried what educated humans might do when they weren't being supervised."

"As you can imagine, Tydides and the others weren't thrilled when they found out," Liz said.

Catalina continued. "Tydides wasn't bothered about the aliens leaving. In fact, he was quite happy about it. But he didn't want to go to the bottom of the ocean, and he didn't want to return to Greece. He was used to hot showers, air coolers, flying platforms, and the rest. I doubt he'd have liked the Bronze Age Mediterranean, even if it wasn't sliding into a dark age. So he hatched a plan to sabotage the alien's departure. Their spaceship formed part of the tower. It's still there, at the core. It's what provides the energy to keep everything running. It's one reason why Atlantis wouldn't survive after it went. The island would become top-heavy and sink. So in order for the spaceship to leave, it had to disengage from the tower. This was the bit the Greeks sabotaged. They waited until the aliens were aboard their spaceship, and then they blew up part of the mechanism. But it didn't work quite as planned. And this is where I need to hand over to Liz."

"Yes, well. I'll try to keep it short and sweet. I let Cat do the lion's share, because I knew if I got going, I might as well be speaking Greek for most of you." Liz smiled. "As Cat said, the spaceship is still locked inside the tower, with the dead aliens on board. The core beneath the pit is labeled, *Comparison of everything driving mechanism*, which I interpret as *Universal Relativistic Engine*. It's Einstein's theory. Nothing can go faster than the speed of light, so the only way to fly between the stars is to either shrink space or play games with time—and there's less difference between these two options than you might think. That's what the aliens' relativity engine does. Except, once it was sabotaged, it couldn't work properly. It keeps trying to manipulate time so it can jump to another star, but it's held here. So it jumps through time instead, taking Atlantis with it."

Liz was right. She might as well have been speaking Greek as far as Sam was concerned.

"So. Now that that's over with, I'll pass you back to Cat."

"Fortunately, the how and why aren't important. There's good news and bad news for us. The good news is we don't need to understand how the spaceship works or do anything clever. The Greeks sabotaged the controls and locked the spaceship in. The caretakers would normally have repaired the damage, so the Greeks changed their programming. This took trial and error, and Meriones, who did the work, wrote it all down in his notes, which we have, as well as the alien hand to get onto the computer system, and a memory stick. All we need is to get to the caretaker control room, and Liz is confident she can—" Catalina looked at Liz quizzically. "What was it again?"

"Reinstall the original command protocols."

"Right. Then the caretakers will repair the sabotage and the spaceship will leave. Once it's gone, Atlantis will start to sink, but Babs's seaplane will be able to fly again."

"What's the bad news?" Floyd shouted.

"The bad news is that when the Greeks blew up the controllers, the aliens were trapped on the spaceship and couldn't leave, which was very quickly fatal for them."

It struck Sam that if the aliens had artificially enhanced human brainpower, they had been a little too successful for their own good.

"Before they died, they managed an act of revenge. The hunters on the outer island were supposed to deal with runaway slaves. The aliens changed their orders so they'd kill everyone on sight."

"Luckily, the aliens were pushed for time," Liz said. "The hunters ignore people up trees, because the outer island wasn't overgrown back then, and there weren't many trees to hide in. The aliens either didn't think so far ahead or didn't have time to write new tree-climbing routines."

Catalina nodded. "I agree the aliens didn't have much time. There weren't any hunters on the inner island or in the tower, and they weren't able to ship any across. However, there were a few other bio-robots they could use. They're based on the aliens themselves. Maybe they were replicas used to test equipment. As you know, Sam ran into one, and from the way it reacted, they're also set to attack on sight. From what I can tell, there are twelve of them, roaming around the lower levels in the tower. They each patrol a particular location, so the upper floors are safe."

"But let me guess, the control room we need to get to is guarded by one," Floyd said.

"Yes."

"How bad are they?"

"They're big, they're strong, and they were built to be indestructible."

"Like a superhero?"

Catalina frowned. "Possibly. If I knew what a superhero was."

"Don't worry about it." Floyd grinned. "If we all jump the Minotaur together, do you think we can overpower it?"

"No. We need a better plan than that."

Yaraha asked, "Supposing we get our better plan and we return to the world. Could we have any idea what year it will be?"

Liz answered. "Actually, dear, I can make a guess. It's the graph. The further back in time you go, the longer Atlantis stays put between jumps, until at about 1150 BC, where the curve crosses the y-axis and the island is stable. That has to be when the sabotage occurred and Atlantis started jumping. At the other end of the line, the jumps get closer and closer together, until there's no time between them at all, and the curve crosses the x-axis. I'm betting that's when Atlantis ends up after its last jump. If I'm right, the year will be 2025, give or take a few."

"There's another issue." Babs looked troubled.

"I know, dear," Liz said. "More than one. Or maybe sides of the same issue. You go first."

"The *Okeechobee Dawn* was a three-seater aircraft. There's a weight limit. Charles and I stripped the spare seat out and everything else we could when we put in the extra gas tanks. Even if we ditch the fuel we don't need, she can only carry six people, seven tops. And there's fourteen of us."

"Thirteen," Liz corrected her.

"Who aren't you counting?"

"Me. The control room is at the heart of the tower. Once the caretakers do the repairs, it'll be minutes before the whole thing goes down. I doubt anyone is quick enough to get out in time. I'm certainly not. I don't run that fast anymore. Once we get rid of the Minotaur, I'll give you time to get to the seaplane, then I'll upload the command protocols."

"No. We'll draw lots." Catalina looked shocked. Clearly, Liz had not mentioned this before.

"We can do that for the other slots on the seaplane. Of course, if half of us get killed fighting the Minotaur, there won't an issue. I understand how to do the reinstall. Plus I'm the oldest. I've had the best years of my life. Gerard and I can go down together."

"I won't let you do it," Catalina said.

"It's not your call, dear."

"We need to talk it over."

"We can talk, but I don't see us finding any other outcome. Either seven escape, or we all stay here for the rest of our lives."

CHAPTER THIRTEEN

Y ou can't just throw your life away." Catalina was outraged. "There
has to be another way. If not, we stay here."

She and Liz were alone in Liz's room after the meeting. Grimacing,
Liz pushed herself up onto the bed. "Then we'll all die before our time.
Atlantis takes a toll."

"There's a difference between taking your chances and giving
up."

"It makes no difference to me."

"You can't say that,"

"I just did, dear."

"But—"

"No buts." Liz's voice was firm. She shifted around on the bed to
get comfy and then patted a spot beside her. "I guess there's no point
asking you to take a pew."

"No." Catalina was too agitated to sit. It was all she could do not
to pace the room.

"I didn't want to say anything."

"About what?"

Liz sighed loudly. The rueful shake of her head looked like part
of an old argument she was having with herself. She lifted her arm and
probed the fingertips of her right hand into the side of her left breast.
"In there. I first felt the lump four years back. Not a bloody thing I
could do about it, except keep checking to see if it was getting bigger."
The corners of her mouth pulled down. "I don't know. No way to be
sure what size it was when I first noticed. Memories play tricks with

you. But it's spreading. Last few months, I've been feeling drained, short of breath. I'm an electrical engineer, not a doctor, but I know a bad sign when I see it."

"What?"

"Cancer, dear. I don't know what they called it in your day. If I'd been in New Zealand in 1980, when I first noticed, maybe the docs could have done something. It's too late now, even if I went back. But here, I won't even have morphine to take the edge off the pain."

"You're in pain?"

"Not too much right now. Mostly what can be put down to old age. But it won't stay that way. So, like I said, it makes no difference to me. I hadn't wanted to tell folk, but I might have to. Just so they know I'm not playing the bloody hero."

❖

Catalina sat on the purple grass listening to the argument go round in circles. Liz had announced a vote would be held on the issue, in a week's time. Which, in her words, "was long enough for everyone to make their bloody minds up." But from the state of the discussion, Catalina suspected the timeline was a little short.

"We can't leave people behind. It would be murder." Babs was adamant.

"So you'll force us all to stay here and rot?" Jorge was equally passionate on the other side. "What do you think, Piracola? Come on, say something. Don't just sit there." He nudged him.

"I agree with you."

"Of course he agrees with you. It's all he ever does." Babs was dismissive. "So, Cat? How about you? You're playing it quiet as well."

It was just as well Catalina did not mind her name being shortened, since everyone, apart from Sam, was doing it. What did that imply about the way Sam saw her?

"I don't know."

"Come on." Jorge turned to her. "You must have an opinion. What does your gut say? What does your heart say?"

I'd rather be talking to Sam. She glanced around the lawn. Sam was not in sight. Catalina returned to the ring of waiting faces—except

Piracola was not looking at her. He was staring at the ground, his face showing confusion and sorrow.

"Is there something you want to say, Piracola?"

"He'll—"

Catalina held up a hand to cut Babs off. "Please, let him speak."

"It is only, none of you have lost family." Catalina said nothing, although Alonzo came to mind. He meant as much to her as her father ever had. "There were eight in the canoe, when we landed. Now it is just Yaraha and myself. My two brothers, Arach—" Piracola broke off, shaking his head. "They are gone. I know if I leave here all our people will have gone also, but the land remains. I want to go home, to stand on our land and sing the song of my brothers, so the trees and the earth and the sky will remember them. I want to go home."

"Do you think Yaraha feels the same?" Babs asked.

"You should ask him, but I'd be surprised if he votes to leave. Yaraha is of my people, but he was the son of a chief, and I'm not. He doesn't always see things the same as me. I lost my brothers, but he casts his net wider. I would have tried to return before now, but he chose to stay, and I couldn't paddle the whole way on my own."

"Supposing your name doesn't get pulled out of the hat?"

"What do you mean?"

Jorge answered. "Babs means, supposing you aren't one of the lucky ones who gets a place on her seaplane? Supposing you get left behind?"

"Then I'll take the *Inflatable* and try to go home that way. It will no longer be needed here."

"Even the *Inflatable* won't be able to battle the undertow when the island sinks."

"You don't know that."

"It's a good guess."

An idea struck Catalina. "Except once the Minotaur is dealt with, there's no reason why some can't leave on the *Inflatable* and get clear before Liz resets the caretakers."

Jorge frowned. "But we won't know what the date is. If Liz is right, when the caretakers do the repairs, Atlantis will make one last jump to 2025, and then the spaceship will disengage and leave. But the *Inflatable* would have to set off beforehand, so we'll have no idea what year it will be in the outside world."

"It makes no difference to me," Piracola said. "The land will always be there."

"It makes a difference to me."

"Why are you arguing against him, Jorge?" Babs said. "I'd have thought it strengthened your side. You must have given some thought to what happens to you if you don't draw a spot on the *Okeechobee Dawn*."

"Is that your problem? Is that why you're so set against going? You're frightened of being left behind?"

"Of course not. I'm the one person who has to be on board. The *Okeechobee Dawn* won't fly itself."

"Couldn't Charles do it?"

"In a pinch, maybe. If you want to take the risk."

"In a pinch? I thought he taught you to fly."

"That was years ago."

"And he's forgotten how to in the meantime?"

"No. But his eyesight is poor. The glasses he's wearing aren't his. They're a pair he found lying around in the Barn. His own got trodden on by accident, not long after we got here. He wasn't just mucking about when he was refereeing the football match. He couldn't see half of what went on."

"So you're worried it's Charles who won't draw a place on the plane?" Jorge said.

Babs's face hardened. "No. Because if Charles isn't on the plane, I don't care how the vote goes, we aren't leaving."

"You don't get a veto."

She stood and glared down at Jorge. "Yes, I do. I won't leave Charles behind. It's my fault he's here to start with."

Jorge watched her stalk away. "Ah. She'll change her mind. You'll see."

Catalina was not so sure.

❖

"I can't believe you're saying that. Listen to yourself!"

Catalina caught the words of a heated argument as soon as she opened the door. Kali and Ricardo sat glaring at each other. Now that the tower was available as a sanctuary, Liz had shared her fears about the caretakers, and Kali and Ricardo had immediately moved to the accommodation there, although they returned to the settlement for meals.

Both looked around at the sound of the door. Confronted by two angry faces, Catalina considered making a quick retreat, although that might make things more, rather than less, awkward.

"I've just come to get a drink of water." This had the advantage of being the truth. Catalina was in the middle of trying out a recently discovered key code on the foyer map to see if it gave access to anywhere new. "I'll be out of your way in a moment."

"No. Come in, sit down." Ricardo beckoned her forward. "Help me talk sense into this crazy woman here."

"I'm not crazy."

"I need to get back to my work." Catalina did not want to get drawn into whatever the argument was about.

"She will not listen to me. See what you can do."

"It's you who are not listening." Kali turned to Catalina. "He has this idea he'll volunteer not to go on the *Okeechobee Dawn* with the condition that I am promised a place."

"It's not just you. It's our child."

"Our child will want a father. Wherever you go, I will go with you. Do you not understand me? I've chosen you. I will not raise our child on no more than a memory."

Catalina filled a cup with water. Did she want to get involved? "I was speaking to Piracola earlier. He has an idea about taking the *Inflatable*. Charles says the seaplane won't need most of the fuel. In fact, they want to ditch as much weight as possible. If we put a tank of gas in the boat, it should be able to get to the mainland."

"I know. My brother has already spoken about it."

"Really? Jorge didn't seem interested."

"He doesn't want to arrive back in time because of his treasures. He wants there to be someone to sell them to."

"But you're not so bothered. Kali is all you want, correct? The two of you could go together in the *Inflatable*."

Ricardo shook his head. "We don't know how far it is to Florida, or what year it will be when we arrive. If it's before the American Civil War, Kali would be seen as an escaped slave. She has no papers to show otherwise. It would hardly be any better for me. We'd have no rights, and neither would our child."

"So what do you think, Cat?" Kali asked.

Catalina sipped the water while considering her answer. "I think Kali will be given a place on the seaplane for certain, for the sake of the baby."

"I won't take it, not without my Rico."

"Then you should wait to have this argument until after the vote. Babs doesn't want to go, and she may not be the only one. There's no point upsetting each other for no reason."

"Yes. Always, you are the clever one, Cat. Atlantis is no place to raise a child, but better both of us here, than for me and Rico to part." Kali leaned across the table and grasped his hands. "I've lost everyone I have ever loved. I will not lose you too. I cannot."

❖

The flying platform could have done with a roof. Catalina eyed the darkening sky. Ominous clouds were moving in quickly, on a strong westerly wind. She ought to get to the Squat before they hit, but on further thought, she wished the platforms had a "go faster" switch as well. Atlantis had an invisible shield that kept damaging hurricanes out, but let lesser storms through.

She tried to distract herself with thoughts of the upcoming vote. It was clear Jorge, Piracola, and Liz would vote to leave Atlantis. Torvold had also loudly expressed a wish to tackle the Minotaur, his desire for a pair of novelty drinking horns undimmed by the lack of beer to drink from them. On the other hand, Babs was opposed, and it looked likely that Kali would talk Ricardo into voting to stay. Yaraha, as ever, was listening to all sides, and saying little, though Piracola was sure he would not want to go. How would the rest vote?

The first hard volley of raindrops landed just as the platform docked. Should she wait the storm out under the station roof or make a bid to reach her room? Then Catalina spotted a familiar figure, sitting on the edge of the deck and watching lightning bolts striking the horizon.

Her pulse sped. "I do wish you wouldn't sit there."

"It's the highest viewpoint around here."

"It's dangerous."

Sam swiveled around. "I've spent half my life dangling over shark-infested waters. This is no different." But she moved away from the drop. "Happier now?"

"Yes."

"Actually, I ought to be going. I'm due to cook this evening."

Catalina made her decision. "I'll come with you."

"Let's go then."

Sam trotted down the steps, leaving Catalina behind, but she stopped at the bottom. The rain was picking up.

"We need to run."

Without thinking, Catalina took the hand Sam held out. The jolt as Sam set off felt as though her arm was about to be wrenched from its socket. Spanish noblewomen did not run. Catalina had seen men and even female servants run. She supposed she might have done it herself as a child, but it was unseemly for a gentlewoman. Apart from anything else, their clothing made it impossible to achieve anything more than a short burst of scurrying.

Towed along by Sam, Catalina was permanently on the point of falling. How did you keep your feet under you? She tried lengthening her stride, and something twanged in her thigh. Her legs started to burn, her throat and lungs were raw.

The heavens opened as they covered the last few yards to the door of the communal house. Raindrops pounded on Catalina's head and shoulders. Sam waved open the entrance and pulled her inside.

"There. Made it." Sam let go of Catalina's hand and turned to her. The smile on her face froze. "Are you all right?"

Was she? Catalina had thought her pulse was racing when she saw Sam, but it was nothing compared to this. Her heart was beating so hard it was making her head shake. Her legs felt as though the bones in them had been replaced by jelly. She staggered to the bench but lacked the strength to climb on, and so collapsed over it, her forehead resting on her arms.

"Catalina, what's wrong? Are you unwell?"

"I...I..." Each gasp rasped at her throat, but the pain was easing. Her head no longer felt as if it were about to fly off her shoulders. "I've never run before."

"Never?" Sam's expression went from surprise to concern. "You have a problem with your health? I'm sorry. You should have said."

"No. It's not my health. I've just never learned how."

Sam opened her mouth, looked confused, and closed it again.

"I should practice. I might need to do it again sometime." Catalina was now able to stand, with just one hand on the bench for support. She pressed the other to her chest. "Tell me, is your heart supposed to pound like this?"

"Depends how far you run."

"You don't look as if you are having trouble."

"It gets easier with practice. You need to build up to it. Would you like me to get you a drink of water?"

Catalina took her hand from the bench. Her body was returning to normal. "It's all right. I can get one for myself."

"Right, 'cause I need to start on the food."

Catalina followed Sam into the kitchen. Cooking was something else she had never done. Although dinner duties were on a roster, Catalina had been excused, on account of the work she was doing with the Greek texts. Perhaps this was another skill worth practicing. She could start by watching Sam, which was an enjoyable activity in its own right.

"Are you all right now?" Sam looked over her shoulder.

"Yes, thank you. Much better. I was watching what you were doing. I should take my turn at cooking sometime."

"In that case, don't watch me. I'm not the best cook here. Try Jorge or Yaraha."

"They might be a bit daunting. You don't mind me watching, do you?"

"No." Sam turned back to her work.

I told him I was the same as him. That when it came to lovers, I wanted my own sex. Those words still shook Catalina every time she remembered them and threatened to bring a hot flush to her own face. The thought of saying anything on the subject to Sam made her stomach flip. How would she ever get beyond this infantile paralysis? Because it had been going on for too long.

Catalina leaned back against the wall and tried to work out what to say, where to start. The heroines in ballads would drop a handkerchief for the bold, dashing heroes to pick up. Whether this would work with Sam was irrelevant, since Catalina no longer possessed a handkerchief.

"Actually, if you want to help, could you get a dozen sweet potatoes?"

The storeroom was close by, and Catalina was soon back. "I could only find this sack with about eight in it. Will that do?"

"It'll have to. We need another expedition to the farm. I'll tell Charles or Liz when I see them."

Catalina's stomach tightened, for a completely different reason. She might be excused from cooking, but nobody was allowed off the hazardous trips to the outer island, and she knew her name was top of the roster. "I could go find them."

"No rush. This will have to do. It's too late to do anything now." Sam began dicing the potatoes.

Catalina moved to where she could study the deft movements. Sam's hands were strong, hardened by work, yet long-fingered and graceful—a blend of masculine and feminine traits that typified her. Catalina remembered running through the rain holding Sam's hand. A shame she had been too busy trying not to fall over to appreciate it.

Could she contrive a way to hold Sam's hand again? Could she turn the moment into something more? Would it be too forward? Too presumptuous? Should she say something first? And if so, what? Catalina was acutely aware of her lack of experience in such matters.

Maybe it would be easier if she found some spare cloth and made a handkerchief.

❖

The first of the castaways arrived in the kitchen. Catalina knew she had run out of excuses to stand about, especially when Sam said, "Go and eat. I'll finish up in here and join you in a minute."

Catalina ladled out a bowl of stew, took a flat disc of cornbread, and went into the common room. As yet, the large circular bench was empty. Unfortunately, Catalina had no sooner sat down than she was joined by Charles and Horatio, who took a seat on either side of her, leaving no space for Sam. Catalina tried not to let her disappointment show.

"How's the research going? Picked up anything new?" Charles asked.

"Mainly confirming what we already know." Catalina dunked a corner of bread in the stew and tasted it. Maybe Sam's cooking did not match Jorge's, but it was far from the worst. "I wish I could talk Liz into delaying the vote."

"Why? You don't strike me as the procrastinating sort."

"Because we don't know enough. We're going to vote on attacking the Minotaur without any information about whether it can be done. There might even be another location where we can reset the caretakers and avoid the Minotaur altogether."

"Yes, well. I think Liz is feeling the pressure of time."

"So am I. There's so much in the books, and most of it's irrelevant. I could spend years going through it all."

"I agree with Cat," Horatio said. "There's no point going off half-cocked. I'll be voting to stay. Not that I want to stay, but we can change our minds later if we find more out. If we attack the Minotaur, and we all get killed, well, it will be too late then, won't it?"

The point was undeniable. Catalina sighed. "From what I've found out, the Minotaurs sound unbeatable."

"Liz said they were based on the aliens," Charles said.

"That's what the Greeks wrote. They should know, as far as body shape goes, but I suspect the real aliens weren't quite so tough."

"I used to read Greek myths as a boy," Horatio said between mouthfuls. "Though only in translation. I fear I was a rather poor student. My schoolmasters tried to teach me Latin, but I was never very good at it. I suppose Latin wouldn't be much use here anyway, although it always seemed a bit like Greek to me. I did like that story about the lady with the snakes for hair."

"Medusa," Catalina said.

"Yes. That was it. How did the story go?"

Catalina and Charles finished off their stew while Horatio fumbled his way through the parts he remembered, interspersed with sections from other myths. It was just as well Catalina already knew the story, because she would never have pieced it together from Horatio's account.

"Anyway. I hope there's none of those awful snake ladies in the tower. I don't suppose you've come across anything about them?"

"No." Catalina put down her empty bowl. "No stone statues either."

At the other side of the room, Sam was talking to Madison. Catalina felt an uncomfortable twinge of jealousy. Sam had confessed to wanting women as lovers. She had not given any clues about whether there was any particular woman she wanted. Sam and Madison did get along well together. The more she thought about it, the less happy Catalina was. Was she being overconfident about her own chances?

Horatio wiped his bowl clean with the last of his bread. "If there's any left, I think I'll have seconds."

He headed back to the kitchen. On past experience, he would probably get thirds as well, despite having a bowl double the size of anyone else to start with. If he drew a place in the *Okeechobee Dawn* would he count as two? Horatio was a good ten inches shorter than Torvold, but had to weigh more.

Charles also finished his dinner. "Not bad. Could have done with more sweet potato."

"Oh yes. That reminds me. Sam wanted to put more in, but we're out. We're a bit low on other things as well."

"Okay, I'll look at the roster."

"It's my turn. I know." Catalina sighed. "Not sure who else."

"Really? Let's see. Ah, yes. Your name's on top." Now that she was aware of the problems with his eyesight, Catalina could see Charles moving his notebook up and down in an attempt to get it into focus. He looked up, blinking. "Except what you're doing is far more important than digging up potatoes. You don't have much time, and you're the only one who can do it. I'm fourth on the roster, so I'll go this time."

"Are you sure?"

"Yes. As Horatio pointed out, we don't want to get ourselves killed by the Minotaur. And now that we can take the flying platforms, it's much safer. No need to trek through the jungle. I'll tell Jorge and Piracola, who'll be with me." Charles patted her knee, then squirmed down from the bench. "See what you can find out. I'm counting on you. Babs is badgering me to vote with her, but I don't think she's going to be on the winning side. In which case, our lives hang on you getting the answers." He smiled. "No pressure."

Now there was plenty of space on the bench, but Sam was no longer in the common room.

"What's cracking?" Madison rolled across the bench and lay on her stomach using her folded arms to hold her head and shoulders up.

"Is that one of those questions I don't have to answer?"

Madison gave a yelp of laughter. "You got it, honey."

"I saw you and Sam talking earlier." Catalina bit her tongue. That had come dangerously close to sounding like an accusation.

"Yes. It's this god-awful vote thing. It's killing me."

"Why?"

"Because."

Catalina waited to see if a longer answer might be forthcoming. "Because?"

"Because it's unfair."

"To you?"

"No. To everyone else. Which puts so much pressure on me."

"I'm not following you." Even by her normal standards, Madison was outdoing herself.

"Because I'm the only one the date works for. It was 2017 when I arrived. If Liz is right about dates, and she's usually right about everything—that woman is amazing—but it's going to be, like, eight years after I left. My mom, my dad, my friends, they'll be a bit older, but not so much. Jorge and Ricardo are next, date-wise. But for them it will be over thirty years they've been away. Their sisters will be ancient, in their fifties, probably grandmothers. After them it's Liz. Well, she's made her part clear. Then it's Floyd, and he's from 1954. He'll have been away over seventy years."

"And this bothers you?"

"Duh, yeah. I keep thinking, the only fair thing is for me to abstain, because, like, I'm the only one who'll be going home."

❖

Catalina flipped to another page. The text discussed how low the temperature needed to be to make a small part of something it was impossible to divide travel through the middle of solid wire without rubbing against it. It made no sense.

"You should take a break," Floyd said.

"I need to—"

"You need to take a break. Go outside and get some fresh air."

Catalina leaned back and yawned. Maybe he was right. "What will you do?"

"Go somewhere quiet, where people won't hassle me, trying to change my views on fighting Minotaurs. The next two days can't go quickly enough for me."

"What are your views?"

"That being a hero isn't as much fun as it sounds in books. I've done the throwing yourself against impossible odds bit. When we're sure we've got a fighting chance, then I'm in. Otherwise, I'll bide my time."

"You're like Horatio then."

"I don't want to bide my time quite that much. I'll take a fifty-fifty shot." Floyd pushed back from the table. "But for now, I'm going for a walk around the island before lunch."

Catalina followed him from the Barn but turned toward the Squat. The previous day's cloud had blown away leaving a pure blue sky. The sun beat down on her with a physical weight, although a cool breeze was blowing from the sea. Where might Sam be?

As she strolled past the docking station, Catalina looked up, but no legs were visible dangling over the edge of the deck. Why would anyone choose to sit in such a dangerous spot? Catalina was about to turn around when she spotted Sam. Instead of her normal perch, she was lying stretched on the grass a short way from the foot of the steps.

Catalina took advantage of the chance to study Sam sleeping. Beautiful was not quite the right word, but was handsome any better? More to the point, would Sam mind being woken? And what would they talk about? Then Sam reached up and scratched her nose. She was resting, not sleeping, and possibly well aware that she was being watched.

Catalina sat down beside her. "I didn't want to wake you, if you were asleep."

"I wasn't."

"I realized when you moved."

"You looked like you were wondering about something."

What word to use to describe you. Thinking quickly, Catalina said. "You're the only person who I don't have a clue about when it comes to the vote." Which was true enough, as well as being plausible.

"Probably because I'm not sure myself."

"You aren't?"

Sam pulled herself into a sitting position. "I've seen the Minotaur once, and I don't want to see it again. So part of me wants to tackle it, just to prove to myself I'm not frightened. But that's a silly reason. For the rest, dumping people on tropical islands was standard for anyone causing a problem on the *Golden Goose*. But even the privateers wouldn't do it, knowing the island was about to sink. And it's not as if anyone here is causing problems. You don't abandon shipmates. I guess my vote's for stay, but I'm having trouble persuading myself it's not because I'm scared." Sam plucked a stalk of purple grass and tossed it into the air, to spiral away on the breeze. "How about you?"

Catalina caught her lower lip in her teeth. "I've done the sums. If we discover a way to defeat the Minotaur, and can convince Floyd and Horatio, I'll have the deciding vote. As Charles said to me, no pressure."

A shadow flitted over the lawn. Catalina looked up. A flying platform was coming in to dock.

Sam shaded her eyes. "If that's the men back from the farm, they finished early."

"Most likely just someone taking a ride."

"I haven't seen any—" Sam broke off sharply.

Jorge was barreling down the steps as if the hounds of hell were on his heels.

Sam jumped up. "What is it? Where's Charles and Piracola?"

Jorge stumbled on the last flight of stairs and literally fell into Sam's arms, gasping. "Hunters. The hunters…they came to the farm. I heard them. We all did. We ran, but…but Piracola was too far from the dock, and Charles. His eyes. I don't think he could see where he was going. They…" Jorge's face contorted in horror. His eyes were blankly focused on nothing. Catalina could see him shaking. "They didn't make it. I waited as long as I dared. But…" He buried his face in his hands. "They didn't stand a chance."

Jorge's legs gave way. Without Sam's support he would surely have fallen. She lowered him gently onto the bottom step.

Catalina's own legs felt weak. She braced her hand on the stair rail, while waves of shock rolled over her. Charles and Piracola, both dead. She would never see either again. Tears stung her eyes. The taste of bile filled her mouth. Jorge was moaning an incoherent prayer in Spanish, while Sam held his hands.

Catalina pushed away from the stairs. She had to do something, tell the others, let people know. But it was unnecessary. Bad news has wings. Even as she turned around, castaways were appearing from doorways and around the sides of buildings, converging on the docking station. Had Jorge's voice traveled so far?

Torvold was the first to reach them. "What is up?"

Jorge was chewing on his knuckle, his eyes fixed blindly on the ground. Sam answered for him. "The hunters. They caught the other two. It's…it's bad news."

Ricardo arrived, with Kali a few steps behind. He knelt at Jorge's side and put his arm across his brother's shoulder. Muttered words passed between them. Kali placed her hands on Ricardo's back, either for comfort or balance.

All the while, the crowd was gathering.

Babs barged her way to the front. "Where's Charles?" She pushed Jorge's shoulder so he was looking up into her eyes. "Where's Charles?"

Jorge's mouth worked, as if trying to form words. "I'm sorry. I'm so sorry."

Forever passed before anyone moved.

"No." Babs stumbled back, shaking her head. "Oh God, no. He can't be. He can't. Fuck it. No." She screamed.

Catalina put her arms around Babs and hugged her while she sobbed.

❖

Catalina did not return to the Barn that day. Once the shock wore off, she spent her time drifting aimlessly around the pathways of the inner island. First Alonzo, and now Charles and Piracola. Why did these last two deaths seem the more shocking? After all, she had known Alonzo far longer, and truthfully speaking, cared about him more. Was it that Alonzo's death had been the closing act of the most turbulent, terrifying period of her life? Whereas the others had come at a time when she felt a measure of control returning? A time when there was hope life could get better?

The sun dropped below the horizon, and the lights over the walkways began to shimmer blue. After the heat of the day, the air felt chill. Time to go to her room and try to sleep, although Catalina was not holding much hope of success.

To her surprise, Catalina found she was at the opposite end of the island from the Squat. She had been unaware that her wandering route had taken her so far. She heard the sound of chanting, rising and falling, with a rhythm not so different from the Benedictine monks in the cathedrals of Spain. But here there was just a single voice, and the words were not Latin, or any other language she knew.

Yaraha stood on the quay, facing the last pink bands of sunset. He was singing of Piracola, of that Catalina was sure. Was it private? Would he object to her listening? Yet she could not leave. Although she did not understand a word, the sorrow and loss in Yaraha's voice touched her deeply.

The last note faded. For a while, Yaraha stood motionless, then he turned to Catalina. "I thought it was you. I heard your footsteps."

"Was it all right, me staying to listen?"

"You grieve for Piracola's death?"

"Yes. Of course."

"Then it was all right. I sang for the stars and the sea to know of his passing. But I could not tell the land—our land." The fading light did not hide the tears running down Yaraha's face. "I've been a coward."

"How so?"

"Hiding here. Refusing to face the world. Piracola wanted to return to our land. As did some of the others, when we first understood where we were. But I held out. I said it was too far, too unsafe. My father was a chief, and so my voice carried more weight. In the end there was just Piracola and me, and we no longer had any hope of paddling our way home."

"You felt responsible for them. Yes, it's dangerous in Atlantis. Today is the proof of that. But a hopeless sea voyage would have been certain death."

"It wasn't that. At first, I held back, deluding myself I might find a way to return to the time we had left. That I might see my family again. But then, when I learned the fate that would befall my people, I could not bring myself to return. I could not bring myself to look on a world where my people's voices were no longer heard. Easier to stay here, with strangers and monsters, than to seek out what should be familiar, but is only the ghost of what has been lost. Had we voted yesterday, I would have chosen to hide here still, like a coward."

"I can understand that, I think. And I wouldn't call it an act of cowardice."

"No. You do not honor the dead, by refusing to say their name. You do not heal a wound by denying it is there. You do not challenge a crime by closing your eyes. I am the last of the Timucua. I should go home. I need to go home."

He raised his eyes. The first stars glinted in the darkening sky. "And I only know this now. Now when I am the last, the very last. Piracola and I were never close. At first, he had his brothers, and by the time they died, I'd made friends with other castaways. Yet he was the last who knew my family, how my mother smiled, what my father's voice sounded like. He knew the songs we sang as we worked. He had seen my son taking his first steps through our village. As long as he was here, there was someone I could talk to, though I never did. The chance is gone forever. It hurts more than I would have believed. Now only I remember."

"So you're going to vote to fight the Minotaur and sink Atlantis?"

"Yes. I will return to the world, to do whatever a man can, to make it a better place. Then that will be the legacy of my people, the Timucua."

❖

Catalina tried to concentrate on the texts, but it was impossible. A sense of urgency had prompted her to come back after dinner. She might as well have not bothered. She had been staring at the same page for five minutes without reading a word. Her mind would not stay on task. She flipped the notebook shut. No point wasting any more time.

Tomorrow morning, straight after breakfast, would be the vote, and she still had no idea which way she would cast hers. She could join Madison in abstaining, although she would need to think of an excuse. Of course, given the current mood among the castaways, her vote would most likely count for nothing. Babs was now demanding to send the whole island to the bottom of the ocean, although she might have changed her mind again by morning. Floyd had also adopted a more militant viewpoint.

Catalina stood in the doorway. The sky was black velvet, sprinkled with stars. A crescent moon hung low in the sky. The purple grass appeared translucent in its silver light, and nearby flowers released a sharp, citrus scent on the night air. She should go home and try to sleep, although Catalina suspected she would have no greater success at this than with reading.

Close to the Squat, she spotted Sam, resting her elbows on a waist high ornamental wall and staring at the sky. They had hardly spoken since the deaths, mainly due to Catalina burying herself in her work.

"Are the stars telling you much?"

Sam looked round at the sound of her voice. "That it's mid March."

"How do you know?"

"Because Perseus is directly overhead, and Orion is coming up there, and Aquarius is right over there."

"You know the constellations." Why should this surprise her?

"Of course. You'd be lost at sea without them. Don't you?"

"I know the names, and I've seen pictures in books, but the stars look so different when they're in the sky, all jumbled together. I know Cassiopeia looks like a W, but I can make out dozens of Ws up there."

Sam laughed softly. "It's over there."

"Right." Catalina tried to pick out the correct stars. "Are you hoping to get advice from them?"

"The stars can tell you where you're going. Not what you'll find when you get there."

"You don't believe in astrology?"

"No. Do you?"

"I went to see an old fortune-teller, back in Spain."

"Did she tell you anything interesting, trustworthy?"

"It was interesting. I'm not so sure how much trust I'd put in it."

"Wise. I've known sailors who put a lot of faith in the stars. From what I could see, they might as well have flipped a coin."

"You mean I'm not going to marry a grandee whose name starts with L and have six children?"

"Was that what the fortune-teller told you?"

"Yes."

Sam shrugged. "You might do it, I suppose."

"Do you think they'll still have grandees in 2025?"

"You'd have to ask Madison."

Catalina settled against the wall beside Sam. "How do you think the vote will go tomorrow?"

"We'll vote to leave. Losing Charles and Piracola has driven home how dangerous life is in Atlantis. Even Kali is less keen on bringing up her baby here. It was another coin toss before, but now I think the vote is settled."

Catalina nodded. The one point nobody was saying aloud, but had to have passed though everyone's head, was the two fewer people wanting a place on the *Okeechobee Dawn*.

"So if you weren't consulting the stars for advice, why were you out here?"

"They're familiar, and beautiful, and I was wondering which one the aliens came from."

"The Greeks thought it was somewhere in Ursa Minor, but I don't know which constellation that is."

"It's to the north."

"Where?"

"Behind you."

Sam put both hands on Catalina's shoulders to turn her around. She pointed with one hand, but her other arm stayed around Catalina's back, holding her steady. Catalina felt her body respond to their closeness. Her stomach did its elevator flip.

She was nestled in the crook of Sam's arm, leaning into Sam's side, with Sam's face scant inches away from her own. She could hear Sam talking about stars, but could not concentrate on a word of it. Ursa Minor was irrelevant. Catalina rested her head on Sam's shoulder, and then turned so she could slip her arm around Sam's waist.

Sam stopped talking.

For the space of several heartbeats they stayed, locked in position, then both Sam's arms enfolded Catalina, holding her close. She leaned into Sam, feeling hard muscle and soft, warm flesh mold against her. Her body was energized, as if summer lightning pulsed through her veins to the beat of her heart, and at the same time, she was swept away on a wave of peace, bone-deep and older than the stars.

Catalina raised her head and looked up. Sam's eyes were closed, her face was getting closer, her mouth slightly parted. Catalina closed her own eyes as their lips met. The effect of the kiss flowed through her, melting her body. Sam's mouth against hers was like nothing she had ever known, or imagined.

"Hey, cool."

They sprung apart. Madison was passing by.

"Oh, don't mind me. Didn't mean to disturb you guys. Sorry."

With a dismissive wave, Madison trotted away down the path. Catalina watched her disappear, then turned back to discover she was alone. Sam had also vanished into the night.

Catalina buried her face in her hands. How quickly you could go from elation to misery. But she had her answer. She had caught Sam by surprise, forced herself on an unwilling target, and made worse than a fool of herself. *I told him I was the same as him. That when it came to lovers, I wanted my own sex.* But that did not mean Sam wanted her.

CHAPTER FOURTEEN

Floor 464 was the same as Sam remembered, the reduced lighting and dimpled green floor, the acrid scent on the air. She strained her ears for a distant roar, or the pounding of heavy feet, but there was only the whisper of air through the grates. She could feel her heartbeat hammering in her chest, and her palms got sweaty.

"Ready?" As the castaway with the most combat experience, Floyd had been put in the role of captain. Both Sam and Yaraha nodded. "Ear protectors on."

Sam adjusted the muffs over her ears and flicked up the switch on the side. All sound vanished.

"Here we go." She had to read Floyd's lips.

He squeezed the trigger on the AK-47. Sam saw the gun recoil, but the shot was just a faint pop through the muffs. She pushed them slightly off her ears to catch the echoes fading away until they were lost in the desolate miles of corridor.

Floyd positioned the safety lever on his rifle at the middle setting, for fully automatic fire, then settled the stock back against his shoulder.

Now Sam heard it, closer than she expected. The booming roar assaulted her ears, as the Minotaur appeared around a corner. It brandished the four axes and bellowed again, before lowering its shoulders to charge. Sam quickly replaced the muffs over her ears, just as Floyd and Yaraha began firing.

The Minotaur lurched to a halt, half stumbling. Its head was knocked back and its body shook with each impact, but it did not fall. The earmuffs muted the rattle of the guns, but did nothing to stop Sam's insides from vibrating from the sound. The explosive volley went on and on, surely far longer than the twenty seconds Floyd had estimated. But eventually, both AK-47s fell silent. Sam pulled the earmuffs from her head.

The Minotaur shook itself and straightened. The only visible sign of the barrage was its loincloth, which was now ragged and hanging askew on its hips. It raised one foot and thumped it down on the ground, hard, and then the other. It shook itself like a wet dog, as if to clear its head and flex its muscles. The first foot moved again. The Minotaur was moving, advancing, building up speed again for the charge.

"Sam, hit it."

Sam punched the color code into the floor selector. The doors whooshed closed, and the elevator started its ascent. Furious roars and the clang of axe blows followed them all the way up.

Floyd blew out his cheeks. "Ugly brute, wasn't it? Didn't seem to mind the bullets. We'll have to come up with something else. Guns aren't the answer."

Yaraha nodded. "I hadn't thought they would be."

❖

No matter how many times she walked into the Barn, the scale never ceased to awe Sam. The ceiling stretched away into the distance, curving to follow the line of the island. It was difficult to pull her eyes away. Not that she was trying very hard.

The night before, suddenly, out of nowhere, she and Catalina had kissed. Or Sam thought they had. In her memory it seemed far too dreamlike to be true. She could ask Madison for confirmation, if she could work out how to get to the question without sounding like a fool. Or she could talk to Catalina. Except the thought of doing that made Sam's knees turn to water and her lungs try to work backward.

Sam clenched her fists. This was stupid. She was going to have to talk to Catalina, and would do so, just as soon as she sorted out the muddle in her head and heart. Then she could find out what Catalina was wanting, and expecting, from her—which was when the real awkwardness took over. Something very close to panic swept through her.

Sam's knees cracked into something hard. The Barn was too cluttered not to watch where she was going. Sam looked down, and there was Catalina, off to the side, hunched over the table and totally ignoring her and the other castaways. The panic dissolved in a swamp of disappointment, but it could return in an instant. All it would take was for Catalina to turn around.

"There has to be something in here that will help us." Floyd claimed everyone's attention.

At the sound of his voice, Catalina raised her head. Sam immediately focused on Floyd.

"What sort of thing are we looking for?" Babs asked.

"Use your imagination."

"Yeah, right."

"No. I mean that. We've just proved guns are useless, except for getting its attention. So think of something less obvious."

"Okay." Babs stopped by of a rack of shelves. "Do you think we can buy it off with Jorge's treasure?"

"Hey. That's mine and not for giving away to monsters." Neither Babs nor Jorge were being serious.

Floyd shook his head, smiling. "Okay, kiddies, separate. And like I said, use your imagination." He waved them away.

Babs and Jorge headed in one direction, while Horatio and Torvold went in another. Sam stayed close to Floyd, getting just far enough from Catalina's table so she could sneak occasional peeks, without being too obvious.

Floyd was playing with the mechanical arm. "If there was a way to get this to the tower, do you reckon it would be strong enough to hold the Minotaur?"

"Maybe, but I doubt it would be quick enough to catch him."

"True." He put down the control glove and moved on. "We could do with hand grenades."

"What are they?"

"Explosives, like gunpowder, but you throw them. The Greeks had something they call apples of destruction, which sounds close." Floyd sighed. "Though there's no guarantee they'll work. The bullets didn't even graze its skin."

Sam stood where she could peer around the screen for the drain. Catalina had her head bent over her books. They had kissed, and they were going to have to talk about it. Maybe after she and Floyd finished in the Barn. Or a bit later. Sam's mouth grew dry and she swallowed. Tomorrow might work.

She sighed and ran her hand though her hair. For now, she needed to concentrate on her task. The rack of swords caught Sam's eye, eight in total. Was sharp the right word to describe them? In Yaraha's demonstration, it was as if they melted a line through whatever the edge touched rather than cut. Sam picked one up.

The weight was well balanced, and the grip was firm. The blade had been crafted to look and feel like a falchion, although it was not made of iron or steel, of that Sam was sure. The blade shimmered, not as sunlight on metal, but like heat rising off baked sand. It seemed alive, as did two more. However, the five other swords were dull and inert.

"What have you found, Sam?" Floyd called from the other side of the screen.

"These falchions."

"The whats?"

"This." Sam held up the sword, then tugged a rusty iron rod free from a pile of scrap metal. It was heavy in her hand, a foot long and three inches in diameter.

"Oh, them. I'm not sure if—"

"Stand back a moment." Sam waved him aside. She pulled back the falchion, then threw the rod high in the air, and sliced at it as it fell. The rod landed on the ground in two pieces. If it had been deflected in its path, Sam had not been able to spot it. "If that can't take a Minotaur's head off, I don't know what will."

"Yes. I'd thought of the swords. Trouble is, you'd have to get inside hitting range. And you'll only have one blade to go at it, while the Minotaur will have four axes to return the favor."

"There's more than one sword here."

Horatio wandered over. "How many people have the training to use a sword? I mean, I do, as a naval officer, but who else?"

"I've been practicing since I went to sea. Nothing formal, but I think I'm all right with one," Sam said.

"So it would be me and you then. I suppose we could have a cutlass each, and the others could distract the Minotaur's attention. Then—"

"Hang on there," Floyd interrupted. "Are you saying you don't think I could handle one of these swords?"

"Do you have any experience?"

"How much do I need?"

"Years," Sam and Horatio answered together.

Floyd measured up to Horatio and flexed his arm muscles so that even the bulges had bulges. "You're saying you think I couldn't beat you?"

"I'm saying you couldn't beat either of us, me or Sam."

"We'll put it to a test." Sam handed the lethal falchion to Horatio, before things got out of hand.

On her tour with Yaraha, she had noticed a box of blunt practice swords and padding. She returned and passed one set to Floyd, then slipped on the quilted jacket and helmet.

Grinning, Floyd waved his sword experimentally, testing the weight. "You seriously think you can beat me? You may be a tough cookie, but..." He flexed his muscles again.

"If you'd spent as much time training as I have, no, I wouldn't stand a chance. As it is..." Sam shrugged rather than finish the sentence. "So come on."

In fact, Floyd nearly made the first hit, because Sam was left dumbstruck by his ham-fisted attack. Floyd swung the sword high over his shoulder and brought it down with an audible shish. Sam deflected it at the last moment, letting her wrist twist so Floyd's sword missed her without losing momentum. The force of his own wild swipe pulled him off balance and Sam tapped her sword on the back of his helmet.

"You're dead."

Floyd frowned and stepped back. "Okay. Try again." He hoisted his sword for another bludgeoning overhead. This time, Sam did not wait and stabbed at his armpit as soon as his body was exposed.

"You're dead."

His third and fourth attacks met the same result.

"You're dead."

Floyd's expression hardened behind the grill on his helmet. The smile was gone. He launched a frenzied onslaught that continued unabated even as Sam tapped out the hits. "You're dead, you're dead, you're dead, and you're dead."

The last inept slash left him again off balance and facing away from her. Rather than let the pointless exercise continue, Sam knocked his legs from under him so he landed on his back and touched the tip of her sword to his throat.

"Do you want me to say it again?"

Floyd's face was set in a dogged grimace, but then it faded. "Okay. I get it. You win." He chuckled and rolled away.

Horatio spoke up. "And that's without Sam pointing out if you'd had one of the alien cutlasses, there were at least three occasions when you'd have jolly well cut your own leg off."

Floyd sat on the ground, with the practice sword balanced across his knees. "So it's just you two with the swords then? The rest of us are distractions. You're happy with that?"

"Happier than I would be fighting the wretched brute with you beside me, waving a cutlass around like a wild thing. You could take someone's head off. Well, we're rather hoping to do that to the Minotaur, but you know what I mean."

Sam tugged off her helmet and shook her hair out. It was getting longer than she was used to. She offered a hand to help Floyd to his feet. "I'm happy with it too."

Catalina had left her books. "You can't. It would be insane."

"It's an idea to play with. Nothing more at the moment," Floyd said. "We need to work out how Sam and Horatio can get close enough to hit the thing without losing their own limbs. And until we've sorted that out, we don't have a battle plan."

Catalina glared at everyone except for Sam, who she pointedly ignored. "Give me that." She snatched the falchion from Horatio and picked at the handle. A flap sprung open. She flipped something inside and the blade became inert, like the dead swords on the rack. "If you're going to walk around with them, you should put them in safe mode."

"Good grief. How did you know to do that?" Horatio said.

"I read about it in a book."

Catalina flounced away, still without looking in Sam's direction. She was angry. That much was obvious. Maybe even furious, and it probably was to do with them kissing. Sam bit her lip. But was it because she ran away afterward, or because they kissed in the first place? They had to talk, and tomorrow was not an option. Sam knew she had to work out what to say and do. And work it out quickly. She needed to think. After returning the practice swords and armor to the box, Sam left the Barn.

❖

The view was not the only thing Sam liked about sitting on the deck of the docking station. Even on the most humid of days, a fresh breeze blew, and it was far enough up so the scent of alien flowers did not overwhelm that of the sea. Sam drew in a deep breath. Normally, it calmed her thoughts, allowing her to sort what was important, but not right now.

Sam pressed her fingers against her mouth. Her lips felt strange, almost as if they were developing a mind of their own and hatching plans to betray her. How would she keep them under control? Those lips had kissed Catalina, and the memory both thrilled and terrified her. She was going to have to talk to Catalina, and maybe even kiss her again, but first they had to talk.

In part it was easy. She needed to apologize for running away and try to explain how, after years of living a disguise, she had been caught off guard and had reacted without thinking. She had spent too long clamping down on her emotions. Her brains had been scrambled when she realized what she was doing.

But what was Catalina thinking, feeling? Sam was certain anger was part of it. Might disgust and outrage also be there? Sam dug into her memory. Who had moved first? Sam thought it was Catalina, but she was not sure. Had she grabbed Catalina without invitation or encouragement? In which case she had a lot more to apologize for.

The last bit was the most awkward. If Catalina had moved first, was it simple curiosity, a spur-of-the-moment, never to be repeated mistake, or was she serious? And how on earth to phrase the questions to find out? Sam needed to work out the answers quickly, because the longer she delayed, the more apologizing she would have to do.

Sam heard footsteps on the steps. Someone was coming to ride a flying platform. She did not turn to see who, in case it was Catalina. Despite the need to talk, she wanted a little while longer, to get her thoughts in order—or was it to build up her nerve?

The new arrival stopped. Sam waited for whoever it was to get in a platform and leave, but instead when the footsteps resumed, they came toward where she was sitting. The sound was soft, as if the person was tiptoeing. A sixth sense sent prickles down Sam's spine. She twisted away from the edge, rising to her knees in the same motion.

"Hey. I was going to say boo. See if you jumped." A teasing smile lit Jorge's face. Had Sam seen another emotion first? Something gone before she could place it?

"You were thinking I might fall in?"

"No. Of course not. Otherwise I would not have done it."

The smile was still in place, but all was not right with Jorge. Sam could feel it. She got to her feet and moved farther from the edge. He had a plan in mind. Was he going to try to kiss her? He definitely carried some intention toward her.

Jorge stood by the edge, in the same spot where Sam had been sitting. He put a fist on his hip, then pointed at the water. "Hey! Look there."

Sam did not move. Something was off with Jorge, and she was fairly sure it had nothing to do with a misplaced romantic impulse.

Jorge sighed. "You're not going to come and look?"

"No."

"Then I'll do it this way." He pulled a knife from under his shirt.

"Jorge!"

"I'm sorry. But you have to understand. I promised to look out for my little brother."

"What?"

"He's set on throwing away his life so his woman will get a place on the plane. I must make sure there'll be enough space for him. Me too, of course, although that truly is a lesser worry."

Sam was struck by an idea. "It wasn't hunters who got Charles and Piracola. You killed them."

"But of course."

"You murdered them."

"If you want to look at it that way."

What other way was there? "Piracola was your friend."

"But Rico is my brother. I promised our mother, on her deathbed, I would always look out for him." Jorge was circling right, cutting her off from the stairs, trying to back her toward the edge. "I really am sorry, but I have no choice."

He genuinely did look regretful, but Sam was unconvinced. From the way he handled the knife, he was experienced in its use as a weapon. Jorge had killed before ever setting foot on Atlantis.

Sam needed to move while she had a chance. She took three dancing steps to one side and then darted back. The sudden switch in direction was almost quick enough for her to weave past him, but Jorge caught her ankle with a glancing kick. Sam fell but rolled back up to her feet. Jorge moved to again cut her off from the stairs. He slashed with the knife, forcing her to retreat, forcing her closer to the edge.

Sam took her eyes from the knife just long enough to check her position. The deck was a good thirty feet up. Falling to the ground was as likely to be fatal as landing in the sea, but could she climb down the side?

"Don't bother looking to see who is there. You cannot shout for help. I made sure nobody was near before I came up."

"Then you did not check well enough." Torvold appeared at the top of the stairs, holding his axe.

Jorge spun to face him. "What are—"

"Ah, Jorge, my grandfather was a very wise man, else Eric the Red would not have chosen him as foster father to young Leif. My grandfather told me to watch and listen well to a man who has lived when all with him have died. If he is telling the truth, I might hear good advice, and if he is lying, I should be very careful. I listened to what you said, and I have watched you, ever since you come back with the tale of the hunters. I also went to the farm and looked for scraps of bone and skin. I did not find them, but I did find blood. What did you do with poor Charles and Piracola? Did you stab them and dump their bodies in the sea?"

"No." Jorge took a step back. "All right, yes, but there are too many of us. I was just—"

Without warning, he leapt at Sam, knife slashing for her throat. Sam threw herself aside at the last moment. A line of fire burned across her left shoulder. She hit the ground and rolled away, but suddenly the deck was no longer beneath her. Her hips went over, leaving her legs dangling in midair. Jorge loomed above her, lifting his foot, ready to kick. Sam's toe touched on a strut. It gave just enough support to let her move and avoid him, although at the expense of slipping a few more inches off the deck. She flailed wildly and grabbed his ankle, stopping her slide.

Now Jorge was the one in trouble. His arms stuck out straight as he struggled to regain his balance. His body arched back. He jerked his ankle free from Sam's grasp, but when his foot came down it was not on the deck. Jorge pitched forward and fell. He hit the sea with a splash.

Sam could no longer find the strut. She was scrabbling, trying to reach anything to pull herself back to safety. And then Torvold was there, clasping her wrist and hauling her onto the deck.

Still on her knees, Sam looked over the edge, at the water below. Jorge had surfaced and was frantically swimming for the embankment. Would he be able to pull himself out? The question was irrelevant. Sam saw a shadow flow under the surface of the waves, changing shape, moving in with lightning speed. Did he sense it coming? Jorge looked up, desperate, imploring. He did not get a chance to cry out before the sea boiled red.

❖

The cut was not deep, little more than a scratch. Sam felt foolish at the amount of attention she was receiving over it. She sat on the edge of her bed, with Babs kneeling behind her. Liz and Madison were also in the room, both watching and offering far more advice and sympathy than was called for.

Babs had insisted on washing Sam's shoulder, and was now dabbing at it with a bloodstained cloth. "It's a clean cut, but could do with a stitch or two. How are our supplies?"

"We have needle and thread, but it's not surgical grade, and we've been out of anesthetic for a long time."

"Hmmm. Still might be a good idea."

"I'll be fine." Sam had gone through the experience of having a wound stitched before and was not overly keen on repeating it.

"You'll need to take this off and get it washed. It's soaked in blood." Babs picked at the band Sam had wrapped around her breasts. The binding had been necessary when she was passing as a boy, and she had kept it for comfort when running and jumping.

"The boob-tube bra." Doubtless Madison was trying to be helpful, although the name meant nothing to Sam.

"I'll do it later."

Sam was already feeling overexposed. The precautions she needed to take aboard ship had become deep-rooted habits. The last person to see her bare chest had been her father, when she was still young enough not to need the band.

There was a knock on the door. "Can I come in? I have to talk to Sam." The desperate voice belonged to Ricardo.

"Yeah. She's decent," Madison called out before Sam had a chance.

The door opened. Ricardo burst in and fell to his knees before Sam. He gave vent to a long stream of Spanish that made as much sense as Madison's English. However, Sam had no difficulty working out it was an emotional apology. Ricardo's tone said it all. Kali followed him in, but hung back by the doorway.

"It wasn't your fault. You aren't responsible for what Jorge did." Sam finally got a chance to fit a word in.

"He is my brother."

"But he's not you."

"Charles and Piracola...he...I don't understand how he could do it. Yes, in the past, Jorge has killed people. I know it. But only when there was no other way."

He would say that. Sam kept the thought to herself.

"He tried to kill you." Tears rolled down Ricardo's face. "I'm so sorry."

Sam reached down and hooked the shoulder of his shirt. She urged him to his feet, then wrapped him in a hug. "I'm sorry for you, too. I'm over the scare, and the cut will heal. But you've lost someone you loved. And you've not just lost him, your memories will be tainted." With all his faults, her father had left Sam with nothing but fondness when she thought of him.

"Why did he do it? Why?"

What should she say? Before Sam could work out an answer, Ricardo returned her hug, which sent a stab of fire though her shoulder. She gave gasp of pain and Ricardo jumped back, hands held up.

"I'm sorry. I'm sorry."

Kali came forward and put her arm around him. "Everyone knows that. Now you have seen that Sam is not seriously injured. You should leave her to be tended."

Ricardo nodded, then looked at Babs. "And I'm sorry for Charles.

I know you were close. I can't believe Jorge would have done that. We were a team. We were all friends. I'm sorry."

"I don't blame you. Nobody does," Babs said. "You should take him home, Kali. See if you can get him to calm down."

"Yes." Kali urged Ricardo to move. "Come, my love. We should go."

The door had barely closed when there was another knock. Catalina entered. Her eyes fixed on Sam, but when she spoke, it was to Liz.

"I've been to a clinic in the tower, to see what was there." She held up several items. "This is what the machines thought we needed."

"Fantastic. What have you got?" Babs held out her hands eagerly.

"I'm not sure." Catalina stood by the bed and switched to looking everywhere except at Sam. She held up a short tube with a lever at the end. "The writing on the side says, *Blow mist with no feeling.*"

"Spray anesthetic. It will take away the pain," Liz translated.

Sam felt Babs move. "Here. You do it, Cat."

After a moment of hesitation, Catalina took Babs's place on the bed. Sam bowed her head, bracing herself for the touch of Catalina's hand on her bare skin. She heard Catalina suck in a breath. "Maybe I should have got more."

"Use what you've got. We can go back to the clinic," Liz said. "That was good thinking."

Sam heard a hiss, and felt a fine rain on her shoulder. Instantly, the burning vanished, but then Catalina's hand brushed the back of her neck, and she had to clench her teeth.

"Sorry. Did that sting?"

"No."

In fact, Sam could no longer feel anything. She heard the hiss of the spray again, but her shoulder was numb. However, the rest of her was not. It took all Sam's self-control not to react as Catalina's hands moved over her neck, arm, and back. Did Catalina have any idea the effect her touch produced? Sam tried to pretend she was somewhere else while the conversation carried on around her.

"I was given these by the machine in the clinic as well," Catalina said.

"What are they?" Liz asked.

"I'm not sure. There's a jar of paste and cloth strips, with glue on one side."

"The paste might be antiseptic."

"That would be a good thing?"

"Very."

"Any idea what antiseptic would be in ancient Greek?"

"I couldn't begin to guess."

"It says the sticky cloth strips have *Defense against cleanliness*."

Liz looked surprised, and then her expression cleared. "Washproof sticking plasters."

"Sticking plasters?" Madison sounded confused. "You mean Band-Aids?"

"Same sort of thing, dear. I very much doubt that Johnson & Johnson had a supply contract with the aliens."

"These look like suture strips." Babs waved something around. "Not as good as stitches, but they'll help."

Sam kept her head down. Finally, Catalina stuck a large cloth strip across the length of the cut. Sam flexed her arm. Thanks to the spray, her shoulder was completely free of pain.

"So, Sam, how do you feel?" Liz asked.

"Much better. Thank you."

"Would you like us to leave you alone now?" Liz's voice held a touch of humor.

"Yes, please." Actually, Sam wanted Catalina to stay.

"You can shower, get clean clothes, and we'll see you at dinner. It says the dressing is washproof, but if it comes off, let someone know and we can redo it."

"Yes. And thank you."

They left. Catalina did not even glance back as the door closed. Left alone in her room, Sam buried her face in her hands. She had been trying to work out what to say to Catalina, but did Catalina want to hear it?

❖

"Okay, folks, listen up." Floyd stood by the fountain in the common room. "Here's the plan. If anyone has any objections or suggestions, now's your time to speak up."

Sam looked around the room. Everything felt very serious.

"I think you all know bits of what I'm going to say, but I want to tie it together, so everyone sees the whole picture." Floyd held up one of the swords from the Barn, currently deactivated. "The only thing we have that stands a chance of hurting the Minotaur are these plasma blades. For the name, you can thank Liz."

"That doesn't mean I have a bloody clue how they work," Liz said. "Cat found out about them in a book. It says there's nothing they can't cut. The plasma bit just stops Sam and Horatio from arguing over whether they're falchions or cutlasses."

Floyd continued. "Although they can't agree on the name, Sam and Horatio both have the experience to use them well, but it means they'll have to get in close and personal with the Minotaur. Even with their training, they won't last long, without help from the rest of us. So next up..."

He put down the sword and held up a coil of the same thin rope Sam had taken with her on the expedition to Old Town. It was, presumably, alien technology since even Madison had no idea what it might be made of. "We have this. And fortunately, we have lots more back in the Barn, a whole bale of it. To date, the only thing we've found that can cut it are the plasma blades. It's super light, but won't break, and won't stretch. Yaraha is going to put his fishing skills to use and make it into a net. If you'd like to volunteer to tie knots, go see him. As I said, it's lightweight. So light it can be carried by..." He glanced at Madison. "Not drains?"

"Drones."

"Right. We'll have four people, each controlling a drone. Those four will need to practice, so they can work together. With luck, they'll get the Minotaur wrapped up, but even if they don't, it won't be able to pay so much attention to Sam and Horatio. On top of that, two others will be armed with rifles. They won't do the Minotaur any damage, but they will get its attention. When I finish here, we'll go outside and find out who're our best marksmen. We don't want anyone hit by crossfire. And as a final point, I'd remind everyone not to leave this equipment lying around when you're not using it. The last thing we want is for the caretakers to blow our plans by tidying stuff away."

Floyd walked to the rear wall and chalked a large circle on it, then drew another, much smaller circle close by and connected the two with a double line. He finished by putting several small hash strokes across the twin lines and a cross on the larger circle, directly opposite.

"Liz and Cat have been able to view the control room using the surveillance cameras in the tower. This is our entrance." He tapped the cross. "The terminal Liz needs is in here, and that's where the Minotaur is." Floyd tapped the smaller circle. "It never leaves this little room, and it's way too cramped to tackle it in there. We need to lure it down the flight of steps in the hall to here." He tapped the bigger circle. "A loud noise ought to do it, but we want the Minotaur to move into the middle of the room and not chase people around the edge. So finally, we need someone to volunteer to be a decoy, to make the Minotaur chase them down the hallway and out into the open room."

"Me." Torvold stood up. "I will taunt the mother-lover."

"Okay, Torry, but I think the word you want is motherfucker."

"I know that. But I was being polite. There are ladies present."

Floyd briefly covered his eyes with his hand. "Right. Last couple of roles. Babs will stay with the *Okeechobee Dawn.*"

"I'd rather come with you guys. I want to do my bit," Babs said.

"We can't risk having you hurt. Getting us away will be enough." Floyd smiled at her. "Kali won't be coming with us either."

"My mother was working in—"

"I know, Kali. You've told us. But you're what, eight months gone now? You can stay and help Babs." Floyd's expression lost all trace of humor. "So last thing before we go for target shooting. The seaplane can only take seven, including Babs. If—and it's a big if—if we all survive the battle with the Minotaur, three people won't be able to get aboard. But that doesn't mean you'll be left to drown when Atlantis goes under. Once we've dealt with the Minotaur, Liz will be able to get into the control room. And, well, she'll be staying there, but the rest of us can leave."

Liz was staring at her feet. She clearly did not want to meet anyone's eyes. Sam could not blame her.

Floyd cleared his throat. "She'll give us two hours to get back here, which should be long enough. Those who haven't got a place on the seaplane can set off in the *Inflatable* and get out of range of the whirlpools. Between Liz's graph and what the Greeks wrote, we expect Atlantis to make one final jump to 2025 before the spaceship departs.

After this happens, whoever's in the boat will be able to use a compass, and ought to make land in a few days. However, there's no saying which year they'll be stranded in. So the only fair thing is to draw lots."

"No." Ricardo spoke up. "I volunteer for the *Inflatable*. We all know what Jorge did. You say it wasn't my fault, but I am his brother, and I know he acted for me, in part." His eyes were fixed on the ceiling. "Just look after Kali and the baby for me."

Kali was clearly about to argue but got drowned out by Torvold. "I volunteer too. I will go in the *Inflatable*. For centuries, there were Vikings living in Greenland, long before this Columbus fellow. If they are there, I can show them the outboard motor. My name will be bigger than Leif's. He will be jealous."

"I also volunteer," Yaraha said. "The year meant nothing to Piracola. It means nothing to the land."

Floyd looked between them. "You three are sure about this?" They all nodded.

The door opened. A caretaker scuttled in and started cleaning the chalk diagram off the wall.

"Okay. That's our cue to go outside and see who's the best shot."

Everyone gathered on the lawn. Floyd held up a rifle. "I know several of you have used an AK-47 before, but this is a bit different. It's called an FN FAL."

"An F-ing fal? Sounds serious," Torvold said.

"No, it's…ah, never mind, buddy. The AK is easy to use and maintain, and we have boxes of ammo in the Barn. Just about every Joe who's turned up since World War Two has had one. The FAL packs more punch. It still probably won't hurt the Minotaur, but it should do a better job of distracting it. However, we don't want anyone getting shot by accident. So let's see how you do for speed and accuracy." He held the rifle out. "Who wants to shoot first?"

Madison stepped forward. "I'll give it a go."

Floyd trotted to the far end of the lawn and placed five sweet potatoes on a low wall, then returned to Madison. "Right. See how many you can hit, taking no more than three seconds between shots." He pointed to the FAL. "You'll want it in semi-automatic mode. The—"

"It's okay. I know." Madison raised the rifle. Five shots rang out with barely a pause. All of the potatoes were gone.

Floyd was silent for the space of a dozen seconds, then drew a deep breath. "So, you've shot one before then, Maddy?"

"Dude, I'm from Texas."

❖

Sam threaded the cord through and pulled the last knot tight. She shook out the corner of the net. It felt light as fine lace. "I think my side's done."

Yaraha was also finishing off. "We just need to attach a drain in each corner."

"Madison said they're drones."

"What does either name mean?" He smiled. "Whatever they're called, we can do it first thing tomorrow, and start practicing. I'll let Liz, Cat, and Rico know."

Sam stood and stretched. Her shoulder felt sore. Fortunately, it was on her left side so would not affect her swordplay, but she wondered if she should get someone to look at it, and maybe spray on more of whatever it was in the tube. She flexed her arm again. The fire was definitely heating up. Hours bent over the net tying hundreds of sheet bend knots had not been good for it, but maybe a night's sleep would sort things out.

"I'll be off then. Good night."

"Good night. And thanks for your help."

Sam grinned. "My life depends on this net. I'll be closest to the Minotaur. I wanted to make sure you did it right."

Outside, dusk was sweeping over the world. The last bands of pink were fading on the horizon. Blue dots sparkled over the pathways, providing just enough light to guide her way. The buildings glowed like honey in the up-lights. Sam breathed in the scent of the unearthly flowers. Atlantis no longer felt so strange to her, so alien.

In a few days, if all went well, she would be leaving, and the island would be on the bottom of the ocean. And if it did not go well, she would be dead. Either way, her time in Atlantis was coming to an end. She would need to make a new home, either in the world of 2025, or in the hereafter. How would she get on with angels? Sam entertained herself with ideas of joining Torvold, drinking and singing in Valhalla.

She was approaching her room in the Squat when somebody

hurtled out of the dark and collided with her—on her left side, as luck would have it. Sam could not bite back a yelp of pain.

"Oh, I'm sorry." It was Catalina. "I wasn't looking where I was going."

Sam straightened up. "I'm fine."

"No, you're not. I should take a look at your shoulder. I've got the things from the clinic in my room, but—" She broke off, pressing a hand against her forehead. "I'm just so angry."

No news there. "Yes, I'm really sorry too. I didn't mean to—"

"No, not with you." Catalina sounded on edge, distracted. Her arm dropped. "I had an idea, the clinic gave the medicine for you. I tried asking about Liz—her cancer. The machine said…" She drew a deep breath. "It said she wasn't worth saving. She should be disposed of. As if she were a broken toy. It wasn't that it couldn't help her. It wouldn't make the attempt. I've spent two hours fighting with the controls, and I got nowhere. In the end I kicked the front." She gave a humorless laugh. "The evil thing diagnosed a bruised toe and gave me more of the pain spray, without even being asked."

"The aliens didn't value human lives. We knew that."

"Yes. But I'd had a flash of hope and then I was angry. Which was why I wasn't paying attention to where I was going." She wiped a hand across her eyes.

Catalina was clearly upset. Sam thought about putting an arm around her, but that was probably not a good idea, even though Catalina had just claimed not to be angry with her. Apart from how the gesture might be received, the fire in Sam's shoulder had cranked up a notch.

"It's all right. I wasn't watching out either."

"I haven't been stabbed. I should look at your shoulder for you. That's if you don't mind." Catalina ended on a tentative note.

"No. I was going to ask someone. The cut has stiffened up. I was on the net, working, and since you've got the stuff, it's um…yes." It would give them the chance to talk, as long as she could string together a complete sentence.

CHAPTER FIFTEEN

Catalina pointed to the bed. "If you could sit there and take your shirt off."

This was going to be awkward. Maybe she should have thought it through first. Catalina busied herself, digging for the medical supplies in her locker while she pulled her thoughts together. They could do with a chaperone to reassure Sam and avoid misunderstandings, but it was too late now. On the other hand, Sam had agreed to come. Maybe they could become friends after all.

When she turned round, Sam was sitting cross-legged on the bed, with her head down. Catalina got up behind her.

"I need to remove the old dressing." She teased the sticky strips off as gently as she could, although Sam still gasped. "Sorry. Did that hurt?"

"No." Sam's voice sounded strained. "How does it look?"

"Not too bad. A little inflamed maybe. No infection."

Sam kept her head down, staring at her ankles while Catalina worked. The trick was to concentrate on the task and not to be distracted by the urge to run her hands over Sam's back. In a short while, the job was finished.

"There. All done. You can go."

Sam did not move. "Catalina?"

"Yes?"

"The night before last, when we kissed—"

Catalina's stomach contracted. "Yes. I know. I'm sorry."

"You're sorry?"

"It was wrong of me."

"Why?" Sam twisted around.

"I gave in to an impulse. I admit, I'd been thinking about you. But I shouldn't have..."

"What?"

"It wasn't something you wanted to do. You ran away."

"I ran away because..." Sam shook her head. "It wasn't because I didn't want to kiss you."

"Then why?"

Sam looked as if she was trying to say four different things at once, without making a sound. Then her face cleared. She leaned forward and pulled Catalina into her arms. Their lips met in a long, soft kiss. It did not make sense, but Catalina did not care. She felt strangely light-headed. She sank back onto the bed, drawing Sam down with her. She needed to hold Sam, to kiss her, and feel their bodies pressed together.

Sam pulled away and stared into her eyes. "Do you..."

"What?"

"It's just, I'm not sure, and I don't know what you, or why..."

"Do you have a question in there?"

Sam looked uncomfortable. "What do you want from me?"

"I don't know. I've never kissed anyone else."

"Nor have I."

"You said you'd had women as lovers."

"No. I said I wanted to. Doesn't mean I ever had a chance to do anything about it. So I'm not experienced, or anything." Sam swallowed visibly.

Catalina laughed. "It probably doesn't help if I said I've read some books."

"Books!"

"My parents would have been horrified if they knew all the things ancient writers committed to paper. But they didn't know Greek, to censor what I was reading."

"What did the books say?"

"They were mainly written to excite male readers." With hindsight, Catalina realized maybe she had found them just a little more interesting than was normal for a demure Spanish noblewoman.

"Like whores outside brothels. Two of them will put on a show to lure in customers."

"You weren't tempted?"

Sam shook her head. "It always seemed cheap and false. And there's nothing false about how I feel right now, but if you're just playing…"

"No. I'm not playing games." Catalina ran her hand though Sam's hair.

Which left the question of what she wanted. They could kiss a while, then Sam could leave, and they could exchange burning looks, the way tortured lovers did in ballads. The minstrels would draw the tension out for twenty verses or more. Then, like as not, it would end in tragedy as one, or both, died. Death or marriage—they were the only options. It did not bode well. There was no church in Atlantis, and death was all too likely. Nor did they have months, or however long twenty verses might take in real life.

So what did she want?

"I'm sure we can work things out." Catalina ran her hand under Sam's shirt, feeling the warmth of her skin.

Sam went to touch her face but stopped. "I've been sweating and my hands are filthy from the Barn."

"You should shower."

Sam sat up. "All right. Do you want me to come back here afterward?"

Catalina was suddenly quite sure what she wanted. "No. I want you to shower here."

Without giving herself time to change her mind, Catalina rolled off the bed, grabbed Sam's hand, and pulled her into the washroom. She slipped her hands under Sam's waistband, eased it over her hips, and let the shorts drop to the floor.

"You're not going to wait for me next door?"

"No."

Catalina tugged her own clothes off, bundled them all together, and dropped them in the laundry bin. She hit the water button.

"Normally, I might have wanted you to woo me for a few months, and then ask my father for my hand in marriage, but we don't have months, we can't go to see my father, and he'd say no anyway." Catalina laughed. The idea was actually quite funny.

She drew Sam close and turned her face up for another kiss. The water streamed over their heads, getting in the corners of Catalina's mouth. It rolled down her shoulders and formed a pool in the hollow where their breasts were pressed together. Hot showers had always been sensual, but this was an entirely different experience. Sam's hands ran up her sides, over her arms, through her hair. The touch sent tingling waves through her.

Sam broke from the kiss. "Are you sure you've not done this before?"

"Yes. I'd have remembered."

Catalina wrapped her arms around Sam, flattening her palms on the hardness of Sam's shoulder blades. The washproof dressing was, fortunately, living up to its name. She slid her hands down Sam's back, examining each bone, each muscle. Sam's skin was hot and slick with the running water. Catalina broke away from Sam's mouth and nuzzled her neck, licking and nipping. Sam gave a whimper.

"Sorry. Did I hurt you?"

"No. But I don't know how much longer I can stay standing. My knees are…"

Catalina's own knees were not as firm as normal, but she was not ready to leave the shower yet. A compulsion was building inside her, a need to be touched, an ache that could not be denied or made to wait.

Catalina turned, so Sam was braced in the corner, then caught hold of Sam's wrist and brought her hand down to where it had to be. The shock coursed through her. Catalina gasped and fell forward, clinging on to Sam to stay upright.

"Please, I want you to…"

There was no need for Catalina to say more. Sam's lips brushed her forehead, even as Sam's fingers moved, exploring, pressing her legs slightly apart to allow better access. Sam's fingers sent waves of pleasure through her, both relieving and increasing the need. Catalina buried her face in Sam's neck.

The waves built inside Catalina, carrying her ever higher, until she hit the top of the crest. Her body shook in time to the pulses, radiating from the touch of Sam's hand. Without the support of Sam's free arm, she would have fallen.

Catalina gasped, taking mouthfuls of air. Then she breathed in water and started to cough and laugh at the same time.

"I need to lie down. Do you think we're clean enough?"

Sam's face held a mixture of tenderness, desire, and wonder. Without answering, she hit the button for the dryer.

Back on the bed, Catalina raised herself on one elbow. She looked the length of Sam's body, considering every inch of skin, and finished, staring into Sam's eyes. "Are you tired?"

"Not really."

Catalina smiled. "Good. Because I've no intention of letting you go to sleep yet."

❖

Catalina woke slowly. She felt warm, comfy, and very safe—ridiculously so, all things considered. What time was it?

Beside her, Sam gave a half snore and rolled onto her back. Catalina turned so she could lay her head on Sam's good shoulder. Their bodies molded together. A wave of peace and joy flowed through Catalina from her head all the way down to her toes, banishing all anxieties. She had not known it was possible to be so happy. No matter how the day turned out, this was a time to treasure. She lifted her head so she could study Sam's sleeping face.

Her parents had put so much effort into planning Catalina's life, her education, introducing her to the right people at court, selecting a husband—no less than three times. Her parents had been fond of her. Could she put it more forcefully than that? Her two brothers had always been more important to them. While a good marriage for Catalina could further the family fortune, it was her brothers who would carry on the family name.

For the Valasco family, Catalina had been a temporary fixture, a political pawn, a commodity in the marriage market. As a child, she had spent more time with her nanny than she had with her mother. When she boarded the *Santa Eulalia de Merida*, there had been little expectation she would see her parents or family home again. She had shed tears on the dock, more because it was expected than from true grief.

Her parents might have wanted what was best for her, but it came second to what was best for the family. Not that they would have abandoned her to a life of hardship and misery. Had everything gone to plan, Catalina would never had been hungry, or alone, or without shelter or a protector. But would she ever have known a moment of happiness as great as what she felt now, looking at Sam's face?

Sam opened an eye. "What are you thinking, Cat?"

"That—"

There was a rap on the door. "Okay, you two lovebirds. Time to roll." Madison's voice.

"That no matter how today goes, these last three days have been the best of my life."

Sam pulled her down for a gentle kiss. "Same here."

❖

The door whooshed open, revealing the large circular room beyond. Cautiously, Catalina stepped inside and paused, listening. The room was familiar from the monitor screens, but now that she was standing there, it was both larger and colder than expected. A chilling draft blew from vents in the ceiling, high overhead.

Directly opposite the entrance was an arched opening, leading to the control room, and the Minotaur. Then, faintly, Catalina heard it, the thump, thump of heavy footsteps, echoing down the hallway. She swallowed and stepped aside, allowing the other castaways to follow her in.

Wordlessly, they moved around the edge, except for Yaraha and Torvold, who carried the net into the middle. While they laid it out, Catalina considered the people she had come to know and care about.

Floyd and Madison had taken positions on either side of the room. Both looked calm, preoccupied, as they checked their rifles and ammunition. Ricardo was leaning against the wall, his eyes on the ceiling and his lips moving. At the end of his silent prayer, he made the sign of the cross with his free hand. In the other, he held one of the drone controllers, as did Liz.

A familiar, wry smile was on Liz's lips. Madison said she spent last night on the roof, at the spot where Gerard's remains had been found. Catalina's eyes blurred. The last three days had been spent with Sam, whenever she had free time. Too late now to wish she had spoken more with Liz, because however the battle went, they would never again get the chance to sit and pass the hours in friendly conversation.

Blinking rapidly, Catalina dropped her eyes to the drone controller in her own hands. She could not afford to let her concentration lapse. The four pilots would mark out the corners of a square, matching the drone they controlled. The alignment was not necessary, but practice had shown it easier to envision where the drone they piloted was in relation to the others.

A pair of feet appeared in Catalina's field of view. She looked up. Sam stood in front of her smiling and mouthing some words. Were they, "I love you"? Before Catalina could reply, Sam kissed her own fingertips, pressed them to Catalina's lips, then turned away and joined Horatio, a few steps into the room.

The laying out of the net was complete. Yaraha took up position and signaled to the other pilots. Catalina pressed the power button on her controller and placed her thumbs on the flight levers. The drones rose slowly to the ceiling, lifting the net. Sam's and Horatio's plasma blades shimmered into life. Catalina heard twin clicks from the setting of the safety catches on the FALs.

Torvold stood alone in the middle of the room. Floyd gave him a thumbs-up signal and whispered, "Over to you, buddy." The first words spoken aloud since the castaways entered.

Torvold swung his axe in a flamboyant figure of eight, then stalked toward the Minotaur's lair. He planted his feet at the entrance to the hallway.

Catalina felt her stomach turn to ice. Her heart pounded against her rib cage. She could feel her legs shaking. She saw Torvold suck in a deep breath, and then his voice boomed out. Catalina did not understand a word, but it had to be something unflattering in Norse. Everyone froze, waiting.

Torvold was drawing another breath when a savage roar erupted, a primal scream of rage, reverberating from the hallway. He shouted again, this time in English. "And the same goes twice for your mother." He swung his axe again. For a moment, Catalina thought he was about to tackle the Minotaur single-handed, ignoring their plans, but then he turned and ran back to the middle of the room.

The monster burst from the hallway. It was bigger and much, much quicker than Catalina had expected. Its movements put her in mind of a large ape that a troupe of entertainers had brought to the king's court in Spain, bowlegged, but powerful. It charged, bearing down on Torvold, ignoring all else. Maybe it had not noticed the other people. Maybe it was too angry to care. Torvold took a step backward.

The explosive crack of a rifle rang out. The Minotaur flinched and broke from its headlong charge. Its head jerked in Madison's direction.

Then a second shot resounded as Floyd fired from the other side. The Minotaur threw its head back and roared a challenge, brandishing all four axes.

Torvold stood his ground, swinging his axe, demanding the monster's attention. "Come on then, you great big booby."

The Minotaur advanced, but slowly this time, step by step.

Catalina looked up. Already the drones controlled by Yaraha and Liz were descending. She swiveled the levers under her thumbs, bringing her corner of the net down on the Minotaur. Gently, the cords settled on the Minotaur's head, snagging on its curved horns. Surely the monster must have noticed, yet it paid no more attention than if cobwebs were falling from the roof.

Was this going to work? Catalina thumbed the control lever, and her drone dropped to waist height. This drew the first reaction. The Minotaur snarled and struck out with an axe, as if to sweep the net away. The end of the shaft caught in a loop, wrenching the axe to a stop, mid-swing.

Now the Minotaur reacted to the threat. It struck out furiously, but all this achieved was to entwine itself tighter. The drones became ensnared. One was clipped by an axe, and Catalina's was crushed when the Minotaur stumbled to its knees, but their task was done. The Minotaur was bound. Catalina lowered her controller. Sam and Horatio were moving in, as was Torvold, while Floyd and Madison circled in search of a clear shot.

Horatio reached the Minotaur first. One hugely muscled arm punched free of the net. Horatio sidestepped a backswing and whipped his sword across, slicing though the Minotaur's wrist. The axe clanged to the ground. The hand oozed yellow blood, yet still gripped the shaft. The Minotaur bellowed, louder, longer, and deeper than before. Was it anger, or pain?

On the other side, Sam stabbed into the heart of the tangled mass of cord, cutting through body and net. The Minotaur surged upward, another hand broke free, but its head and feet were hopelessly entangled, and the Minotaur crashed back to its knees. Horatio was there, ready. His sword flashed out, plunging deep between the curved horns. The Minotaur lunged at him, its momentum causing the blade to effortlessly slice its own head in half.

Still the monster moved.

Horatio jumped back out of the way, but his foot caught in the net and he went down. Sam moved in closer. Her next strike severed the left leg. The Minotaur collapsed, but its one free hand continued to flail wildly. It was only bad luck that the axe struck Horatio's thigh. Catalina heard the sickening crunch of breaking bone. Horatio had been trying to stand. He collapsed in a spray of red.

Torvold stood behind the monster. He grabbed the net in both hands, hauling it away from Horatio, while Sam continued her attack. She chopped off the hand that had struck Horatio, and then sliced through the Minotaur's neck. The head swung around, trapped in the net by its horns.

And still the Minotaur fought on.

Madison took aim, firing four shots directly into the raw neck stump, producing a splatter of yellow, and at last the monster's movements began to weaken. Torvold picked up Horatio's sword and joined in. The plasma blades were turning the net into lengths of loose cord, but the battle was won. The Minotaur was no longer a threat. Yet, even after it had been cut into a dozen pieces, the fingers still twitched and the eyes rolled in its head.

The castaways gathered around Horatio.

"How is he?" Liz asked.

"'Fraid I won't be able to run very fast," Horatio answered through gritted teeth.

"Broken leg. Losing a lot of blood. But he caught more of the flat than the edge of the axe," Yaraha said.

"He'll need a splint before you move him. Luckily, I thought to bring this." Liz tossed over the tube of pain-relieving spray.

"I will carry you, my friend." Torvold patted Horatio's shoulder.

"Dashed decent of you to offer, old thing, but you might need a bit of help."

"While you sort him out, I'll check on uploading the program." Liz tapped Catalina's arm. "Come with me and help."

The upper room was a tenth the size of the lower one. It was dimly lit, with walls covered in static display screens and control panels. The rows of blinking lights seemed bright in the gloom. Liz pulled Meriones's notes from her bag, along with the memory stick and the alien glove.

She passed the notes to Catalina. "Where's the interface we need?"

"Over there."

The screen flickered to life when Liz placed her gloved hand on it. An aperture, the right size for the memory stick, opened up. Catalina needed only a minute to work through the notes. Having the controls before them made Meriones's instructions far easier to follow than the usual cryptic Greek texts.

"It's all set. You just need to press here. The upload will start, and then..." Catalina bit her lip to stop it from trembling.

"You're not going to start a pointless argument, are you, dear?"

"No. I just wish there was another way."

"So do I, dear. So do I. But at least I'm going to achieve something worthwhile. Go out on a high note."

Catalina wrapped Liz in a hug. "I can't think of anything to say." *Take care*, or some similar trite phrase, would not work.

"Then don't say anything." Liz returned the hug. "Come. Let's see how the others have got on."

Horatio's face was pale. His leg was splinted, using a deactivated sword and several pieces of cord. Another length was tied tightly around his thigh, slowing the flow of blood.

"I'm all set with the upload. I'll give you two hours before I get it running," Liz said. "Now, I want you to bugger off, because I hate big good-byes."

Despite this, the castaways showed no urge to leave. Floyd shuffled his feet. "You can't expect—"

The door opened. Catalina spun around, dreading another Minotaur, even as she recognized the "Meea, meea, meea."

The spider-like caretaker scuttled across the room to the Minotaur's writhing torso. A blaze of brilliant blue-white light spluttered from its front appendages as it started to reattach a piece of leg, for all the world like one of the metalworkers Catalina read of in the Greeks books.

"Shit." Floyd spoke for them all.

Liz's shoulders slumped. "I didn't think about whether caretakers can repair other bio-robots. But I guess it's obvious, really. The buggers can't keep going forever. They're bound to break down from time to time."

Floyd stood over the caretaker, holding his rifle. "There's no point in shooting this one, is there?"

"No, we'll just get more turning up. All we can do is slow down the repair work. Though I don't doubt more will arrive, when this one fails to make progress. You need to go. Now. Run. I'll wait until the Minotaur is getting to a dangerous state, before I start the upload. After that, you'll have as long as it takes the caretakers to repair the sabotage." Liz waved her arms. "So what are you waiting for? Run."

"We can try again another day."

"And hope the Minotaur hasn't learned from this defeat? You're never going to get a better chance. Go. Now." Liz pushed the nearest two people, Ricardo and Madison. "Go."

Floyd resisted a moment longer, but then sharply raised his right hand, palm down, to touch his eyebrow. "Yes, ma'am." He tossed the rifle to her, then turned to the rest. "Okay. Come on, folks. Move out."

He and Torvold bent to pick up Horatio.

"No. Leave me. I'll stay with Liz. Even you two can't carry me and run." Horatio pushed their hands away. "My own silly fault. Too many second helpings."

"You are not serious."

"Yes, I am. You need to run like the clappers. I'll slow you down."

"But—"

"YOU'RE WASTING BLOODY TIME." Catalina had never heard Liz shout before.

The shared paralysis broke. Everyone rushed to the exit, except for Catalina, who stood, refusing to accept they were out of options. There had to be another way. Then Sam grabbed her hand and towed her away. At the door, Catalina grabbed the frame, hanging on for one last look back.

Horatio had slid across the floor to where the caretaker was working. He had reactivated the second plasma sword and was chopping at the Minotaur.

Liz stood in the entrance to the hallway, rifle in hand. "So, tell me, what was your honest impression of Charles Darwin?"

"Well, if you want the truth, he was a bit of a bore. Kept going on about these wretched little birds on a group of islands he'd visited."

The door whooshed shut. Catalina would never see either of them again.

Sam jerked her away. "Come on."

Already, the others were far down the corridor, turning a corner. The control room was deep in the heart of the labyrinth. Catalina put an effort into running. The intended practice had not happened, but this time it was easier to keep her feet under her. Was fear making the difference? Even so, Catalina felt her heart was about to burst by the time they rounded the final corner and saw the others, waiting in the elevator.

Torvold's outstretched arm was holding the door open for them. It clipped Catalina's heel as Sam dragged her in. She had just about regained her balance when her insides lurched and they started the ascent. Sam held her up. Nobody spoke, but she could read the same question on everyone's face. How long did they have? Catalina could imagine the elevator, inching its way up the tower. Surely it had never taken so long before.

The door opened. They spilled out and ran on, through the foyer and out into the pit. Catalina's lungs were on fire. Her breath rasped in her throat and her legs burned. She did not know how she would manage the stairs on the docking station. Then Torvold picked her up and carried her to their goal. Floyd was tapping in the destination code as they piled aboard.

After the frantic race, the flying platform drifted serenely on its journey. Catalina elbowed her way to the control panel. Was there really no "go faster" button? But would she dare press a cryptic Greek command, knowing it might do the opposite of what she expected? The platform glided into the tunnel.

Catalina closed her eyes. What was happening back in the control room? Had the Minotaur been repaired yet? It would surely kill both Horatio and Liz in an instant. Catalina imagined Liz, finger hovering over the upload button, listening to the pounding footsteps, climbing the steps, getting closer. Liz would wait until the very last second. Tears ran down Catalina's face.

Never had the flying platform been so slow. Eons passed before they emerged into sunlight again, but at last they were clear of the tower. Just a quarter mile to go. Catalina could see the docking station and the *Okeechobee Dawn* moored nearby.

They were halfway across the innermost sea when a low, throbbing whistle began. Catalina looked back. The outline of the tower was blurring, shimmering as though seen through a heat haze. A blast of wind buffeted the platform. The sky changed from blue to gunmetal gray, and fog erased the horizon. The reprogrammed caretakers had repaired the Greek sabotage. Atlantis was jumping, a precursor to the alien ship's departure.

The throb got faster, while the pitch of the whistling rose, climbing so high it was pressure, rather than sound. A light blossomed deep inside the tower. Within seconds, it was so bright it turned the walls incandescent. Catalina turned her face away, but felt the heat on the back of her neck. The whistle snapped like a whip-crack, so loud it hurt her ears.

And then nothing. The wind dropped. The sky turned blue.

When Catalina looked back at the tower, at first it seemed nothing had changed, but then it began to crumple inward, like a sand castle on the beach when the tide comes in. The platform coasted to a halt.

"We're falling," Madison shouted.

The platform was sinking, steadily gathering speed, dropping toward the waves. Catalina hit a button. There was no longer anything to risk by the attempt. A jolt, and the platform steadied and continued its flight.

"What did you do?" Floyd asked.

"*Reserve potency in extreme situations*. I started the emergency backup power supply."

Would it be enough? Atlantis was already starting to topple. The islands ahead were thinning as sea washed over the land, while behind the crumbling tower, the other side of the rings were lifting. Eventually, no doubt, the entire island would go under, but for now, as one half sank, the other half rose.

Catalina looked at the newly exposed substructure. It had always been obvious that Atlantis was artificial. Now its true form was revealed, as what had been below water level lifted into view. The island rings were D-shaped bands in cross section, set on the rims of two massive bowls.

Catalina thumped her fist on the control panel. On backup power, the platform was going even slower than before. They glided over the flooded inner island. The docking station was now mere yards away, but the base was submerged. Waves broke around the bottom of the steps, and the seaplane was no longer moored nearby. Surely Babs had not abandoned them.

The flying platform docked, but the deck was tilted at an angle. Catalina clung to a rail to prevent herself from sliding off. Would the piranhas still be active? Or would they be lifeless, without a supply of energy? Catalina gripped still tighter. Regardless, where could they go? Around them, treetops and buildings jutted above the waves, but the lawns and paths were gone.

Atlantis was sinking faster, the slope of the deck getting more acute. Its edge was nearly touching the waves. Catalina looked down at a series of mini-whirlpools forming in the backwash. Then she heard a buzzing. The sound grew louder, closer. The *Inflatable* was coming across the raging water, bouncing from crest to crest, with Kali at the helm.

The spinning whirlpool were getting ever wilder, deeper, faster. Waves surged back and forth, crests splashing spray. Yet, somehow, Kali avoided all hazards, without losing speed. She brought the boat closer to the deck than Catalina would have thought possible, pulsing the motor to keep the boat in place.

"You'll have to jump."

Ricardo went first. Three long steps down the slope and then off. He landed in the boat. Madison, Yaraha, and Torvold followed.

"Will you be all right?" Sam shouted in Catalina's ear.

"One way to find out."

Catalina loosened her grip on the rail. On her last step, her foot slipped on the wet deck and she fell rather than jumped forward. She crashed into the side of the *Inflatable*, head inside, legs in the water. Before she had a chance to move, Torvold grabbed the waistband of her shorts and flipped her in. She landed painfully on a sack containing small hard objects.

Sam and Floyd arrived last. "We're all here."

"Where's Horatio?"

"He got hurt. Stayed with Liz."

"Sit tight then. Here we go." Kali turned up the motor, full throttle. The *Inflatable* leapt forward, across the churning sea. Waves broke over the bow. The inner sea had always been calm and gentle, but not now. The sea was boiling as Atlantis sank. Catalina clung to Sam with one hand and the bench with the other to stop herself from being pitched overboard. Through the salt spray stinging her eyes, she saw the *Okeechobee Dawn* ahead, riding the surf.

"What happened? Did something go wrong?" Kali shouted over the chaos.

"Kind of," Floyd answered. "We didn't allow for a caretaker turning up to repair the Minotaur."

"We wondered about it. When the island started to sink, Babs moved the seaplane away from land, where the waves aren't so wild."

The waters were indeed becoming less violent, although still far from smooth. Yaraha leaned over, "Torvold, you can go. Take Horatio's place in the plane."

"No. You take his place. I will stay in the boat."

Kali cut the motor. "No. You're both going."

"There isn't room."

"Yes, there is, because I'm not leaving that damn fool man of mine."

Ricardo looked shocked. "Kali! You said you'd go on the plane."

"I never did. You're mine. If you think I'm letting you get away, you don't understand me at all."

"But—"

"But nothing."

Babs was waiting in the open door. "Systems are up and running." She grabbed the mooring rope Floyd threw to her.

The castaways scrambled into the seaplane, until only Torvold, Kali, and Ricardo were left.

"Torvold. Get in the plane now. I'm staying with Rico."

Torvold patted Ricardo's shoulder. "My grandfather was a wise man. He told me never to argue with a woman when she uses that tone of voice."

Ricardo closed his eyes. "Okay, go. I'm going to marry a crazy woman."

Torvold pulled himself into the seaplane. As he closed the door he shouted, "And let her drive."

But already Kali had set off, racing the *Inflatable* across the wild water.

Babs called out. "Sit tight. This will be a rough takeoff, if we make it. We don't have seat belts, so just hang on."

"To what?" Torvold asked.

"Anything."

Catalina was wedged into a space on the floor. A noise grew, similar to that of the outboard motor, but deeper—a roar, not a buzz.

Catalina felt the seaplane shake. It was accelerating, faster and faster. Even without being able see out, Catalina knew the speed surpassed anything she had ever experienced. The force squashed her into Sam. The *Okeechobee Dawn* jumped as if it was being kicked by giants. The frame rattled, sounding at the point of falling apart. Then a jolt, bigger than any that had gone before, followed by the sensation of being in an elevator. The front of the plane rose, pressing Catalina still harder into Sam. They were flying.

Torvold could not restrain himself. He struggled to his knees so he could look out the window. "Oh yes. Oh yes. Look. We are like birds."

Catalina joined him. The sea was dropping away below. The last of Atlantis poked through a huge disc of raging water and white surf.

"Can you see the *Inflatable?*" Sam asked.

"No."

"Do you think they'll be all right?"

"I hope so."

The *Okeechobee Dawn* climbed higher. A wisp of fog blurred the scene, and then cleared briefly before more fog swept by. No, not fog Catalina realized. The *Okeechobee Dawn* was flying into the clouds. She looked back for a last glimpse of Atlantis, and then it was gone.

❖

A row of lights appeared on the horizon, beneath the last faint glow of sunset.

"Is that a city?" Catalina asked.

"Yes."

The cockpit was cramped. She and Madison stood behind Babs's chair, stretching their legs and trying not to tread on anyone.

"How big is it?" The lights continued unbroken as far as Catalina could see.

"Depends which city it is. Do we know how far north we are?" Madison asked Babs.

"I'd guess at somewhere around Daytona Beach, but I could be off by miles." She grinned at them. "Shall we say between Jacksonville and Miami?"

"Home sweet home." Floyd was sitting in the chair beside Babs.

His face looked strange, lit only by the instrument panel. "I grew up in Jacksonville, before my folks moved north. I reckon it'll have changed some."

Catalina sat back down beside Sam, making space for the others to look. The size of the city was unsettling. Would this world be home? It was not the one she knew. Then Sam put an arm around her, and the fears vanished. Whatever this world was like, they would face it together.

"How's the gas holding out?" Floyd asked.

Babs tapped the glass over a gauge. "We're fine to make land, but we won't be able to go much farther inland. Safest if we beach first chance we get."

"Okay. I was hoping we could avoid attracting too much attention. But since we can't sneak in without anyone noticing, what story do we give? Any ideas anyone?" Floyd looked around.

"Hey. Wait a minute," Madison said. "You were thinking we could keep Atlantis a secret?"

"It was always a long shot, I guess."

"Duh. Why? My daddy works for cable news. He'll know people. We'll need agents. We're going to be huge, mega-huge, beyond mega-huge. They'll be lining up for us. Press, films, magazines. We can write books. Be on talk shows. Oprah will want us as guests, if she's still going, that is." She smiled back at Catalina and Sam. "Celebrity wedding of the year. Take it from me. We are so made."

"Madison, will everybody be talking like you?" Torvold asked.

"Don't worry. You'll catch on."

Catalina snuggled closer to Sam. The only thing Madison had said that made any sense was the part about books. She had read so many, maybe she could write one. It was more promising than being a guest singer at the opera. Despite all the childhood music lessons, her voice was not good.

Suddenly, a new voice sounded in the cockpit, unfamiliar and strangely distorted. "Attention unknown light aircraft. This is air traffic control. You have entered controlled airspace. Please identify yourself and your destination."

Floyd snatched up a fist-sized object at the end of a coiled line. He pressed a button on the side and held it at arm's length. "So we just tell them the truth?"

"Maybe break it to them gently."

Floyd released the button. "We're requesting permission to make a water landing. Not bothered where, but we're getting low on gas."

"Who are you?" the crackling voice asked.

"Sergeant Floyd Lombardi of the US Coast Guard."

"What was your point of departure?"

"Believe me, buddy, it's a long, long story."

Catalina rested her head on Sam's shoulder and smiled. It was indeed a long story, and it was not over yet.

EPILOGUE

Out in Print Books

Author Event

This Friday, 7:30

Come and hear bestselling author duo

Valasco and Helyer

read from the latest installment of their Pirate Princess series.

Don't miss out on your own signed copy.

Tea, coffee, and light refreshments available

Your Saturday Evening TV

7:00 pm. *Escape From Atlantis*

Celebrity host Madison McDowell makes a welcome return for another series of the hit action game show, bigger, faster, and more extreme than ever before. Madison has promised favorites such as the flying platform slalom and hunters' chase will stay, while adding exciting new challenges for the teams of contestants. Expect a generous serving of fun, thrills, and upsets. In Madison's own words, "Watch out for that minotaur!"

ATLANTEAN SET FOR RECORD PAYOUT

Former US Coast Guard Sergeant Floyd Lombardi is expected to receive the largest ever payout of backdated salary in military history.

Regulations entitle all POW or MIA servicemen to receive full pay, and all eligible promotions during their time of enforced absence. It is believed the government intended to compensate Sgt. Lombardi only for time he spent in Atlantis. However, it has proved impossible to configure the payroll computer to accept the elapse of just 22 years since 1954.

AUCTION MYSTERY GROWS

A new batch of reputedly Atlantean artifacts have been released for auction, fueling speculation. Unconfirmed sources have identified the sellers as a Mr. and Mrs. Garcia, currently residing in the Cayman Islands. A spokesman outside the couple's luxury home where they live with their infant daughter, Elisa, refused to respond to reports that they wish to retain their anonymity until it is confirmed Mr. Garcia will not face prosecution for alleged drug trafficking offenses.

CROWDS TURN OUT FOR ROUND THE WORLD HERO

It was standing room only on the shores of Lake Okeechobee yesterday to see Barbara "Babs" Weinberg complete the last stage of her epic round the world flight in her restored 1930s seaplane, the *Okeechobee Dawn*.

A visibly emotional Ms. Weinberg thanked everyone who had supported her on her historic flight and dedicated her achievement to her friend and former navigator, Charles Wooten. She refused to comment on her plans for the future, except to say, "The adventure won't end here."

SUPREME COURT RULING DUE

Senator Yaraha Timucua is expected to move one step closer today to securing his party's nomination, when the Supreme Court rules on his eligibility for office. What is not in question is that he was born in the region that is now Florida. Arguments have centered on whether this makes him a natural born citizen. However, most legal scholars have described it as "unthinkable" for the ruling to go against him, clearing the way for Senator Timucua to become the first full Native American president of the United States.

Open Lecture

◇————————◇

Leif Ericson as I knew him.

The man, the myth.

by

visiting lecturer Torvold Olavson

Professor of Norse History

University of Reykjavik

4:00 p.m. in lecture hall D

From: Chris.Peterson@DeepwaterVentures.com
To: Michael.Belinski@DeepwaterVentures.com
Cc: Susan.Jacobs@QDKlegal.com

Hi Mike

Just seen the sonar results. We've found it, ▮▮▮▮°N ▮▮▮▮°W, depth 2000m. Good news, it's international waters, but we all know who wants to get their hands on the alien tech. I'm setting up a meeting with our legal guys 2:00 p.m. tomorrow to make sure we're up to speed and know what to expect. We don't want an injunction slapped on us before we can send the sub down.
Regards
Chris

About the Author

Jane Fletcher (www.janefletcher.co.uk) is a GCLS award-winning writer and has also been short-listed for the Gaylactic Spectrum and Lambda Literary Awards. She is a recipient of the Alice B. Reader Appreciation Awards Medal.

Her work includes two ongoing sets of fantasy/romance novels: the Celaeno Series—*The Walls of Westernfort, Rangers at Roadsend, The Temple at Landfall, Dynasty of Rogues*, and *Shadow of the Knife*; and the Lyremouth Chronicles—*The Exile and The Sorcerer, The Traitor and The Chalice, The Empress and The Acolyte*, and *The High Priest and the Idol*. She has also written two other stand-alone novels, *Wolfsbane Winter* and *The Shewstone*.

Her love of fantasy began at the age of seven when she encountered Greek mythology. This was compounded by a childhood spent clambering over every example of ancient masonry she could find (medieval castles, megalithic monuments, Roman villas). Her resolute ambition was to become an archaeologist when she grew up, so it was something of a surprise when she became a software engineer instead.

Born in Greenwich, London, in 1956, she now lives with her wife in southwest England, where she is surrounded by enough historic sites to keep her happy.

Books Available From Bold Strokes Books

Against All Odds by Kris Bryant, Maggie Cummings, and M. Ullrich. Peyton and Tory escaped death once, but will they survive when Bradley's determined to make his kill rate 100 percent? (978-1-163555-193-8)

Autumn's Light by Aurora Rey. Casual hookups aren't supposed to include romantic dinners and meeting the family. Can Mat Pero see beyond the heartbreak that led her to keep her worlds so separate, and will Graham Connor be waiting if she does? (978-1-163555-272-0)

Breaking the Rules by Larkin Rose. When Virginia and Carmen are thrown together by an embarrassing mistake, they find out their stubborn determination isn't so heroic after all. (978-1-163555-261-4)

Broad Awakening by Mickey Brent. In the sequel to *Underwater Vibes*, Hélène and Sylvie find ruts in their road to eternal bliss. (978-1-163555-270-6)

Broken Vows by MJ Williamz. Sister Mary Margaret must reconcile her divided heart or risk losing a love that just might be heaven sent. (978-1-163555-022-1)

Flesh and Gold by Ann Aptaker. Havana, 1952, where art thief and smuggler Cantor Gold dodges gangland bullets and mobsters' schemes while she searches Havana's steamy red light district for her kidnapped love. (978-1-163555-153-2)

Isle of Broken Years by Jane Fletcher. Spanish noblewoman Catalina de Valasco is in peril, even before the pirates holding her for ransom sail into seas destined to become known as the Bermuda Triangle. (978-1-163555-175-4)

Love Like This by Melissa Brayden. Hadley Cooper and Spencer Adair set out to take the fashion world by storm. If only they knew their hearts were about to be taken. (978-1-163555-018-4)

Secrets On the Clock by Nicole Disney. Jenna and Danielle love their jobs helping endangered children, but that might not be enough to stop them from breaking the rules by falling in love. (978-1-163555-292-8)

Unexpected Partners by Michelle Larkin. Dr. Chloe Maddox tries desperately to deny her attraction for Detective Dana Blake as they flee from a serial killer who's hunting them both. (978-1-163555-203-4)

A Fighting Chance by T. L. Hayes. Will Lou be able to come to terms with her past to give love a fighting chance? (978-1-163555-257-7)

Chosen by Brey Willows. When the choice is adapt or die, can love save us all? (978-1-163555-110-5)

Gnarled Hollow by Charlotte Greene. After they are invited to study a secluded nineteenth-century estate, a former English professor and a group of historians discover that they will have to fight against the unknown if they have any hope of staying alive. (978-1-163555-235-5)

Jacob's Grace by C.P. Rowlands. Captain Tag Becket wants to keep her head down and her past behind her, but her feelings for AJ's second-in-command, Grace Fields, makes keeping secrets next to impossible. (978-1-163555-187-7)

On the Fly by PJ Trebelhorn. Hockey player Courtney Abbott is content with her solitary life until visiting concert violinist Lana Caruso makes her second-guess everything she always thought she wanted. (978-1-163555-255-3)

Passionate Rivals by Radclyffe. Professional rivalry and long-simmering passions create a combustible combination when Emmet McCabe and Sydney Stevens are forced to work together, especially when past attractions won't stay buried. (978-1-63555-231-7)

Proxima Five by Missouri Vaun. When geologist Leah Warren crash-lands on a preindustrial planet and is claimed by its tyrant, Tiago, will clan warrior Keegan's love for Leah give her the strength to defeat him? (978-1-163555-122-8)

Shadowboxer by Jessica L. Webb. Jordan McAddie is prepared to keep her street kids safe from a dangerous underground protest group, but she isn't prepared for her first love to walk back into her life. (978-1-163555-267-6)